# Murder Frames the Scene

## A HAWAI'I MYSTERY

### VICTORIA NALANI KNEUBUHL

A LATITUDE 20 BOOK

UNIVERSITY OF HAWAI'I PRESS
HONOLULU

**Library of Congress Cataloging-in-Publication Data**

Names: Kneubuhl, Victoria N. (Victoria Nalani), author.

Title: Murder frames the scene : a Hawai'i mystery / Victoria Nalani
Kneubuhl.

Description: Honolulu : University of Hawai'i Press, 2016. | "A latitude 20
book."

Identifiers: LCCN 2015038299 | ISBN 9780824855291 pbk. : alk. paper

Subjects: | LCGFT: Detective and mystery fiction

Classification: LCC PS3561.N418 M883 2016 | DDC 813/.54—dc23

LC record available at http://lccn.loc.gov/2015038299

University of Hawai'i Press books are printed on acid-free
paper and meet the guidelines for permanence and
durability of the Council on Library Resources.

# ACKNOWLEDGMENTS

I would like to thank my editor, Masako Ikeda, and the University of Hawai'i Press for publishing this book. My special thanks to John Donohue, Andrew Katz, and Marisa Campbell for smoothing out the many bumps in the manuscript, and to managing editor Cheri Dunn for overseeing the final product. Mahalo also to Carol Abe, Debra Tang, and all of the people at the UH Press who helped to transform a story into a real book. Thank you to my dear partner, Phil, who is always there for me. And last but not least, thank you to all the people who have read my books and asked for more.

# SHANGHAI, OCTOBER 1935

**THE AIR TURNED** cold, and the Shanghai rain drizzled down on the October afternoon as Ned Manusia walked along the waterside of the Bund. The change in the weather did nothing to stop the chaos that swirled around him—cars, trucks, limousines, streetcars, vending carts, arguments, loud conversations, beggars calling for alms, the cries of rickshaw drivers angling for fares, and sometimes in the distance, a ship's whistle. The dampness increased the already pungent assault the city had on his senses, as all at once he inhaled expensive perfume, roasted pig, flowers, fish, and the body odor of human poverty, and with the next breath took in another colliding set of scents. It was here on the graceful curve of the Whangpu that the Western-styled city of Shanghai had grown from the mud of the riverbanks—a vision of foreigners made manifest over decades through the backbreaking labor of thousands upon thousands of Chinese workers and now appropriately nicknamed the Paris of the Far East.

The rain was getting heavier, and Ned wrapped his coat closer, lowered his head, and hurried past the Public Garden toward the arched steel trusses of the Garden Bridge. On the pedestrian causeway, he looked down into Soochow Creek, the murky-green water spreading like a thick glaze toward the Whangpu. He could feel the raindrops getting bigger, hear them hitting the brim of his hat, and see them falling into the water below in infinite patterns of intersecting circles. People everywhere began to dash for cover, and Ned broke into a run toward the Astor House Hotel, arriving at the entrance just as the rain poured down in thick sheets, washing the city in a flood of liquid gray.

He stepped into the wood-paneled lobby of the hotel with its vaulted white ceiling and brilliant chandeliers, a warm and welcoming contrast to the dismal weather outside. Taking off his coat, he plunked himself down in an overstuffed chair. He had tried to work all morning in his room, but writing in a hotel room rarely went well for him. He'd gone for a walk after lunch, planning to kill an hour or more sitting in the Public Garden watching the river traffic, but now it was raining. He was tired of waiting, and he could feel the malaise of boredom seeping into him. He could never appreciate Shanghai and its decadent excitement the way others did. The ingrained blindness of the foreign community, with its wealth and colonial privilege, to the culture, language, and poverty of the people around them grated on him. He'd come at the request of his "unofficial" government office. His series of lectures to the Shanghai Dramatic Society had been very well attended. As a successful playwright from Britain, he had a ready made cover for his "other activities." He'd been given passwords and told someone would contact him so he could complete his commitment. But nearly a week had gone by, and no one had turned up. He felt impatient and bored and missed Mina Beckwith, his fiancée in Honolulu, but if there was any hope at all that his childhood friend Nigel Hawthorn was still alive, he'd stay here as long as it took to get him out. He was more than sure Mina would understand. The lobby clock said three when he finally got up and checked the front desk for messages, and as he felt he couldn't face going back to his fourth-floor suite, he decided to wander into the bar for a little fortification. He had a sinking feeling when he remembered that tonight he had to go to the soiree Mrs. Worlan-Burke was hosting for the Dramatic Society. As he sat down on one of the stools along the virtually empty teak bar, he groaned quietly to himself thinking about Mrs. Worlan-Burke with her turbans, her long cigarette holder, and her shallow, mindless chatter.

"Everything all right, sir?" A distinct American accent broke Ned's thoughts. It was a big-city accent, Detroit or Chicago. He couldn't quite place it.

"Oh, sorry, yes, I'm quite well, thank you. Just a small unpleasant thought," Ned smiled.

"Can I get you something to cheer you up, sir?"

"Yes," Ned answered, "I'll have one of the Astor House Specials. Still made with real absinthe, I hope."

"*La fée verte*—just what you want when you've got the blues." The bartender smiled, expertly mixed the cocktail, and set it before Ned in the blink of an eye.

"Thank you," Ned said and took a sip. "It's as marvelous as I remember."

"You staying here, sir? If you don't mind my asking." The bartender brushed his hand over his crew cut and then began to wipe the already spotless surface of the bar.

"That's right," Ned answered, "and I don't mind you asking."

"It's just that most of the Brits are all for the Cathay Hotel."

"Too stuffy. Too 'see and be seen' for my taste."

"I'm with you there, sir."

Ned extended his hand. "You can drop the 'sir.' My name's Edward, but please call me Ned."

"Jon Jones, but everyone calls me Jonesy." The bartender gave Ned a hearty handshake.

"Been in Shanghai long, Jonesy?" Ned asked. He was enjoying his drink and having someone to talk to.

"I been here awhile," Jonesy answered. "It's quite a town."

"Never a dull moment?"

"Not unless you're *looking* for some dull moments. Everything's available here, if you know what I mean."

"I'm certain I do," Ned said, "but what brought you here, Jonesy, to Shanghai?"

"Same as almost everyone else," he said with a chuckle, "trouble at home and the yen to make some money. Say, aren't you the playwright that's come to talk to the Drama group?"

"Guilty as charged." Ned raised his hand. "How did you know?"

"I help build the sets for some of the plays, and I hear people talk. This is a great town for talkers. You're here for an hour, and they know your underwear size on the other side of the city. I heard you were born in Sāmoa, and you were part Samoan."

"I was born in Apia, and my father was half Samoan. He was the harbor pilot. My grandparents still live there."

"I spent a few months in Apia once. I had the time of my life." Jonesy beamed. "I even took a jaunt over to Savai'i, I stayed with my pal in his village, Sala'ilua."

"I'm astounded," Ned said. "I wouldn't think anyone in Shanghai had ever even heard of Savai'i."

"I was in the merchant marines back then. So, if you don't mind my asking, how did an Apia boy happen to become a playwright? I don't recall theater being a big pastime in Sāmoa."

"My mum took me back to Britain when I was a boy, after my father died." Ned looked out the window and saw that it was still raining. The drink was casting a haze over the afternoon, and he felt a wave of sadness sweep through him as he thought about his friend Nigel, hoping he wasn't lying lifeless somewhere in this unfathomable city or, worse, being tortured in some dank secret prison.

"Hey there," Jonesy said, "you look like you could use another drink."

"I don't know if I should," Ned replied. "I don't usually drink this early in the afternoon, and I have to be somewhere tonight in a sociable condition."

"Don't worry, you have plenty of time to sleep it off, and this one's on me. It's not every day someone from Sāmoa walks into the bar."

It was nearly eight in the evening when Ned went down to the lobby from his hotel room. In evening dress, with his overcoat slung casually over his shoulders, as he descended the grand staircase, he failed to notice that his tall and handsome looks caught the gaze of several women. His Green Fairy–cocktail afternoon nap had lasted almost three hours. Mrs. Worlan-Burke's chauffer was due to arrive in just a few minutes. Ned waited quietly in a corner chair and tried to mentally prepare himself for what he was sure would be a long and tedious night. He wondered what Mina was up to in Honolulu and thought that he might enjoy the city a little more if she were here. Still, he could very well be called on to do something dangerous, and even though she had the courage of a lioness when things got tough, the last thing he wanted was to put her at risk. He found it hard to believe she'd agreed to marry him and harder still to discover that he found himself so eager to be married to her. He was thirty-one years old now. Most of his friends were married with children, and he had begun to think he might be contented becoming an eccentric old bachelor. But almost overnight, she had changed everything.

One of the bellmen approached and discreetly informed him that Mrs. Worlan-Burke's car was waiting. Ned still couldn't figure out how some of the staff kept track of visitors' faces and names. But this was the hotel frequented by Americans, so perhaps his British accent made him stand out. He walked with no little reluctance out the front door and was met by a uniformed driver, politely standing by the open door of a gleaming black limousine. He was more than surprised to find Mrs. Worlan-Burke herself, sitting in the backseat, smiling up at him.

"Ned, darling!" she greeted him with a loud, horsey laugh and her usual exaggerated enthusiasm. She extended her right hand with its long, perfectly polished nails. On several of her fingers, she wore rings with glittering stones.

"Mrs. Worlan-Burke," he smiled and took her outstretched hand as he got in and the car door closed after him, "this is a surprise."

"I thought I would pick you up myself," she said, "so we could have a chat before the party." She adjusted her dark-green turban and tucked up a strand of blonde hair that had escaped. Ned guessed Mrs. Worlan-Burke must be in her mid-forties, but it was difficult to tell, as her makeup always made her look like she was about to go on-stage. She addressed the driver. "Wu, dear, take your time. We'll go down the Bund and then past the racecourse."

"Yes, madam."

"Thank you, dear," she said.

The limousine pulled away from the hotel, and Ned, thoroughly irritated, looked out the window in silence. As they stopped at the corner, before turning across the bridge that would take them back along the Bund, a group of Japanese soldiers marched by under a street lamp. Their faces were set at a grim and determined angle as they cut their way along the sidewalk. Other pedestrians stepped aside to let them pass.

"Ah, yes," Mrs. Worlan-Burke said as she observed him watching the soldiers, "the shadow of the Japanese army hangs heavy over our city."

"No one seems to be worried about it." As soon as the words left his mouth, Ned realized he sounded a bit sarcastic and maybe impolite.

"I see you've heard about the famous 'Shanghai mind' we're all supposed to be afflicted with. Here we are, obliviously fiddling away like Nero, with our silly, extravagant amusements, while Rome burns around us."

"I'm sorry if I sounded insensitive," Ned said.

"We haven't much time. So let me change the subject for a moment, Mr. Manusia." She pressed a lever that raised a privacy screen, closing them off from the driver. "I'm sooo dying to talk to you alone, darling!"

"Really?" Ned looked at her. "Whatever for?"

The privacy screen clicked into place, and Mrs. Worlan-Burke leaned back against the plush dark leather. She surprised Ned by turning away from him. She sat, watching the city going by, as if she suddenly wanted to be by herself. With her hands folded placidly on her lap, her whole person seemed to become both relaxed and contemplative. She was silent for a few minutes and then spoke to him in a calm and intelligent tone of voice that sounded completely out of character. "I'm sure, as a writer, you must enjoy reading?"

The question caught him off guard, and it took a moment before he could reply. "Of course," he answered carefully. "I've enjoyed reading since I was a child."

"And as a child," she said as she looked at him, "what was your favorite book?"

"*The Wind in the Willows*," he answered.

"Really? I loved that one too. What was your favorite part?"

He laughed. "The part when Toad falls in love with motor cars. And yours?"

She laughed too. "Why, when Ratty comes back to his old home and begins to feel nostalgic. Honestly," she sighed, "I don't know why we have to go through this silly rigmarole."

"We've met so many times. Why is it you've waited so long to let me know you're my contact?" Ned was both exasperated and puzzled.

"Why?" she repeated. "Because we had to make sure you were safe, that you weren't being watched. The metropolitan police are in league with the Kuomingtang, the Nationalist Party, and we're very suspicious of the relationship between the Nationalists and the Japanese. Chiang Kai-shek has concentrated his efforts on a brutal put-down of the Communist Party, particularly in this city, and has ignored and actually made, in my humble opinion, foolish concessions to the Japanese. We're just not sure how far these concessions extend or who the metropolitan police might be spying for—not to mention the hundreds of Japanese consular police, who say they're only keeping an eye on their own people, but we know they're up to other things. They're already in Manchuria, and it's to their benefit that this internal struggle between the Communists and Nationalists continues. There are eyes everywhere in Shanghai, Ned, so we can't be too careful."

"Is there any word on Nigel, then?"

"I'm sorry to say, I don't know much more than that he's been hurt but is still alive." She now looked careworn, as if the turban and the glittery rings had become a burden. "They fix it so none of us know too much about anything—in case we get picked up by the wrong people. Of course, then, we're expected to spring into action at a moment's notice. You'll meet a young woman tonight who's playing the piano at the party, Mei Lien Chen. She'll tell you what to do next. I'd say, if you have a chance to get Nigel out of here, the sooner, the better."

"I've made some tentative plans. I'll just have to see where he is and what shape he's in."

"Well, I don't know if I'll see him again. He's such a lovely man. My husband and I both adore him. Take good care of him for us, will you?" She wiped a few tears from her eyes. "Oopsy now, mustn't spoil the disguise. I'm just so tired of worrying about everyone."

"You were the last person I would ever have expected to be my contact," Ned said, handing her his handkerchief.

"I guess from now on you'll have to think twice about shallow and dithering social butterflies who flit around Shanghai in ridiculous turbans."

"If you would ever like to be in one of my plays, Mrs. Worlan-Burke," Ned nodded at her, "you won't even have to audition."

"Thank you, Ned. Lately I've been seriously thinking about changing careers."

Ned became charming and sociable, asking Mrs. Worlan-Burke all kinds of questions about Shanghai. She pressed the lever again, lowering the privacy screen so that they could have a better view of the city as it floated by the limousine. Ned recognized the racetrack, the YMCA, and the Park Hotel and knew they must be nearing the place where Nanking Road became Bubbling Springs Road. He remembered there were some stunning residences out this way. But it was now dark, and so rather than struggling to view the scenery, he gave his attention wholly to Mrs. Worlan-Burke's descriptions of Tsingtao—what a shame it was, she lamented, that he didn't have time to visit the lovely seaside town. She then moved on, resuming once again her animated and embellished personality, to recount the wonders of Suzhou—its gardens, its canals, its artistic and cultural heritage. Ned listened, content not to say a word, relieved and revived by the thought that he had just taken the first real step on the journey to finding and shepherding Nigel to safety.

The limousine finally pulled off the main road to a tree-lined drive festooned on either side with white lanterns. From a bag next to her, Mrs. Worlan-Burke produced two velvet masks. They were partial masks that only covered the top half of the face, and they were done up with sequins and sparkles. She handed Ned one that was black and silver and kept the lacey, blue feminine mask for herself.

"I forgot to tell you, this is a masked party," she chuckled. "It's nearly Halloween."

"How charming," Ned said as he put on his mask. "How do I look?"

"Devastating, darling, simply devastating," she replied as she donned her own mask.

The limousine sailed along the driveway up toward a two-story home with long, low horizontal lines built with limestone on the lower façade, bold sand-stucco planes on the second story, and a red shingled roof. They came to a stop under a porte cochere that sheltered the front entrance. A valet opened the car door, and another attendant was right on hand to take Ned's coat from him and give him a small card with a number on it.

"This house is reminiscent of that American architect, whose name escapes me," Ned commented as he graciously helped Mrs. Worlan-Burke step out from the backseat.

"You're so clever, darling. It's a Frank Lloyd Wright copy," she said, standing and taking his arm as they made their way to the front door. "The couple who built it had seen some house of his in America— Graystones or Graytrees or Graycliffs, Gray-something, I can never remember. Well, they simply had to have one like it, so they built this. It's quite a nice place, actually. Now listen, darling," she said, turning to him just after they crossed the threshold of the house, "if you need any help before you leave, you just call me."

With that said, Mrs. Worlan-Burke wished him luck, kissed his cheek, let go of his arm, and drifted away. The party was in full swing, and apparently no one had even noticed the absence of the hostess. Beautiful people of varied nationalities swirled around him, dressed to the nines, masked for the most part in stunning bohemian style— sparkling and lively, but Ned, fond of well-made houses, was fascinated by the architecture of the home: the warm wood, the wide airiness of the windows, and the feeling that the rear gardens were actually part of the living space. He wandered out to the back, where just off the patio, on the lawn, several jugglers dressed as harlequins were tossing silver plates and goblets about with skill and abandon to the sweet music of a string quartet. Ned accepted a flute of champagne from a waitress clad as a glamorous witch. After the juggling, despite his mask, several people recognized him from his lectures, and soon he had quite a crowd around him chatting him up and asking questions about plays and the London and New York theatre scenes. Suddenly a gong sounded, and one of the witch waitresses announced the piano performance of Miss Mei Lien Chen in the music room. Ned excused himself and arrived just in time to hear Miss Chen begin what Ned thought to be one of the finest solo piano arrangements for *Rhapsody in Blue* he had ever heard. The dim lighting of the room, the mood and feeling of the music, transported all the listeners to another place, a place permeated by rhythm and melody, transcending the everyday world. When the piece was over, there was a long period of silence before everyone in the room jumped to their feet, clapping and cheering. There was an initial rush toward the pianist, so Ned waited patiently until everyone had gone and she had started to put her music away into a black carrying case before he approached her. Ned could see right away that she was part Caucasian. She was taller than most Chinese women. Her hair was a beautifully black, but her eyes were definitely hazel.

"Excuse me, Miss Chen," he said softly. "I'm wondering if I might have a word with you."

"Please, call me Mei. You're the playwright?" She said as she donned her eye mask of two matching monarch butterflies.

"Yes, that's right," he answered. "And please call me Ned."

She looked around the room before she spoke again. There were a few groups of people milling around and talking. "Perhaps we could find a drink and take a stroll. I need to unwind a bit after playing, and Crandall always does up the garden so beautifully for a party."

"Crandall?" Ned gave her a quizzical look.

"Crandall is Mr. Worlan-Burke," she smiled. "Haven't you met him? He's a very nice man. So would you like to see the grounds?"

"Very much," Ned nodded.

"We'll need to keep warm." She waved at one of the witch waitresses and gave her their coat numbers. "I'd like a tumbler of cognac, please, double. Would you like one too, Ned?"

He nodded.

"Make it two," she said to the waitress.

They made some small talk until the waitress returned with their coats and their cognac, and then they ventured out into the garden, along a gravel path, lighted on either side by glowing lanterns that hung from thick bamboo poles. Flowering azaleas with white, purple, and pink blooms lined the path. The garden, Mei told him, covered about three acres and had many side paths that wound through different sections, including a wonderful maze. They walked along one path that led uphill to a clearing and a bench lit by a lantern, where they could look down over the garden and view the house in the distance. They could also clearly see if anyone was approaching. Mei sat down and raised her mask up. From what Ned could see of her in this dim light, she had a lovely face with delicate features. She wore her hair pulled back into a simple chignon, as if she did not want to call attention to her good looks—a practice Ned had noticed many female musicians held in common. He had always suspected it was because they longed to be recognized for their ability and not for their looks. As Mei pulled her cloak over her legs to ward off the night air, Ned couldn't help but notice that she had been blessed with long, tapering fingers—very handy if one wanted to be a pianist.

"I think it's safe to speak freely now," Mei said. "I know you must be anxious to hear about Nigel. He's in hiding, recuperating from a gunshot wound. His partner was killed. He nearly wept when he heard it was you who'd been sent to help him. Of course, now it is imperative to get him out of the country and out of the reach of the Nationalists and the Japanese."

"I've been instructed to make arrangements for our departure, but I would need to know when he can safely travel."

"This is Friday, and if all goes well through the weekend, I think he could leave next week."

"That's great news," Ned said. "I'll go ahead and make arrangements for the two of us. If he needs more recovery time, I can always cancel."

"You'll need to make arrangements for the three of us," Mei said.

Ned frowned. "The three of us?"

"I'm afraid Nigel wouldn't hear of leaving without me. You see, we were married last week. I'm his wife."

"Congratulations, Mei," Ned turned to her and smiled. "I had no idea of course, but I am happy for both of you."

"He said you would be. He's talked and talked about you."

"I'm engaged now myself," Ned said shyly.

"Really?" Mei smiled. "Who's the lucky girl?"

"I think I'm the lucky one. Her name is Mina Beckwith. She lives in Honolulu and is part Hawaiian."

"A real island girl."

"She's also a very capable journalist," Ned added. "I hope you'll meet her soon, but when can I see Nigel?" Ned asked.

"First, we'll go around a bit, as if we've become friends, and I'll show you the sights. We'll see if we're followed or observed too closely. I think Mrs. Worlan-Burke told you something of the dangers."

"Yes, she did," Ned said.

"And because of my charitable work, I've been branded a Communist sympathizer, so we'll have to be extra vigilant. I'm afraid my social politics have complicated an already dangerous situation. If we're sure everything is safe, we can set up a meeting. If it turns out we're being followed, then we'll just have to figure out how to handle that too."

"My main concern is Nigel's health and safety and, of course, yours also."

"Shall we begin?" she said seriously. "Let's go back to the party, dance for a while, and then let everyone see us leave together."

"That sounds like a very appealing assignment," Ned said as he stood up. "Much more pleasant than sitting on this cold bench."

They returned to the house, where a small orchestra was playing dance music. After an hour or so of dancing and socializing, Ned and Mei left together and headed for the French quarter. It was well after midnight, but the streets were bustling and lively as if the evening were just beginning. They strolled up and down Avenue Joffe with its leafy trees and European cafés and stopped at a couple of smoky cabarets where Mei said the jazz musicians were particularly good. At the second cabaret, she was invited by the bandleader to play the piano and did a remarkable rendition of *I Got Rhythm* that nearly brought the house down. Ned noticed quite a few Russian women, members of the sizable Russian migration to Shanghai precipitated by the Bolshevik Revolution, making themselves available in the cabarets and even on the streets. He and Mei decided to end the evening in a Russian café. Though the walls could have used a paint job and the red-checkered tablecloth looked threadbare in some spots, they ate some of the best stroganoff Ned had ever tasted while being serenaded with authentically sad Slavic melodies by the restaurant's minstrels, who wandered from table to table. When Ned asked Mei if she were a Shanghai native, she looked at him for a moment before she answered.

"It's funny," she began, "Nigel has told me so much about you that I feel as if we've known each other for many years, but of course, you know nothing about me."

"I'm sure you must be someone special," Ned replied, "if Nigel chose you for his life's companion. And I do know you're awfully good on the piano."

"I've been playing since I was a girl," she said. "I've studied abroad too, with different teachers, but never at a conservatory."

"But you were born here?"

"Yes," she said, pouring herself a glass of red wine from the bottle they had ordered. "I'm the love child of a Chinese courtesan and a very wealthy white businessman." She paused to see how Ned would react.

"That's a fascinating and unusual way to come into the world," he said with interest.

She studied him as if she were making her mind up about something. "Would you like to hear my story?" she finally asked.

Ned could see that though the wine may have loosened her tongue, it had not impaired her judgment. "I'm always interested in people's stories," he answered as he poured himself another glass of wine and settled back in his chair, "especially yours, since you're now married to my dear friend, and it's likely we'll know each other all our lives."

"I didn't think of that," Mei smiled. "It *is* likely that we'll know each other for many years . . . if we all manage to get out of here in one piece."

"We will," Ned said firmly.

"Well then," Mei began, "my mother belonged to an elite group of women. They were trained artists—trained to sing and play musical instruments, to tell stories, and to provide companionship to wealthy men. Some who became very popular, like my mother, were like film stars and would arrive for their engagements in style with a retinue of servants and musicians. These women were very independent, and the successful ones also had their own lavish establishments where they lived, held banquets, and entertained. They were not prostitutes, but many of them did choose a lover when and if they wanted one. My father said my mother was the most beautiful woman he had ever seen. He was from a family of Sephardic Jews who had made fortunes here in China, and of course, he was married when he met my mother. He wasn't much to look at, my father, but he was kind and funny, and she chose him over all the handsome, rich men she could have had. She became pregnant with me and died a few days after I was born. My father named me Mei Lien, after my mother. He had me placed with a foster family, a Chinese business associate who owed him favors. They were very kind to me, and my father would come and visit at least twice a week, sometimes more. He told me the truth about everything as soon as he felt I would be able to understand. He made sure that I was well raised and cared for, well educated, and before he died, he saw to it that I was well provided for too. My mother had made a good deal of money that she left to me, and my father turned it into a small fortune."

"He must have been a remarkable man," Ned said.

"Why do you say that?"

"Because you could easily be angry and resentful about such an upbringing, yet you speak of him with great affection in your voice," Ned answered.

"You noticed the tone of voice I used when I talked about him?" She seemed surprised.

"I'm a playwright. In the theatre, a tone of voice, a facial expression, a gesture, a tilt of the head— they tell us a lot about the emotion behind the words."

"It's true," she smiled sadly. "I think he was an exceptional person, and of course, I always knew he loved me. And he always made it clear to me how much he loved and admired my mother. I think it makes a great difference as a child, to feel secure in your parents' love. It's like a rock, and many other, unconventional things don't matter so much if you have that security."

"And how did you and Nigel get together?"

She tilted her head slightly. "You know how Nigel loves music? He saw me playing the piano one night, and I won his heart through the keyboard."

## 2

# HONOLULU, OCTOBER 1935

"OH, NO," MINA Beckwith groaned. "Don't tell me you're in on it too."
    "I have no idea what you're talking about," said the petite and spunky Cecily Porter, née Chang, one of Mina's closest friends since childhood. Cecily leaned against the high wooden back of the restaurant booth and folded her arms. Her short black hair made her look much younger than her twenty-eight years.

Mina and Cecily were at the Harbor Grill in downtown Honolulu, one of their favorite haunts. A waitress appeared in a white uniform with a few stains that looked like they'd been through several washes and hadn't come out. She set down a teriyaki steak sandwich with macaroni salad in front of Mina, a club sandwich with potato salad in front of Cecily, and glasses of iced tea for each of them, and then she rushed off.

Mina tucked a stray strand of dark-brown hair behind her ears, picked up her knife, and sliced her sandwich in half. "Don't be ridiculous. You know exactly what I'm talking about."

Cecily broke out in a grin. "Okay, so I'm in on it, and I do know exactly what you're talking about. But Tamara Morrison has just hired Tom as the manager of her gallery, so can you blame me for ganging up on you?"

Mina rolled her eyes. "More pressure. Now my best friend's husband's new job has entered the equation."

"Well, it hasn't really," Cecily said as she picked up her fork and fiddled with her salad. "It's just an extra attraction. Besides, Tom would love to work with you."

    "I don't know." Mina shook her head.

"Why? Do you have some other work?"

"No."

"What then?"

"I just don't know if doing an art catalog for some rich lady's gallery is going to be very interesting. She might be fussy and interfering." Mina took a sip of her iced tea.

"It's not going to be at her gallery."

"So where is it going to be?"

"It's at the Honolulu Academy of Arts. She's bankrolling it, so she gets to be in charge."

Mina furrowed her brow. "Oh, well, I still don't see why she's so keen on me."

"She's smitten by your writing. It's what you get for doing those great articles for the paper."

"I guess I should feel flattered."

"Is Chris Hollister still angling to get you back? To the paper, I mean." Cecily asked cautiously.

"Yes," Mina answered, "but unless there's a big change in the editorial policy, I don't see how that's possible. It's so one-sided."

"Meaning antilabor?"

"Meaning anti anything that doesn't support the wealthy elite— of which, yes, I know I'm one—but regardless of social position, a responsible journalist *and* a responsible newspaper should be ethically bound to reporting both sides of an issue."

Cecily waited for a moment before she continued. "I think you should at least talk to Tamara Morrison. She doesn't appear to be fussy, and I know she's ready to shell out the bucks to make this publication look tops."

"Really?"

"Yep." Cecily picked up half of her sandwich. "Plus the artists she wants you to write about are an interesting lot. I wish she were begging me to do it." She took a bite.

"Begging me? She hasn't even asked me to do this job."

"You're kidding," Cecily said with genuine surprise.

"Nope." Mina shook her head. "I've gotten a call about it from Violet Lennox, her friend and supporter, from my Grandma Hannah, my father, my sister, Sheila Halpern, because her brother Andrew belongs to their artist's group, and now you're talking to me about it, but not a peep from the dowager herself."

Cecily laughed. "She's priming the pump!"

Mina smiled. "She's an operator."

"My dad wants you to come for dinner at their place tomorrow night with me and Tom. He's making duck l'orange, and then crêpes suzette for dessert."

"You're so lucky your dad can cook. All ours can do is steaks on the grill."

"I know I shouldn't complain, but I liked it so much better when he just cooked Chinese food. At least we're having duck. That's kind of Chinese."

"What are you doing this afternoon?" Mina asked.

"I'm getting my hair done," Cecily answered, pulling at her short black curls. "Time for another perm."

"I think about cutting my hair every once in a while," Mina said. "But what stops me is that I'd look just like Nyla, and no one would be able to tell us apart."

"How is the twin sister?" Cecily wiped her mouth with her napkin. "How come she's not here with us?"

"She had a doctor's appointment. Her tummy is getting really big, and she's already felt kicking."

Cecily arched her eyebrows. "Let's hope it's only two legs, not four."

Mina burst out laughing. "She's having a baby, not a puppy."

Cecily laughed too. "Twins, I meant twins! But speaking of puppies, is my favorite Portuguese water dog waiting for you in your car?"

"No," Mina answered. "Mrs. Olivera is giving him a haircut, and then Mr. Olivera is giving him a bath."

"Pretty convenient to have a housekeeper and a gardener who will groom your dog," Cecily said just before she took a sip of her iced tea.

"You know, they wished they could have kept Ollie themselves, but their landlord doesn't allow dogs."

"Wasn't he given to them as some kind of collateral?"

"Yeah," Mina nodded her head. "Their nephew borrowed thirty bucks, skipped town on a freighter, and left Ollie behind with a note to sell him. The Oliveras love him. That's why they bathe and trim him."

"Great!" Cecily grinned. "He'll be sweet and clean for your visit to Tamara. She's a big supporter of the Humane Society. She adores dogs."

The very next afternoon, having received a phone call, Mina found herself driving up the winding Pacific Heights Road to the home of Tamara Morrison. The fall sky was a clear, brilliant blue, and the air became cooler as her Packard coupe climbed the mountain ridge. The humid days of late summer and early fall, with their sharp and blinding sunlight, now gave way to gentler days, when the sunlight lost its hard edges and everything had the look and feel of a French impressionist painting—bathed in soft light and defined by a certain luminosity. Mina's dog, Ollie, sat beside her next to the open window. She didn't allow him to hang his head out anymore, even though he loved it, because he'd once gotten an infection from a piece of dirt or gravel that had flown into his eye. She'd discovered, after she'd bought him, that Portuguese water dogs were quite rare now, and she felt very lucky to own one. He was mostly black, but he had a white patch around his nose and one on his chest. His feet and lower legs were white too, as if he were wearing socks, and his hair was impossibly wavy. His expressive eyes were a deep, melt-your-heart brown, and his nose was shaped like a teddy bear's. Mina downshifted as the road became steep. She thought perhaps she'd missed the house as she was nearing the end of the road. But the road turned, and she found the house and parked on the street.

With Ollie trotting beside her, she walked, as instructed, to the wooden-paneled gate in the middle of the high, white wall that faced the street. A set of bells jangled when she opened the gate, and leaving behind the sunny sidewalk, she stepped into the shade of a restful courtyard. Ollie bustled up to a tiled pond in the center of the garden that was surrounded by short grass inset with smooth stones. The ferns, heliconias, and other tropical plants that bordered the garden walls looked freshly watered, and above, the spreading branches of a jacaranda tree cast lacey shadows over the inner garden.

Mina looked up at the house, a fusion of Mediterranean and Asian architecture. Reminiscent of a pagoda, the roof of dark-blue clay tiles took a slight but graceful curve upward at the corners of the eaves. Casement windows were set like mysterious eyes on the thick, white stucco walls. The cool and deep lanai sheltered a dark, gleaming front door in the shape of a Chinese moon gate, and on either side of the front door were two decorative masonry screens carved through the wall to look like calligraphy characters. Just as she stepped onto the stone-block floor of the lanai, the moon-gate door suddenly swung open, and Tamara Morrison stood there smiling with her odd but friendly freckled face. Her nose, set between two large gray eyes, was somewhat beaky, and her silver hair was held up on top of her head by two lacquered chopsticks with unruly strands sticking out in different directions. She was dressed in an indigo Japanese *happi* coat, slightly wrinkled, worn open over a white blouse and dark silk pants. The whole effect made Mina smile back, and before a word was exchanged, she felt welcomed.

"Oh, what a sweet-looking dog," Tamara exclaimed as Ollie strolled toward her wagging his tail.

Mina had noticed that Ollie possessed a sixth sense about approaching people. He seemed to put on exactly the right demeanor to please strangers. Sometimes he bounded toward them, sometimes he waited until they approached him, sometimes he quietly sidled up next to them, and sometimes he simply avoided certain people. Inevitably, it turned out to be the right thing to do, as it was today. In less than thirty seconds, he had turned Tamara into a friend for life.

"Come in, Mina. I'm so glad you came, and your dog too, of course. What's his name?"

"Ollie," Mina answered.

"Is he friendly with other dogs?"

"If they're friendly," Mina said. "Ollie could wait out here. He'd be quite happy."

"No, no," Tamara shook her head. "Bring him in, and we'll go out to the back garden. He can play with my dog, Jocks—who is probably off digging up the most expensive plant in my garden." She let out a laugh and beckoned Mina to follow her into the house.

They passed through the large, cool living room with its high ceiling, then up two stairs and through an opening, cut in a mirror image of the front door, leading into the dining room, then out through French doors to a terrace overlooking a sloping garden and the city. There was a table set for two with a glass pitcher of lemonade and a plate of cookies. Tamara picked up a whistle from the table and blew it sharply, and a minute later, a white West Highland terrier came rushing up with a bark and sat at her feet. He had traces of dirt on his muzzle and paws. Tamara reached into her coat pocket and gave him a tidbit of something. He had already glanced over at Ollie, who was sitting politely and watching.

"All right, Jocks," Tamara said, "say hello to my new friends."

Jocks sniffed Ollie, who sniffed him back. Then Jocks let out a bark, ran partway down the lawn, turned, and barked again at Ollie, who bounded toward him, and the two of them took off out of sight. Tamara watched them run down the hillside.

"It's good for dogs to have acquaintances of their own kind, don't you think?" Tamara cocked her head to one side to see what Mina would say.

"Yes, I guess so," Mina answered thoughtfully. "It's probably true for all creatures."

Tamara nodded. "I'm considering getting another dog. I think it would be good for Jocks. Lemonade?"

"Yes, please."

"I made it myself from the lemons in the garden," Tamara said as she placed ice cubes into two tall glasses that were etched with tropical leaves. "I made the cookies too. Peanut butter. They were the children's favorite when they were little."

"Do your children live here in the islands?" Mina asked as she helped herself to a cookie.

"No, they've both moved away. Massachusetts and San Francisco. They're always trying to get me to move, but I won't. I was born here, and I plan on dying here."

"Not for some time, I hope," Mina smiled.

"I'll be sixty-one in January. I'm old but not completely over the hill."

"You hardly look your age," Mina said, sincerely.

"Why, thank you, dear," Tamara said, handing her a glass full of lemonade. "But let's not talk about how we look. I bet you're like me. Doesn't it bore you to tears to be with a group of women who go on and on about their looks and their clothes?"

Mina gave her a wry smile. "As a matter of fact, when I find myself in those situations, I usually try and think of an excuse to leave."

"And so you should," Tamara agreed. "Life's just too damn short."

"This lemonade is delicious," Mina said after taking a sip. "So are the cookies."

"I'm so glad you like them. I haven't made them for ages."

"This is a lovely home you have," Mina said as she reached for a second cookie.

Tamara sighed. "Yes, it's lovely, but I'm afraid it's starting to feel too big for just one person."

"Did you want to tell me about your project?" Mina asked.

Tamara smiled. "In a bit. Enjoy the lemonade and cookies, and then we'll go into the library and talk. Will Ollie be all right if he doesn't see you?"

"He won't even notice. I'm sure Jocks is much more fun than I am."

After each of them had a second glass of lemonade, they went back into the house. While going back through the living room, Mina stopped to admire a display of several Japanese prints on the wall. She recognized the work of several *ukiyo-e* masters—Hokusai, Hiroshige, and Yoshitoshi. They climbed a staircase just to the left of the door, and Mina was amused at the things she failed to notice when she had first passed through this space. The library occupied a loft above the entrance and was built over the front lanai with a lovely view of the courtyard. A half wall separated the library from the living room— very convenient if one wanted to look down, but if one were looking up from below, most of the library would be blocked from view. The walls were white stucco, and the floors and ceiling were all out of dark wood. There were bookshelves filled with books, oriental carpets on the floor, a library table, a desk, a window seat, and an overstuffed chair with an ottoman. As Mina gazed around, she thought of Ned and how he would be so happy in a room like this, surrounded by books and overlooking a garden. The thought of finding a big house and of creating such spaces suddenly appealed to her.

"What a lovely room this is," Mina said in almost a whisper as they sat down at the library table.

"Oh, I've made a thousand plans and dreamt a thousand dreams in this room," Tamara mused, "and after all these years, I still think it's one of the best places to be. Now, let me tell you about the catalog and the exhibit. You know I have a gallery in Waikīkī."

Mina nodded. "Of course, and I understand you're something of an artist yourself."

"Let's just say I've been trying to learn how to watercolor for years. Now, I'm in charge of putting together a show for the Honolulu Academy of Arts. It features local artists who live and work in Hawai'i. It opens in the spring, and I want the catalog to be something special."

"Yes," Mina nodded, "several people have told me about it."

"Well, I'd like to go beyond just having photographs of the pieces in the show with the usual write-ups. I want to have a biography of each artist and a kind of statement about their philosophy or their approach to their work. I thought at first perhaps they could each write a statement themselves, but what most of them turned in was not very articulate. I think some visual artists find words very difficult. So I was hoping that maybe you could look over their statements, interview them, look at their artwork, and write a kind of article about each one of them, with biographical information, of course. You know, the kind of lovely articles you've written in the past for the paper. Of course, we're having some professional photographs done of each one of them. They've dreamed up a scheme—they're going to be in poses of famous paintings, and they're even creating theatrical setups for themselves."

"How many artists are there in the show?" Mina asked.

"They're seven all together." Tamara opened a folder on the table. "This is the list. I'm sure you'll be familiar with many, if not all, of them. There's April Fraser. She works in various media, but she's known the most for her beautiful paintings of island flora, particularly the flowers."

"Of course I know April," Mina smiled. "We were at school together, but we always called her Appy."

"Yes, most people still do."

"I heard she went to the Art Student's League in New York."

"Did her a world of good," Tamara said. "She worked hard to get there, you know. Paid for most of her education all on her own. Her mother is a schoolteacher and could only help a little."

Mina frowned. "Yes, I remember my mother telling us that Appy's father walked out on them when she was a baby."

"Well, Appy's come out just fine. She's a wonderful and determined young artist. Now, there's Desmond and Molly Rivers. You know Desmond is a printmaker, and his wife, Molly, is a sculptor. Bas-relief is her current interest."

"I've heard of Desmond," Mina stated. "I've never met him, but I think he used to do some commercial artwork for the newspaper."

"Oh, he hates commercial work now," Tamara nodded, "but I'd say he was lucky to have something to fall back on when he needed to make money."

Mina laughed. "I'll say. I've known quite a few would-be artists who tended bars and waited on tables."

"If I understand his current financial situation, he won't have to ever do commercial work again." Tamara paused as if she'd said too much. "Desmond and Molly are an attractive couple," she continued, "and are developing quite a following. They're also the backbone of many artistic activities in town, including our Halemana studio events."

"Halemana," Mina repeated. "Is that the name of the artists' group?"

"Yes," Tamara answered. "We just started it last year. But not just anyone can join. It's by invitation only. I know that sounds snobby, but really we would invite any serious, experienced artist to join if they expressed an interest."

"Where do you meet?"

"We just got a big studio space on Black Point, right next door to Desmond and Molly's house," Tamara said excitedly. "It's more like a big shack. It used to be a school camp, but the school sold it to build a gym and a pool. When Dez and Molly decided to move to Black Point, they suggested we look into acquiring it. Well, I acquired it actually, but I intend to bequeath it to Halemana. I wanted people to have a real place to work—so many of them have to live in such cramped quarters—and a place where we could have classes too."

"I know that school camp. It belonged to St. Agnes Elementary School. I live just on the other side of Black Point—at Ka'alāwai."

"Perfect. We're having a housewarming—I should say studio-warming—party on Halloween. I hope you'll join us."

"Oh, I see Bill Hitchins is on the list," Mina said, changing the subject. "He's an awfully talented character."

"I think he's something of a genius—as long as he's sober. When he's not sober, he's a fool. And if he's not careful, he'll lose that pretty little wife of his to someone more dependable."

"He got married?" Mina tried not to sound too surprised. "He always seemed to never want any responsibility."

Tamara laughed. "He still doesn't want any responsibility. He married a beautiful young girl he met in Tahiti. She adores him. In fact, she mostly supports him by dancing in Waikīkī. You know how all the tourists are wild for Tahitian dancing these days."

The next name on the list caught Mina's eye. "Tilda Clement—her paintings of Hawaiian women are so distinctive."

"I just wish she didn't have such a blunt way about her." Tamara shook her head. "You just never know what's going to pop out of that woman's mouth. I always feel I have to warn people."

"And this name," Mina continued, "Akira Nakasone—I've heard of him, but—"

"Oh, Akira!" Tamara broke in. "He's a fabulous *sumi-e* artist, a master. You have to see his ink-brush paintings."

Mina pointed to the last name on the list. "I don't think I've ever heard of Raymond Morgan."

"He's a photographer. He and his family just moved here recently, about a year ago. He's a man of leisure—made some clever investments when he was younger, so I hear. He'll also be taking the photos for the catalog, so you'll be doing some work with him—and with

Tom Porter, my new gallery manager. I understand you and Tom's wife are friends."

Mina smiled. "Since forever. I was the maid of honor at their wedding. I'm looking forward to working with Tom."

"Yes," said Tamara thoughtfully, "he's bright and ambitious. His letters of reference say he works well with artists. I just hope he's able to work well with local people as well. You know some of these mainland types can be so arrogant and impatient. They just can't assimilate into our island ways."

"I think he'll be fine," Mina replied. "I don't think Cecily would have it any other way."

"That's a big point in his favor, being married to an island girl. She looks Chinese-Hawaiian. That's just my guess. I'm pretty good at it." Tamara looked at Mina, expecting a confirmation or correction.

"A most accurate guess."

"And you," Tamara looked at Mina's face, "don't tell me, now. Let me guess. I'd say Hawaiian—of course, I know your grandmother—and English—well, Beckwith is a giveaway—but I suspected you've got a touch of Irish in you from somewhere too."

Mina grinned. "How did you guess that? My grandmother on my father's side was from Dublin."

Tamara winked. "It's your eyes. I see the Irish hills in them. Well, so you will take my job, won't you?"

"I couldn't very well refuse, now that I see how interesting it might be."

"I've budgeted three hundred dollars for your services. I hope that's enough."

"It's more than generous," Mina assured her. "I'll probably ask you to donate it to a charity."

Tamara nodded. "You just let me know which one. I was hoping you could come to the group meeting we're having for the exhibition. It's just before the Halloween party. The meeting is at five, and the invited guests start arriving around six. We're all wearing costumes, and please bring Ollie. I'll have Jocks with me." Tamara took out another list and scanned it. "Lots of potential donors are invited, and of course, Tom and his wife will be there. Cecily, is that right?"

"Yes, that's right."

"And of course, your fiancé is more than welcome." Tamara looked embarrassed. "You know how small town we can be here. I just happened to hear. I'm so glad you're doing this."

"Unfortunately, Ned is out of town right now, but I'll look forward to being there."

"Well," said Tamara, "now that we've gotten things rolling, shall we go and see how much of the garden those four-legged boys have destroyed?"

# 3

# SHANGHAI, OCTOBER

**O**N A LATE Sunday afternoon, an overcast sky hanging above, an autumn breeze spread an unfriendly chill over the city. There were few people in the Public Gardens as Ned sat reading. He lifted his eyes from the book to the steely cold waters of the Whangpu, now windblown and choppy. People glided by in their sampans, grim faced, hunched over, and buttoned up against the weather. He had only been there a few minutes when a young rickshaw driver appeared. Dressed in knee-length breeches, a clean long-sleeved shirt with frog closures, and a jaunty Western-style shooting cap, he presented a cheerful contrast to the gray weather.

"I take you for nice ride, mister. Cheap fare," the boy smiled.

"And where would you be taking me?" Ned asked.

"I take you where wind blows."

Ned stood up. "Then I guess we should be going."

He followed the young man and got in the rickshaw. The bonnet was pulled up and fastened, which gave Ned protection, not only from the wind but from prying eyes as well. They rolled off down the Bund, and Ned could feel the strength of the young man as the rickshaw started to move, like a runner leaving the starting block, slowly working up some steam, and finally hitting a comfortable stride. Ned marveled at the way these men made a living. Not only was it hard physical labor, but the pay was little more than a slave wage. It cost about fifty cents an hour to hire a rickshaw, and by the time the poor puller had paid off the company, he had precious little left over. Still, there were over eighty thousand rickshaw pullers in Shanghai, and if the average man provided for a family of three or four, the job supported a significant part of the city's population. Ned had been told that most of the pullers were not Shanghai born but former peasants making a go of it in the big city, hoping for something better to come along. He realized that this young man who was pulling him might not be a real rickshaw driver. More likely it was someone Mei had hired, someone she trusted. They had come to the section known as the Old Chinese City. It was a city built before the onslaught of foreigners and had once been walled. Although the old walls had long since come down, the Old Chinese City was still a maze of narrow streets and alleys, reflecting a time long before the advent of the automobile, the bus, and the tram. The rickshaw driver swiftly navigated through twists and turns, past the street hawkers and sidewalk barbers, and came to a stop outside a shop in what looked like a dusty, forgotten section of the city.

"Go quick inside," the driver instructed Ned.

Ned obeyed, dodging into the old shop's entrance with his head down while the rickshaw driver hurried off. Once inside, an old man with a long, scraggly beard scuttled toward the door, locked it, and pulled down the shade, and then he beckoned Ned toward the back of the shop. It was crowded, dark, and musty—full of old furniture, porcelain plates, small and larger statues, ginger jars, chests, vases, old clothing, and antique jewelry in cases. A group of masks stared down ominously. The whole place was jammed with so many things that Ned had the distinct feeling everything might collapse at any minute, fall inward, and smother him. The grizzled old man didn't comfort him either. He kept motioning Ned to go further and further into the rear of the store, which proved to be quite deep. In a far corner, the old man pointed to a staircase and rudely grunted as if he wanted Ned to go up. A young girl of about ten or eleven came down the stairs and motioned to him to follow. They went up one floor and then another to a small landing, where the girl pointed to a door at the end of a long hall.

Ned walked down the hall, opened the door, and entered a large, dimly lit room. An ornately carved opium bed stood against the wall. It was draped with silks and spread with soft cushions. Ned recognized Nigel, lying there, covered with a rich red quilt. There were chairs and tables grouped artfully around the room, and Ned guessed they were all cleaned-up pieces that had come from the grimy shop below. This room, in contrast, was neat and well scrubbed. Ned pulled up a chair next to Nigel's bed, and Nigel stirred in his sleep and then opened his eyes.

"Ned, Old Trout, it really is you." Nigel shifted a bit and managed to sit up.

"I'm afraid it is. You'll never be completely rid of me." He leaned over and took Nigel's hand. "How are you? You old beast."

Nigel chuckled. "I know I look a fright, but you should have seen me before."

"It's good to see you," Ned said sincerely, "and you don't look half as frightful as I expected."

"Mei's got me patched up, but it was touch and go for a while. I guess you've met the missus and made a good impression."

"I'm the one who's impressed. I don't know how a tramp like you managed it."

"Well," sighed Nigel, "I wish I could count on everyone to feel as you do, but you know what snobs people can be. If we stayed here, there would be quite a few people who would cross us off their list forever for marrying across the forbidden lines."

Ned looked at his friend. "Everyone who matters will feel as I do, and those who don't weren't worth your time in the first place."

"Shanghailanders can be extremely cruel and unenlightened, Ned."

"Then it's a good thing you're leaving this all behind."

Nigel laughed. "Well, it hasn't been all bad."

"Oh, make up your mind," Ned teased. "And speaking of leaving, do you think you could manage in three days?"

"I'll make myself be ready by then. What is the plan?"

"The plan is, we sail on the *Vanguard* in three days. I'll come round and get you at seven thirty in the morning. Mei will meet us on board. We'll be going to Sydney."

Nigel frowned. "Mei's warned you how dangerous getting me out might be, hasn't she?"

"Don't worry about it. I'll get us out of here, and in a few days, we'll be tossing one back in Sydney."

"Say," Nigel broke in, "I've forgotten to offer you a drink. There's some fine whiskey in that cabinet over there. Why don't you pour us a couple?"

"Maybe you shouldn't be drinking," Ned cautioned him.

"I'm allowed one double a day, and I'm electing to have it now."

Ned went up to the ornately painted cabinet, found the whiskey, and poured two doubles. He returned to Nigel's bedside, and as he handed Nigel his drink, he said, "And while we enjoy this fine whiskey, you're going to tell me exactly how you wound up lying like a wounded prince in all this oriental splendor."

Nigel grumbled. "Trying to be a bloody patriotic hero, that's how."

"But you *are* a bloody patriotic hero, and there *are* things worth for fighting for—or against. And as the world stands, I would say it's against."

"Anyway," Nigel went on, "I was asked by my employers to infiltrate a Japanese men's club and try to ferret out secrets."

"A Japanese men's club? You mean like a British men's club? I didn't know there was such a thing."

"British culture is horribly insidious, isn't it? It's a very exclusive club for officers. I had a partner from the Philippines, Enrico Balban. They hired me to teach fencing, cricket, and squash, and Enrico got hired as a janitor. He worked cleaning up the showers and locker rooms. What no one knew is that we both had crash courses in Japanese. So these blokes would chatter away in front of us thinking we didn't understand a thing. Eventually we were found out."

"And how did that happen? Getting found out."

"This German doctor started visiting the club, Dr. Hirsch. It was a little over a year ago. I knew that blond, snotty bastard was trouble from the start. I don't know what his business was with the Japanese, but he was always in the company of the higher-ups—the officers, the diplomats, and the really wealthy Japanese businessmen. I only saw him a couple of times myself, but each time, they were absolutely fawning over him. He was particularly chummy with this one young officer who was equally as arrogant and cocky. The doctor wasn't here that long, and I've learned since that he was the one who said we should be under surveillance. He may have overheard Enrico and me talking—although I don't see how. We were so careful. Eventually they had us followed."

"Do you know anything more about this doctor?" asked Ned.

"No, as I said, he was here for about two months, and then he vanished. They must have been watching us for a long time before they made their move. I got a call from Enrico one day. He said he was sure that someone had been in his flat, and he'd seen a Japanese officer he recognized just outside on the street as he came home. Enrico kept notes. I told him not to, but he insisted that it was the only way he could be thorough. Anyway, he called to warn me. And right after that, he left the flat, and they took him down. They beat him to death and threw him in Soo-Chow Creek. The official report said he was drunk, and a gang attacked, robbed, and dumped him. He was a marvelous person." Nigel paused to stifle his anger and grief.

"And you?" Ned asked.

"I was leaving my flat for a car that was to take me out of the city when they came after me. I was shot, but I managed to lose them. It was quite a feat. I ended up hiding in a bakery that belonged to some friends of Mei. I lost a lot of blood and passed out before they could get me picked up. With Mei's help, they had me moved here. I just can't believe I'm still alive, and Enrico is dead. I think he had a family somewhere."

Ned was quiet for a minute and then looked at his friend. "Lately, I've felt like the whole world is tumbling toward a huge, dark something. I have these moments when I think I sense a terrible presence lurking around—in the same way we used to think about the bogeyman under the bed when we were kids. But I'm quite sure this thing isn't the figment of a child's imagination. It's something real. And I'm afraid that many more lives, like the life of your friend, will be extinguished before it goes away."

Nigel chuckled. "You're still operating with a writer's psyche, I see."

Ned laughed. "Can't help it," he said and then downed what remained of his whiskey. "So, on top of everything else, you're now a married man."

"She agreed to marry me, even though we both thought I might not make it. And Mei tells me you're about to enter the esteemed state of matrimony yourself."

"It's true," Ned answered, "and I'm both delighted and surprised at the same time."

"Tell me about her. I know Mei's told you all about herself."

"Well, her name is Mina Beckwith. Like me, she's part Polynesian—Hawaiian, to be specific. She's a journalist on a bit of a hiatus right now. She's beautiful, smart, funny, and kind, and she has a dog named Ollie and an identical twin sister."

"And how did you meet this paragon?"

Ned gave him a boyish smile. "I met her during a murder investigation. She'd just come upon a dead body."

"How romantic—a body and a murder investigation."

"Her brother-in-law happens to be the chief of detectives in Honolulu. He's an old friend of mine. I visited him several times in Hawai'i, and his wife kept going on about how I should meet her sister. I kept making polite excuses, but when I finally did bump into her—"

"Over the dead body?"

"It wasn't *right* over the dead body, you know. Now where was I? Yes, when I finally met her—well, when I first met her, she was all dressed up like a harlequin, and I didn't know who she was—but when I actually met her, I think I was lost in about ten minutes." Ned looked down into his empty glass. "That's awfully good whiskey. I think I might pour myself another."

"I think I'll cheat and have a half, if you don't mind."

"Only half," Ned frowned. "You need to be well enough to leave in a few days."

"Only half, Old Trout."

On the designated morning of departure, Shanghai was once again blanketed with rain—not a heavy rain but a lingering kind of drizzly rain, enough to make Ned decide to wear his Burberry raincoat and carry an umbrella. He had hailed a taxi in front of his hotel to

meet Mei for breakfast at the Cathay on the Bund. After confer-
ring with her about their final plans, they parted, making a show
of saying good-bye, as if it were a final farewell. Earlier in his hotel
lobby, Ned had made sure that anyone within earshot had heard
him ask the desk clerks to have his luggage sent to the SS *Vanguard,*
a cruise ship that was to leave that afternoon, and had anyone
checked, he would have been told there was a first-class cabin booked
in his name.

He now stood in the Old Chinese City, looking out the back-alley
doorway, on the watch for the car and driver that would be picking
him and Nigel up. The doorway was set back from the street with a
small weed-and-rubble yard between the doorway and the rickety
back gate that opened right on to the alley. Nigel sat beside him, but
out of sight, as Ned scanned their surroundings. Backs of houses,
shops, and restaurants of two and three stories opened onto this rough,
unpaved lane that was barely wide enough for both car and pedestrian
traffic to safely share. The old city was a maze of these byways, and
Ned imagined that it would take quite some time to memorize all
the routes one could follow to arrive at a chosen destination. The rain
had cast a dull and muddy pallor over the morning, and the normal
potholes that dotted the alley were quickly becoming puddles. There
appeared to be only normal activity—a storekeeper sweeping rub-
bish out of his back door onto the street, a rickshaw driver wearily
making his way towards the main road. A young man walking along
with a cage of chickens in each hand had stopped to fuss with one of
the cage doors as an old beggar woman wrapped in rags and carrying
a gunnysack slowly made her way from the opposite direction picking through trash bins as she went along. Despite the peaceful scene,
Ned was on high alert, and he had a tense, sinking feeling that, from
experience, he knew would not subside until their ship was leaving
Shanghai in the distance and Nigel was safely tucked into his cabin.
Nigel was still weak and could walk unsteadily with a cane but needed
assistance to negotiate steps and stairs.

Ned spotted a dark sedan rolling slowly up the alley. It pulled up
and stopped near the gate. Ned helped Nigel to his feet, and they made
their way toward the car.

"This is the first time I've been outside in weeks," Nigel commented. He was making a great effort to try to walk without assistance.

"Careful on the uneven ground," Ned said, prepared at any second to steady his friend.

They reached the car, and just as Ned was about to help Nigel into the backseat, the young man who had been carrying the chickens made a dash toward them, pulled out a long, sharp knife, and held it against Nigel's side.

"Tell car go," the boy said in broken English.

Ned stood facing the boy as he clutched Nigel, and they both froze in position. "What did you say?" Ned asked, pretending not to understand, stalling for a few seconds to try to think.

"I say tell car go," the boy said in a loud voice. "Some men come for you. You do what I say or he dead man."

Over the boy's shoulder, Ned saw the old beggar woman only a few feet beyond. She seemed to have scurried up close to them quickly and quietly.

"You want me to tell our driver to go? Is that it?" Ned spoke slowly and deliberately.

"Yes," the boy almost yelled. "You do it now!"

The old woman had stealthily approached and was just behind the boy. From under her cloak, Ned saw a billy club rise in the air. Just as the woman brought the club down on the boy's head, Ned gave Nigel a shove toward the car and jumped back to avoid the knife blade that came forward and then dropped to the ground as the boy fell into a heap. The old woman, wrapped in rags, raised the brim of her hat, and as she winked, Ned recognized the face of Mrs. Worlan-Burke.

"Let's get our arses out of here," she said. "His friends can't be far behind."

Ned jumped in next to Nigel, and Mrs. Worlan-Burke climbed in beside the driver, ordering him to step on it. Just as they lurched forward, another car turned into the alley behind them and sped up in pursuit. Mrs. Worlan-Burke glanced at the vehicle behind them while giving directions and encouragement to the driver in Chinese. They gained some time by speeding across a main thoroughfare to another alleyway, but Ned could see that they were still within sight range of their pursuers. At the next thoroughfare, when Mrs. Worlan-Burke had the driver turn into the oncoming traffic, Ned thought he might just die of a heart attack, but they quickly turned into another alleyway and made another left turn and then a right turn coming into a dead end. Ned thought she might really be crazy, but she ordered them all out of the car. And with Nigel supported between them, they hurried down a small, dark passage between two buildings, while the driver ran away in another direction. The passage made some confusing twists, but Mrs. Worlan-Burke seemed to know exactly where she was going. They came near a kind of open market littered with stalls where people were selling everything under the sun, from live rabbits to silk dresses. Mrs. Worlan-Burke stopped and stripped off her beggar garb.

"Pardon me, but we don't have time for niceties," she said as she reached into her gunnysack and dove into a dress and some expensive shoes. She whipped out a matching purse and umbrella and then reached into the purse for her sunglasses and scarf. "See that stall over there?" She pointed a few yards away from the passage to a stall that was selling vegetables but had a kind of closed tent behind it. "Get Nigel in there as quickly as possible and duck down. Leave the rest to me. I'm going round the other way. Lie low, because in a few minutes this place could be crawling with Kuomintang, their Japanese allies, or both."

Ned managed to get Nigel quickly into the back of the stall. There were smelly crates and bins of old vegetable trimmings from cabbages, turnips, onions, potatoes, and other kinds of vegetable garbage, and Ned and Nigel crouched behind them so that no one from the street could see them. After what seemed like an hour but was actually only about ten minutes, a rickshaw cart, designed for hauling, pulled up behind the tent. Two Chinese men stuck their faces in the tent.

"Mrs. Lady says to get your arses in rickshaw. Hurry up, and lie down," one man said.

"Are you okay?" Ned asked Nigel.

"Let's do whatever Mrs. Lady says," Nigel replied.

"Okay?" said the Chinese man.

Nigel said something in Chinese to the man and then asked Ned if they should go straight to the *Vanguard*.

"Not straight there," Ned said, and he named an out-of-the-way place on the river.

"Why there?" Nigel asked.

"That's for me to know and you to find out," Ned grinned.

Nigel rolled his eyes. "Oh, Jesus. This is going to be a day to remember, isn't it?"

Ned gave the directions to Nigel, who gave them to the two men in Chinese as they lifted him up and placed him in the cart, motioning Ned to follow. It was a cart built with a flat bed, and Ned and Nigel lay down while the men covered them with filthy blankets. Next they heard lots of voices and felt things being thrown over them. There was a split in the wood on the side of the cart—just enough for Ned to see through. The men were throwing on a thick layer of garbage. After a few minutes, the cart began to move. As they rolled along, Ned could see brick cobbles, dirt, and the feet and lower legs of people going by. The bad smell was overwhelming, and the rain was dripping over the garbage and leaking down through the blankets. Ned felt something sticky dripping and spreading over his favorite Burberry raincoat.

"Are you all right, Nigel?" Ned asked in a muffled whisper.

"Lovely transport you've arranged," Nigel answered.

"Don't thank me. Thank Mrs. Worlan-Burke."

"I hope I don't heave."

"Do your best, will you?" Ned said. "I thought things couldn't smell much worse, but perhaps I just wasn't using my imagination."

The rickshaw driver said something in Chinese, and Nigel responded. "He said to be quiet and still," Nigel whispered to Ned. "Military patrol."

Ned held his breath as the rickshaw came to a stop. From between the slats, Ned could see several pairs of polished boots and the muzzle ends of rifles pointed at the ground. The seconds passed like hours as the rickshaw drivers answered questions. Ned closed his eyes and thought about Mina. He imagined her playing happily with her dog,

Ollie, outside her house on the beach. He saw her moving toward the water's edge with Ollie beside her and pictured them wading into the calm, blue ocean. He saw Mina start to swim, gliding through the water with her long, graceful strokes, Ollie following, while a seabird swooped around them overhead. He was jostled from his daydream and back to being covered in garbage as the rickshaw began to move. The drivers mumbled something, and Nigel reported that they were away from the soldiers but still within sight distance. They turned onto a main thoroughfare with heavy traffic. Ned could see car and bus tires whizzing by, streetcar tracks, and the legs and feet of all kinds of pedestrians as they made their way across town. The dirty coverlets over them were getting wet, and the dampness, laden with the odors of rotting vegetables, was seeping down and permeating Ned's coat and hair.

"We're going to need a good scrubbing after this," Nigel commented, as if reading Ned's thoughts.

"Oh, I don't know," Ned responded. "Perhaps we might just set a new trend in men's cologne."

Ned could tell when they pulled off the main streets, as the traffic thinned out, and just when the road became very quiet, the rickshaw came to a stop. The drivers said something, and Nigel told Ned that they should get out as quickly as possible. Once the rickshaw drivers were rid of their passengers, they hurriedly pulled away, and Ned and Nigel found themselves standing in a deserted alleyway just south of the Bund, only a few yard from the banks of the Whangpu. There were old, abandoned warehouses on both sides of the narrow street and a set of stairs that led down to a dock, where a small sampan sat bobbing in the water. Ned helped Nigel on board and got him settled on the bench under the hood. He took off his now-soiled coat and wrapped it around his shivering friend, who looked as if the morning adventures were taking a toll on his already delicate health. Ned then donned a tattered coat and large straw hat. He took a revolver from under the bench and put it in one of the oversized pockets of the coat. He cast off and, standing on the stern of the craft, took the oar and began to steer them across the river toward the opposite shore.

The air was turning cold. The rain began to come down harder, and as clouds of mist swirled across the water, Ned had to work to keep his destination in sight. The rain pelted the gray-green water as he expertly worked the oar in long, powerful strokes, moving the sampan along at a neat clip. They were nearly halfway across the river when Ned heard the sound of a small outboard motor. The sound got louder, and Ned could soon see the prow of another sampan approaching. He had barely spotted the boat when the first bullet ripped past his legs and through the hood.

"Get down on the floor, Nigel," Ned shouted, as he pulled out his pistol and returned fire.

Ned could see the sampan approaching. There were three men, one steering the outboard and two with guns. Another bullet flew past his head. It was impossible to row and shoot at the same time, and he knew the mist and rain were the only things that were saving him from being hit. He gave the oar a couple of powerful strokes and dove under the hood. Lying on the floor, he took another shot at their pursuers, this time hitting their prow only a foot away from where one of the gunman lay. In the background, he could hear the sound of another engine, bigger and more powerful than the outboard, and he feared the worst—that the sampan that was in sight had more powerful reinforcement behind it. There was more gunfire as the sampan with the outboard moved in on them. A bullet hit the deck, and wood splinters flew, some of them just missing Ned's face. The roar of the more powerful boat drew closer, and in the confusion, Ned couldn't tell exactly what direction it was coming from. The gunmen were close, about thirty yards and closing. The roaring engines were nearly on them. Out of the mist came a shiny, blue launch about fifteen feet in length. It flew between Ned and the pursuers. Taking a tight turn, it doubled back and headed straight for the gunmen, ramming their sampan and sending them flying into the murky river. The launch came about next to Ned and Nigel and cut its engines.

A dark, smiling Polynesian face peered down at Ned. "Malo le soifua."

"Oliva!" Ned shouted back. "Just in time."

"Ia, fa'avave!" Oliva motioned Ned to hurry.

They got Nigel in the launch and sped away into the shroud of mist and rain, leaving the three men to flounder in the river. In a few minutes, the launch pulled up to a dock near an old freighter bearing the name *South Sea Trader*. Ned and Nigel disembarked, and Oliva told them he would see them later, as the launch was to be abandoned far away from the ship. The pair were hustled on board by some stevadores, strong island men who swept Nigel into their arms and carried him up the gang plank and into his cabin, where Mei waited anxioulsy. Ned, carrying a soiled and smelly Burberry raincoat, stumbled into his cabin, stripped off his clothes, and went directly to the shower. Just as he finished dressing, he felt the ship under way, first moving away from the dock and then foward on the Whangpu and out toward the open ocean. He wanted to thank the captain but knew he had best wait until they were out at sea, as the ship now required the captain's full attention. He knocked quietly on Nigel and Mei's door. Mei opened the door, and inside, he found Nigel bathed and settled in his bunk.

"You all right, old man?" Ned asked.

"That was a close call, Trout," Nigel smiled weakly.

"Trout?" Mei grinned.

"You never heard that." Ned frowned.

Mei laughed and looked at him. "Trout?"

Ned groaned. "Nigel, I should have left you to drown in the river."

"Then I wouldn't have the pleasure of finding out how we ended up on this lovable scow," Nigel said.

"Captain Clarke is an old family friend from Apia. He and my father were very close, and I've known him since I was a boy. He's taken this ship all over the Pacific. When I checked out the shipping schedule and found out he was in port, I arranged for him to help us out. I used the *Vanguard* as a blind, and it's worked out perfectly. Well, almost perfectly."

"And the man who saved us?"

"Oliva? He's been Clarke's right hand ever since I can remember."

Overcome with emotion, Nigel took Mei's hand. "I didn't think Shanghai would ever let me out alive."

"You need a new job, darling," Mei said as she kissed him on the forehead. "No more cloak and dagger."

Nigel looked at Ned. "So, if you don't mind me asking, where are we really going?"

"We're headed first for Sāmoa," Ned answered. "Then you and Mei can decide whether you would like to go on to Sydney or whether you'd like to try your luck in Honolulu. Personally, I think you two would love Honolulu."

# 4

# HONOLULU, HALLOWEEN

**MINA WATCHED FROM** the window as Cecily and Tom's car came down her driveway while Ollie barked excitedly. Her bungalow was on the beach, tucked away in the neighborhood of Kaʻalāwai, a short ways from Waikīkī, just around the side of Diamond Head, and although it was only a short jaunt from the famous beach, it seemed a million miles away. There were two identical bungalows on this two-acre piece of property. The other was just across from Mina's and separated by a large hau-tree arbor. It belonged to Mina's identical twin sister, Nyla. But Nyla and her husband, Todd Forest, who happened to be the chief of detectives in Honolulu, had their own house up in Maunalani Heights and used their bungalow for guests and parties. It had been Ned's home base for a good part of the year, and his things were still there waiting for his return from Shanghai.

"Thank you for warning me, Ollie." His goofy behavior always brought a smile to her face. "But I can see them on my own. Be quiet now."

At the words "be quiet," Ollie immediately stopped barking and sat at attention looking out the window. Mina saw him sniff the air and tremble slightly with excitement when he recognized Cecily stepping out of the car. Cecily was dressed in a harem outfit with ballooning pants, turned-up shoes, and a very fetching veil. Mina could vaguely see Tom in the car, and it looked like he was wearing a turban. She came out of the house, pulling the patch of the pirate costume down over her left eye. Her hat had the skull and crossbones painted on it, a white, silky blouse bloomed over a pair of puffy, black silk pants, and a sword was held in place by a crimson sash. Her black boots made her look even taller. She had her hair tied back in a braid and a huge golden loop dangling from her left earlobe. Ollie scampered behind her with his own matching pirate hat and eye patch.

"Oh, Mina!" Cecily exclaimed. "I love the penciled-in mustache—the way it curls up at the ends. And Ollie!! Look at you!"

"I don't think he likes that eye patch," Mina said as she motioned Ollie into the car. "I had to coax him to not paw it off. You look too gorgeous for words."

"Thanks," Cecily said as she got into the car. "It was Tom's idea."

"More like your fantasy, huh, Tom?" Mina winked at Cecily's husband with her unpatched eye as she climbed in beside Ollie.

"Women are sassy troublemakers, aren't they, Ollie?" Tom smiled at the dog, turned the car around, and drove them all off to the Halloween party.

It only took them a few minutes to get there as Black Point, a lava headland that pushed out into the sea, was just next door to Kaʻalāwai. Mina had not been to the old school camp in many years, but the grounds seemed as familar to her as if time had hardly passed. She thought how quickly places in the islands could change and become unrecognizable, while over the years, others seemed to hardly change at all. She recognized the layout of the compound and the two large rooms under the long roof that once were dormitories for girls and boys. Perpendicular to the dormitories was the sprawling meeting room with its stage, stone fireplace, and attached kitchen. The paint was peeling off the aging wooden structures, but they were perfectly situated to take advantage of the the ocean views and breeze. Covered porches connected all of the spaces, creating an open-air hallway, while the lawn, wide and long, stretched from the buildings all the way to the craggy black lava cliffs and the constantly breaking waves. A stand of ironwood pines had been planted around the back and sides of the building so that one had to walk through them when approaching from the parking lot. The trees were much taller than Mina remembered. Long needles had dropped from the trees and dried out, forming a thick carpet of brown that covered the ground. Small, rounded cones were embedded in the needles, and Mina could feel them beneath her shoes as she walked. The sensation made her think about the many hours she and her sister had spent as children at so many different island beaches, gathering these cones and twigs to fashion animals, trees, miniature figures, and all kinds of imaginary creatures. A breeze from the ocean swept through the trees, rustling the branches and making a lonely whistling sound that filled the air. Ironwoods were imported, foreign trees, considered by some residents as plant pests. But they were part of her childhood, and like so many other things from the background of her past, she had formed an unintentional attachment.

"Hello, I'm so glad you could come, Mina," Tamara said as she walked from the veranda towards their party, Jocks trailing after her. Tamara was dressed as a Scottish highlander, and Jocks wore a miniature kilt and matching tam. His tail wagged furiously as he bounced up to Ollie. "We're meeting in the painting and drawing studio, formerly known as the girls' dorm. The real party is in the meeting room, but the decorators—that would be the men—say we can't see it until all the business is out of the way. Very mysterious if you ask me."

It amused Mina to be attending a meeting where everyone wore a costume. At one end of the room, a row of drawing benches had been shoved to one side, and chairs were placed in front of a platform that she guessed was usually used as a model's perch. There was a similar platform at the other end of the room with an arranged still life of driftwood, shells, a fishing net, and some glass balls, but it was surrounded by several easels. All along the top of the back wall, figure drawings in charcoal, graphite, and conte crayon were carelessly tacked up. Cubbyholes and shelves sat beneath them, crammed with rags, boxes, and various implements of art. The side of the room that faced the sea took full advantage of the view.

A man, dressed as some kind of Greek god, Mina guessed, came striding toward them, and she imagined, even before he spoke, that his handsome good looks could charm the good sense out of many a mortal woman. He had a striking, energetic presence, and with a hint of gray at the temples, Mina thought he looked like he could be Johnny Weissmueller's older brother.

"You must be the writer who's going to save us all from looking like we don't know what we're talking about." He smiled at her with what appeared to be genuine warmth.

"Yes, dear." Tamara laughed. "She's going to spin straw into gold."

"And here I was thinking it was a lost art." He took Mina's hand. "I'm Desmond Rivers, and I'm so pleased you're going to help us."

Mina thought his hand felt very sure of itself. "I hope I'm able to help make everything a success," she said.

"Is this Mina Beckwith?" A lovely woman dressed as a Greek goddess glided up next to Desmond. She was tall and shapely with a striking blonde streak in her lovely light-brown hair. Together they looked like a formidable pair, beautiful, strong, and capable of persuasion. "I miss your articles in the paper. We always counted on you to keep us informed. I so hope you might go back."

"That would depend on a number of things changing," Mina said with a smile.

"This is my wife, Molly," Desmond said. "I guess you can tell shyness is not one of her problems."

Molly winked. "I'm sure it's not one of yours either, is it, Mina?"

Mina laughed. "No, it's a big handicap if you want to chase a story."

"Go do something else, Dez dear," Molly said as she took Mina's hand. "I get to take her around and show her off."

Molly spirited her away to meet Bill Hitchins and his Tahitian wife, Tevai. Bill was dressed up like Hermes, in a helmet with wings and a cloak over his tanned and taut bare chest, and instead of pants, he had chosen to wear theatrical tights. His suede boots were also adorned with wings, and Mina thought his flirtatious grin looked especially mercurial. His wife seemed shy in her Cleopatra costume. She said hello but hardly anything more, and although she smiled serenely, Mina thought she looked lost and stranded.

"Yo ho ho, it's Mina Beckwith."

Mina turned around to see a slim figure completely swathed in black with velvet ears, a slinky tail, and a velvet mask that gave her a whiskered nose and covered the upper part of her face but left her red lips and perfect chin on display.

"Meeow." The figure twitched her nose.

"Appy?" Mina said. "Is that you?"

"Shucks, you recognized me," Appy answered, giving Mina a hug. "I'm so glad to see you."

"Don't tell me," Molly said in a comical drawl, "you both know each other from that dreadful school everyone went to."

Appy laughed. "We won't mention it, Molly."

Molly rolled her eyes. "Please. I'm so sick of lilyponds and who-knows-who. Everyone here can just go on and on. It's one of the curses of not being raised in the islands."

"Well," Mina said, "it can also be one of the curses of *being* raised here."

"Depending on who you're talking to," Appy added.

Molly frowned. "I have no idea what you mean. Oh, look, there's Raymond. Come along, girls."

Molly steered them toward a man outfitted in black and red, wearing a skull cap with horns on his head and holding a pitchfork in his left hand. He had a perfect goatee, and Mina had a hard time figuring out if it was real or pasted on.

"Ray," Molly called out to him, "I want you to meet someone."

Ray came obediently toward them and gave Molly a slight bow. "I can't very well disobey a goddess, can I?"

"This is Mina Beckwith," Molly said. "She's the writer you'll be working with on the catalog. Mina, this is Raymond Morgan."

"My pleasure," he said with a smile.

"Oh my God!" Appy blurted out before Mina could offer a polite response. "Look at that!"

They all turned to look at the woman who had just walked in the door. Jocks started barking at her, and Tamara had to hush him up. The woman wore a long, gray gown crisscrossed with black velvet ribbons, and her high-heeled shoes made her seem unnaturally tall. Her long hair, which looked like it had been sprayed gray, was arranged in calculated disorder, sticking out in some places and hanging down in scraggly strands in others. Her face and arms were covered in some kind of grayish-white makeup, but the most startling and frightening thing about her was the way she had painted her face. She had painted dark deep circles around her eyes and emphasized the hollows of her cheeks. Her lips were black, but near the right corner, there were tiny drops of painted blood. She carried a basket of fresh, raw beef bones. The whole effect was so unearthly and real that everyone in the room fell silent. The woman stopped and surveyed the crowd.

Finally the woman started laughing. "There'd better be a prize for the best costume because this took the whole damn afternoon to put together!"

Everyone in the room responded with a laugh and went back to their conversations. Molly walked up to the woman.

"What are you, Tilda? Some kind of devouring ghost? The makeup is simply amazing." Molly admired her for a moment. "Come here and meet Mina Beckwith."

Molly introduced Tilda Clement to Mina but then was called away by her husband.

Tilda observed Molly as she floated toward Desmond. "The God and Goddess. I wonder if that's how they see themselves or how they want others to see them."

"Maybe both," Appy giggled.

"Where's that friend of yours?" Tilda asked Appy. "The one who makes those twisted metal things?"

"Are you talking about Andrew Halpern?" Mina asked.

"Appy is dying to reel him in, aren't you, dear?" Tilda's tone was carefully poised between sympathy and ridicule.

"I—I don't know what you mean," Appy responded, obviously taken off guard. "I mean, I don't think I even want—I haven't ever—"

"You're so easily rattled, Appy," Tilda interrupted. "Try to say what you mean, darling."

Desmond called the meeting to order, and everyone took their seats. Mina saw a young, wiry Japanese man slip in and take a seat. He was not wearing a costume, and Mina guessed it must be Akira Nakasone. There were the usual kind of reports at a business meeting— the approval of the last meetings minutes, a membership, treasury, and old-business report. When the new-business discussion opened, it centered around the upcoming exhibit. Mina was introduced, but then she got confused by the disorderly proceedings. She was able to gather that each artist was going to be photographed in some kind of setup of a famous painting of his or her choice, and she was to meet and interview each artist at the photography session. The first on the list would be Desmond, who was scheduled the day after tomorrow.

Appy whispered to Mina, "He probably needs to take the day off tomorrow to nurse the big hangover he's going to have after the party."

When the meeting concluded, Desmond announced that everyone should gather at the meeting-room door in ten minutes. During the interval, other guests were arriving, and Molly was rallying everyone together on the lawn until the appointed time. Mina noted Akira Nakasone walking directly toward the parking lot. She saw that Andrew Halpern had come with his sister, Sheila, and her husband, Sam Takahashi. Sam wore a wolf mask and a tuxedo, and Sheila wore a black evening gown and a long red cape with a hood. Andrew was dressed as Robin Hood, all in green, carrying a bow, with a quiver full of arrows slung over his back. Appy was glancing over at Andrew and then looking away. Perhaps, Tilda was right, Mina thought. Appy *was* interested in Andrew and appeared to be very anxious about it. Mina waved as she saw her friends Louis Goldburn and his wife, Doris, walking through the grove of trees. Dressed in Renaissance costumes, they looked as if they'd stepped out of a Shakespeare play.

"How are you, Mina?" Louis smiled as she went up to them. "And where's your brilliant fiancé?"

"I'm fine," Mina smiled back. "And his brilliance is in Shanghai."

Louis frowned. "Shanghai?"

"He was invited to give a series of talks at some Dramatic Society," Mina said.

"I don't think Shanghai is a very safe place to be right now." Louis looked concerned.

Mina pouted. "That's why he said I couldn't go along."

"Sounds fishy," Doris said. "You never know what these men might really be up to, eh?"

"Are you a supporter of this art group too?" Louis asked. "They do some wonderful work."

"Not yet," Mina answered. "I'm helping with the catalog for an exhibit at the Academy."

"I keep trying to get Duncan MacKenzie to join," Louis said, "but he doesn't seem interested."

"Oh, Louis dear," Doris said in her droll manner, "it's far too bourgeois for him."

An older man, dressed in the cap and gown of an old-fashioned professor, approached them.

"Louis and Doris," the man said with a distinctly Germanic accent, "I am so pleased you could come tonight. It will be quite a nice gathering."

"Have you made that strudel we hear you're so famous for?" Doris asked.

"Just for you, my dear, I have made some for the dessert table," he answered.

"We'll be the first in line," Louis said. "Ari, have you met our friend Mina Beckwith? Mina, this is Ari Schoner."

He was a stout man with gray hair, wire-rim glasses, and a bushy mustache. "So pleased to meet you," Ari said as he gave Mina a warm handshake. "I will speak to you all later. I must make sure everything is going well in the kitchen."

He turned and bustled away toward the meeting room.

"Ari left Germany several years ago, but he's only been in Hawai'i for around a year," Louis reported. "He was a professor in Munich. He left because he knew the persecution of Jews was only going to get worse under Hitler."

"It's terrible," Mina said.

"Just last month, they declared that Jews were no longer citizens. Overnight, people have lost citizenship in their own country and the rights that go with it. I'm afraid to think what might be next," said Louis with a tremor in his voice.

"Come on now," Doris took her husband's arm. "You promised me an evening of fun, and I'm going to hold you to it. Why look, they're finally going to let us into the hall."

Mina was one of the last to go in. Ollie and Jocks had been romping in the ironwood grove, and she had to spend a few minutes picking needles out of Ollie's curly black hair. The sun had just set and the fleeting twilight cast a pale-pink glow over the clouds when she strode toward the doorway with Ollie by her side. Over the entry, spindly dead branches had been twisted and tied into an arch, and a sign that read "Black Point Cemetery" hung down from the apex. The letters looked like they had been scrawled in blood. Mina stepped into the great hall, which was dimly lit with candles and lanterns. An artificial tree stood in the center of the room. Its bare branches stretched out in a looming canopy and were painted to look like they had been scorched in a fire. Several stuffed black birds with evil red eyes glared down. A faux Egyptian coffin stood upright beneath the windows that faced the sea. It was surrounded by tombstones, and some kind of green fabric had been cleverly arranged with grasses, sticks, and dead shrubs to create an artificial graveyard. There was a narrow pathway that led up to the coffin, and as Mina approached, she saw a sign on the coffin door that said, "Open if You Dare." She pulled on the rope latch, and immediatley the door swung open and the figure of a mummy fell toward her. She shrieked and jumped back, and then burst into laughter as the mummy stopped itself just before it touched her, held back by some kind of tie. Desmond, who was standing nearby, let out a cheer.

"Let's toast to Mina," he shouted as he raised his glass. "The first one brave enough to take the dare."

"That was very clever," Mina said to him.

"Come and see something else, my dear," he said.

Desmond steered her behind the artificial tree to the stage that rose from the main floor and was recessed in the east wall. There were two sets of stairs on either side of the curved apron. The front of the stage was lined with jack-o'-lanterns, and behind them sat several grotesque figures at a banquet table.

"Up here," said Desmond, leading her on to the stage. It's meant to be looked at from all sides."

Mina and Ollie followed him up the stairs. In the center of the long table sat a skeleton with a golden crown and several dead lei. Its arms were stretched out on the table on either side with the palms of the hands turned upwards. The skeleton was flanked by twelve figures, six on either side in groups of threes. The groups were all of different materials. One was a group of dressmaking forms with wire rib cages. Ghoulish masks on sticks served as heads, with long protruding tongues, horns, and narrowly shaped eyes. Thin arms formed from rags bore claw-like hands that grasped at decaying food. Another group were three store mannequins done up with fangs and black capes like vampires. Another group were evil-looking scarecrows, and the last and most omnious were figures formed from papier-mâché that looked like demonic children's dolls. Mina thought the way the smiles were painted on their faces was especially disturbing. Candelabras cast a flickering light over the table, which was strewn with rotting vegetables and stale bread. Although she found the whole thing very well planned and executed, it seemed like underneath the creative fun, there was an unintended motif of something not very nice at all. She stared at everything for a moment and then turned to Desmond.

"It's the *Last Supper*," she said. "You've patterned it after Da Vinci's *Last Supper*."

"Very good, Miss Beckwith," said Desmond, clearly impressed. "No one else has recognized our joke."

"And who exactly would the jokers be?" she asked.

"Me, Andrew, Raymond, and Bill," he said. "We thought we would fool everyone, but I guess we might have to get up pretty early in the morning to fool you."

Mina laughed. "I guess you might."

"Now, how is it you don't have a drink? I think we need to do something about that."

After Mina had gotten a drink, she wandered through the crowd of costumed guests. Raymond Morgan introduced his Swiss wife, Marguerite, who was dressed—appropriately, Mina thought—as a milk maid. She seemed to Mina an unlikely partner for Raymond. He was the cosmopolitan type—tall and athletically slim, with dark hair and lively brown eyes. He had a way of holding his head and appeared to be looking down on everything. Deserved or not, it gave him an air of sophistication, while his wife, by contrast, was a blue-eyed blonde, short, pudgy, and looked like she could have run a bakery. Mina couldn't help thinking about the Jack Sprat nursery rhyme. Their daughter, Eva, however, had inheirited the best traits of both parents. She was tall and well formed like her father, with the bright blue eyes and golden-blonde hair of her mother. Mina guessed her to be about eighteen or nineteen. In counterpoint to her father's devil outfit, she was dressed as an angel with gossamer wings and a halo. Her much younger brother, Paul, looked very bored in his sailor uniform. They spoke for a moment and then turned to watch a group of modern dancers who suddenly swept into the room wearing long scarves and performing to the eerie melody of *Danse Macabre*. When the dance concluded, a gong sounded to announce the opening of the dinner buffet. Mina got herself a plate of food and made her way to one of the tables that had been set outside, sitting down with Ari and Tilda. They were soon joined by Eva Morgan.

Ari was going on about someone in Germany named Gibble or Gobbel—how bad he was and all about his voracious sweet tooth for young girls. Ari said something about his newspaper files and the pictures he'd collected of Gibble/Gobbel with girls young enough to be his daughter. But while he was talking, Mina noticed that Eva had the strangest look on her face and was staring intently at Bill Hitchins, who was flirting audaciously with Molly. Eva's face turned crimson as she saw Bill place his arm around Molly's waist and playfully nibble at her earlobe. Molly walked away from Bill, but not before she pinched him and laughed. Eva stood up abruptly and left the table.

"That was very sudden, don't you think?" Ari commented.

"It's just as well she sees what Bill is like before it's too late," Tilda said before she licked the spare-rib sauce off her fork. She had only been half listening to Ari.

"Does she have a crush on him?" Mina tried to sound nonchalant.

"He's been flirting with her and teasing her like crazy," Tilda said, "like he does with anyone he catches admiring him."

"Where is his wife, Tevai?" Ari asked. "I saw her earlier."

"She probably went home," Tilda answered.

"Do they live near here?" Mina asked.

"They live on the far side of the point," said Tilda. "Her brother lives with them too. He's as beautiful as she is. There's a path through the pine trees over there to the lane that leads to their place."

"Yes," Ari said, "and Desmond and Molly have their house on the other side of the parking lot. It's very convenient to the studios."

Tilda winked at Mina. "Very convenient. Well," she said, crumpling up her napkin and putting it on her empty plate, "Tevai will be back with her brother. She seems to know just when Bill is about to pass out or make away with some woman, and they appear out of nowhere to shepherd him home."

Mina couldn't help but notice a distressed Eva talking to her father. He led her into the meeting room, and soon Eva returned with a glass of punch and sat back down.

"I hope you are feeling better, my dear," Ari said.

"Yes, thank you," Eva said as she smiled politely.

Just as everyone was finishing dinner, dance music began in the hall. Tilda and Eva excused themselves, but Mina decided to linger outside for a while as the night was clear and full of stars, and the ocean waves were breaking in peaceful white ribbons. For a few minutes, Mina was lost in thought, thinking about Ned and what he might be doing. Ari had also remained behind, saying he was far too old for dancing. From inside his professor's robe, he took out a cigar and a lighter.

"I hope you don't mind," he said softly, as if he might be intruding on her thoughts.

"Of course not," she said.

"This is a lovely spot," he reflected. "Hawai'i is a lovely place."

"Yes, it is," Mina replied. "Still, it must be hard for you to be away from your home."

"I do miss it sometimes," he confessed. "But everyone here is so kind, and you see, I could not stay there. I had already made too much trouble."

"What kind of trouble?" Mina asked.

"For years, I made it very clear—how I felt about the Nazi Party, at the university, in public speeches, in letters to the newspapers. Then, when they came to have so much power . . . well, you can imagine why I had to leave. Fortunately, I have only one sister, whose husband is dead. She left years before me to live with her daughter in New York. So there is no one to worry about at home. I mean, no close family, but of course we all worry about everyone else."

"What are you doing out here, Mina, when all the fun is going on inside?" Cecily appeared from behind.

Ari chuckled. "She is taking pity on an old man."

Mina laughed. "Hardly pity."

"You should go inside and enjoy yourself," Ari said.

"You should come and taste the apple strudel Ari made," exclaimed Cecily. "It's out-of-this-world good."

"Now that sounds completely irresistible," Mina said.

As Mina was following Cecily into the hall, she saw Molly Rivers walking purposefully over to Ari. Mina paused on the porch and observed what she thought might be a heated discussion between them. Molly's face contorted, and she stood quickly and rushed away from Ari. Mina turned and walked through the door, not wanting to be seen watching.

Inside, the music swirled while couples took to the dance floor, whirling around the scary tree in the center of the room. While Ollie played with Jocks inside and outside, Mina danced a bit, visited with old friends, and chatted with the people she had just met. She thought Desmond was paying her a little too much attention. He asked her to dance several times, and she felt relieved when Raymond cut in on him.

"I think sometimes Desmond can be overwhelming," Raymond said as he moved expertly accross the dance floor.

"Thanks for rescuing me," Mina said.

"I'm just glad I was right," he replied. "Some women enjoy his attention."

"I'm engaged to be married," Mina informed him.

"My congratulations," he said, "but where is your young man?"

"He's away on business," she answered. "I hope your daughter wasn't too upset by Bill Hitchins."

He looked surprised. "Eva?"

"Perhaps I shouldn't have mentioned it," Mina said apologetically. "I saw her watching him with Molly, and then she seemed so . . . unhappy."

He shook his head. "He's a rogue, but I suppose it's better that she saw for herself. Maybe now she'll be more sensible."

As the evening wore on, Mina felt a bit tired of it all and wandered back outside to sit down away from the drinking and dancing. An exhausted Cecily and Tom sooned joined her, and just as they were about to head for the parking lot, they saw a determined Tevai, followed by a young man who could have been her twin, come from around the building headed for the party.

"Gosh, where do think she's been?" Tom asked.

"At home," Mina said sadly, "waiting until it's time to collect her wayward husband."

Two days later, rain and wind swept across Honolulu. Mina pulled her coupe into the small parking lot at the Black Point art studio. There were a couple of other cars parked there, and she thought they must belong to some of the artists who used the studios. She was here to do her first interview for the art catalog with Desmond Rivers. A south swell was rolling in, sending waves crashing against the lava headland, and she couldn't help but feel unsettled as she watched large white plumes of water shooting up in the air with each set of waves. She did as she had been instructed and followed the sandy path on the ʻEwa side of the parking lot through the beach morning-glory vines to a gray and weathered wooden side gate with a string of several rusty cowbells. She went through and then around to the front door. She walked onto the porch, which was littered with shoes and sandals, and knocked on the door, but no one came to answer it. So she knocked louder and then sat down on a small bench. After ten minutes of waiting, she was about to leave when Desmond came walking around the corner of the house. He seemed surprised to see her sitting there.

"Didn't Molly let you in?"

"I don't think she's at home," Mina said as she stood up.

"I'm so sorry," he said as he opened the door. "I had an errand I couldn't put off. She was here when I left. I hope you haven't been waiting long."

"Not long," Mina answered as she followed him through a small foyer and down a hallway that opened up to a dining area on the right and a large living room that faced the sea.

"I wonder where she went?" he frowned and looked around as if she might be hiding somewhere. "Oh, well, I guess we don't need her to get on with it, do we?" he grinned at Mina.

Just outside, framed by the large glass window, the huge waves were breaking on the cliffs, and she found herself having to almost shout sometimes in order to be heard over the roar of the crashing surf. They sat together on the plum-colored sofa trying not to be distracted. After about fifteen mintues, Molly showed up, somewhat startled by the two of them. Her hair looked damp and bedraggled. Her face was flushed, and she was out of breath.

Desmond frowned at her. "Where have you been? Didn't you remember Mina was coming?"

"Sorry," she quickly replied. "I was out walking and forgot about the time. When I remembered, I ran home as fast as I could. I'll make some coffee."

She rushed out of the room but soon returned, composed and serene, to hover around them—first with coffee and then with warm muffins—pretending to be disinterested but all the while keeping a trained eye on their exchanges. Mina wondered if Molly was simply curious or if she felt like she had to monitor her husband's behavior. The living room was tastefully but simply furnished—the plum sofa, a coffee table, a couple of chairs, and a large Persian carpet. The spare décor brought one's attention to the artwork—Molly's sensuous bas-relief, her curving statuettes; Desmond's prints, primarily of Hawaiians doing traditional tasks: fishing, pounding poi, or weaving lauhala. Mina particularly liked one of a group of women quilting under a breadfruit tree because it reminded her of her Grandma Hannah.

"Oh, yes, I was a commercial artist in San Francisco when we first moved here," Desmond leaned back against the arm of the sofa, crossed his legs, and gave her a satisfied smile. "Now, I'm only doing fine art."

"And what brought you to the islands?" Mina asked.

"I was offered a job with the newspaper, doing commercial work, which I did for a number of years, but then, I decided to make a go of it on my own, as an artist."

Molly snickered. "His grandmother died and left him a pile. He doesn't *have* to work anymore."

Desmond laughed. "And neither do you, darling."

"Oh, but I actually *like* teaching—grown-ups, that is," Molly retorted.

"Printmaking," Mina continued, not wanting to veer too far off the subject, "how did you decide to choose that as your medium?"

"Of course, I already knew all about mechanical printing." Desmond languidly stirred his cup of coffee. "Because I'd worked for so many newspapers as an illustrator and a draftsman. So when it was introduced to me as an artistic medium—I happened into a class in San Francisco at the Art Institute—I was immediately smitten."

"I know you especially like Hawaiian subject matter," Mina commented.

"When we first moved into this neighborhood, there were so many Hawaiian families—fishing, some farming, but mostly fishing. They were so good to us, and I was taken by them. And after all, this *is* Hawai'i." Desmond's brow furrowed slightly. "I can't understand these artists here who want to pretend they're somewhere else and prefer to paint a phony European-styled still life or contrived scenes of ladies in Dutch costumes. It's ridiculous."

Molly smiled as she refilled Mina's coffee cup. "Desmond has a few favorite soap boxes he likes to climb up on."

While Desmond was going on about how artists in Hawai'i should be representing Hawai'i, there was a knock at the door. Molly went to answer it, and Mina could see Marguerite Morgan standing on the threshold. Molly left Marguerite standing in the open door while she dissappeared down the hall. Marguerite gave Mina and Desmond a wave just before Molly returned and handed a box to Marguerite, who immediately left.

Desmond grinned. "Ari and Raymond are putting together the setting for my photo in the painting studio. I've decided to stay with the Zeus theme."

"So which art piece did you choose?" Mina asked.

"I've got the painting right here." Desmond reached for a book on the coffee table and flipped to an already marked page. "It's *Zeus and Thetis* by Ingres. Molly has agreed to pose as Thetis."

"He's just dying to have me grovel before him," Molly said with a wry smile.

Mina couldn't help thinking about his previous rant over artists pretending not to be in Hawai'i, but she glossed over these thoughts as she scanned the reproduction of the painting in the book. Zeus was seated on a throne in the heavens. Square shouldered, upright, and masterful, he stared ahead while his left arm rested on a cloud. A bird that looked like an eagle peered around the left side of the throne. Thetis crouched in submission near his right knee. She had some filmy fabric draped around her, but it was very revealing. Her arm reached up as if to entreat him by caressing his face. He barely seemed to acknowledge her.

"Of course," Molly said, peering over Mina's shoulder, "I'll have more covering."

"What is it she wants?" Mina ran her forefinger over the image of Thetis.

Molly answered before Desmond could. "She wants Zeus to protect her son Achilles in the Trojan War."

"That's right," Mina nodded as she remembered the myth. "Thetis was the mother of Achilles, and she dipped him in the river Styx."

"Except for his ankle," Molly reminded her, "his Achilles' heel."

"And didn't Achilles die in the Trojan War?" Mina couldn't quite remember.

"He did," Desmond interjected. "Paris shot him in the ankle with an arrow."

"See," Molly said to Mina, "it never pays to beg a man for anything."

As they sat ruminating over the picture, Mina thought she heard, over the surf, a woman yelling or screaming in the distance. In a few seconds, Desmond and Molly heard it too. Molly moved instinctively to the door as Mina and Desmond followed. As Molly flung the door open, Marguerite came flying in.

"Help!" she said frantically. "Call for the ambulance! Come quickly! The meeting room! They have been shot."

Mina ran for the phone while Molly and Desmond dashed out the door after Marguerite. After calling for the ambulance, Mina called the police station and asked to be put straight through to her brother-in-law, Todd Forest. She quickly told Todd where she was, that someone had been shot, and asked him to come, and then she raced through the rain toward the meeting room.

When Mina got there, she heard Marguerite screaming and crying in the kitchen and Molly yelling at her to calm down. Mina ran straight to the kitchen and found them huddled over Raymond, who lay on the floor with blood oozing from his leg. He let out a groan of pain, and she knew that it meant he was still alive. Molly pushed the hysterical Marguerite out of the way and sat her down at a small table in the corner, while Mina bound up what she thought was a gunshot wound and managed to curtail some of the bleeding. Although he seemed to be in shock, she saw that he was breathing steadily.

"Take her outside," Mina said to Molly, "and go and wait for the ambulance. With some quick attention, I think he'll be okay."

As Mina ushered them out the door, she saw Desmond standing frozen on the stage, his face a ghastly white and his eyes glued to the Halloween spoof of the *Last Supper*. Instead of the skeleton on the center throne, Ari Schoner sat slumped on the table, his arms stretched out and his palms turned up in the pose that mimicked Christ. She ran up on the stage. She could see that blood had seeped out from under his chest, making a wide, damp spot across the black tablecloth. Even before she checked for his pulse, she knew he was dead, but in a gesture of formal respect, she gently lifted his wrist and searched for it to be sure. A huge wave crashed against the cliffs, sending a fine salty mist over the lawn and blowing a damp chill through the room.

"Don't touch anything," Mina said to Desmond as she lowered Ari's arm back to its resting place. "There's no more we can do for him."

She went back to the kitchen to stay with Raymond, and it was then she saw that the cupboards and drawers were all flung open and their contents strewn around the room. She quickly went to the doorway and scanned the meeting room. Every closet and cupboard in that room had been opened and ransacked as well. It had all the appearances of a burglary, committed by a very violent and angry person or persons.

Todd arrived in a squad car just behind the ambulance. Before Raymond Morgan was taken to the hospital, the ambulance team assured them that although he was in considerable pain, his condition was fairly stable, and Maguerite then consented to stay behind to answer Todd's questions. After a preliminary look at the crime scene, Todd called in the homicide team and asked the two duty officers to do a quick check around the grounds. At Molly's suggestion, they all retreated to the house for a shot of brandy and some strong coffee. Once inside, Todd sat Marguerite down and asked her to tell him what had happened.

"You pardon my accent," Marguerite began. "I am Swiss, and my English is not so perfect."

"Please don't worry." Todd assured her. "This isn't an English-language test. I just need to know what happened. I'm sorry to keep you from your husband, but the more we know right away, the better chance we have of finding the criminals."

"What would you know?" Marguerite asked.

"Just start from the begining," Todd answered, "when Raymond got here, when you got here."

"Well," she said, "Raymond comes here earlier to meet Ari. They are going to fix up the scene for the photograph—for Desmond's photograph. Raymond is photographer, you know. Then I am coming later to help them, maybe one hour, because I am busy at home making breakfast for the children and seeing Paul off to school. My daughter, Eva, drives me here, and I come first to this house to get the box of . . . the box of—what do you say?" She looked at Desmond.

"Props," Desmond prompted.

"Yes," she continued, "I come to get the props, and then I go to painting studio, where we will make the scene. Raymond and Ari are not there, but I don't think anything is wrong. I think perhaps they are in meeting room doing something because I see door is open when I come. So I am in painting studio, and I want to sweep off place where we will make scene because there is too much dust. I get broom and begin to sweep when I hear noise like Raymond yelling, but I don't think it's anything bad, so I just keep cleaning. Then I think I hear noises again, and I feel something must not be right. So I run toward meeting room, but right away and when I get near door, I hear something from kitchen, so I go there. I see my husband and blood, and first, I'm afraid he is dead, but I see him breathing, so I know he's . . . he's—you know, his eyes are closed."

"Fainted?" Desmond suggested.

"Yes, yes, fainted. I don't know what to do. I put my handkerchief on the leg where Raymond is bleeding, and I run here for help. I didn't know—I mean, I didn't look to Ari. I didn't see him. I just—Raymond is my husband!" She burst into tears.

"There's nothing you could have done, Mrs. Morgan. Mr. Schoner was already dead. There's no need to blame yourself for anything."

"Here, Marguerite," Molly handed her a shot glass of brandy. "Drink this."

"Did you see anybody at all?" Todd asked.

"No," Marguerite said before she downed the brandy. "I know they took my husband's ring, his watch, because I don't see them on his hand, his wrist. His wallet—I don't know because I didn't see his pockets." She was quiet and looked at Todd.

"Thank you, Mrs. Morgan," Todd said. "That's enough for now, but I may need to speak to you again. Let's go outside, and I'll have an officer take you straight to the hospital."

Todd took Marguerite outside and returned to question Molly, Mina, and Desmond. He then excused himself with the same caveat he gave to Marguerite—that he may have to question them later.

Mina decided she'd had more than enough for one morning. She mumbled something vague to Molly and Desmond about going over her notes and calling in a few days. She could see that they needed some time to be alone just as she did. She drove home without really thinking about where she was going, as if the car were a horse returning to the barn all on its own. She soon found herself coasting down the drive to her bungalow, where Ollie stood on the deck barking out his excited welcome and furiously wagging his tail. It was still raining, and the south swell was still rolling in. But here at Kaʻalāwai, the waves did not smash against cliffs, and though the shore break was sometimes loud, it was never threatening. And she felt a sense of relief to be at home and further away from the merciless pounding of the surf. Once in the house, she made a cup of tea and sat down while her mind went over the scenes of the morning. Everything had happened so quickly. She tried to slow down the progression of her thoughts and review everything in slow motion, rewinding her memory when she wanted to retrieve another detail. She wasn't sure how long she had been sitting and thinking when Ollie jumped up and barked, alerting her to a car coming toward the house. She looked out the window and saw that it was a police car driven by Todd. He came to the door and asked if they could talk.

Only a year ago, she and Todd would not have shared their thoughts about anything. He had once resented her interest in crime, sneered at her career as a journalist and what he called her "unfeminine attitude." But she and Ned had helped Todd when he was in deep personal and professional trouble during the affair of the portrait murders—trouble that he escaped only through their help and understanding. And earlier this year, she had proved a dependable asset in the recent murders that had begun at the Haleiwa Hotel. Their trust was now approaching steady ground, and she hoped that one day he would come to think of her in the same way he thought of Ned—as a valued confidant and peer.

"Want a tuna sandwich?" she asked him. "I like plain-old food when something bad happens."

"Don't go through any trouble for me," Todd said as he sat in one of her rattan chairs.

"It's not trouble. I made a big bowl of tuna yesterday, and I'm making one for myself. I have potato chips too."

In less than ten mintues, as the rain pattered on the roof, Todd and Mina were sitting at her dining-room table eating their sandwiches, munching on potato chips, and sipping colas.

"Your guys find anything interesting?" she asked as she took a bite of her sandwich.

"They found two discarded wallets," he answered. "I'm sure you can guess who they belonged to. That looks like some strange party they had in that meeting room. Didn't you say you were there?"

She shrugged. "They're artists. It's Halloween. But I have to admit, that setup on the stage gave me the creeps at the party. Ditto for this morning, only worse."

"It was like a nightmare from my Catholic-school days. Why are you mixed up with these people anyway?"

She was amused by Todd's natural suspicion of artistic types, and she wondered how he and Ned had ever become friends. She explained the art show and catalog and how she got involved in the project.

Todd raised his eyebrows. "So you're going to get to know all of these people?"

"By the time the catalog is done," she said with a note of weariness, "I'll probably know more about them than I ever wanted too." She paused for a moment to take a sip of her cola. "Do you really think that was a robbery?"

He shook his head. "No. Not unless I'm Cary Grant. Do you?"

"Nope," she replied with conviction.

"All the evidence is there. Why don't you buy it?"

"Why don't you?"

"To tell you the truth," he said as he reached for a chip, "I can't really say exactly why."

"For one thing," she began slowly, "it seems so violent for your average Honolulu burglary."

"You're right," he agreed, "way too violent."

"Maybe you'll find something else to go on when you talk to Raymond," she suggested.

"Maybe," he said, "but everything appears to be pretty straightforward right now."

"On the surface," she added.

"On the surface," he repeated. "On the other hand, there just may be a homicidal burglar on the loose in town. That would be terrible. I'm asking for extra patrols in this neighborhood. You probably should lock your doors."

She laughed. "I have Ollie to protect me."

At the mention of his name, Ollie got up and came toward her, wagging his tail.

"Oh, yeah," he chuckled. "I forgot about your vicious Portuguese water dog."

"He saved Ned." She cooed at her dog. "Didn't you, Ollie? Yes you did. You brave boy."

"I guess you might learn a lot by hanging around with that crowd," he said.

"That's right. Listening to them is actually my job."

"And do you think you might try to fish around and report anything interesting you might learn to me?"

She smiled. "Of course. What's a sister-in-law for if she can't do some fishing around?"

"We got a cable from your handsome playwright," he reported. "He's in Sāmoa."

"Really?"

"He asked if it was okay for him to bring a couple of friends to stay in the bungalow with him. Of course, we told him it was fine."

"Did he say who they were?" She felt put out that he hadn't cabled her and wondered how he got from Shanghai to Sāmoa.

"He didn't say."

"Sounds mysterious." She sighed and then furrowed her brow. "Todd, what do you really think that business this morning was all about?"

He put down the last bit of his sandwich. "I don't know, but it was ruthless and twisted. I think you should be very careful."

# 5

# HONOLULU, LATE NOVEMBER

**I**T WAS LATE morning, and Ned had just finished looking over the first act of a new play he started some months ago. He sat on the front lanai of his bungalow, absentmindedly gazing across the hau arbor that separated his bungalow from Mina's. The hau leaves made heart-shaped shadows on the gray bricks beneath the trellis, and as Ned watched the shifting leafy patterns, he realized it was the first morning he had all to himself since he arrived. Nigel and Mei decided to try their luck in Honolulu, and for the last two weeks, they had all been roommates. Nyla Forest, Mina's identical twin sister, had thrown herself into helping the new couple settle into Honolulu. She had found a wonderful secondhand car for them, and today she and Mei were looking at several houses for rent. Nigel had mysteriously gone off in his newly acquired car to Fort Ruger, the military installation just behind Diamond Head. He had a phone call early in the morning, mumbled something about a meeting, and left abruptly after breakfast—leaving his wife to house hunt without him.

Ned propped his feet up on the outdoor table and leaned back in the chair, looking up at the muscular white clouds parading across the sky. The sun had nearly reached its noontime apex. But at this time of year, a sunny day was bright without being as glaring and oppressive as it could be in the summer, and today he found it especially luxurious to be sitting outside in the warm sun. A slight breeze was blowing, and in the background he was vaguely aware of the distant sound of waves breaking and the hum of bees busily feeding somewhere in the garden. A great sense of relief washed over him, as the strain and danger of his Shanghai sojourn faded away, and he hoped he would never find himself in a situation like that again. It threatened all of the things he envisioned in the future for himself and Mina. He wanted to promise himself he would never intentionally take another risk like that, unless it was for someone he dearly loved, someone in his family circle or a dear friend, like Nigel. But life played its tricks, sometimes thrusting unwelcome situations on you, and then there was nothing you could do but ride out the current and hope you survived. He sensed that he was drifting. The warmth of the sun, the bees, and the quiet garden lulled him into closing his eyes and sailing seamlessly off to sleep.

The next thing he felt was a pair of soft lips, gently brushing his cheek. He opened his eyes to see Mina. She had pulled one of the chairs up and was sitting next to him.

"How long have you been sitting here?" he asked.

"A little while," she answered.

"I didn't even hear your car pull up."

"I think you were in a very deep sleep," she said.

"And how did I look," he chuckled, "in this very deep sleep?"

"You looked like you were eight years old," she smiled.

"I think you just made that up."

"I didn't."

"I don't even remember falling asleep," he said. "The last thing I remember is feeling like a collapsed balloon."

"You haven't really told me what happened in Shanghai," she paused. "You don't have to if you don't want to."

"It was hard," he frowned. "It's not that I don't *want* to tell you. It's just that I'd rather not think about it now."

She gazed thoughtfully at him and said, "I know what you need. Get your swimming trunks on and meet me down on the beach."

A few minutes later, he found himself with Mina, launching a small outrigger canoe that she borrowed from her neighbor and gliding off and out past the surf. They cleared the breakwater and paddled toward Diamond Head, past the houses and along the cliffs. The sea was calm and placid, and after a while, they stopped paddling and drifted, both of them sitting in silence, looking back at the shore. The cars winding up along the cliff road and the few people walking along the beach seemed so small and far away, and the lighthouse looked like part of a toy set that one could easily pick up and place somewhere else. He felt so pleasantly removed, as if he'd taken a giant step away from his life and was floating in another world. Mina slowly turned the canoe toward home. She lazily paddled a few strokes and then stopped again, fascinated by something she saw in the water, and in the same languid rhythm, they paddled and drifted, slowly making their way back home, at an unhurried and idle pace, as the hours of the afternoon slipped away.

When they returned, Nyla, Mei, and Nigel were sitting on Ned's deck eating sushi and drinking iced teas. It struck Ned, as it had before, how much Nyla and Mina resembled each other—the thick dark hair, the pale green in their eyes, the honey-brown color of their skin. Yet they each emanated a different kind of energy. Mina had a mercurial quality about her, a quickness that sometimes made you feel like she knew or saw vital things that she wasn't letting you in on. Nyla, on the other hand, appeared calm, collected, and reassuring, and now that she was pregnant, she had assumed the aura of a modern Madonna.

"We couldn't figure out where you'd gone," Nyla said as she stirred her tea. "We brought some sushi for you too."

"We've had a lovely paddle," said Ned as he helped himself to a cone sushi.

"And we've had great luck," Mei said with a smile. "I think we've found the perfect house. It's in—what is the name of that valley?"

"Mānoa," said Nyla.

"Where in Mānoa?" Mina asked.

"It's on Huelani Drive, near the Tea Room," Nyla reported. "Two stories, four bedrooms, a study, and beautiful back lanai and garden that backs up to the hillside. Very private."

"Have you seen it?" Ned asked Nigel.

"We're on our way over in a few minutes," Nigel answered. "Seems we could move in tomorrow if we like it."

"If *you* like it, darling," Mei said. "I'm already in love."

"Do you have furniture?" Mina asked. "I mean, are you shipping anything here?"

"Not much," Mei sighed. "I have a few things that belonged to my mother. Nigel lived like a camping bachelor. I guess we'll have to buy quite a bit. Although I'm not very good at house decorating."

Nyla and Mina looked at each other and laughed.

"You're in terrific luck," Ned explained. "Nyla just happens to be one of the best decorators on the island, and Mina has previously served as her intrepid assistant."

"And I'm volunteering my sister's free services," Mina said with a laugh.

Nyla smiled at her sister. "Ditto."

"We wouldn't dream of imposing on you, Nyla," Nigel said somewhat timidly. "I mean, you've been so gracious about letting us stay in your bungalow, and you've helped us to find this new place."

"If you like it, Nigel," Ned reminded him.

"Yes, well," Nigel continued, "we just wouldn't dream of inconveniencing you by—"

Nyla turned to Ned, interrupting. "Are all you Brits so thoroughly polite?"

Ned nodded. "Nauseatingly polite. We all got our bums whacked if we even thought about being impolite."

"Waiting for a baby to arrive is absolutely boring," Nyla said to Nigel. "It would be a relief to have something interesting to do." She looked at her watch and frowned. "We have to leave. The rental agent is meeting us."

"Better get going," Mina said. "Ned and I will take care of the rest of the sushi."

"Wish me luck," Mei whispered to Ned and Mina as she followed Nyla and Nigel to the car.

"They're very nice people," Mina commented as she poured herself a glass of tea. "Just like you said. I hope they like it here."

"Nigel will need something to do," Ned said as helped himself to another sushi. This time he picked one of the rolled pieces. "He's talked about starting a fencing school. He's absolutely marvelous. Say, you didn't mention how your interview went this morning."

"It was a just a follow-up," she said as she stirred her tea. "I did most of it a few weeks ago. We're just starting up again since the . . . incident."

"Ah yes." He drummed the table with his fingers. "The incident. It seems there haven't been any more such incidents in the neighborhood or even anywhere on the island."

She shrugged. "I know, it's disconcerting, but there's nothing more to go on as far as I know—or as far as Todd has told me—which could be two very different things."

"I have a very uncomfortable feeling about the whole thing," he said. "For several different reasons, not the least of which is your close proximity to the affair."

"I didn't set out to stick my nose in anything, darling." She smiled at him.

"No, but once you've had a whiff of an unsolved crime, I know it's hard to pull you off the track."

She raised her eyebrows. "Are you comparing me to a bloodhound?"

He laughed. "I would never do that, darling. I think you're much more of the beagle type. But really, how was your morning?"

"Well, if you want to know, it was a bit like visiting another planet. It's a good thing that eccentric people amuse me."

He gave her a quizzical look. "What happened?"

"I got there as Raymond and his wife, Marguerite, were setting up for the photograph. I told you about the photographs, right? How Desmond picked this one where he's Zeus sitting on a throne, and Molly, as Thetis, is submissively begging for protection for her son? I had to get my questions answered while all this preening and posing was going on, and every five minutes, Desmond would stop and ask me if I thought something would look better one way or another. I think it irritated Molly that he kept asking my opinion."

"Not another male who's dying for your attention, I hope."

She ignored him and continued. "So Raymond Morgan keeps fussing with the camera and the pose, and the thing is, Desmond is so focused on himself and getting his head at just the right angle, he doesn't even notice that Raymond is spending an inordinate amount of time lingering over Molly's body, touching and arranging her in just the right way—in front of his *own* wife, Marguerite, who appears to be equally oblivious."

"Maybe she is oblivious," he said, "and maybe this Desmond person doesn't care."

"And then there was the pose itself." She shook her head in disgust. "The handsome Greek god, so strong and confidant, and the groveling female begging, literally at his knees. I mean, honestly, how can he not see how, how—"

"How the image that he's selected for himself is so shallow and egotistical? And how obvious it might be to others?"

"Exactly."

"Sounds like he's blind on several accounts."

"*He* is," she said as she leaned her elbow on the table, cupped her chin in her hand, and looked directly at him. "But nothing escapes Molly, nothing at all."

A few hours later, Ned found himself sitting with Nigel on the back lanai of an almost empty house perched on the western hillside of Mānoa Valley. They had gravitated to one of the only pieces of furniture—a built-in puneʻe overlooking a garden, green and verdant from frequent rain. Beyond, a tangle of jungle met the steep valley walls, enclosing and containing the garden in its own world. Darkness was settling over the island, but the light had not completely faded. And a chorus of birdsongs and crickets filled the air. Mina, Nyla, and Mei had gone downtown to pick up Todd and some food for dinner that they had agreed on in a secretive conversation. Ned and Nigel sat without speaking, as if absorbing the chemistry of the house with its wide-open rooms, wainscoted walls, polished floors, and high ceilings, its dramatic staircase that led to the upper bedrooms and screened sleeping porch. Ned thought he could almost feel the house breathing. He had always had an attraction to vacant spaces—empty houses waiting to be filled, bare stages anticipating the next play, deserted streets—spaces that lay open to endless possibilities.

"Thanks for coming over here at a moment's notice," Nigel said, breaking the silence.

"Mina was dying to see the house," Ned replied. "I was too actually. I expect we'll be doing this before too long—looking for a place to start our married life."

"Did you ever believe it would happen to you, Trout? I never thought it would happen to me. Most of our friends have been married for ages. It's a lovely place, don't you think?"

"I wouldn't mind living here myself," Ned admitted.

"The agent said they might be willing to sell. Of course, we have to give Honolulu some time to see if we *really* like it."

"Of course," Ned agreed.

"I'm glad we have a few minutes alone," Nigel began. "It's about the meeting I went to this morning."

"Oh?" Ned cocked his head. "Not more cloak and dagger. You've only been here a couple of weeks."

"*They* called *me*. It's not like I went out looking for it, and it doesn't sound dangerous at all."

"Why do I feel we've had this conversation before?"

"No, really," Nigel insisted, "it's not that dangerous. And you were the one who gave me that eloquent speech not long ago about the terrible darkness descending on the world and how we ought to do something about it."

"We," Ned repeated. "I should have known what follows would be—we!"

"Well, if you won't hear about it," Nigel said sulkily.

Ned laughed. "Don't pretend to be petulant. Of course I want to hear about it."

"Hah! I knew you would. To be brief, there were two naval representatives at the meeting. They belong to the Office of Naval Intelligence, and they seemed to know all about my previous work. They're troubled by recent information that the Japanese government is receiving regular reports on the installations here—ship movements, troop movements, weapons, defense plans. Someone is doing an excellent job of spying on the navy in Hawai'i. They believe it's all going through the Japanese counsel. They're not sure exactly who is doing it, and they need to be very discreet because they can't destroy diplomatic relations with Japan to find out."

"But," Ned cut in, "they want *you* to—figure it out."

"Actually, they said our *British government* wants me, to help them figure it out."

"And how did they hear about me?"

Nigel chuckled. "I told them. Listen, you know this place so much better than I do. I can hardly find my way to the beach."

"I don't know it that well either, but tell me, why aren't they using their own people?"

"One, they don't have anyone out here with much experience; two, if we were discovered, it's better for American diplomacy that we're British; and three, they mentioned something about a domestic spying dilemma that I didn't quite understand, but most importantly, our "unofficial" office has volunteered us. Volunteered *me*, I should say. You will be *asked* to join me officially by tomorrow. I had no choice because apparently I haven't been relieved of duty."

"You mean you haven't officially resigned. They've got you on a technicality."

"The other thing," Nigel confessed, "is our visas. I don't think we'll have any problem staying in the Territory, or anywhere in America, for as long as we want, if we do this work for the military. At least that's what they're telling me."

"That's quite an enticement for both of us." Ned was quiet for a time, staring into the garden and thinking. "It doesn't sound that dangerous now, but you have to see that it could become dangerous."

"The world *is* dangerous, and people need us, Trout."

"Well," Ned said, still looking out at the garden, "at least we won't have to leave the islands."

"Who's talking about leaving the islands?" Mina's voice came from behind. "It better not be you, Ned." She switched on some of the lights in the living room. "What are you doing sitting out there in the dark?"

"Solving world problems, love," Ned answered.

"Well, we have a more immediate puzzle—there's eight for dinner and no table, so we need some genius improvisation."

"Eight?" Ned asked.

"Yep," she answered. "We wrangled Cecily and Tom. It's your first dinner party, Nigel."

The others all streamed into the house, carrying boxes of food and bottles of wine, and everyone in the group threw themselves into the spirit of being inventive. Cecily had the foresight to bring along a worn but large tablecloth that she spread in the center of a carpet that Ned and Todd hauled down from upstairs and placed in the center of the living room. Mina and Nyla managed to break off some sprays of purple bougainvillea (without getting scratched) from a bush near the driveway and arranged them in the center of the cloth. Nigel poured Chianti into paper cups, and they all sat down in a circle on the carpet. Mina and Mei passed out the paper plates laden with spaghetti and meatballs that had been ordered from the Mermaid Cafe—the proprietors, Duncan and Maggie, were friends and had carefully included napkins and wooden chopsticks along with some very tasty garlic bread.

"I hope everyone is able to eat spaghetti with chopsticks," Mei said as she passed them out.

Cecily laughed. "This is Hawai'i. We can eat anything with chopsticks."

Ned raised his paper cup. "Here's to Nigel and Mei, to their new home and new life in Hawai'i, may it be happy and full and everything they hope for."

After the toast, everyone dove in eagerly, if somewhat clumsily, into eating the especially delicious spaghetti.

"You'll never guess what I heard today," Cecily said between bites.

"What did you hear?" Nyla asked.

Cecily looked around at everyone and said, "Christian Hollister and Lamby Langston got married."

A pronounced silence fell over the gathering.

"I guess Mei and I must be missing something here," Nigel said after a few moments.

"Christian Hollister is the editor of the daily newspaper," Ned said as he tried to observe Mina's reactions without being obvious. Hollister was her former boss, and Ned knew that even though Hollister kept a discreet distance, he had been more than a little sweet on her.

"And Lamby Langston is a gorgeous . . . a gorgeous—" Nyla couldn't think of what to say.

"Nitwit!" Todd rejoined.

"Todd," Nyla scolded. "Nigel and Mei will think we're heartless gossips."

"Only until they've met her," said Tom, Cecily's husband, causing everyone to burst into laughter.

"It was very hush-hush," Cecily reported. "They got married at his family home, and they're postponing the honeymoon until summer, when they can go to Europe."

"I'm surprised," Nyla said. "She's definitely what I would call the big wedding type."

"I'm sure the most important thing to her was just to get that diamond ring on her finger," Cecily said. "They've been going out forever. I'll bet she was giving up hope."

"I wonder why he finally decided to do it?" Tom asked.

Todd shrugged. "Who knows? Maybe she's, you know," he reached over and stroked Nyla's pregnant tummy.

"I doubt that," Nyla said as she picked up a piece of garlic bread. "She's too self-serving for that."

"Welcome to the intrigues of island life," Ned said to Nigel.

"Of course, now we'll be dying to actually meet them," Mei said.

"I'm sure you will," Ned said. "He loves to fence, doesn't he, Mina?"

"I don't know, does he?" she replied with an air of disinterest.

Ned tried to read Mina's reaction to the news. She seemed to be hanging back from the conversation as if she were processing the information in private. Or was he just imagining things?

"And speaking of getting married," Cecily said, turning to Ned and then Mina, "how come the engaged couple hasn't set a date yet? We all went through with it. Now it's your turn."

Ned looked at Mina. "I think we're being put on the spot, darling."

Mina wrinkled her brow. "I guess first we should decide *where* we want to get married."

"See, I told you," Nyla said to Cecily. "They're in bad need of supervision. They haven't even gotten to square one in the planning department."

# 6

# LATE NOVEMBER

"A NY OTHER INTERLOPERS for Thanksgiving?" Mina asked as she poured herself a cup of coffee.

Nyla thought for a moment. "No, just Nigel and Mei. What's Cecily doing?"

"They're going to some dinner with her mom's family," Mina replied.

The sisters were sitting at Nyla's kitchen table in her Maunalani Heights home. The house overlooked the city, commanding a sweeping view from the back of Diamond Head to Barber's Point. At about a thousand feet above sea level, the temperature in the heights was almost always cool and pleasant and, during these months, even chilly. Mrs. Olivera, Nyla's housekeeper, who also worked for Mina one day a week, fussed over Ollie while she cleaned up the breakfast dishes—giving him scraps of leftovers from the plates.

Mina sighed. "You're spoiling him, Mrs. Olivera."

"But he is such a good boy. Aren't you, Ollie?" Mrs. Olivera bent down and let Ollie lick her face. "He looks so happy, Mina."

"Come here, you shameless beggar," Mina said to the dog. He responded by walking over to her and wagging his tail. "You are the best happy dog on the island, aren't you?"

Nyla laughed and rubbed her tummy. "Geez, I hope my baby gets this much attention."

"Come with me, Ollie," Mrs. Olivera said as she was leaving the room. "Let's go upstairs and look for dirty towels." Ollie trotted after her as if he understood.

Mina watched her sister drop a couple of cubes of sugar in her coffee, add some cream, and slowly stir the steaming liquid. The silver spoon made clinking noises as it hit the side of the cup. Mina could always tell when her sister was about to bring up something serious. She had a certain way of moving and thinking, as if she were first trying to calm everything down before she introduced the delicate subject.

"I was wondering," Nyla began, "what you thought about Christian Hollister getting married."

Mina was quiet for a few seconds and looked back at her sister. "Why are you asking me this?"

"Because I think it's odd that he goes out with Lamby for years and then marries her shortly after you and Ned get engaged."

"Oh, please," Mina said in an exasperated tone.

"I just don't understand how you can be so smart and observant about some things and so blind about others."

"I just think you're wrong, that's all," Mina said.

"Me and half the island?" Nyla cocked her head like a saucy bird.

"Look, it's none of my business why he married her. He married her, and now he's going to have to live with her."

"Hmmm," Nyla said, "that sounds like a disapproval."

"Well, aside from her being a—what was the word Todd used for her?"

"A nitwit."

"Right. Aside from her being a nitwit, I just don't think he really loves her."

"Tell the truth," Nyla leaned forward, "did you never, ever think he might be in love with you?"

Mina shrugged. "What difference does it make? I'm in love with Ned." She reached for an apple banana from the bowl of fruit on the table and started to peel it.

Nyla persisted. "But if Ned weren't here."

"But he *is* here," Mina said. "Ned exists, and I love him. And anyway, Chris Hollister and I are political opposites, and I'll never be one to believe that love can conquer all, not in the long run anyway—which is why I think he made a big mistake marrying her. She's going to bore him to tears, and in a year or so, he'll be out prowling around the town looking for someone to have an affair with."

"I agree," said Todd, who had been standing in the doorway. Nyla frowned. "Todd, have you been listening to our private conversation?"

Todd yawned. "Some of it. I couldn't help it if you didn't hear me coming."

"You could have made a discreet cough or something," Nyla said.

"How come you're not at work?" Mina asked.

"Late night," Todd answered as he poured some coffee. "I got to sleep in."

"I suppose now you're going to want something to eat." Nyla got up and headed for the Frigidaire.

"Don't talk to Ned like this when you get married, Mina."

Nyla laughed. "You know you love it, Detective Forest."

"You'll never guess what happened," Todd said to Mina. "You know that guy who got killed at your artist's studio?"

"Ari Schoner?" Mina gave him her full attention.

"Yeah, Schoner," Todd nodded. "Yesterday, somebody tried to break into his house."

"Did they steal anything? What were they after?" Mina asked.

"They didn't even get in," he said. "One of the neighbors saw someone forcing the cottage door and raised a ruckus. Then he, or she, ran away."

"That's odd," Mina said. "Don't you think it's odd?"

"Could be odd," Todd answered, "could be coincidence."

"Could be that was a fake burglary at the art studio and actually a premeditated murder," Mina said as she leaned back in her chair.

"Could be," Todd agreed, "but I would have to emphasize *could*."

"So what's happening to his house? To all his things?" Mina asked.

"Apparently he owned the cottage," Todd said. "I would have thought he would have left everything to his sister on the East Coast. But according to Louis Goldburn, he left it to someone named Matilda Clement."

"Tilda?" Mina gave Todd a puzzled look.

"You know her?" Todd asked.

"She's one of the artists," Mina answered. "I think she and Ari were friends."

Todd grimaced. "Figures. Anyway, she's going to do something about it. Stay there or have somebody stay there." -

"I guess by now you've had a chance to question Raymond Morgan," Mina said, trying her best to sound casual.

"I have indeed," said Todd. "He wasn't much help. He was looking for a screwdriver or something in one of the kitchen drawers. He heard someone approaching the kitchen but thought it was Ari. He glanced up and saw a hooded figure with a gun. He remembers the gun going off, a sharp pain in his leg, falling over, and then passing out. He can only remember the figure was tall as opposed to short, dressed in black with a black cloth hood covering the head. He couldn't see any eye color, and he can't even be sure if the person was a male or female."

"So are you looking any further into things?" Mina tried to sound casual.

"My sister is interested," Nyla said as she placed a plate of scrambled eggs and Portuguese sausage in front of Todd. "Can you tell?"

"It's one of those things," Todd said as he sprinkled salt and pepper on his eggs. "I can't really do any more unless something else happens."

"And don't tell me," Nyla said as she gave Mina a wink, "you want my sister to keep a watch on those degenerate artists."

Todd nodded. "Yep. I want her to watch them like a hawk."

Ned looked out the car window as the driver, Reginald Rankin, slowed down. The Japanese embassy stood on the well-shaded corner of Nuʻuanu Avenue and Kuakini Street. In keeping with the older, well-established neighborhood, the consular residence was a grand two-story house with a porte cochere and wide steps that led up to a gracious doorway. Next door, the embassy offices occupied a neat white building that looked more like a home than a place of business. The grounds of the embassy and residence were tastefully planted with tropical shrubs and immaculately kept. Reginald continued on Nuʻuanu Avenue and then turned left into a small alley behind some houses that led to a secluded garage behind a store.

"It's just up the back stairs here," Reginald said as he eagerly led the way. "It's the whole floor above the store."

Ned and Nigel followed and found themselves in the airy parlor of a second-story flat. The windows in the parlor and dining room faced Kuakini Street and had a clear view of the embassy offices and the consular residence. There were doors off the parlor that opened onto a wooden-railed veranda running the length of the building along the street, screened in and shaded by the overhang of the roof. Ned registered this as a very fortunate feature, as it would be very difficult to see into the flat from the street.

"How long have you had these rooms?" Ned asked.

"I think they rented them about six months ago, sir," Reginald answered. "The great thing is we can drive in the alley, park in back, and no one sees us coming or going."

Ned smiled. "I think we can drop the 'sir' business. Call me Ned."

"And I'm Nigel and not Mr. Hawthorn."

An impish smile spread over Reginald's freckled face. "I guess that would make me Reggie."

"So what exactly has gone on up here, Reggie?" Ned asked as he looked out across the quiet street. The tall shower trees swayed in a gust of wind, and small green leaves and pink flowers fluttered and twirled, raining down on the gray sidewalks.

Reggie looked embarrassed. "I'm not quite sure. I think they were just taking pictures, and then they were told to back off."

"Really?" Nigel raised his brow.

Reggie removed his cap to reveal a head of very short but very red hair. "I guess now would be the time to talk to you about what I understand our orders to be."

"I think that would be a very good start," Ned said.

"Well, first of all, I'm working for the ONI, and my assignment is to assist you. That's all I can tell you about my real background. My cover is that I'm a semilazy, part-time college student at the university living in this apartment, but I'm just getting settled and won't really be starting college until January. I'm being bankrolled by my wealthy and indulgent widowed mother. I know you've already been briefed about what our mission is, but there are a couple of other things they wanted me to tell you. Through the work of the people who were here taking pictures, several suspects were targeted. We will have to identify them, but from what I was told, all of them, with one exception, appear to be Americans—which brings me to the second thing I'm supposed to tell you. It's about the Office of Naval Intelligence. See, the ONI is almost exclusively focused on trying to serve the fleet in outlying areas."

"You mean spying *outside* the United States?" Nigel asked.

"Yeah," Reginald nodded, "because the navy has this intelligence dilemma about secret domestic operations—snooping, to be frank—violating the constitutional obligations that every naval officer is pledged to defend."

"But this problem at Pearl Harbor, which is on home territory, poses quite a serious threat to the navy," Ned said.

Nigel chuckled. "So they want the British to do the dirty work so the naval officers won't be violating what they've sworn to uphold, because they now see it will most definitely involve spying on American citizens."

"That's about the size of it," Reggie said. "When they saw that the suspects were most likely Americans, they just stopped what they were doing."

"Interesting," Nigel said.

Ned looked around the flat. The old wooden building was the kind found in any town around the world, with a store on the street level and what once were the family living quarters above. Although the flat was worn from decades of life passing through it, it was well maintained. The wide-planked wood floor, painted gray, squeaked slightly as he walked from the parlor through an archway to the spacious dining room and then beyond into the kitchen. There was an ancient table, scarred with knife scratches from chopping and slicing, a kerosene stove, and a screened food safe—the kind of kitchen he often saw in Sāmoa. A window with faded flowered curtains looked out above the white enameled sink and across the street. He guessed that the officers had installed the Frigidaire. When he pulled the curtain back, he could see a group of boys walking down the sidewalk in their school uniforms. One of the boys, the one who stood with his hands on his hips and looked like he was giving orders to the others, seemed very familiar. Ned stood there for several minutes watching him. It was interesting, he thought, how some boys, even at a young age, had an instinct for leadership. The boy wasn't even the biggest or the brawniest one in the group, but there he was, cocksure of himself, telling the others what to do while they eagerly listened. Ned smiled to himself before he turned away to finish looking over the flat. On the other side of the parlor, there was a bathroom and three bedrooms, one of which had been set up as an office. He went back to the others, and they all sat down at the round table in the dining room.

"Is there a boys' school near here?" Ned asked Reggie. "I saw some boys in uniforms."

"On the other side of the embassy from here is a Catholic boys' school," he answered. "I think they just moved here recently."

"So," Ned continued, "from the school yard, you can see the back side of the buildings? The side we can't see from here?"

Reggie nodded. "That's exactly what you would see."

Ned looked lost in thought for a moment and then turned to Nigel. "I really think it would be unwise for you to show yourself too much. You've just had a close call with the Japanese army."

"I'd have to say the same for you," Nigel replied. "I'm sure by now our friends in Shanghai have figured out who you are."

"But hopefully not *where* I am or where *you* are," Ned said.

"Not bloody yet," Nigel mumbled.

Reggie looked at both of them with a tinge of awe and excitement. "You mean someone's after you?"

Ned chuckled. "Let's just say we're counting on them not wanting to bother with us anymore. The point is, Reggie, Nigel and I should not be seen lurking around the Japanese embassy. I think we're well out of sight up here, but we'll have to be very cautious about our coming and going as well."

"But we're going to have to find some way to keep watch besides sitting up here," Nigel said. "You can't see any of the back or side doors from here. We need people on the ground."

"Well," Ned said. "I have some ideas. We'll be depending on you to help us coordinate everything, Reggie."

"Oh, I'm on assignment to you, night and day," Reggie said with marked enthusiasm.

"And you're actually living here?" Ned asked.

"Yes, sir. I mean, yes, Ned." Reggie answered.

"And you said we have money?" Ned asked Nigel.

Nigel nodded. "We do have a generous allotment deposited in an account under my name. We'll need to keep some kind of ledger, of course. I'm sure there will be background checks to do, and at some point, we'll need help following suspects. And there's equipment to think about."

"They've left some things in one of the rooms." Reggie jumped to his feet as if he were ready to run and fetch things. "Some binoculars and several Ansco Memo cameras."

"Cameras," Ned mused. "They'll love it."

"Who'll love it?" Nigel narrowed his eyes and looked at his friend. "What are you talking about?"

Ned laughed. "I'm talking about the gang of boys we're going to get to help us watch the embassy. We can call them the Kuakini Street Irregulars."

Mina walked with Ollie through the ironwood grove toward the art studios. There was no wind this afternoon, and the long, green pine needles hung perfectly still, drooping down as if they had been abandoned and stranded in limbo, longing for the arrival of the wind or even a breeze that would stir them to life and awaken their stilled voices. Ollie lagged behind and tried chewing one of the round pinecones but immediately spat it out and trotted back to Mina's side. Under the overcast sky, she thought the old, weathered buildings looked like part of a ghost town, and she could almost hear the echoes of the shouts and cries of children who had run and played here when it was a school camp. She put her things down on a bench outside the painting studio and peered in through the screened window. No one was there. The drawing benches on one side and the easels on the other stood poised and ready, as if a class had just left the room but might return at any second. She heard noises coming from the printing studio and went there to find Desmond hard at work. She had to clear her throat before he noticed her.

"Oh, Mina, hello." His eyes lit up when he saw her standing there. "Tilda said to watch out for you."

"I'm supposed to meet her for an interview." Mina hoped this wasn't going to be a waste of time.

"She's down on the lava with Raymond," Desmond said. "They should be just finishing her photo. You should have a look. I'm sure it's going to be a stunner."

Ollie ran around Mina, jumping and pouncing for pleasure, as she crossed the lawn to the lava shoreline. Today the sea was glassy and still. She could see Tilda and Raymond a short ways down the coast near a tide pool, so she removed her sandals and made her way over the lava. She wasn't sure, but she thought she saw Tilda slip her arm back into her dress to cover her right breast when she noticed Mina approaching.

Tilda's tall and large-boned figure was posed, barefooted, on a smooth, black lava rock in the middle of a still turquoise tide pool. A long, silky gown of dark blue, loosely belted at the waist and printed with a pattern of luminous peacock feathers, clung to her pale and perfectly proportioned body. Her luxuriant reddish-brown hair billowed around her, and in her hands, she held a bowl of brilliant green water. Her lipstick was blood red.

"I hope I'm not disturbing you," Mina said as she neared them.

"You're not disturbing us at all," Raymond said with a smile. "We're just waiting for the right shade of light," he said as he looked up at the sky.

Tilda gave Mina a smug and self-satisfied look. "Can you guess what painting I've chosen?"

Mina inwardly bridled but knew better than to show it. "No," she said, "but I'm sure it's a lovely one."

Tilda tossed her head and smiled. "I forgot you were raised here, so you've probably never heard of John Waterhouse. This is his painting, *Circe Individiosa.*"

Mina bit at her lower lip and turned away, pretending to look for Ollie. She'd heard remarks like this before about people from the islands, remarks designed to try to put you in your place—always a notch below the speaker.

"There's a book in my bag," Raymond said to Mina, as if trying to smooth things over. "The page with the painting is marked, if you care to have a look."

She took the faded-blue art book out of the leather bag, glad to have something to do, and opened it to the marked page. She stared at the painting and back again at Tilda. The painting had an entirely different backdrop—a kind of tangled dark forest—and the Circe figure was standing in some sort of lake or river.

"Okay, get ready," Raymond called out to Tilda.

Mina looked up to see Tilda strike the pose. Tilda lifted up the bowl of green water and fixed her gaze intently on it, as did the woman in the painting. It didn't look exactly like the painting, Mina thought, but they were capturing the feeling of it. Her mind fumbled to clarify exactly what it was that she saw and felt. She wished she had paid more attention in her college art class. She glanced down again at the book and then up again at Tilda standing there with that intense look on her face. For a split second, she had a feeling of revulsion, and she closed the book. Of course, she thought to herself, as beautiful as it appears, it's really a portrait of focused maliciousness. She put the book back into the bag as if any more contact with the picture might leave a residue of poison on her, and she remembered what both Todd and Ned had said about being careful.

"Just let me grab my other camera for a few quick shots," Raymond was saying to Tilda. "I want to try this new Kodachrome. It's the latest thing."

"Isn't that color film?" Mina asked him. "I heard they just came out with it."

"Yes," he answered with enthusiasm. "Some of my fellow photographers are saying that color is vulgar, but I'm dying to try it out."

When the photo session ended, Tilda went ahead to the studio to change while Mina helped Raymond carry his gear back to his car. She could see that he was tired and thought he probably wasn't a hundred percent recovered from his ordeal.

"How are you feeling?" Mina asked as they walked along.

"I'm getting back to normal," he replied, "although when I'm tired, my leg feels heavy. I'm sure it makes my limp more pronounced." Mina stopped and waited for him as he put down his bag in order to catch his breath. He then took out a handkerchief and wiped his brow before they continued on their way.

"I'm sure it was frightening," she said, "the robbery and the shooting, I mean." She couldn't help but recall the terrible incident she was involved in during the summer—at a weekend party, she had taken a bullet in the shoulder, and another woman had been killed. Raymond sighed, and she thought he looked rather attractive with his dark hair combed back and his air of vulnerability.

"I look at it this way," he said. "I could have ended up like poor Ari."

"Yes," she said quietly, "that was a real tragedy. He and Tilda must have been close. I've heard that he's left his cottage to her."

"Really?" Raymond gave her a look of surprise and then grinned and shook his head. "That Tilda certainly gets around."

"Pardon?" She gave him an innocent look.

"Nothing," he replied quickly. "I meant nothing."

After she had helped Raymond put his things in his car, he thanked her and drove off. She returned to the painting studio to find Tilda emerging from a room off the main studio with a hairbrush in her hand. She left the door open, and Mina caught a glimpse of a single bed, a clothes rack, and a makeshift vanity.

"It's our resting room," Tilda explained. "The models use it. Shall we get started?" There was a note of impatience in her voice. "I'm trying to move, and I really don't have much time."

"Oh, you're moving?" Mina asked casually, as she opened her notebook.

Tilda began brushing out her long hair. "To Ari's cottage, if you must know. He left it to me. His things are still there, but I'm moving in anyway. I'll sort everything out as I go along."

"The statement you wrote about yourself and your work was the best of the batch," Mina said. "I really don't have much to ask."

"I can just imagine what the others wrote." Tilda rolled her eyes. "None of them realize how important really strong promotion is. Selling your work is a business."

"Of course." Mina nodded in agreement, eager to see where this was going.

"I have my things in reputable museums, as you know from reading my statement. I sell. People know my name because I work at it." She continued brushing her hair vigorously. "Now, what is it that you want to know?"

"Well," Mina began, "since you've been in the islands these last four years, you've primarily painted Hawaiian women. What is it that attracts you to the subject?"

"I've always favored portraiture." Tilda put down her hairbrush and sat on one of the drawing benches in what looked to Mina like a kind of pose. "And as I'm sure you've noticed, I have my own distinctive style. For my subjects, I only choose—I only want to paint the real Hawaiian women, the ones who truly represent the Hawaiian race."

Mina pretended to look confused. "The real Hawaiian women?"

"Yes," Tilda said in an authoritative tone, "the ones who represent true racial type. Not—no offense to you, of course—but not the mixed type, the hapa-haole types. I want to create a visual record of the real Hawaiian women, the ones who are quickly fading away, so their images can be saved on canvas for posterity."

"I see," Mina said, looking down at her notebook.

"I see my painting as an urgent mission, because, as we all know, the Hawaiian race is a dying race, and it's imperative that something of the strength and majesty of these women—I won't say beautiful because to our Western sensibilities they are not beautiful—be preserved. They represent something primitive, powerful, and ancient that is passing out of our world." Tilda paused and looked at Mina. "Is that enough for you?"

"More than enough," Mina said as she stood up. "I don't want to keep you when you have so much to do, so if I have anything I need to clear up, I'll call you."

"Of course, you're going to show me what you've written before it's printed," Tilda said as she examined her nails. "I have to have final approval."

"Of course," Mina said as she edged toward the door. "See you later."

As she turned to go, Mina nearly ran into Desmond, who was coming through the doorway.

"Finished with Tilda?" he asked.

Mina simply nodded and went outside, where she whistled for Ollie. He came charging around the corner of the building with a piece of driftwood in his mouth that looked as if he had been chewing it. As soon as she saw him, she walked as quickly as she could to her car. When she got there, to her great irritation, she realized that in her haste to get away, she'd left her bag on the bench outside the painting studio door. She put Ollie in the car and went back to retrieve her bag. As she picked up the red satchel from the bench, she was surprised and relieved to find that Tilda and Desmond were nowhere to be seen, but then she heard Tilda's unmistakable voice coming from the room off the studio. Her cries and moans left no doubt in Mina's mind about what she and Desmond were up to. Mina turned away in disgust and stomped off to her car.

It was nearly five when her car rolled down the driveway at Ka'alāwai. A sense of relief washed over her as the high hedge and the gardens surrounded her. She parked the car and walked up to the hau arbor that separated the bungalows. She could see Ned sitting on his deck reading something, and she wandered over. He stood when he saw her, and a look of concern spread over his face.

"What's wrong, darling?" he asked in a soothing voice.

"Do I look that bad?" she said as she brushed a stray strand of hair away from her face.

"You look like a schoolgirl who's had a really discouraging day."

"Which means?"

"Which means you look like you've been exposed to something hurtful."

"I don't know whether to cry or go out and buy a gun."

Ned looked at her and cocked his head. "Why don't you go and put your things down, splash some cold water on your lovely face, and come back here, and I'll serve you one of the best cocktails you've ever had."

"I'll be right back," she said as she turned and walked toward her house.

When she returned a few minutes later, somewhat calmer, Ned had spread a white tablecloth over the outdoor table. A bowl of fragrant plumerias sat in the center and, next to them, a plate of crackers—some spread with salmon paste, some with cheese, and a few with what looked to Mina like caviar. No sooner had she taken a seat when Ned appeared with two cocktails in chilled stemmed glasses.

"Sidecars," he said, "made with Armagnac, Cointreau, and lime juice."

"How did you do all of this so quickly? It's remarkable."

"That's me," he replied, raising his glass, "the Old Remarkable."

"The Old Remarkable might make some lucky girl a great husband."

He laughed. "I think you may be right. Try your cocktail."

She took a sip and said, "This isn't one of the best cocktails I've ever had. I think it might be *the* best cocktail I've ever had."

"And now that we have that established," he said as he leaned back and made himself comfortable, "the bartender is waiting to hear your tale of woe."

"Oh, the tale of woe," she said in a half moan, raising her forearm to her forehead, "but where, oh, where to begin?"

"Start with when you got there," he suggested.

She recounted the afternoon step by step, repeating every word of the conversations she could remember, and as she recounted it out loud and relived it in her mind, she found she had gained an emotional distance. She wasn't sure if it was due to the presence of Ned or the effects of the cocktail, but now she felt protected and separated from the sordid and insulting events. When she finished her story, Ned excused himself, took their two empty cocktail glasses, and returned with seconds in newly chilled glasses.

"I'm sure you can tell I did a bit of preparation before you got home," he said as he set the frosty glasses down.

"You're saving my life," she said as she reached for a cracker with caviar.

"To say I understand how you feel, Mina, would be an understatement. The woman sounds ghastly and oblivious to her own feelings of superiority."

"I just get so sick of it," she complained. "These people who move here from the mainland and treat us like we're stupid."

"And like many Pacific visitors," he said thoughtfully, "she's under the self-aggrandizing illusion that her work is saving the natives."

"What's terrible," Mina said, "is that anyone who knows little or nothing about Hawai'i will listen to Tilda's spiel and think she's wonderful—when to me, all it looks like is someone fishing for an angle, trying to make a name for herself. I mean, it would be different if she would just shut up and paint, but when she turns it into some noble humanitarian mission, it's sickening. Honestly," Mina shook her head, "Tilda wouldn't know the real Hawai'i if it came up and bit her on the 'okole."

"She sounds like she doesn't care much for other women," he commented.

"And ugh! I just can't stand it when people describe us as a dying race. It's psychologically demoralizing—as if we're not quite real or we don't count because we're on our way out."

"Speaking of psychology," he added, "I'm sure our friends Dr. Freud or Dr. Jung would have a field day with her for choosing that painting as a self-image."

"I have to admit, I know nothing about the painting, except that it gave me the creeps." She took another sip of her cocktail as if for fortification.

"But your instincts were excellent," he began. "Waterhouse's *Circe Individiosa,* or 'Jealous Circe,' illustrates a particular story of Circe taken from Ovid. In the story, a handsome man denies Circe because he's in love with someone else. When Circe can't have him, she changes the innocent girl into a dreadful monster out of spite and jealousy. She does this by pouring a powerful potion into the place the poor girl bathes."

"Tilda is sick."

"That doesn't appear to bother that Desmond person, does it?" He took the last sip of his cocktail.

"Double sick. The whole mess makes me want to give myself a good scrubbing."

"Just the thing!" he said. "Let's clean up, put on our evening rags, and forget our troubles in a night of dinner and dancing at that lovely rooftop place downtown."

She grinned at him. "Please promise you'll still be like this after we've been married forever."

"Don't worry, darling," he said. "I won't change a thing."

# 7

# THANKSGIVING EVE

**M**INA HOISTED THE canvas carry bag up on her shoulder and left the Chinatown marketplace. Nyla had given her a list of things to buy for tomorrow's Thanksgiving dinner, and now Mina wished that she had parked the car closer. It was just after noon, and she was headed to the Mermaid Café and her lunch date with Louis and Doris Goldburn. After a couple of blocks, she began to feel an ache in her shoulder from the weight of the bag, as if the pain from her old gunshot wound was about to wake up. She wished she hadn't let that lady at the vegetable stand talk her into buying more sweet potatoes than she needed. She stopped, dropped the bag from her shoulder, and then took a moment to wipe her face with the handkerchief from her purse. She was glad she had decided to leave Ollie at home. With everyone getting ready for the holiday, the streets around the fish market and produce stands had been hot and bustling, and the swirling smells, the loud cacophony of languages, and the crowds of people, sometimes overflowing into the street, had left her feeling exhausted. But now, only a few blocks away, the street was quiet, and even though the breeze that blew down from the mountains was slight, it felt calm and cooling. The Mermaid Café was just around the corner, and she put her handkerchief back in her purse, brushed off her plaid blouse and navy-blue slacks, lifted the canvas bag onto her other shoulder, and forged on—hoping she didn't look as disheveled as she felt.

She turned right onto the boulevard, pushed through the swinging gate of the café yard, and made her way up the red-brick walkway that divided a small but very green patch of lawn. The restaurant was frequented mostly by seamen and dockworkers because of its excellent and reasonably priced food as well as its proximity to the harbor. The tables on the patio were all taken, and judging from the noise and clatter coming from inside the café, she was afraid it might be full too. But as soon as she opened the screen door, red-headed Maggie McKenzie, who owned the café with her husband, Duncan, whisked her to an empty table in the corner and pulled off the piece of paper that said "reserved."

"I was saving it for you and Louis," Maggie said before she kissed her on the cheek. "He called to say he would be a few minutes late. Want some iced tea?"

"Please," Mina answered, "and can I use your restroom?"

"Follow me," Maggie said.

Maggie marched Mina through the kitchen, where Duncan and a helper were working at a frantic pace to fill orders. Duncan raised a tattooed arm to give her a quick wave as she went by. Maggie directed Mina up a long wooden staircase to their living quarters.

"First door on the left off the hall," Maggie told her. "You don't want to use the head down here—too messy from all the guys."

Mina climbed the stairs and found the immaculate bathroom. She washed her hands and face, brushed back her wavy brown hair, and reclipped her barrettes. As she walked back down the stairs, she couldn't help but remember that it was only months ago that she and Ned helped to clear Jack Carstairs, a close friend of the McKenzies, from murder charges. She wondered how Jack was doing. Back in the restaurant, she sat down and sipped her iced tea. It was cool and refreshing with a hint of lemon and mint, and she felt like the chaos of Chinatown was a million miles away. She scanned the room for any new mermaids Duncan might have carved and put on display. She couldn't find any, but her attention was drawn to the life-size mermaid near the entrance. There was something about that particular carving that seemed to capture everyone's attention—as if the lovely female form was trying so hard to tell you something. The screen door opened, and Louis Goldburn stepped in, looking somewhat out of place in his white shirt and tie. He spotted Mina in the corner and walked over.

"Doris sends her apologies," he said as he sat down. "She has a terrible cold, and all she wanted to do was stay in bed."

"I'm sorry she won't be here," Mina said.

"And I'm sorry to be late," Louis said. "Have you ordered?"

"Not yet," Mina answered. As if reading their minds, Maggie stopped at their table on her way to the kitchen with an armful of dirty dishes. "Duncan made something special for you this morning. I'll just tell him to fix it now. I hope you like it." Maggie vanished as quickly as she appeared.

"I guess we're getting the special treatment," Louis said to Mina.

Before long, Maggie was serving them each a lobster roll with a side of potato salad. The buns looked like Maggie had baked them herself. "Duncan bought this lobster fresh, this morning," Maggie said.

After Mina and Louis had gotten started on their lunch, she asked him if he would tell her about Ari Schoner.

He grinned. "Aha! I knew this would be more than just a social event. Is there any special reason?"

"I'm sure you've heard about the attempted break-in at Ari's house?"

"No, I haven't." A worried look passed over his face. "What's-her-name didn't mention it when she came to pick up the keys the other day."

"What's-her-name could use a good slap on the head."

"I thoroughly agree," he said. "I didn't approve of him leaving his house to her, but then I'm just the guy who draws up the papers."

"I wonder if she wheedled it out of him?" she mused. "Or if she even knew he was leaving it to her?"

"I'd put my money on wheedling," he said as he stirred some sugar into his iced tea, "but I don't know for sure." He paused, put down his lobster roll, and looked at her. "Jesus, I completely forgot. You were practically right there when it happened—when he got shot during the robbery."

"That's what bothers me," she said, leaning forward and lowering her voice. "I mean, it was so violent, and there were no other burglaries like that anywhere else on the island, and then someone tries to break into his house."

"I see how it could seem very suspicious. What do the police say? Let me guess—not enough to go on."

"Exactly," she said before she took another bite of the lobster roll.

"God, this is delicious, isn't it?" he said before he took another bite.

After they had finished and asked Maggie to thank Duncan profusely, they each ordered a dish of vanilla ice cream with sprinkles of candied ginger and cups of coffee.

"Well," Louis began, "here's what I can tell you about Ari. Like me, he was Jewish and not very religious. He was a professor of art history at the University of Munich, hence his interest in art and artists. He was a rabid and outspoken opponent of the Nazi Party, and in 1930 or 1931, with the rise in power of the Nazis, he saw the writing on the wall and decided to leave."

"That was smart," Mina said.

"It was timely too," he added, "because a couple of years later, Hitler became the chancellor of Germany, assumed the powers of a dictator, and began to imprison political 'subversives' in special prison camps. Anyway, Ari was able to leave and immigrate to the United States—no small feat since the Immigration Act of 1924 pointedly discriminates against Jews. It drives me crazy. The government *says* it's concerned about the plight of Jews in Germany, but it refuses to give people shelter."

"Because?" she looked confused.

"They say they can't change the Immigration Act because of the Depression and high unemployment, but I'm sure anti-Semitism is playing no small part. Ari's niece is married to a wealthy man on the East Coast who pulled some strings to help get him in. Ari told me there were several Washington politicians who couldn't have gotten elected without her husband's contributions. Ari came to Hawai'i on a trip with his sister and decided to stay."

"Can you think of any reason why someone would want to kill him?" she asked.

"Other than being anti-Nazi? I can't see the Nazis sending someone all the way to Hawai'i." Louis paused. "And I really don't know why someone would want to kill him. He was an extremely kind and gentle soul with a real social conscience. He contributed so much time and money to all kinds of good causes in the short time he was here."

"No dark secrets? No gambling debts? No wicked eccentricities?"

"No, that would hardly be him," Louis shook his head. "His only eccentricity was his files. He kept these files—newspaper and magazine clippings mostly, but some items were facts he'd gathered written on note cards. I never saw all of the files, only a few folders. He got newspapers from all over, including Germany. Don't ask me how. He kept tabs on a lot of things—events and people, odd things you wouldn't suspect—and he had his special interests, of course, most of them political."

Intrigued, she asked him if he knew where the files were now.

"I imagine," he said with a grimace, "they're in his house and now the possession of what's-her-name."

Ned sat at the old dining table in the Kuakini Street flat and watched as twelve-year-old Alika Napili impressed Nigel by expertly mastering the use of the Ansco Memo camera in about twenty minutes. It was mid-afternoon, and Alika had come straight from school, happy to see Ned again and to be doing what he called "spy work." Alika's sister and guardian, Kaleinani, was a friend of Mina's, and Alika had once helped out on another case by watching a house. On Ned's first visit to the flat, it was Alika he had recognized on the street as the leader of the group of boys. Ned had spoken to Kaleinani the day before, and after listening and asking questions, she said she would allow him to help. Kaleinani was ten years older than her younger brother. She worked managing the classy Wahine Surf Lounge in Waikīkī, and Ned suspected that she liked Alika having responsible company at night. Ned assured her that they would more than watch out for him. She laughingly said that it might keep his busy mind out of trouble, and as long as he did his homework and did well in school, it was okay with her. Ned and Nigel had decided that Reggie would coordinate the boys' activities from the flat. Reggie would also be in charge of putting together the photo and log files and doing any other jobs that might come up. Alika was just snapping a picture of Ned and Nigel when Reggie came in the door with colas and almond cookies from the store below.

"So do you think you can help us out?" Ned asked Alika as he placed an almond cookie the size of a small saucer in front of the boy.

"Sure," Alika answered as he aimed the camera at the cookie and took another picture.

"The boys will have to keep everything a secret," Nigel reminded him.

"They can keep secrets," Alika said as he broke a piece of cookie off and began to eat it.

"Alika helped Mina keep an eye on a house," Ned said. "He did an excellent job.

Alika's large brown eyes brightened. "I saw a dead body and the murderer!"

Nigel looked at him in surprise. "Weren't you scared?"

Alika shook his head. "No, but I almost fell out of the tree I was hiding in."

"Well," Nigel said as he popped the cap of a cola and handed it to Alika, "I hope you won't see any dead bodies on our job."

They showed Alika a very neat map of the neighborhood that Reggie had drawn with pen and ink. It showed where the back of the consulate grounds abutted the school and how the schoolhouse and playground stood in relation. Alika told them that the classroom he and his friends were in looked out that way, and they could see the embassy grounds even when they weren't outside on the playground. Along the western side of the property ran Nuʻuanu Stream, and the banks of the stream grew thick with grasses, trees, and bushes. To the east ran Nuʻuanu Avenue. They explained to Alika that they would like the boys to watch the back of the embassy as much as they could and to remember whom they saw coming and going and that there were certain people they were especially interested in. They also told him that they would like it if he could come to the flat before school, around seven, and right after school in case they needed someone to help take a picture without being noticed.

"I can come here when I get up," Alika volunteered. "We live in the lane just behind here."

"That will be splendid. I didn't realize you were that close," Ned said.

"We moved in the summer," Alika said. "Kaleinani said we had to live in a better neighborhood, and I had to go to the parish school. And now she even makes me go to church on Sundays."

"You don't like the school?" Ned asked.

Alika shrugged. "I like it, but Brother Jacob gets really mad if I don't do my homework."

Nigel turned to Reggie and laughed. "I guess you better add making sure Alika finishes his homework to your list of duties."

After they finished their colas and cookies, Alika took Ned, Nigel, and Reggie out to the alley. It was a short dead-end lane off Nu'uanu Avenue with five or six small houses. Alika showed them where he lived and then led them on another path at the end of the lane that went down to Nu'uanu Stream. As they descended to the streambed, the ambient noise of the traffic receded, replaced by the sound of flowing water. Trees, hedges, and a barrier of green hid the houses, separating the stream from the outside world, and for a few minutes as Ned walked behind Alika, he was transported back to his own boyhood—when an afternoon outside could unfold like this, in the warm sunlight beside a clear running stream, when there was nothing to do but whatever caught your fancy. A pair of dragonflies were gliding over the water. Ned stopped and watched as they looped back, swooping down several times before they disappeared downstream. The men followed the boy, and just under the Kuakini Street bridge, they took off their shoes to cross Pauoa Stream where it flowed into Nu'uanu Stream. On the other side, Alika showed them how easy it would be to sneak up on the back of the embassy residence and peek in the windows. With the high, uncut grass and a thick patch of koa haole, he said it would be easy to make some hiding places where you could stay for a long time with no one seeing you.

Back at the flat, Alika gathered up his things and set off to assemble his gang. The following day was Thanksgiving, but he promised to bring the boys by on Friday afternoon, as school was not in session. He also promised to be there himself before and after school and on the weekends, except when he had to go to church. When Nigel told him that all work and no play made Jack a dull boy, Alika looked at him like he was crazy and said that this was better than any game anyone could think up.

"The lad is certainly exceptional," Nigel said just after Alika had run out the door.

Reggie laughed. "I just hope I remember how to do algebra. He said he could use some help."

## 8

# THANKSGIVING

MINA WAS HAVING a bad dream that involved Tilda. In the dream, Tilda was some sort of military officer, and she had arrested Mina for writing something bad about her in the art catalog. In one hand Tilda held a rope that wound around Mina's neck, and in the other she held a whip that she kept cracking at Mina's heels. Rain pattering on the window woke her from the unpleasant scenario, and she felt relieved to be looking over the side of her bed at Ollie, who was curled up and sleeping peacefully on the oval, red Persian rug. As soon as she sat up, he popped out of his slumber, his tail wagging even before he was fully standing. He did a playful doggie stretch and moved over to greet her, looking up with his large brown eyes.

"Who could ever resist such a sweet boy?" she said as she scratched the favored spot under his muzzle. "Too bad you can't bring me coffee in bed."

She threw an old silk robe over her nightgown and headed for the kitchen to make a cup of coffee. She then sat on the pune'e in her living room, looking out the windows that faced the beach, and watched the rain. Soon she found that her thoughts had turned to Ari Schoner's death and to the attempted break-in of his house. She tried to think of how she could push things further, what avenue she could pursue to find out how the two things might be connected. She wished she could actually see Ari's files and question Raymond further to see if he remembered anything significant. She remembered too how late Desmond was for their appointment that morning and how Molly arrived even later, flustered and out of breath. And she hadn't forgotten the scene between Molly and Ari at the Halloween party.

The rain beat harder against the glass, and the wind seemed to be rising. She wondered as she watched the tops of the trees sway and bend why her mind gravitated to these problems of crime. What drew her to these dark goings-on? She slouched back on the cushions and took a sip of coffee. There was always the danger element. Todd had spoken to her about it just the other day, and Ned had cautioned her too. But they both exposed themselves to danger all the time. They didn't shrink back mentally or emotionally when there was a risk. But it wasn't danger per se that she found attractive. People who really loved danger became race-car drivers or went off to climb Mount Everest. No, danger was an element but not the main attraction. Even now she couldn't stop herself from sifting through the possibilities of why Ari might have been killed. Perhaps he was blackmailing someone with the information in his secret files. Perhaps it was a professional assassination for something he did in Germany. Perhaps Tilda and possibly an accomplice just wanted his house. Yes, it was the puzzle she wanted to solve—not just any puzzle but a high-stakes puzzle, a puzzle that mattered, a challenging puzzle that ended in some kind of justice, some kind of order. She suddenly realized that Ned was knocking at her door, and she jumped up to let him in.

"It took some time for you to hear me," he said. There were tiny raindrops in his hair. "You looked like you were a million miles away."

She kissed his cheek. "I can't believe I didn't hear you."

He touched her arm. "And you're cold. You'd better go and put something warm on. It looks like it might rain all day."

By the time she returned wearing a pair of navy slacks and a striped long-sleeved jersey, he had poured himself a cup of coffee and refilled hers.

He placed her cup in her hands. "Weren't your father and Grandma Hannah arriving from Hawai'i yesterday?"

"Yesterday evening."

"Do they come for this dinner every year?"

"Yes, they always come for Thanksgiving. Grandma Hannah stays and visits with her friends all over the island and goes shopping. Then we usually all go to the ranch for Christmas, but this year we won't because of Nyla."

"It's lovely of your sister to have everyone over."

"Yes, and I'm sure she'll be calling us any minute now," she said, in a way that was both amused and exasperated, "wondering where we are."

He chuckled. "Really?"

"Yep. Every Thanksgiving she wants her minions up there bright and early and under her supervision. Better get used to it."

"Have you eaten yet?"

"Oh, no, never eat before you go! Nyla will have piles of food for the help to snack on."

"Sounds like a major production," he said as he stroked her cheek with the back of his hand.

"I shouldn't be grumpy about it," she said. "It makes her so happy to have everyone there and to boss us all around. And poor thing, she's fat and pregnant like a pumpkin."

Just as he leaned forward to kiss her, the phone rang, and they both burst into laughter.

A few minutes later, with their dinner clothes packed and Ollie in the backseat of Ned's sedan, they were headed along through the rain and wind to Maunalani Heights. As they drove around Diamond Head, they could see that the top of the hill was covered with clouds, and they knew that Nyla and Todd's house was likely to be shrouded in mist. Mina was looking out at the rain-slick streets and the puddles.

"Ned," she said, still looking out the window, "why is it exactly that the Nazis are so down on the Jews? I know there is this race-hatred element, but isn't there something else, some kind of political thing?"

"Are you thinking about Ari Schoner?"

"I can't stop thinking about him," she said. "He came all this way to protect himself, and he ends up getting murdered."

He was quiet for a moment and then said, "Do you remember the war?"

"Not really," she answered. "I was in the second grade when it started, and we're so far away. I remember people talking about it, and one of our neighbors had a son who died. I was eleven on Armistice Day, but that year, everything is eclipsed in my mind by the influenza epidemic. My parents moved us all up to the Big Island that summer, and we stayed on the ranch for a whole year. It was one of the best years of my childhood, but you must remember the war more clearly. You were older and closer."

"I was ten when it started," Ned began, "and fourteen when it ended. If it had gone on much longer, I might have been fighting in it. It was a terrible time. Almost every family we knew lost someone in that blood-drenched gutter."

"But why are you asking me about the war?"

"Because your question about the Nazis and the Jews has some roots in the war. There were labor strikes in Germany during the war that affected the military industries, and some people—conservatives, nationalists, military types—blamed the strikes on the Jews and felt that they were responsible for Germany losing the war. So yes, there was a political element. Lots of Germans blame the Jews for their defeat."

"I guess I didn't pay much attention to European history in college."

"Then," Ned continued, "after the war, the financial penalties imposed by the Treaty of Versailles created near-impossible economic conditions in Germany. But in addition, there was the unforgivable— at least in the minds of many Germans—and humiliating clause in the treaty that made Germany say it was responsible for starting the war."

She frowned. "Didn't the war start because some Austrian duke was assassinated by a Serbian, causing an Austro-Hungarian invasion of Serbia?"

"Well, I see you paid *some* attention, darling."

"Maybe some," she admitted.

"So after the war, in Germany there is terrific economic hardship and collectively this feeling of humiliation and resentment born out of a sense of a grave violation of honor. The Weimar government that signed and agreed to the hated treaty was unable to get the economy back on its feet, and the atmosphere became ripe for a fanatic like Hitler to exploit all of these feelings of economic hopelessness, humiliation, and resentment, which he does. And as part of his plan, he makes the Jewish people a collective scapegoat to carry the blame for everything that has gone wrong in Germany."

"It's never a good idea, is it? Humiliation and the inevitable anger it causes on a personal or collective level. It leaves people vulnerable to vindictive and frightening behaviors." She rolled down her window a few inches, as the car was getting excessively humid and the windows were fogging.

"Yes," he said sadly, "I'm afraid it does, and has."

They were three-quarters of the way up the hill and nearly a thousand feet above sea level when the mist wrapped around them. Sometimes on rainy days, banks of water-laden clouds would wind themselves around Maunalani Heights, cloaking the hilltop for hours. Mina shivered and put on her sweater. The temperature at her sister's house was always about seven degrees cooler than at the bottom of the hill, and today with the wind and rain, it seemed particularly pronounced. They pulled up into Nyla and Todd's driveway to see smoke cheerfully rising out of the chimney. Ned reached over and took Mina's hand.

"When we leave this car," he said, "you have to promise to leave the weight of the world behind—for your sister's favorite holiday."

She leaned over and kissed him. "Okay, but I have to warn you. Thanksgiving is not her most favorite holiday. It's only her warm-up exercise for Christmas."

The kitchen door flew open, and Nyla stood there, voluptuously pregnant, with one hand on her hip while she licked some substance from a wooden spoon held by her other hand. "Hey," she called out, "are you two coming in, or are you just going to sit in the car and smooch all day?"

"Hey, shut up, fat lady," Mina answered. "You're just jealous!"

In the house, there was the initial chaos of greetings followed by eating on Ned and Mina's part, as the others had already had breakfast. Nyla had assignments for everyone. She put Ned and Todd in charge of setting the table and laying out the decorations. She had drawn out diagrams for the table, the buffet, the top of her baby grand piano, and the mantle. Charles Beckwith, Mina and Nyla's father, sat on the couch with the diagram and watched them. He was a handsome man in his mid-fifties with the definite look of someone who worked outdoors. He had sold the family business, the lucrative Island Ironworks, and traded his career in Honolulu years ago for the life of a paniolo, managing Uluwehi Ranch on the island of Hawaiʻi. His father had started the ranch on a whim, and it had turned out to be not only a profitable enterprise but also a place that the next two generations of Beckwiths felt passionately attached to.

"Nyla said I'm to supervise you two," Charles grinned as he looked over his daughter's diagrams.

"Does that mean she doesn't trust us?" Ned asked as he looked over a box of pumpkins in various sizes.

"No," Charles answered, taking out his glasses from his shirt pocket. "I'm sure it means she thinks I'm too clumsy. What do you boys want to start with? Why don't you start with the mantle and work your way up to the table?"

"Sounds good to me," Todd said, peering over Charles' shoulder. "Hmm, candles, pumpkins, Indian corn, and pinecones."

"This thing on the piano looks a bit more complicated," Ned said, joining them.

"Yeah, you can do that," Todd said. "You being one of those artsy types."

Ned laughed. "Of course, that means you'll be doing the fancy napkin folding, since you're a copper and good at solving puzzles."

"Now, now, boys," Charles gently scolded, "let's see congenial co-operation or no beer with lunch."

"Better step lively." Todd tossed a pumpkin at Ned that was expertly caught just before it knocked over a vase. "Or there might be hell to pay!"

"Todd, I need your help with something." Mina walked into the living room with a pair of clippers. "I need you to cut some monstera leaves from the garden. It's for the front-door arrangement, and we can get some for the piano top too."

Todd followed her out into the garden while Ned worked on the mantle.

"I don't really need your help," Mina said as they walked to where a large patch of monstera grew. "I wanted to tell you something I found out about Ari, Ari Schoner."

"What's that?" Todd's interest piqued.

"Louis Goldburn told me that he kept these files," Mina said as she started to look for leaves with no blemishes and a deep green color. "Files about people and events, with pictures and notes and newspaper clippings. Louis said Ari knew a lot about people, odd facts and other things."

Todd frowned. "That's a pretty strange hobby."

"He seemed so sweet, but it sounds like he was a compulsive busybody, collecting information about people."

"Like a blackmailer?"

"It crossed my mind," Mina said. "That would neatly explain the attempted break-in."

"How extensive were these files?" Todd asked.

"Louis didn't know. He said he'd only seen a few folders."

Todd glanced up at the house. "Nyla's peering out the window. Look busy."

Mina bent down, clipped one of the large leaves at its base, and handed it to Todd. "I wish we could get a look at those files."

"There's no way I can get a search warrant," Todd said. "Couldn't you sweet-talk that Tilda person into letting you have a look?"

"The very thought of being sweet to her nauseates me," Mina answered. "But if I have to, I will." Mina clipped another leaf and handed it to Todd. "I only need two of these leaves. How many of these do you need for the piano arrangement?"

"Three," he answered. "And better hurry it up. We don't want Nyla coming after us with her rolling pin."

By four in the afternoon, everyone was dressing for dinner. The preparations had finished at around two, leaving enough time for a rest and a shower. The wind had died down, but the rain and mist still hung onto the mountaintop, and although the temperature never seriously dropped during these spells, the dampness that seeped into the fiber of the house could turn it cold. It was on days like this that Todd would keep the fireplace lit and logs stacked neatly in the basket beside the hearth. Ned sat in one of the overstuffed chairs reading a magazine while Ollie lay happily curled up on the rug near the roaring fire, sleeping contentedly by Grandma Hannah's feet. Hannah's bright-white hair was expertly swept up and pinned, framing her flawless brown face like a halo. Her knitting needles worked swiftly and rhythmically on a pair of what Ned thought must be baby booties. Grandma Hannah lived with her son-in-law on the ranch and ran his household. Mina and Nyla's mother had died some years ago, and Ned suspected that Charles had wanted Hannah nearby, not just to see him through the loss of his wife, a loss they both shared, but to ensure that the family stayed safely anchored for his two daughters and to give Grandma Hannah, someone he was extremely fond of, a home and a useful purpose.

"Are you analyzing me, my dear? Or just fascinated by my knitting?" Grandma Hannah asked without looking up.

"To tell you the truth," he replied, "I was thinking about how lucky Charles is to have you managing his home front."

"Oh, I love it, you know," she said. "There's always something interesting happening on a ranch—a new colt, a wild bull, a cattle drive—and I don't do everything myself. You know what we say here: many hands get the job done."

"Just as we did today," he smiled.

"Just as we did today," she repeated.

"And how is Mrs. Shimasaki, your new cook, getting on?" he asked, remembering how Mina had talked them into giving the young widow a chance.

"She's working out perfectly. Her child is being spoiled by everyone, and many of the paniolo admire her, if you know what I mean."

"She must be very grateful to be in such a secure position and away from plantation work."

"You know," Grandma Hannah confided, "at first I was afraid the ranch might be too isolated for her—that she might feel too uncomfortable surrounded by so many men. There's only one other woman who comes to do the cleaning and helps with serving meals—but Mrs. Shimasaki has taken to ranch life like a duck to water."

"That's very good to hear," he said as he recalled the tragic death of Mrs. Shimasaki's husband.

"What's good to hear?" Mina asked as she entered the living room. She wore a lovely long, black, satin evening dress that was slightly shaped but simply cut. The only adornments on the dress were the small layers of ruching along the ballet neckline and on the cuff of the puffed sleeves. She wore a single strand of pearls and matching earrings. Ned thought that she looked casual and comfortable in this island setting, but she would just as easily fit into a dinner party in a New York penthouse.

Ned smiled at her. "You look lovely."

"Thank you," Mina said, genuinely touched by his compliment.

Shortly after everyone had gathered in the parlor, Nigel and Mei arrived. A feast at the beautifully set table followed the cocktails. There was a first course of oysters Rockefeller, then a green salad with alligator pears and fresh crabmeat. Thanksgiving favorites came next—turkey and gravy, stuffing, Grandma Hannah's sweet potato casserole, green beans, stuffed mushrooms and asparagus spears with hollandaise sauce. Nigel and Mei were delighted by the novelty of their first American Thanksgiving.

After dinner, while the others cleared the table and put things away, Mei entertained and impressed everyone on Nyla's baby grand piano. Eventually dessert was laid out on the buffet. There was a pumpkin pie, a coconut cake, and several kinds of cookies. Around eight o'clock, when they were all lounging around the living room, remarking on how wonderful the meal was and how full they were, Charles suggested opening the bottle of brandy he had brought. Mei finally took a break from the piano, helped herself to a piece of pumpkin pie, and joined them.

"I've never eaten pumpkin pie before," Mei said just before she took a bite. "Umm, it's lovely."

Todd had brought out the brandy snifters and the bottle as Nyla, who was now thoroughly exhausted, collapsed into an easy chair and put her feet up on an ottoman—a sure sign that she expected to be waited on for the rest of the night. Charles poured brandy for everyone except Grandma Hannah and Nyla.

"So tell me," Charles said as he handed Mina her drink, "how is the project for Tamara Morrison coming along?"

"The one you helped to talk me into?" Mina asked.

Charles laughed. "She and Jonah were good friends of ours. I just told her I'd put in a good word with you. I hope you didn't take the job because of me."

"That's not likely, Dad," Nyla said with a sly smile.

"You know those people?" Mei asked. "Tamara and Jonah Morrison?"

"Do you?" Mina asked.

"I do," Mei answered. "Not well though. I met them many years ago before my father died. I'm not sure how my father knew them, but I know they went to Shanghai at least once a year for a while. I'd forgotten that they lived in Hawai'i."

"Jonah died a couple of years ago," Charles said.

"Oh, dear," Mei replied. "I'm sorry to hear that."

"What were they doing in Shanghai?" Mina asked.

"I think my father said Jonah did business there, but I don't know what kind."

"Jonah represented several American manufacturing companies," Charles said as he swirled the honey-colored brandy around in his glass. "No one was ever sure how many pies he had his fingers in, but he was a very nice man, socially."

"I seem to remember they had a lot of Japanese friends in the upper echelons of Shanghai society," Mei said thoughtfully. "I remember they liked Japanese art, especially ink-brush paintings and *ukiyo-e*."

"Did the upper echelons include the military?" Ned tried to sound casual, although he knew it was a bit awkward to ask.

"That would be a given," Mei said.

"A given," Nigel said as he glanced at Ned.

"I know they spent quite a bit of time in Japan too," Mei added.

"I'm sure he must have had business interests there," Charles said.

"How is Mrs. Morrison?" Mei asked Mina.

"Oh, she's fine," Mina answered. "And she still loves Japanese art."

"You should call on her," Nigel said to his wife.

"I could arrange for us to eat lunch," Mina offered. "I'm sure you would enjoy meeting her again. She's kind of a character."

# 9

# EARLY DECEMBER

**NED SAT IN** the Kuakini Street flat looking over the photographs of the suspects provided by the Office of Naval Intelligence. There were several of people arriving and leaving the embassy. The faces of the suspects had been circled with a black wax crayon, making them all look guilty. In the first photo, an older Caucasian woman was stepping into the embassy car. There were a couple of other pictures of her entering a teahouse with two Japanese men, one older and the other younger, both quite distinguised and handsome. Ned thought the older man looked like he was in his sixties and the younger man in his forties. He could tell just by looking that they were both diplomats. There was another series of photographs of a young, wiery Japanese man and a pretty Caucasian woman carrying boxes and bundles of greens and flowers into the embassy buildings. The last group of photos showed the same handsome young Japanese diplomat in the first group of pictures getting into a car with two American-looking men. In the next pictures, all three of them were at a golf course, and there was another picture with the three of them on a sailboat. A young woman with long, dark hair had joined them. He could only see the back of her head, and it was not circled. Ned could not tell exactly where they were. The last picture was a single one of a tall, forceful woman who looked like she could be in her early thirties, stepping out of a sports car at the embassy. She was carrying two rectangular parcels wrapped in brown paper and tied up with string.

"Looking at our gallery of possible rogues?" Nigel asked as he and Reggie entered. Nigel snatched up a picture of the older woman and the Japanese diplomats and frowned as he sat down. "The things people think they can get away with."

"What?" Ned looked at him in confusion.

Nigel let out a laugh. "Don't you remember? *I never make sense in the morning until after my third cup of coffee.*"

Reggie set down a box that held three cups of steaming coffee and pastries. The aroma of the fresh coffee was nearly intoxicating, and the box contained what Ned had come to recognize as *malasadas,* Portuguese doughnuts, one of Mina's favorite treats.

"Where did you find these?" Ned asked Reggie.

Reggie grinned. "I have my secret sources. I've learned a useful thing or two while living in Hawai'i."

"Hmm," Ned said as he helped himself to a *malasada,* "maybe you've gone and fallen for a nice Portuguese girl."

Reggie looked stunned. "What makes you say that?"

"It was a jest, Reggie, a joke, a smart remark, as you say in America." Ned looked at him and took a bite of his pastry.

"Oh," Reggie said, narrowing his eyes and looking at Ned.

Ned had already turned his attention back to the photos. "Any idea who these people are?"

"No," Reggie replied, "but I'll tell you everything I was told. It isn't much. This guy here, the older Japanese man, that's the ambassador, and this younger guy is some kind of diplomat. He travels back and forth all the time, so there's a good chance he's taking the information back to Japan. The older lady goes to lots of social occasions at the embassy and goes out to lunch, sometimes dinner, with the ambassador and his wife." Reggie moved on to the next photo. "Okay, this guy who looks more like a local Japanese man, he and this lady go there every week with all these flowers and sticks and things. They might be florists, but they're regular visitors, like clockwork, and they stay for several hours, so they could be doing the flowers and passing information. These two younger guys with the Japanese diplomat— every time he comes to town, they play golf, and I was told sometimes they go sailing. And the lady with the car, she goes out with that diplomat guy when he's here, and she takes parcels like this every once and a while to the embassy."

"They know these people do these things, but they don't know who they are?" Ned asked in disbelief.

"I know," Reggie shook his head. "I thought that was strange myself. All I can figure is maybe they do know who they are, but they want us to find out on our own so there's no question of the navy being involved."

"Honoring their pledge and all that," Ned commented.

Nigel frowned. "But they gave us these photos."

"My final instructions were to burn them three days after I showed them to you," Reggie said.

Ned laughed. "Which you may or may not do, right?"

"I don't see how hanging onto them as long as we need them would hurt," Reggie answered. "Just so long as we always keep them here."

"At any rate," Nigel said, "we need to quickly figure out how to identify people without arousing suspicion."

Ned sighed. "So that means we can't involve the Honolulu Police Department. I don't know of any private investigators on the island, except my fiancée. She seems to know everyone, and if she doesn't, she can easily find out."

Nigel shook his head. "I don't want to involve Mina. It's too close to home for me. As you said yourself, these things can seem so safe and harmless and then quickly turn into something dangerous like—" Nigel stopped himself.

"Like what?" Reggie's eyes were as big as saucers.

Nigel gave Reggie a look. "Like nothing."

"Well," Ned said, "we'll either have to hire someone, since we are all virtual outsiders to Honolulu, or we'll have to follow them home the next time they make an appearance. Do you know where this is?" he asked, pointing to the picture with the boat.

"I think it's the Pearl Harbor Yacht Club," Reggie answered. "I've been there.

"There's a yacht club out there?" asked Ned.

"Yep," Reggie nodded. "It's a club out on the peninsula, the Pearl Harbor Peninsula. Some of the Honolulu elite have holiday houses out there, and some bigwigs who work out that way have made their homes there too. Parts of it are pretty swank. But now there's some modest homes and military people, navy people mostly, living on the peninsula. There's a ferry that goes over to the military installations, so it's convenient for navy types."

"What about this place?" Nigel asked.

"It looks like some kind of teahouse," Reggie said.

Nigel frowned. "We really need someone to help us find out who these people are. Someone trustworthy."

Ned thought for a moment. "I know just the person. He's local. He's trustworthy. He knows everyone. He loves a bit of cloak-and-dagger, and best of all, he owes me a few favors."

Ned walked over to the desk with the telephone and dialed a number. "Hello," he said, "is this the Aliʻi Theatre? Yes? I'm hoping you can help me. I'm looking for Johnny Knight."

Mina and Ollie pulled into the parking area at the Black Point studios at about two in the afternoon. A steady breeze had been blowing all day with an occasional heavier gust. Breezy days always enlivened Ollie, and when Mina let him out of the car, he pranced around while looking at her, then gave a leap and ran into the ironwood grove. Mina had just decided it was too windy for the hat she was wearing and was chucking it in the backseat when Tilda came into the parking lot carrying a box of what looked like Halloween decorations from the October party.

"Here to watch the baby being photographed?" Tilda gave her a crooked smile.

"Yes." Mina felt immediately irritated and contrary. "But Appy is hardly a baby."

"She acts like she just got out of high school." Tilda opened the trunk of her car and threw the box in. "And that painting she's chosen, *Symphony in White,* how could you get more virginal?" She slammed the trunk closed to emphasize her point.

Mina shrugged. "Actually, I think it suits her." She had made a point of looking up the picture last night and was very sure of herself.

"Yeah," Tilda smirked as she stepped into her car, "all those sad-looking pre-Raphaelite women are right up her alley."

Mina ignored her, pretending to busy herself by getting her hand-bag and her notes. She let Tilda back out and roar away without any further conversation. Good riddance, Mina thought, as she watched the red MG disappear down the drive.

As she walked up the path through the ironwoods, she saw Ollie running around furiously with a stick in his mouth and decided to just leave him to his own devices. He never wandered out of earshot and hardly ever got into trouble, and if he got scared or felt threatened, he always made a beeline to her. As she approached the buildings, Molly came rushing out to meet her. Mina could tell by the look on her face that something was wrong.

"Mina," Molly said in a low voice as she took her arm and steered her toward the main building, "I'm so glad you're here."

"Is something wrong?"

"Yes," Molly answered, "but not terribly wrong. Come and put your things down in the meeting room, and I'll tell you."

In the meeting room, Raymond waved to Mina as he adjusted the lighting for Appy's photograph. Mina was amazed at the accuracy of the setup—the white drapes, the floral carpet, the wolf-skin rug. The small, somewhat obscure, group of flowers that lay on the rug looked like it had been lifted from the painting.

"That is amazing," Mina said.

"Yes," Molly replied. "Raymond likes Appy, and he's really gone the extra mile for her. The trouble is, she's in the painting studio in a fit and is saying she just wants to go home."

"Why?"

"I don't know. We're not that close, and she won't tell me, but I suspect it probably had to do with something that beastly Tilda said to her." Molly's face flushed with rage. "Honestly, I hope someday Tilda gets what she deserves."

"And you want me to go and talk to Appy?"

"Didn't you know her in school? You see, we just can't waste Raymond's time or get behind on our schedule."

Mina sighed. "Okay, I'll see what I can do, but Tilda-damage control is not what I signed up for."

"Thanks, Mina." Molly forced a smile. "I really appreciate it."

Mina approached the painting studio and could see Appy pacing and crying through the screen. "Appy?" Mina called out as she opened the door. "Appy, what's happened?"

Appy stopped in her tracks and turned to face Mina. As Mina looked at her, a silent tear streamed down Appy's cheeks, and Mina instinctively went to embrace her.

"I hate Tilda. I hate her," Appy sobbed. "She's a witch, and I wish she were dead!"

"What did she do? What did she say?" Mina held her gently by the shoulders and looked at her. When there was no reponse, Mina shuttled her to a bench and made her sit down. "Now, you don't have to tell me if you don't want to, but it might make you feel better."

Appy took a deep breath. "Did you know my father left my mother when I was a baby?"

"Yes," Mina answered. "I'd heard somethng like that."

"He's an artist too, you know. He's a sculptor on the mainland. He does a lot of bronze statues for parks and things. We don't really talk much because he left my mother and never cared a fig for me. He never helped out or anything."

"I can understand why you wouldn't want to have much to do with him."

"Well, Tilda knew him. He's older than she is, of course, but he's handsome, and women are always fluttering around him. Tilda wanted to tell me all about how she had an affair with him—like she was so proud of herself or something. I got mad and told her I didn't really want to hear about it. Then she got really nasty and said that my father told her the reason he left my mother was because she was sleeping with all of his friends, and he wasn't even sure if he was really my father or not. And when I told her to shut up about my mother, she said she just might tell everybody all about it." Appy paused and caught herself before she started to cry again. "Mina, my mother would never do anything like that. I know her. She's never even had a single date or a boyfriend all these years, and not because men haven't asked her out. She said she loved my father, and he hurt her so badly that she never wants to be in love again. If Tilda goes around lying like that about my mother, I'll kill her!"

"Look," Mina said, "I don't think she'd dare say anything like that to anyone but you. She's just trying to bully and scare you. That's how she is. I'll bet you anything she made all that up, and if she didn't, I'm sure your father made it up and told it to her to make himself look good. And anyway, everyone here has known your mother for years and would never believe malicious gossip like that."

Appy was quiet for a minute. "Do you think so?"

"I know so. Come on now, wash your face, put on some powder and lipstick, and step into that gorgeous white dress."

It took about half an hour, but Appy was able to present herself in the meeting room, ready to have her photgraph taken. Mina watched as Raymond, who was being very kind, fussed and fawned over Appy—telling her how lovely she looked and how beautiful the photos were going to be. It was true, Mina thought. Appy did look lovely, and also, while she hated to admit it, there was a grain of truth in what Tilda had said. Appy acted much younger than her years, and even though she had been to art school in New York, she seemed overly sheltered and protected for someone who was at least twenty-four years old. Girls like Appy would always be picked on by women like Tilda. Mina could see how Appy's seeming naivete must irritate Tilda by making her more aware of her own jaded nature. And to add fuel to Tilda's fire, Appy was a more sensitive and imaginative artist than Tilda could ever hope to be. In Mina's estimation, there was something shallow about Tilda's portraits, and even though they were technically faultless, they somehow lacked the depth and life that shone through in Appy's work.

"This was definitely the right choice you made," Raymond was saying to Appy as he made a small adjustment to one of the lights. "You look like the first day of spring."

Mina wondered if in this day and age, looking like springtime was a good thing or a bad thing. Tilda might be right about that too. The world was growing more complicated and competitive every day, and girls like Appy were so easily trodden underfoot by the increase of people with ambitious, self-serving attitudes. It didn't surprise Mina that Appy would be attracted to someone withdrawn and wounded like Andrew Halpern—someone who would need an endless supply of sympathy and cheering. Appy probably romanticized his dark personality as proof of his noble, artistic suffering.

When the photo session was over, Mina went back to the painting studio to help Appy out of her dress and start her interview, while Molly and Raymond broke down the set.

"So, Appy," Mina began, "I just wanted to straighten a few things out. I have what you wrote for your statement—"

"Oh, I know it was horrible," Appy interrupted her. She was buttoning up her blouse as quickly as she could.

"It wasn't horrible. There's all kinds of information in it. It's just a touch jumbled up." Mina thought that was much better then saying it was nearly impossible to understand. "So I need to clarify a few things."

"Oh, okay," Appy answered as she sat, pulled back her long auburn hair, and began to braid it.

"Now, when did art first interest you?" Mina asked.

"Gee, um, I don't know. I always liked drawing from when I was a kid. My mother has saved all these things I drew. She has hundreds of drawings of all the cats we've ever had and every flower that grew in the garden. When I got older, I got some colored pencils and then some pastels. Then at Punahou, Mr. Wells, the art teacher, really helped me and took extra time. That's when I started painting, and then I just decided I was going to be an artist."

"And how did you get to the Art Students League in New York? That's a pretty big achievement."

"Well, I don't know. I just sent them my portfolio, and I got in. Saving the money was harder than getting accepted."

"How did you do that?" Mina was curious.

"I worked two jobs for a year and saved all my money. I worked at Liberty House doing window displays on weekends, and during the week, I worked at the desk at the Moana Hotel. Then, when I got to New York, I stayed with my mom's sister. She runs a really nice boardinghouse, so she let me stay in one of the rooms, and I helped her with the cooking and cleaning."

Mina stopped taking notes and looked at Appy. "That took quite a bit of focus and discipline."

"For the second two years, I won a scholarship, so that helped a lot."

"Still, just getting accepted there is really something and then working so hard to be there."

"I guess it just didn't seem that way to me. We were supposed to be in the studio for eight hours every day, and some of the other students thought that it was hard, but I loved it. I would even go in sometimes on the weekends to work. And it was actually fun to help my Aunt Rita. She's way younger than my mom. She rented a lot of rooms to actors, and they would give us free tickets whenever they were in a play."

"I'm surprised you came home," Mina smiled.

"Oh, I always wanted to come home. All the things I really want to paint are here."

"I've seen a few of your landscapes, but flowers and plants seem to be what you like most."

"I could paint plants and flowers forever. I've even been asked to do some botanical illustrations for textbooks. I'm getting into painting birds too. They're hard to make sketches of, though, because they move so fast. I like to hike into the mountains and try to spot the rare birds. You know, the real Hawaiian birds that you hardly see anymore. And sometimes you can come across really rare plants too." Appy paused for a moment and then said in a softer voice, "Andrew likes to go hiking."

"Appy," Mina said cautiously, "doesn't Andrew have another girfriend?"

"You mean Jay-ling?"

"Uh-huh."

"They broke up, and she went to the mainland. Andrew said he was glad she left because all she wanted to do was sleep during the day and go to parties at night." Appy's face clouded. "Of course, as soon as Tilda found out that I liked Andrew, she tried to flirt with him, but he doesn't like her at all. He calls her a cow. She loves to flirt with other people's boyfriends, and married men too."

"Really?" Mina decided to find out what Appy knew.

"Yeah," Appy lowered her voice. "I think *maybe* she's slept with Bill and Raymond, but I know for sure she has with Desmond."

"Desmond?" Mina pretended surprise.

"Yes, and Tilda and Molly were having a big fight when I got here today. I bet that's why she decided to be so mean to me."

Johnny Knight, artistic director of the Aliʻi Theatre in Kaimukī, sat behind his desk, looked over the photographs Ned and Nigel had brought, and burst out laughing. When he saw Ned's frown, he stopped laughing and said, "I thought you were going to show me some real desperadoes." Johnny smiled. "You're going to die when you find out who these people are."

"Don't tell me they're all cast in your next production," Ned said.

"They're in a kind of production, but it's not mine."

Ned looked puzzled. "So are we going to play a guessing game?"

Johnny eyed Nigel. "Ned's told you that Mina and I are distantly related, right? We're related on her mother's side."

"I guess that's where your handsome island looks come from," Nigel commented.

"I would not want to tell you anything Mina might be hiding from you." Johnny was clearly in one of his more mischievous moods and enjoying being cagey.

"What has Mina got to do with it?" Ned asked.

"Quite a bit," Johnny said. "I'm surprised you don't know these things, Ned. Things that are right under your nose."

"Please," Ned couldn't help but be amused, "can we get to the climax of the scene?"

"These people are all artists. They're all in that art show Mina is working on for Tamara Morrison. In fact, that gray-haired lady *is* Tamara Morrison!"

"If I didn't know you, Johnny, I wouldn't believe you." Ned found it hard to disguise his surprise.

Nigel sighed and turned to Ned. "Well, Trout, it looks like we might not be able to keep your beloved out of this."

"Trout?" Johnny's grin looked like the crescent moon.

"Oops," Nigel grinned too, "a slip of the tongue."

Ned frowned at Johnny. "You never heard that."

"Trout?" Johnny teased again.

"Johnny," Ned said in an even voice, "if you ever repeat that, I will not work with this theatre again, and yes, that is a blatant threat. Now please tell us about these people."

"Okay, okay," Johnny chuckled, "the threat is duly noted. So these two guys—that's Desmond Rivers and Bill Hitchins. I bet this girl with them is Appy, April Fraser. This lady carrying the box of flower stuff is Desmond's wife, Molly, and she's with Akira what's-his-name. Oh, and this one here, with the car—she's a piece of work, I can tell you—that's Tilda, the ogress. They all belong to that Halemana gang of artists."

Ned looked again at the photographs, now aware that these were all the people Mina had been talking about. The characters in his mind now had faces, and like a slap on the face, the first thought that crossed his mind was that the brutal murder at the art studio was connected to what he and Nigel were investigating. "Do you know any of them personally? Do you know what they're like?" he asked with an unbidden urgency.

"Well," Johnny said, leaning back in his chair, "Tamara is from Hawai'i. I think she was a McClintock before she got married to this Morrison guy. She has the house to die for up in Pacific Heights. The husband was a big businessman. He left her a cartload of money when he passed away. I know they were big art collectors, traveled all over the Orient, but their great passion, or greed—however you see it—is for Japanese woodblock prints, *ukiyo-e.* Those men with her in the tea-house photo—one is the ambassador, and the other is some young diplomat. I hear he's quite a dandy and loves Caucasian women. And by the way, Ned, Tamara is a theatre subscriber and a very generous patron."

"In that case, I guess she can't be all bad," Ned commented.

"Desmond and Molly live out on Black Point. Word is he's a rover, if you know what I mean, and his wife just puts up with it. Although, I'm sure you can tell by looking at her, she certainly doesn't have to. Desmond is pretty stuck on himself, but he is a very talented artist. Well, all of these people are talented artists. I don't know what Molly is doing here with Akira. He's a master with the ink brush and also has a flower shop. He teaches *ikebana* to interested people. He's got quite a reputation for that too and for having an eccentric personality. Maybe Molly is learning *ikebana*. Now, if you ask me, Bill Hitchins here is probably the most talented and the most disreputable of the lot but able to turn on the charm like nobody's business. He drinks a bit too, I hear, and is always in financial straits. His young and adorable Tahitian wife is the one with the steady job. She and her brother dance in Waikīkī. He and Desmond look like they're at the yacht club."

"The Pearl Harbor Yacht Club?"

"Oh, yes, the Pearl Harbor Yacht Club," Johnny nodded, "founded by Tamara's late husband, your soon-to-be father-in-law, and a host of other prominent Honolulu businessmen and ocean enthusiasts."

"Charles Beckwith likes sailing?"

"Before he moved to the ranch, it was one of his main diversions." Johnny pulled out a cigarette and lit it. "He used to win lots of regattas too. You know, Mina and Nyla probably have cards."

Ned looked perplexed. "Cards?"

"The gentlemen members are allowed 'cards' for their female tribe, so they can use the clubhouse. It's actually quite beautiful, and the food is top-notch."

"I must get Mina to take me there."

"Tamara probably has a lifetime card, since her husband was one of the founders and poured a small fortune into it. I bet she still gives them dough. Desmond could be a member, and maybe Bill too. They're a bit bohemian for the membership, but I hear they're good sailors, and the club likes talent. It's one of those clubs where you see the paupers rubbing shoulders with the princes. Most of these Honolulu clubs are race prejudice and class prejudice about membership, but the yacht club will forgive your low-class origins if you can sail really well—but not your race, unless you're really an exceptional."

"An exceptional?" Nigel looked puzzled.

"Like Duke Kahanamoku, athlete extraordinaire, or Edward Manusia, famous writer. Or," Johnny went on, "an exceptional could be of any race, really, if he was filthy rich and well mannered. There's a huge subjective gray area with these yachtie people."

"I guess we should count ourselves lucky," Ned said. "But what about the ogress, the infamous Tilda I've heard so much about?"

Johnny laughed. "She's a hungry one. She's ambitious, and she has a knack for getting what she wants. Don't say I didn't warn you."

"I stand warned by you *and* Mina."

"Oh, she's the kind of person who would drive Mina crazy." Johnny paused, leaned forward, and lowered his voice to a very confidential tone. "So just what have all these people done, Ned? Are they part of an art-forgery gang or what?" Johnny cocked his head. "And are you going to let me play cloak-and-dagger too?"

# 10

# SATURDAY, DECEMBER 7

**W**HEN MINA HAD offered to drive Ned's car out to the yacht club so he could enjoy the scenery, Ned had quickly agreed. Nigel and Mei sat in the backseat, intrigued by the landscape of their new island home. The dark-blue sedan traveled along the road through Pearl City, past rice and watercress farms. They rolled smoothly by taro and lotus flourishing in ponds, tilled hillsides of sugarcane and pineapple, banana patches, papaya groves, and innumerable family farms growing all kinds of table vegetables. Seeing so many neat but ramshackle-looking houses, it was easy to imagine tired men and women returning to these humble homes after many long and backbreaking hours of work. Along the way there were also lots of children—playing with beanbags, walking on homemade stilts, or engrossed in games of marbles or milk caps. Mina smiled to herself, thinking how the children of the world could bring lightheartedness and a sense of fun into the hardest living conditions. It was just after noon on Saturday, and the country town with its stores, barbershop, soda fountain, and movie theatre was mostly shut down and the streets all but deserted.

The dark-gray sky had become heavy, and the air carried the distinct promise of rain, as Mina turned the car off the main road toward the Pearl Harbor Peninsula. Tall kiawe trees grew along either side, with their spreading canopies, carpets of thorns, and long, pale beans. They saw two small boys collecting the beans in a gunnysack to sell, Mina guessed, or to take home to feed their own animals.

"Thanks so much for arranging this visit to the yacht club, Mina," said Nigel from the rear seat. "I'd love to meet some other people who like to sail."

"Save your thanks for Tamara," Mina answered. "She's the one who's treating us to lunch, and she's dying to see you, Mei."

"I'm surprised she remembers me," Mei said.

"I'm not," Mina said, glancing at her in the rearview mirror.

"Why is this yacht club so far away from the city?" Ned asked.

"Well," Mina began, "they started yacht racing in Honolulu Harbor but then decided it was too small and too crowded with commercial vessels, so they moved out here. They got this clubhouse in about 1928, just a few years before my father moved to the ranch. It used to belong to one of the Afong family."

The car emerged from the kiawe groves into a neighborhood of large houses and mansions, with rolling lawns and meticulously kept gardens—the kinds of houses that required a flotilla of servants and gardeners.

Mina laughed. "I know what you're all thinking. It happens to everyone the first time they see this place and wonder how in the world this happened in what seems like the middle of nowhere."

"So tell us, darling," Ned said, "how in the world did it happen?"

"It was part of Ben Dillingham's land-colonization scheme. He brought the railway out to Pearl City—that was an essential part of the plan too—in the 1890s and made a special line that ran down to the peninsula. This bottom half of the peninsula, especially on the water, is where all the well-to-do people bought lots and set up vacation estates, although some people retired out here and a few live all year round. My father used to bring us to the club when he went sailing, but I haven't been out here in years. It's one of those lovely, tucked-away places."

A light rain had started as they arrived at the yacht club, and the two couples walked hurriedly from the car to the shelter of the two-story clubhouse. Wide white columns supported an arbor that encircled most of the ground floor. Thick bougainvillea vines bursting with purple blossoms covered the arbor, creating a natural, shady ceiling over the red-brick floor of the veranda. It was easy to tell that at one time this had been an impressive mansion, and even though it had been extensively renovated, it still retained the feeling of a grand country home. The French doors at the entrance led to a foyer with a staircase and large doors on either side, one to a bar and another to a dining area. Tamara Morrison came down the stairs just as they stepped inside.

"Hello, everyone," Tamara smiled. "And Mei," she said, embracing her. "I have so many fond memories of your father. It's really wonderful to see you." She guided them into the dining room and to a table near the back doors with a magnificent view of the harbor. "I thought we should stay inside, because it looks like it might rain. Please go ahead and order a drink. I just have to finish up this meeting for our art show, and I will be right down."

"For the art show?" Mina asked.

Tamara sighed. "I made the mistake of having a group meeting of the artists to get their opinions on how to hang the show. Now they're upstairs squabbling." She laughed. "They'll argue and insult each other, and then they'll come down and, after the first drink, be as chummy as ever. Your arrival will be the perfect reason for me to break up the meeting."

It was just afternoon, but the dark, low sky made it seem like evening. They ordered drinks and ventured out onto the veranda, as the rain was still very light and not penetrating the arbor of bougainvillea. The lawn, dotted with coconut trees, stretched out before them, seamlessly merging with the water of the harbor, which lay motionless and so tranquil that Mina thought she might be able to kick off her shoes and run across the loch to the other side. She had always remembered this place as if it were another world—cut off from the mainstream, surrounded by these peaceful waters, part of the dream-like realm childhood becomes once you leave it. She remembered the day Grandma Hannah brought them down here to swim while her father was sailing. After hours in the clean and clear water, she wrapped them in towels, and they all lay down on a wide lauhala mat while Grandma told them the stories of Ka'ahupahau, the shark who guarded the harbor. Mina couldn't exactly recall the story, but she remembered looking up at the fronds in the coconut trees and watching them move back and forth, wondering where the wind went when it wasn't blowing, as she listened to the warm sound of Grandma Hannah's voice. She did remember part of one story about an arrogant girl who sat near the shore here making a lei. An old woman came by and asked her if she would make one for her, but the girl treated the old woman scornfully and humiliated her.

"If I can't have my painting in the entrance, then I don't want to be in this stupid show!" Mina instantly recognized Tilda's voice. It was coming from the stairs in the foyer. "And don't give me this kindergarten talk about being fair to everyone."

There was a short silence, as if someone were answering her but not loud enough for anyone to hear. Then Tilda spoke again. "Well, how would you like it if I told everyone exactly how your husband made so much money?"

They all caught a glimpse of Tilda stomping off to the bar and then Tamara Morrison heading for the ladies' room. There was an awkward silence at the table, and then Mina shook her head and laughed. "She's so . . . so . . ." She paused, trying to think of a word to describe her.

"So contentious?" Ned guessed.

"Yes," Mina frowned. "Yes, and she's entangled with the others in some twisted ways too."

"It's very interesting," Mei volunteered, "how people in different groups deal with each other."

Some of the other artists drifted down the stairs and into the dining room. Mina introduced them as they straggled in, and soon an informal party was well under way. When Tamara entered, she was her cheerful self, as if the scene on the stairs had not happened. She had arranged a lunch buffet of sandwiches and salads, and with the rain and a haze of alcohol, an unhurried afternoon began to unfold, one careless moment after another. Tamara, obviously wanting a private visit, took Nigel and Mei aside to an out-of-sight table in the corner, where they had her full attention. Into the room strolled Tilda, drink in hand, followed by Raymond, who was still walking with a slight limp. He had a sly, self-satisfied look on his face, and the first thing Mina thought was that it might have something to do with Tilda. Raymond took a quick glance around the room and went out the front door. Tilda had spotted Mina and walked over to her. "I've been meaning to call you, Mina," she said, trying to be very friendly. "I've finished looking over what you wrote. You can have the copy back with my changes, if you like."

Mina managed a pleasant smile. "Fine, I can pick it up from you anytime."

"Why don't you stop by tomorrow, on Sunday? I'm meeting someone around six, but you could come earlier."

"I'm going to Molly's photography session tomorrow afternoon. Maybe I can stop by on my way home," Mina suggested.

"Perfect." Tilda turned her head to appraise Ned. "Is that your friend I've heard so much about?"

"That's him. Would you like me to introduce you?"

"Oh, no, don't bother. I can introduce myself." Tilda gave her a wink and turned away.

Mina watched as she sidled up to Ned, who had the attention of most of the group. She could see they were all intrigued by him, probably not just by his charm and good looks but by the whole idea of a playwright, born in the South Seas, and now well known in London and New York theatre circles. They were all talking and laughing and waving their hands around. She wondered how long it would be before they were sloshing their drinks. The humidity suddenly made her feel uncomfortable. The atmosphere in the room felt oppressive, and all she could think of was getting away from this crowd of people and their chatter. Ned was deeply involved in conversation. He surely wouldn't notice if she slipped out for a walk in the fresh air.

The rain that had fallen ever so lightly had now stopped, leaving the grass damp and the leaves of the colorful crotons that bordered the veranda draped in tiny droplets of water. She touched one of the leaves and watched the water drip away. She wove her way over the neatly trimmed lawn and through a grove of coconut palms. Their fronds hung perfectly still as if all the trees had fallen into a quiet sleep. Down near the shore stood a white gazebo. Tevai Hitchins, with a garland of yellow plumeria encircling her head, sat on an Adirondack chair sewing and singing to herself in Tahitian. She stopped as she saw Mina approaching.

"Hello, Tevai," Mina said, trying to be friendly.

"Hello, Mina," Tevai replied with her pretty French accent.

"What are you sewing?" Mina asked as she stepped into the gazebo.

"I make a tifaifai for me and Bill, for our bed cover." She reached over and showed Mina her handiwork.

"A tifaifai? Why, it looks like a Hawaiian quilt."

"Yes," said Tevai, "only we don't make it thick—you know, we only make the top with the pattern."

"You don't quilt it?"

"No," Tevai shook her head, "we only make it like this. I sew the uru."

Mina admired the breadfruit appliqué that Tevai had nearly finished stitching down. The light-green breadfruit leaves spread out in a beautifully executed pattern over a darker-green background, with very small and even stitching. "This is really lovely, Tevai."

"Bill drew out the pattern for me. He is very good. I'm going to make him do another for me when I finish this one."

"Aren't you hungry?" Mina asked. "Don't you want to go in to eat?"

"I brought some food for me and Rahiti," she said, pointing to a covered dish on the table. "I made taro and fish for us. He's diving out there." Tevai pointed into the water and in the distance to a small buoy. The tip of a spear appeared, then a head emerged, taking a breath of air before it disappeared again into the smooth water. "I don't like to go inside—too much drinking, and I don't like the way Tilda talks to me. She talks loud—as if I cannot hear."

Mina laughed. "I don't like the way she talks to me either."

"Sometimes she makes Bill very angry."

"Why?" Mina couldn't help asking.

"I don't know, but he says she plays bad games, and she better be careful."

Someone laughed behind them. "Who better be careful? I hope it's not me."

Mina and Tevai turned to see Eva Morgan standing behind them. She was dressed simply in dark-blue pants and a pretty green pullover. Her blonde hair hung in two braids, and she looked much younger than she had at the Halloween party. It dawned on Mina that Tevai and Eva must be around the same age.

"I didn't know you were here, Eva," Mina said to her with a smile.

"I just got here," Eva said as she entered the gazebo. "I dropped my dad off earlier, and now I'm waiting to drive him home. My mother says he always drinks too much when he comes here. I brought movie magazines, Tevai—*Silver Screen, Photoplay, Movie Mirror.* I went to get them from the beauty shop."

"Eva is working in a beauty shop in Pearl City," Tevai said, as if Mina should be impressed.

"I didn't even know there was a beauty shop out here," said Mina.

"It opened some time ago," Eva told her. "I only work a couple of days a week. I just shampoo hair, do comb-outs to get the customers ready for the real hairdressers."

Mina smiled. "That must be fun for you."

"It's mostly military wives. It's pretty boring, actually, but it's something to do." Eva's eyes squinted as she scanned the water. "Is Rahiti fishing?"

"Yes," said Tevai, "and I hope he brings something good for dinner."

Mina left the two girls to their movie magazines and walked out to the pier. It was so still that no one appeared to be sailing. Off in the distance, Ford Island nested in the harbor. The US Army had purchased the island during the war, but now, the navy owned the island. It was an aviation center, and navy ships moored there too. A ferry carried people back and forth. Mokuʻumeʻume had once been its name, but like so many places, officials had changed its Hawaiian name to an English name. She thought she remembered that Ford was some kind of doctor. As she sat on the pier and watched the fish swim around the pilings, she wondered what Hawaiians had found so fascinating about the islet to give it a name that meant enticing and alluring. She thought her grandmother had told her something about the island that she couldn't remember. Anyway, Mokuʻumeʻume was a much better name than boring Ford Island. The sky had turned a silvery blue-gray, with the water mirroring the same hues. The air hung breathless and still, as if the whole afternoon was dangling in suspended time, and as she looked once more toward the little island, she was sure she could see a large fin gliding over the surface about a hundred yards away. She stood up and watched the fin sweep slowly out of sight, and then she got up and headed back to the clubhouse. On her way back to the clubhouse, she saw Raymond talking to Eva a short distance away from the gazebo. Their voices were raised, but when they saw her walking their way, they quickly quieted down. Eva said a few more words to her father, then turned and walked back to the gazebo. Raymond came walking toward Mina, with a definite scowl on his face.

"I'm sorry you had to see that," he said when he reached her side.

"Nothing serious, I hope." She tried to sound casual.

"I've asked her so many times not to smoke cigarettes." He shook his head. "Oh, I know she's old enough and everyone else does it, but I don't approve of young girls smoking. Eva forgets that Tevai is a married woman, even though she is only a year older than Eva. I suppose it's hard for me to see her grow up," he sighed. "Good God, listen to me. I must sound like an old-fashioned boor."

Mina laughed. "No, you sound like a father."

"Well, I told her to collect her things and take me home." He looked back as if to make sure his daughter was complying. "It was nice to see you here."

When she got back to the clubhouse, she saw that Tilda had cornered Ned and was pouring on the charm. Mei had found a piano in the corner, and Tamara was in deep conversation with Molly. Mina decided to help herself to some lunch and picked out some petite sandwiches of shrimp paste, some of egg, some potato salad and coleslaw. When Mei saw her, she stopped playing, got a plate of food, and joined Mina.

"I'm so glad you're back," Mei said. "Nigel has gone off with Bill and Desmond. He's now totally enthralled with the idea of sailing."

"You didn't know he liked to sail?"

"Well, he mentioned something about it once, but to hear him to-day, you'd think it was his grand passion."

"Ned seems enthralled too," Mina said dryly.

"That woman doesn't seem real," Mei said, glancing at Tilda.

Mina laughed. "I don't think she is."

"Maybe Nigel and Ned are up to something," Mei said just before she took a bite of one of her sandwiches.

The fork full of potato salad Mina was raising stopped midway between her mouth and her plate. "What do you mean? Up to something?"

"I meant Ned and Nigel. It's just this sense I get when I think Nigel is working instead of just being himself."

Mina looked over at Ned, who was smiling and nodding at Tilda. Was it her imagination, or did she detect a hint of insincerity under his pleasant smile? "I see what you mean."

"This is an interesting twist to a leisurely afternoon." Mei gave Mina a conspiratorial smile.

Mina smiled back. "Very interesting."

# SUNDAY, DECEMBER 8

**Y**OU SAID I would do what?" Ned looked at Nigel in disbelief. "I haven't fenced in ages."

"I'm sure it will come right back to you, Trout," Nigel assured him.

"We'll have to have a few practice sessions first. I don't want to make a fool of myself. And don't ever call me Trout in front of Mina, or our friendship will be off forever."

"Don't complain. Tamara said she would get us both temporary memberships to the yacht club. It's the least we can do to reciprocate."

"Next you'll be wanting me to sail," Ned complained.

"Can you?"

"No."

"Oh, don't worry," Nigel said with a wave of his hand. "I could teach you all you need to know overnight."

It was early afternoon, and the dark clouds of the morning were breaking and shifting, letting intermittent spots of sunshine spill over the garden. The two friends were sitting on the lanai at Ned's bungalow. Just before Nigel arrived, Ned had seen Mina off to a photography session for Molly Rivers. Nigel was happily biting into a cold chicken sandwich that Ned had made him. Glistening tears of water ran down the two cold bottles of beer that sat on the table alongside a dish of boiled peanuts and a tray of cheese and crackers.

"So what did you think of our first encounter with the suspects?" Ned asked.

"What really amazes me," Nigel confessed, "is how anybody and his grandmother could go sailing around in that harbor and keep an eye on all the comings and goings of those navy ships. My God, they even have races around that island—Ford Island, is it?"

"Ford Island," Ned repeated, "although I'm sure there's another, older name for that place." Ned poured his beer into a glass. He just couldn't get used to the idea of drinking beer straight out of a bottle. "Desmond and Bill could be quite a team—leisurely sailing around and taking notes."

"Yes, well," Nigel began to agree, "but Tamara and that Tilda creature both look capable of sailing a boat and doing the same thing. This is a perfect sandwich, Trout."

Ned frowned and picked at the label on his beer bottle. "I really wish you would train yourself not to use that name."

"Sorry," Nigel grinned. "It's a splendid sandwich, Edward."

"I wonder," Ned mused, "just what Tilda meant about Tamara's husband and his business dealings."

"Actually, I had a discussion with Mei on the very subject last night."

Ned raised his eyebrows. "And?"

"Mei said she thinks—she's not one-hundred-percent positive—that some of the things Morrison manufactured and sold to the Japanese, possibly also to the Chinese, were vital parts to weapons."

"Arms manufacturing—that could explain why he had friends in high places."

"If it's true," Nigel continued, "there could have been a lot of favors being exchanged for big contracts. She remembers Morrison was an avid art collector."

"Avid," Ned chuckled, "sounds like a euphemism for ruthless or greedy."

"Could be," Nigel nodded and took another healthy bite of his sandwich.

"Could be she's still exchanging favors."

Nigel chewed thoughtfully, swallowed, and looked at Ned. "If we didn't know any better, if we hadn't been in this shady occupation for so long, we would never suspect such a sweet older woman."

"We're in a permanent state of suspended disbelief."

"I have no idea what that means," Nigel said as he polished off his sandwich.

"Applying it to our situation, it means our judgment is permanently suspended concerning the implausibility of any narrative we might perceive."

Nigel laughed. "What you mean is that we've seen so many impossible things, now we'll believe anything is possible."

"Precisely," Ned said just before he reached for some peanuts. "I spoke to Tilda for quite some time yesterday. I think she's the type that could easily be seduced by money and by the idea that she was in a position of some power."

Nigel closed his eyes and inhaled. "Ah, the ambrosia of money and power."

"I believe she'd have a steady diet of it, if she could."

"Actually, I quite like Desmond and Bill," Nigel said. "I hope it isn't one or both of them, but Bill's hard up, I think. He might do it for money or fun or both."

"I understand from Mina that Desmond is financially set, but I think he's a bit of a bounder."

"I could see him romanticizing his role as a daring mercenary participating in world-changing events."

"His wife, however," Ned continued, "is more of an enigma. I wasn't able to speak to her at all."

"She could be in league with the Japanese fellow," Nigel said as he reached for a cracker with cheese.

"Mina is meeting with Molly as we speak," said Ned. "Perhaps I can . . ." Ned's voice trailed off, and he paused before he spoke again. "I just don't like using Mina this way without letting her know. It's deceitful."

Nigel was quiet for a moment. "Our whole job revolves around being deceitful. I didn't like asking Mei about Morrison either, but the less our family and friends know—"

"The safer they are. The old motto."

"The old motto may be a cliché, but that doesn't mean it isn't true. It's for their protection."

"Well, if there's one thing I know about Mina," Ned said, "it's that she would bristle at the idea of not being informed because I thought she needed to be protected."

Mina pulled her Packard left off the main road as she approached the Nuʻuanu Pali lookout and followed the dirt track until she saw Raymond Morgan's car. She could see them off in the distance in a small grassy area near a huge boulder. It was close to a cliff edge but just back far enough to be safe. The clouds moved swiftly overhead, a passing breeze rolled over the grass, and Mina felt they were fortunate to be here on a day without the strong winds that usually whipped up the cliffs. Nuʻuanu Valley rose gradually to this one traversable pass in the Koʻolau Mountains, and then the land dropped suddenly down at least a thousand feet. In ancient times, over four hundred men had died here in the great battle of Nuʻuanu. When Kamehameha's men forced the Oʻahu army up the valley, many of the warriors perished, jumping or being pushed over the precipice to their death. It was a magnificent and lonely place that felt wild, as if it were its own country, separated from the settled parts of the island by its elevation, its cooler air, and its remoteness. She inhaled the scent of the surrounding forest as she walked slowly down to the grassy area where Marguerite Morgan was dressing Molly up as Brunhilde. Molly had chosen to pose as the Valkyrie from a work by the illustrator Arthur Rackham. She could see that the costume was very detailed, with a winged helmet, elaborate sandals that climbed up Molly's legs, a tunic, a skirt with a kind of long breastplate over it, a cape, and a spear. There was also some kind of horn tied around her waist. Mina was immediately struck by the incongruity of a woman dressed like a Nordic shield maiden in this place. It often grated on her that people came to live in the islands, didn't care about where they were, and did their best to pretend they were somewhere else. One of the major events in Hawaiian history had taken place here, and part of Mina felt as though these people were dismissing a past that was important and valuable to her by coming here and imposing an outlandish foreign image on the landscape. Nyla would accuse her of being intolerant if she shared these thoughts with her, and maybe Nyla would be right. There were people who imposed things and other images on the islands in ways that were far more harmful, and anyway, Mina thought with a good-humored, cynical smile, at least she's dressing up like a warrior.

"Oh, Mina, you're just in time," Molly waved.

"That's some costume." Mina forced herself to be kind.

"Marguerite made it," Molly said.

"I made it for Eva," Marguerite said as she stepped back to survey Molly. "One year she wanted so badly to go as a Valkyrie to a costume dance. Of course, I had to alter it for Molly."

Molly winked. "She means I'm not as slim and lithe as Eva."

"You look strong and lovely," Marguerite said, "as if you just stepped out of the storybook."

"Why did you choose Brunhilde?" Mina asked Molly.

"I'm a friend of Arthur Rackham's daughter, Barbara. I met her at a party when I was in art school in London. We hit it off and got to be very close. I went to her parents' house quite a bit too, so I got to know and meet her father. This has always been one of my favorite illustrations."

"How interesting to know such a famous illustrator," Mina said.

"Poor man," Molly sighed. "Barbara tells me he's quite ill now but still working. He's doing *The Wind in the Willows*."

Raymond, who had been absorbed in setting up his camera, finally asked Molly to climb up on the boulder and take her pose. She looked quite striking with the dramatic backdrop of the mountains behind her. Raymond looked down at the book and then through his camera lens, all the while asking Molly to make minor adjustments. When he finally had her posed just the way he wanted her, a slight breeze blew her cape, and it needed straightening.

"Marguerite," Raymond yelled. "The cape. Fix it."

Mina watched as the slightly overweight and uncoordinated Marguerite struggled to try to climb up on the boulder, but when her foot slipped and she nearly fell over, Mina decided to intervene. Marguerite gratefully let Mina take over, and Mina easily scrambled up to Molly and fixed the cape. Over the course of the next half an hour, which seemed like three, Mina had to make several more adjustments to the costume because of one thing or another. But at one point, the clouds parted and allowed the sun to shine at an angle that illuminated Molly on the boulder, while the background remained in shadow, and Molly was suddenly transformed. The blonde streak in her hair glistened, and her eyes glowed. And it seemed to Mina that she might just rise up and fly away into the clouds. Just as quickly as it had begun, the clouds passed over the sun, the light faded, and Molly was once again just a woman in a costume.

"I got a very good picture," Raymond said with a beaming smile. "I'm sure of it."

"Are we finished?" Molly asked.

"Finished," Raymond answered.

"Great," said Molly with a sigh of relief. "These sandals are choking my legs. I must have tied them too tight."

"You looked beautiful," Raymond gushed. "So strong and perfect."

Mina and Marguerite helped Molly to change while Raymond packed up. Molly had left her car at a friend's house down in the valley and said she had packed a picnic for all of them. When everyone was ready, Molly rode with Mina while Raymond and Marguerite followed behind. They wound back down along the twisting Pali Road, and when they reached the area where residences began, they turned off onto a long driveway covered by a canopy of trees and surrounded by an intense growth of tropical foliage. They reached a large white house, and Molly directed them to park next to her car. Soon, several picnic baskets in hand, they were headed off across the manicured lawn, which sloped down to Nu'uanu Stream and a waterfall pouring into a pool. The force of the water was not so strong as to be loud and unpleasant, so they were able to set up very near the water's edge for their picnic. On the opposite side of the stream, a bamboo forest fringed the banks, and when the wind blew, the woody stalks clapped and clattered as they swayed back and forth.

Molly had prepared a sumptuous spread of cold ham and turkey, bread, pickles, mustard, and a dish of baked beans. Marguerite had made some kind of European potato salad that tasted of vinegar, and Mina thought it was especially delicious. Right after they ate, Raymond and Marguerite said they had to leave to pick up their son from his Boy Scout activity, but Mina and Molly stretched themselves out on the grass and talked as they watched the clouds sail by and listened to the falling water and the bamboo. They spoke, not looking at each other but staring up at the sky.

"The biographical information that you wrote down is great," Mina began, "but I thought it would be good to include something about what fascinates you as an artist—the things that push you into your work."

Molly laughed. "Hmmm, why not start off with something deep, Mina?"

"Sorry," Mina said, "I like to cut to the chase."

"Let's see," Molly began. She ran her fingers through her long hair, and her eyes had a faraway look as she spoke about her work. "I can tell you that because I'm working on dimensional pieces, of course I'm attracted to forms, and with that comes a love of line and the balance of weight. And I guess you could say, looking at the large body of my work, that the female body fascinates me, because most of my work depicts women. I love that here in Hawai'i there are so many different kinds of women, different ethnicities, I mean. It seems to me that each of these groups has a different physical language, a way of moving, a way of standing still, a way of holding the head. But to tell you the truth, I could never put my finger on what inspires me to start a piece. I only know it when it happens, and it's different every time. And that's okay with me. I like it that my own creativity is a mystery, and I can't tell you how it works. I guess the best thing I can tell you about it is that there are certain conditions that seem to help it along—the most important being free time. I need time by myself to think, to daydream, to ponder over things. Although there have been times too when an idea has just smacked me in the face, jumped out of me full blown, the way Athena popped out of her father's head."

"I'm sure it must be a big help to be married to an artist." Mina couldn't pass up the opportunity to fish.

"I would never call Desmond a big help," Molly said. Her face clouded over, and she frowned. "Oh, he understands my need to work, but he can also be extremely self-centered and infantile."

"I didn't mean to hit a nerve." Mina tried to say it in a way that sounded sympathetic.

"Sooner or later someone would tell you about us, so it might as well be me." A minute ago, Molly had been poised and composed, but now her voice sounded hard and quavered slightly. "Desmond is a philanderer. I knew it when I married him. I thought I could live with it, but now he's getting out of hand. I just don't like it when he throws it in my face. One of these days, he'll push me too far."

Mina, amazed by this sudden and personal revelation, reached for a bottle of cola, opened it, and took a sip. "Maybe he hasn't quite grown up yet."

"Hah! That's an understatement if I ever heard one." She paused, looked away, and took a deep breath to regain her composure. "I shouldn't be talking like this to you about marriage. I know you've just recently gotten engaged."

"It's perfectly all right," Mina said. "I know most marriages aren't happily ever after. My worry is feeling stifled."

"Well, I have to say, Desmond has never made me feel stifled."

"So what else do you like to do?" Mina asked. "When you're not working on your sculptures?"

"I like teaching—adults, that is—and now I'm studying *ikebana*. It's very much like sculpture but in a different, less permanent form. Akira is teaching me. He's such a kind and patient man."

"I don't suppose he's going to pose for a photograph the way the rest of you have."

Molly smiled and shook her head. "No, he's doing a self-portrait."

"Does he give classes in *ikebana*?" Mina inquired.

"Not really," Molly said. "In his shop, he teaches people who are interested. You just go by, he gives you some materials, you do something, and he critiques it. I mean, he does explain the principles, once or twice, but after that, it's learning by doing. He has different clients he does regular arrangements for—offices, some homes, different places. Sometimes I help him."

They were both quiet for a while and watched the waterfall. "This is a lovely spot, isn't it?" Mina said in a soft voice

"Yes," Molly answered. "I love coming here."

"And the bamboo makes a wonderful sound."

"That's just what Ari said the last time we were here," Molly said, transfixed by the water.

"It's so sad—the way he died, I mean." Mina watched Molly carefully.

"I warned him to be careful," Molly said as if Mina weren't there, "but he wouldn't listen."

"Careful of what?"

Molly was so far away, Mina doubted that she even heard the question.

"Molly?" Mina tried to get her attention.

"Oh, sorry, what? I just got so lost in thought." Molly was both flustered and embarrassed.

"Are you okay?" Mina asked with genuine concern.

"I'm fine, just fine," Molly said with feigned confidence. "I just have these weird spells sometimes."

"Mina," Ned called out as he knocked on the door of the bungalow. "We'll have to hurry if you want to stop off to pick up those papers."

It was evening, and the sky was losing its light. The dark clouds had returned, the wind had picked up slightly, and the promise of rain increased by the minute. Ned and Mina were expected for an informal dinner at Todd and Nyla's house, but before going there, Mina wanted to stop at Tilda's cottage in Waikīkī to pick up the written biography she had forgotten to collect on her way home from Nuʻuanu. Ned, who always liked to be punctual, even for informal dinner invitations, thought if he stood outside, it might hurry her along. Ollie was lying just inside the door, and he looked up at Ned as if to tell him it was hopeless to try to rush her.

"Ned," Mina called back, "could you get the pie I made and put it in the car? I'll be right there."

When Ned opened the door to her bungalow, Ollie immediately jumped out of his way and followed him with interest to the kitchen. Sitting on the counter was a warm pie dish wrapped in a fresh dish towel. Ned caught the unmistakable smell of baked apples and cinnamon, and resisting the urge to pull out a fork and devour the pie then and there, he dutifully walked it out to the car with Ollie at his heels. He had just closed the car door and turned around when Mina came out and walked down the stairs toward him. She was wearing a belted silky dress with flounced sleeves and a two-tiered ruffled skirt. The fabric was dark with a palm-leaf print. She looked so disarmingly lovely to him that he felt himself hanging there, suspended in midair with what he thought must have been a silly grin plastered on his face. In the next instant, he found he had taken her in his arms and kissed her.

"Why, Mr. Manusia," she whispered, "I thought you were so worried about us being late."

"I wasn't so worried that I couldn't spare the time to kiss you," he whispered back.

"If we don't leave now," she said, "we really will be late."

"Your wish is my command," Ned said as he gave her a nod and opened the car door. "What would you have me do with Ollie, your fearsome beast?"

"He can sit in the back," she answered as she climbed in the car.

"Are you going to trust him with the pie?"

"Ollie doesn't like sweets," she said as she smoothed out her skirt. "If it was a tray of meatloaf, I wouldn't trust him for one second."

They headed off with Ollie and the pie in the backseat and took the road around Diamond Head, passing the lighthouse and a view of the windblown sea. As they came around the crater, just before the park, Mina directed Ned to turn left into a neighborhood of cottages. She checked the address she'd written down, and when they were sure they had found the right one, Ned parked in front on the street. It was a small, one-story wooden house painted white, with a lateral wing that paralleled the street and another perpendicular wing on the left. There was a small, separate garage on the right. The front yard was unremarkable, with one plumbago bush in the center of the front lawn and a stand of scraggly banana trees nearer the house. The grass looked dry and unmanaged, and there were a few wilted plants in pots near the front porch. Tilda's shiny red car was parked in the driveway.

Mina looked over at Ned and grimaced. "She might throw a fit because I didn't call, but who cares? I just want to get this over with so I don't have to deal with her anymore."

Ollie whined when Mina left the car. He watched as she followed the curved concrete walkway up to the door and knocked. The wooden inner door was open, and Mina looked through the outer screen door into the living room. The daylight was fading quickly, and she could make out only the dim shapes of objects.

"Tilda?" Mina called out. "Are you here?"

The only response was a decided silence. Mina thought that maybe she was in the backyard and couldn't hear her, so she opened the screen door and stepped inside. The living room was paneled in bleached wood, and the ceiling vaulted up to open beams, making the space surprisingly large. She could make out a kitchen and a dining room behind the living room, and through the opened top of a Dutch door, she saw a small patio and, beyond that, darkness, blotting out the backyard.

"Tilda?" Mina called again.

To the left was a door to a hall, with the bathroom nearly straight ahead and two doors at either end leading to bedrooms. Mina was drawn to the front bedroom, by a halo of light that flooded onto the polished-concrete hall floor. She reached the door, which stood slightly ajar, pushed it open, and froze at the sight before her. Tilda sat in an ornately carved wooden chair at a large antique desk set in the center of the room. She was wearing the dress with the peacock-feather pattern that she had worn for her photo. The bowl she had used in the photo sat before her on the desk. She was slumped forward, her head down and immersed in the bowl of water. Mina did not want to get any closer, but she stepped up and felt for a pulse before she turned away. On her way out, a file folder on a small table in the living room caught her eye. It was the folder she had given Tilda to look over. She opened it and saw by the pencil notes that Tilda had gone over it.

She knew she shouldn't remove anything from the house, but she impulsively picked it up, tucked it under her arm, and then ran out to get Ned. When Ned went back inside to have a look and to call Todd, she quickly stuffed the folder into the glove compartment.

As they waited in silence for the police to arrive, Mina sat in the passenger seat of the car with the door open, facing the house, her feet on the running board. Ned leaned his back against the hood, arms folded, also staring at the house, with Ollie by his side. They were both so lost in their thoughts that they almost didn't see the woman who had started to walk toward the front door, but Ollie let out a bark. Ned intercepted the woman, turning her around and escorting her back to the sidewalk. Mina could tell from a distance, by her dress and by her cloth tote bag made of printed cotton scraps, that she was Japanese.

"But I must talk with her," the lady was saying to Ned when Mina joined them.

"I'm afraid there's been—" Mina hesitated for a second, "an accident, and you won't be able to speak to her. We're waiting for the police to arrive."

The lady looked frightened. "Oh, oh, this is terrible," she finally blurted out.

"Do you know the woman who lives here?" Mina asked.

"I clean house for Mr. Schoner. He's very nice man," she said. "After he die, lawyer ask me to keep house clean, so I do. Then the lady comes, but I no like work for her, so I come tonight to tell her I cannot. What's wrong with her?"

Ned spoke quietly. "I'm afraid she's dead."

"Maybe the police will need to speak to you," Mina said kindly.

The woman looked horrified. "But I must go home," she pleaded. "I have things to do and the streetcar. I no like stay out late."

"We'll make sure you get home safely," Mina assured her.

Just then, Todd arrived and, right behind him, two police cars with the doctor and the photographers. Ned stayed back with the Japanese woman, who introduced herself as Mrs. Kaneshiro, while Mina spoke briefly to Todd. A police officer took Mrs. Kaneshiro's name and address and told her she would be contacted later. After

Todd talked to Mina and Ned, he suggested that they go up to the house and wait there with Nyla. Mina got the distinct impression that he was hurrying them away from the scene of the crime, but she was more than happy to leave. Mrs. Kaneshiro said she lived in Pawaʻa, and Ned and Mina drove her to King Street in Moʻiliʻili, where she could easily catch the streetcar home.

They drove up Sierra Drive in silence. As they neared the top of the winding road, it started to rain, transforming the smell and texture of the air. The lights of the city below twinkled in the night through the veil of the passing shower.

"It looks like a jewel box, doesn't it?" Mina said.

"An encounter with death can make everything look beautiful."

When they reached the house, she let Ollie out the back, and the three of them stood there in the rain under Ned's umbrella for a few minutes before they walked toward the warm lights of the hilltop home. Nyla held open the kitchen door and kissed her sister and Ned as they entered.

Nyla sighed. "Bad way to begin the evening. Was it horrible?"

"It was very disturbing," Mina said, "but it wasn't a bloody mess, if that's what you mean."

"She looked like a dead queen sitting on her throne," Ned said.

"Drowned on her throne," Mina added.

"Her head may have been in that bowl of water," he said, "but I'm quite sure I saw telltale marks on her neck. I think she was strangled first."

"Is Grandma Hannah here?" Mina asked.

"No," Nyla shook her head. "Last I heard from her, she was headed out to Punaluʻu to visit some friends. She'll probably turn up in a few days."

Mina sighed. "I need a drink. Maybe two drinks. Maybe two martinis?"

"Go and sit in the living room," Nyla instructed, "and I'll make your martinis. Ned?"

"I could use a shot of whiskey, thanks."

In the living room, Mina watched as Ned placed another log on the embers in the fireplace. She surmised that Todd had built a cheerful fire for their dinner before he was called to the crime scene. Nyla had turned the lights down low in the living room, and Mina stared at the orange flames dancing around the edges of the log and glowing embers. She took the drink her sister handed to her and drank it quickly, eager for the alcohol to dull the impact of the image of Tilda's head stuck in that bowl of water. Her sister took the empty glass and went to make another. Ned, who had wandered over to the window, sat on one of the easy chairs that faced the fire.

"Are you all right?" he asked her.

"I am," she answered, "just a bit stunned. How about you?"

"Same," he answered.

"I couldn't stand her, but still, I would never wish that on anyone."

"I'm sure your not liking her had nothing to do with her death. I found her unlikable too."

"Are you talking about the deceased?" Nyla asked as she handed Mina another martini and sat down. "I'm breaking my own rule and having a drink," she said as she sipped from a glass of wine. "The deceased," she repeated. "It's an official term I learned from Todd."

"Did he tell you who the deceased was?" Mina asked.

"You know, he never tells me anything," her sister answered. "Who was it?"

Mina swished her martini with the olive on the toothpick. "Tilda Clement."

"That artist?"

"Yep," Mina answered.

"There seems to be some very bad luck in that group," Nyla commented.

"I don't think luck had anything to do with either of those deaths." Ned was frowning and staring at the fire.

"I think I met her once at a party," Nyla said as she sipped her wine. "I thought she was kind of vulgar."

Mina looked at her sister. "You mean rude and uncouth?"

Nyla smiled. "I was trying to be nice."

The rain began to come down harder, silencing the conversation, as if they were all listening to the sound of the water dropping down from the sky, hoping it could tell them something. Mina felt like a cold, dark fog was moving over her. It suppressed any real emotion she may have been starting to feel, but the picture of Tilda sitting there came back—her hair, wet near her face and the rest of it streaming out dry and glossy over the table, her arms hanging limp and lifeless by her side. The life that had pulsed through her was obviously gone, and her body was hunched up in the chair like an empty husk. Somewhere in the background of these thoughts, Mina heard Todd's car pull into the garage. She heard the car door slam and his heavy tread through the kitchen and into the living room, where the three of them sat with their faces all turned to his as he entered. He walked straight to the whiskey bottle to pour himself a drink.

"No sign of any break-in," Todd began as if he had prepared for their need of an explanation. "Looks like she was strangled about an hour before you found her and then placed in that peculiar pose. We might know more after the boys give the place a once-over and the coroner goes over the body, but I doubt it."

"Anybody see anyone?" Ned asked.

"Nope," Todd answered. "The neighbors saw and heard nothing."

"I wonder why she was wearing that dress?" Mina said as if talking to herself.

"What dress?" Nyla asked.

"It was the dress she was wearing when she had her picture taken for the exhibit catalog. It was this elaborate silky thing all printed with peacock feathers."

"Sounds pretty fancy to be lounging around the house in by yourself." Nyla drank the last of her wine. "Well, is anyone hungry? I could pack up some fried chicken and potato salad for you to take home and eat later if you like."

"That would be great, Ny," Mina said, "if you didn't mind."

"I don't mind at all," she said. "Nothing like murder to ruin the evening, is there?"

"Let me help you," Ned volunteered.

Nyla maneuvered her pregnant body into a standing position. "I don't really need any help, but your charming company would be appreciated."

Todd poured himself another shot and went to join Mina. He spoke quietly. "I had them comb through the house for those files, and they aren't there. We need to talk."

"Not now," she whispered, "but soon."

# 12

# MONDAY, DECEMBER 9

**M**INA WOKE UP on Monday morning with a headache. She glanced out the window and saw that Ned's car was already gone. She let Ollie out and stumbled into the kitchen and found a pot of coffee with a note under it from Ned saying he'd gone to meet Nigel. Mina sat down with her cup of coffee. She remembered getting home last night and asking Ned for another martini, and she couldn't remember anything after that. She did, however, recall putting some of Nyla's fried chicken and potato salad in the Frigidaire and realized she was starving. She had just eaten two pieces of chicken and some of the salad and was about to swallow two aspirins when the phone rang. Assuming it was Todd, she let it ring while she took the aspirins and then answered, but it wasn't Todd. It was her former Japanese nanny, Setsu.

"Setsu-san," Mina said, "what a surprise. Good morning."

"Good morning, Mina," Setsu replied. "How are you? And how is Nyla? You know, she asked me to help when baby comes. I am so happy for the new baby."

"We're fine. We're all fine, and you?"

"I'm very good, very good, but Mina, my friend would like to speak to you. She's very nervous, you know. I hope you can help her. She's a very good friend of mine."

"What's she afraid of?"

"Oh, you met her last night—where the woman was killed—Mrs. Kaneshiro. So terrible what happened to that woman! My friend said you were very nice to her, and Ned was very nice too. I told her you good girl, and she can trust you. She said she has something at her house, something that belonged to the man who died and then the lady who died. She doesn't want it in her house anymore. She thinks it must be bad luck. She wants you to help her."

"But what is it?" Mina had her suspicions, but she wanted to be sure.

"It's papers. Many papers in boxes. You can come today?"

"I need to shower and get dressed. Where does she live?"

"Maybe you pick me up, and we go together. She lives in Pawaʻa. If I go with you, she won't be so shy."

"I'll meet you in one hour."

Mina hung up the phone and ran for the shower. Before she left, she fed Ollie on the deck and gave him a special treat of some canned salmon. "Sorry, boy," she said as she was leaving. "You'll have to be on your own today."

Setsu was on the porch of her neatly kept cottage in Mānoa Valley and walked quickly out to the street as soon as she saw Mina's car coming. Setsu had taken care of Mina and her sister from the time they were babies and, later on, their younger brother. When their mother became ill, Setsu had faithfully nursed her until she passed away. Their mother had provided generously for Setsu in her will, enabling her to buy a cottage and live independently.

"So good of you to come for me, Mina," Setsu said as she climbed into the car. "I brought you a jar of lilikoʻi jelly. I have one for Mrs. Kaneshiro too. I don't know if she likes it, but she can always give to her son and his family."

"Thank you," Mina said. "I'll get Ned to make some scones so we can really enjoy it. So, now, where does Mrs. Kaneshiro live?"

"You just go down Punahou and then turn left onto Young Street. Her house is over there." Setsu sighed and leaned back. "She so frightened after last night, and then this morning she broke a comb, and now she thinks her luck will be very bad."

"You said she had some boxes that belonged to Ari Schoner?"

"Yes, she cleaned house for that man, and he paid her to keep them in a spare room. He told her not to tell anyone. She said he used to go there and put things in them. Then he dies. Next that woman goes and wants to look at them. Mrs. Kaneshiro wasn't sure what to do, but she let the lady look. Next thing, the lady is dead too, so she wants those things out of her house. She doesn't know what to do."

They drove down out of the valley, past Punahou School with its rock wall covered in night-blooming cereus vines, past the Christian Science Church, the Frear Estate with its tall trees and green lawns, and past Central Union Church. Just across Beretania Street, Mina turned left onto Young Street, and Setsu pointed out the house. Mina pulled up in front of the picket fence that surrounded the house. A row of sunflowers was planted just behind the fence, and the yard was nicely kept. On one side, a mango tree shaded a pretty collection of anthuriums that surrounded its trunk. On either side of the plain concrete path that led up to the front door stood planting boxes with a variety of well-tended vegetables including several beanpoles with beautiful string beans that looked ready to eat. In contrast to the tidy garden, the paint was peeling off the fence and the house, and one of the front windows was boarded up.

"Mrs. Kaneshiro needs to get after her lazy son to fix her house," Setsu said as if reading Mina's thoughts.

Mrs. Kaneshiro was standing at the open door, beckoning them to come in. As Mina stepped up onto the porch, the boards under her feet gave a loud squeak. Inside the house was dim and cool, sparsely furnished, and although the house was old, everything in it looked scrubbed and clean.

"Come, come inside here." Mrs. Kaneshiro skipped any niceties and marched them straight into the spare room. She pointed at about ten cardboard boxes. "See, see, here. Please, Miss Beckwith, look inside. Go, look inside!"

Mina opened one of the boxes. It was stuffed with files, and Mina lifted one out that was labeled "Sonoma Institute for Research." It was newspaper clippings, copies of papers, and notes about a hospital in California that promoted eugenics and experiments in that field. The whole box seemed to be filled with things and people connected to the eugenics movement. Another box had files on people prominent in the Nazi movement in Germany, and another box on American Nazi sympathizers.

Mrs. Kaneshiro had worked herself into a state. ""What? What? What's inside? It's bad things, no?"

"How long have you had these things?" Mina asked.

"I don't know," Mrs. Kaneshiro answered, "maybe six months, maybe little bit more."

"Did Mr. Schoner come here often?"

"Maybe one or two times every week, but just before he died, he come more."

"And Tilda, Tilda Clement, did she come?"

"Only two times," said Mrs. Kaneshiro. "One time was last week. I no like show her, but she threaten me. She say maybe I stole these things. I no like her, but I let her look. Both times she was here long time, looking and writing down so many things. After that, I no like clean for her anymore, and I want her to take these things away. That's why I saw you last night. I was going tell her, but now, cannot. I don't know what to do! I don't like this business. First Mr. Schoner, and now that lady. I don't like these things. Maybe I will be next!"

Mina remained calm and spoke in her most soothing voice. "There's nothing to worry about. These are just files about people and other things. I think we should take them to Mr. Schoner's lawyer until we know who they belong to now that Mr. Schoner is no longer alive. His lawyer is a friend of mine. I should call him right now. Do you have a telephone?"

"No, no, but get pay phone just down the street." Mrs. Kaneshiro took Mina to the front door and pointed out the booth a couple of doors down. "Yes, you call now. Thank you. Thank you so much."

"You see, Tatsue," said Setsu, "I told you Mina could help you. Come, let's go and sit down while she calls."

Setsu steered her friend into the living room. Mina returned and told them that she had called Louis Goldburn, the lawyer, and he had asked her to bring the boxes down to his office. Mina suggested that Setsu and Mrs. Kaneshiro might like to go to the nearby *okazu-ya* and pick up something for lunch while she loaded the boxes in her car, but the two ladies would not hear of her doing it by herself. So the three women made several trips back and forth until Mina's car was packed and the room was cleared. Then Mina insisted that they all go and get some lunch to bring back to the house to eat. She knew that the *okazu-ya* just a block away on King Street had excellent food, and she felt herself craving some tempura and noodles. She also wanted a chance to try to find out if Mrs. Kaneshiro knew anything useful about Ari Schoner or Tilda Clement. People who cleaned houses knew all kinds of interesting things about their employers. When they arrived at the lunch spot, Mina asked Setsu and Mrs. Kaneshiro to order (not forgetting to tell them about her tempura craving) and insisted on paying for everything. The walk to and from the *okazu-ya* did much to restore calm to Mrs. Kaneshiro's frayed nerves.

Back at the house, they sat in the kitchen. Mrs. Kaneshiro unwrapped the brown paper from the food and placed all the items on her own serving dishes. They were white and heavy like restaurant dishes, with sinuous blue carp painted around the rims. She brought out real plates that matched the serving dishes, blue napkins, lacquered chopsticks, and chopstick rests in the shape of eggplants. She also made some tea, and Mina thoroughly enjoyed the lunch.

"My, my, Miss Beckwith," Mrs. Kaneshiro chuckled, "you eat very well."

"She always eat like that, you know," Setsu laughed. "And she never come fat. Her sister just like her too."

"Mrs. Kaneshiro," Mina said, ignoring their comments, "what can you tell me about Mr. Schoner? What kind of man was he?"

"Oh, he's very nice man," she answered as she poured more tea into Mina's cup, "very polite man, very neat in his habits—easy to clean for him because he likes everything in its place. He's always busy, and he has many friends. But that Clement lady, she's always calling him, asking him for this and that. He was too kind, you see, and likes her because she always makes like she's sad and needs help."

"Yes," Setsu added, "some men like women who always need help."

"And these boxes?" Mina asked.

Mrs. Kaneshiro shrugged. "I don't know. One day he just ask me if I can keep them for him. He doesn't want anyone to know where he has them. He pays me to keep them. I don't read English very good, so I don't know what it's all about."

Mina sipped the warm tea. "Did anyone else besides Tilda, Miss Clement, come and ask about them?"

Mrs. Kaneshiro shook her head. "No, nobody knows. I don't know, maybe one day he told her about the boxes. I don't know how she knows. I don't like her. She's not nice—such a sloppy person—throwing her things all over. I know she had men over too."

"Really?" Mina pretended to be shocked.

"Yes," Mrs. Kaneshiro nodded. "I can tell because, you know, the bed smells funny kind."

"You mean she was murdered?" Reggie said in wide-eyed disbelief.

"Yes, Reggie," Nigel said as he calmly poured a cola into a glass. "I'm afraid she was."

Ned came to the table in the Kuakini Street flat after getting his own cola and glass from the kitchen. It was after noon. But school had not yet gotten out, so Alika and the other boys weren't there. They had wanted to inform Reggie while he was alone.

"But why?"

"We don't know why," Nigel answered. "We need to try to find out. All of those people in the photographs belonged to that artist's group we told you about, and she's the second one to be killed within nearly a month."

"We have no idea if it's related to what we're investigating here or not," Ned added. "But it's not good."

"Don't you want some ice with those colas?" Reggie blurted out.

Ned and Nigel glanced at each other and laughed.

"No, Reggie," Nigel answered, "we think you Yanks are ice obsessed."

"Sorry," Reggie blushed, "I didn't mean to change the subject. It just seems so strange."

"If you were loading up your glass with ice cubes in Britain, we would laugh and think you were strange," said Nigel. "Drinking things that are too cold is bad for your stomach. That's what my mum always said."

"How was she . . . I mean, how did it happen?" Reggie asked.

"She was strangled in her house," Ned told him. "My fiancée and I found the body when we went to pick something up from her last night."

"I guess I knew this work was risky," Reggie said nervously, "but I didn't think it would involve murder."

Nigel sipped his cola and said, "Neither did we."

"So what should we do?" Reggie looked perplexed.

"Nigel and I are going to try to find out more about her," said Ned. "You carry on watching the embassy and taking any information that the boys give you. I think you said you can have their photos developed for us."

"Yeah," Reggie nodded. "I'm setting up a darkroom in one of the spare bedrooms, and I can do it myself, so we don't have to go to a photo shop."

Nigel looked impressed. "That's great. I'm sure the Irregulars will be dying to help you."

Ned stood up and walked to the window. "I wish there was some way we could find out what's going on inside the embassy. Then we would know what all those people were up to when they went in there. We have no idea what she was doing there."

Nigel shook his head. "I don't know how we would do that. I mean, the only people who work there are Japanese, and even if we did know a Japanese person who would be willing to work with us, we'd still have the problem of getting them an embassy job."

"I think maybe we should tell Mina what we're doing," said Ned. "She's working with all of our suspects."

"Who's Mina?" Reggie looked confused.

"My fiancée," Ned answered.

"No," Nigel said, "not yet. Let's try to find out about them on our own. We've met all those people ourselves, so we don't have to rely on her. I'd rather not involve her unless we absolutely have to. We can chum up to Bill and Desmond. We can charm Tamara. Maybe you can get interested in *ikebana*, Reggie."

"Icky what?"

"*Ikebana*," Nigel repeated. "It's some sort of Japanese flower arranging. I'll try and get a book."

"Flower arranging?" Reggie looked disgusted.

Nigel chuckled. "Welcome to the world of intelligence work, laddy."

"Technically, all this stuff is evidence in a murder investigation," Todd said as he sat across from Mina at a table in Louis Goldburn's office.

"I know," Mina sighed. "But in all the excitement, I just didn't think about police procedure. Anyway, I've saved you a few hours of searching and reading by going through everything first."

Mina sipped the cup of tea that Doris Goldberg had made for her and took a bite of one of the cookies that had come with it. Doris was from New Zealand and always made a cuppa around four o'clock. Todd grumbled about how she should have called him right away, but Mina took it to be a weak but obligatory performance of duty and just listened without saying anything.

"So what did you find?" Todd finally asked.

"I went through everything pretty quickly, but I think thoroughly. You might have your own people do it again just to be sure. It looks like he kept files on almost everyone he knew. But he was preoccupied with anything and anybody he knew that might have connections to anti-Semitic movements or organizations, and of course he was especially interested in anyone with connections to the Nazi Party. He has big files on all the Nazi Party leaders. Most of the files are on people we don't know, but there was a section called "Halemana." He had files on everyone in the exhibition. Most of the files are just regular things, you know, things you would keep in a scrapbook on someone—art openings, exhibits, stuff like that—but there's other things too, things you need to see."

"Oh, Jesus," Todd rolled his eyes, "don't tell me it's a secret society or something."

"No," Mina chuckled, "but most of these people now could have a motive for killing Ari and/or a motive for killing Tilda—who once she saw this stuff might have been sorely tempted to blackmail people."

"Did she?" Todd asked. "See this stuff, I mean."

"Yep," Mina nodded. "Mrs. Kaneshiro said she went over twice and demanded to look through it."

"Okay, so what would she have found?"

"Well," Mina began, "let's start with Desmond Rivers and Bill Hitchins. In 1925, they both joined the New York unit of what was then called the Free Society of Teutonia."

"The what?"

"The Free Society of Teutonia. They're a pro-Nazi group that up until a few years ago collected dues and sent money to the Nazi Party in Germany. Most of the group are German immigrants, but there are quite a few people who just like the Nazi ideals. You can't join unless you swear you have no Jewish or Negro blood. Anyway," she said as she opened one of the files, "here's a couple of pictures of our boys at a meeting and another of them passing out leaflets. Then there's a membership roster for 1925 with their names on it."

"So do we know if they still belong to this group?" Todd looked at one of the pictures and saw Bill and Desmond smiling and in the company of two beautiful blondes.

"We don't know. At least these files don't tell us."

"And Desmond's wife, Molly." Mina opened another folder. "She's the daughter of Dr. Adam Madison, who has dedicated his life to the study and promotion of eugenics. There are lots of articles in here about his career and some pictures of him with German doctors and researchers. The Nazis are big fans of eugenics."

"Okay," Todd frowned, "remind me what this eugenics business is all about."

"Basically, it is an applied science, some might say pseudoscience, or biosocial movement that wants to genetically improve society and the human population. Unfortunately, the worst of their methods can include marriage restrictions, segregation, compulsory sterilization, and forced abortions, and some of them even advocate extermination of certain segments of the population. They probably would not have approved of my parents' marriage or your marriage to Nyla."

"Great," Todd said with undisguised sarcasm.

"Some of them are into experiments," Mina added. "I don't even want to think about what they might be, but you can see the big attraction Nazis would have to all of this, with their emphasis on racial purity and the glorification of the Aryan race. And California is a big leader in the eugenics movement in the United States. Molly's father has his clinic in Sonoma County."

"There's a eugenics movement in the United States?" Todd seemed genuinely surprised.

"Yes. Some large and well-known corporations and institutions have funded research, and some respected scientists from big universities are followers."

"How do you know all of this?" Todd asked.

"I did an article for the paper once."

"Yeah? Well even to a flatfoot like me, it sounds ominous."

"Because it is ominous." She looked at him with a frown. "Then there are these clippings and pictures of Tamara and her husband with pieces of artwork and Japanese diplomats. Here's another one of them somewhere in China. It looks like they're with some Japanese military officers. There are pictures of her at the embassy here. I don't know what they mean, and my guess is Ari didn't either."

"It means she's chummy with bigwigs from Japan. Anybody else?"

"There's a file on April. Aside from her art achievements, there is an article from a mainland paper about her father. Apparently he's doing time in an Arkansas prison for participating in some kind of art fraud. There are a few things on Raymond Morgan, the photographer, but it's only mundane stuff about his photography and an interview when he first arrived. There's a newspaper photo of two Japanese military officers and an obituary here with "Akira" written on it in pencil, but I can't read kanji, so I don't know what it says. It's a few years old, and neither man looks like Akira. I'll ask Setsu what it means, if you don't mind me borrowing it. I swear I won't lose it."

"Was there anything on Tilda?"

"I bet she destroyed it, because she is the only one who's not here."

"I wonder how he collected all of this?" Todd flipped through one of the file boxes. "You would have to have dedicated discipline and a driving obsession."

"He was such a sweet man," Mina mused. "I can see Tilda using this for blackmail, but I'll be very disappointed if he was doing it too."

"We need to keep quiet about this for now," Todd said. "Do you think we can leave these things here? Can we trust your lawyer friend and his wife?"

"I'm sure we can," Mina said quietly. "Louis was very fond of Ari and will do anything we ask if it helps find his killer."

"Mina," Todd said seriously, "don't tell anyone, even Ned. Any leak could be dangerous for you. And you need to make sure Setsu and her friend keep their traps shut tight."

Mina smiled. "So I guess I'm still on the job, huh, boss?"

Todd raised his eyebrows. "That's right, doll, and the body count stands at two, so you have to be twice as cautious as before."

# 13

# TUESDAY, DECEMBER 10

**I KNEW IT** would all come back to you, Ned," Nigel said as they put away their foils, "but I didn't think it would be in the first five minutes."

Ned grinned. "You know what they say, about riding bicycles and all that."

"Do you suppose you could let me win on Saturday—since I'm the one who would like to make a living at it?"

"Maybe," Ned laughed. "You'll have to be very nice to me between now and then, and under no circumstances can you call me Trout."

They had just finished their first practice for the fencing demonstration on Saturday. Tamara had arranged for them to use the pavilion at the yacht club. The pavilion was set some distance from the clubhouse and included a large empty room with a seasoned wooden floor and sliding glass doors. Another part of a building also housed the locker rooms. Being a weekday morning, the club was empty. Through the glass doors, Ned could see the roof of the clubhouse in the distance, shrouded by trees and tropical verdure, and the green lawns and gardens that surrounded it. He could also see Bill Hitchins and Desmond Rivers walking across the grass toward them. They had just put away their fencing jackets and trousers when Bill strode into the room.

"Tamara said to look out for you," Bill said cheerfully. "Looks like we just missed out on the excitement."

"I hope you'll come on Saturday morning to the demonstration," Nigel said. "To watch me whip Mr. Playwright here into shape."

Bill looked at Ned and winked. "Sounds like a challenge."

Ned smiled. "He'll be begging for mercy, Bill."

"Desmond and I are about to go for a sail," Bill said. "Would you like to join us? We're taking out a very sweet yacht that Desmond is thinking of buying. There are lots of old swim trunks and T-shirts you can use."

Less than half an hour later, Ned found himself sitting on the bow of a yacht sailing through Pearl Harbor with a beer in one hand, which he was forced to drink without a glass, and a stick of dried swordfish in the other. They had left the L-shaped pier on the west side of the peninsula and sailed around to the east loch of the harbor. On the east side of the peninsula was one of the largest Hawaiian fishponds Ned had ever seen, and he thought in the distance he could see other fishponds all along the loch. It was a shame the way these resources for the farming of fish were disappearing. Not only were they engineering marvels, Ned thought, but they provided people with healthy food that was so much better than the tinned food everyone was mad about these days.

Nigel was chatting up Desmond at the wheel, while Bill, shirtless, sat a few feet away from Ned with his sketchbook and a beer bottle held expertly in place between his two feet. They were circling Ford Island, where several naval ships were berthed, and Ned recognized how easy it would be for Bill or Desmond to sail by once or twice a week and take an inventory of ships. When Bill saw that Ned was looking at Ford Island, he began to point out and name various vessels, telling Ned how many men they carried and how they were armed.

"They have an air base on the island too," Bill informed him, "but I guess they thought it was inadequate because they just built a new one over there." Bill pointed to the flat stretch of land just to the south. "It's called Hickam, and they just finished it this year."

"And how is it you know so much about the navy?" Ned asked.

"I did a stint in the navy when I was much younger, but I hated it."

Ned watched and listened as Bill opened his sketchbook and began to draw. Bill wasn't looking at Ford Island but back toward land, where the island rose up into the cloud-capped Ko'olau Mountains.

Bill kept up his conversation with Ned as he drew, as if his hand and eyes had an independent telegraph system. He had the kind of skin Ned had seen on countless Caucasian men who had spent most of their lives in the sun—a bronze brown, with premature wrinkles around the eyes and on the neck and hands, and he had a certain beachcomber smell to him that Ned recognized too—dried saltwater and perspiration tinged with alcohol. Bill told Ned that he and Desmond had met one summer, long ago in New York, hadn't seen or heard from each other for a number of years, and then renewed their friendship when Bill moved here from Tahiti about two years ago. Ned looked on at Bill's pencil gliding effortlessly over the paper, making the landscape before them take shape out of gray marks and swirls. It was appearing like magic on the blank white page—the pressure of his hand making light and shadow, depth and contour. He was sensitive, Ned saw, to the whiteness of the paper itself as a space and a color, using it expertly and automatically.

"That's a wonderful drawing," Ned finally said.

"Oh, it's nothing," Bill said. "I do several of these a day, and every once and a while one of them turns into a painting."

"I'd be very interested in seeing your work sometime."

"Anytime you like, just come by the house, have a beer or two, and look," he grinned. "Tamara tells me we're practically neighbors."

"I'll look forward to it."

Bill was silent for some time, concentrating on his drawing. Suddenly his pencil stopped. He looked blankly out at the water and then turned to Ned. "It's terrible about Tilda. I heard that you and Mina found her."

"We did," said Ned. "Believe me, it was a shock to us as well. We can't figure out why anyone would want to kill her, but I suppose that's a job for the police."

"Well, she certainly was a piece of work, wasn't she?" Bill tapped the end of his pencil on the drawing paper.

"I only met her once. She did seem, how should I say it, overwhelming."

"That's very polite of you," Bill said. "Most people might not be so kind. The fact is, she could really lean into people. She was always pushing to get what she wanted."

"Maybe she pushed someone too hard." Ned tried to sound perplexed.

Bill heaved a sigh. "I would not be surprised if she did."

"Sounds like she may have been dangerous."

"I think she liked it that way, living dangerously, and look where it got her." Bill went back to his drawing and said no more.

It was overcast, and the breeze was slight. Ned watched the bow of the boat cutting through the water, as they sailed around the island and then out toward the mouth of the harbor. Another, much larger peninsula separated the middle and east lochs from the west loch and stretched into the narrow passage that connected the harbor to the sea. Once they entered the passage, Ned could see the new air base more clearly. Naval ships, air bases, and military housing—this area was fast becoming a stronghold for US forces and sure to be their nerve center for the Pacific. It was easy to see, historically, how the islands had been coveted for military purposes because of their strategic location, and he understood that during the kingdom of Hawai'i, there was strife and controversy about this area being used by America for its military.

He wondered what it might be like to live in a world without a need for all of this. Throughout history men had devised ways of killing each other for land, power, and dominion over others, and even though he certainly knew that he would never see a world without war during his lifetime, he felt it important that he could imagine it.

"Hey, Bill," Desmond shouted, breaking Ned's reverie, "your turn to take the helm while I lounge around."

"Aye, aye, Captain Bligh," Bill laughed. "I'll be right there."

Bill moved with the grace of a ballet dancer toward the stern, and Desmond came up to the bow and stretched out near Ned.

"You look lost in thought." Desmond smiled his charming smile at Ned.

"I was just reflecting on how the American military has established itself in this area. I knew their presence here was big. I just didn't realize how big."

"Yes, indeed," said Desmond, "we're very well protected."

Ned wanted to say that the big protective presence also created a big inviting target, but he thought better of it.

"America has been great for these islands," Desmond went on. "They've come a long way."

"You don't look old enough to know what things were like before," Ned said, doing his best to sound innocent.

"Well, of course, I'm not," Desmond laughed, "but I know some of these old kamaʻāinas, and they've told me what it was like under the monarchy. You know, how it was corrupt and backward." He was speaking with the kind of bravado that never failed to grate on Ned's nerves.

"Really?"

"I know some people have these sentimental feelings about the past, but really, you're an educated man. Surely you can see how prosperous things are here in the territory, how much opportunity there is—all thanks to America."

"I am an educated man." Ned couldn't help himself. "I've been to Oxford and Harvard, and one thing I've noticed is that things aren't so prosperous for Hawaiians in what used to be their own country."

"Yes, but they were living under a despotic monarchy. Now they have democracy."

"Did you know," Ned tried to sound matter-of-fact, "that the kingdom was actually a constitutional monarchy and that there was a legislature of officials that were elected by voters?"

"No, I don't know anything about the old government." Desmond paused and for a fleeting second looked like he realized he might not know what he was talking about and had to think quickly about how to cover his tracks. "But, anyway," he said with a benevolent smile, "I love the Hawaiian people, and I know they're so much better off than they used to be. The way I see it, it's for us to lead the way, to show them how American values are the way of the future, and those that catch on will do well, and those that don't—well, maybe they just weren't meant to, if you know what I mean."

"No," Ned said, just to see what Desmond would say. "I'm not sure I do know what you mean."

"Well," Desmond replied thoughtfully, "I guess I mean that the people with the energy and intelligence to take advantage of opportunities are the ones that deserve them. People who can pull themselves up by their bootstraps will always succeed, and people that can't will always fail."

"Coming about," yelled Bill. "Watch the heads."

Ned had been aware for some time that they had left the harbor passage and were out in the open sea. The main sail swung around, and the boat turned so that he now looked toward the land instead of the horizon. This was the second time in just a few weeks that he found himself offshore, looking back at the land—today, in a very different location. From this point of view, he could see and feel this island, Oʻahu, as a living, breathing entity, firmly planted and growing out into the sea. Ned had come across people like Desmond before—people who wanted Polynesians to exist only as living folklore. They would never be able to grasp anything real about being Polynesian. He reflected on how often people asked him if being part Polynesian caused him any confusion, and he always wanted to laugh because he felt that it gave him an advantage. He understood two very different points of view of the world, and it gave him twice the insight. Under ordinary circumstances, he would have a lot more to say to Desmond. But he had a job and a larger goal, and he couldn't lose sight of it even for the very great satisfaction of cutting an untrue and ill-conceived argument to shreds.

As they sailed back toward the L-shaped pier, Ned lost himself in his surroundings. The way the mountains flowed down with their valleys and graceful ridges reaching toward the sea, the remains of the ancient fishponds, and the palm trees swaying patiently and steadily along the shore were a stark contrast to the airplane runways, battleships, and aircraft carriers. He imagined the island being overlaid with a veil—a veil that was still transparent but becoming more and more opaque, obscuring what was under the surface. But the things that were under the surface would still be there. They were unerasable, because they were the first things. They grew out of this place, and like a careful underpainting, they would always remain, scenting the air and giving depth and dimension to whatever might follow. They were things that could wait silently for years and years to be discovered and revealed again.

They were just gliding toward the pier, and off in the distance, slipping along into the middle loch, Ned was sure he saw the fin of a shark.

"Oh, yes," Setsu nodded, "I know who this man is and why Akira's name is written here. This Japanese army officer, I don't know him, but this man next to him, that is Akira's father, Dr. Nakasone. I understand at one time he was a military doctor in Japan. He was very high up."

That morning, Mina was sitting with Setsu on the back porch of Setsu's cottage in Mānoa Valley. The back porch of the cottage overlooked a lovely garden enclosed by a high fence that was draped in thunbergia vines. Just over the edge of the porch was a small pond, and Mina could see several colorful goldfish swimming around the lily pads. Ollie lay next to the pond, transfixed by the fish. Irises, now not in bloom, wrapped around the pond, and in the corner of the garden, a mountain apple tree stood, with its leaves still glistening from a morning shower.

"Does the caption say anything interesting?" Mina asked.

"Not really," Setsu answered thoughtfully. "It just talks about a big meeting for army officers and army doctors to talk about health for the Japanese army. This was in those papers from yesterday?"

"Yes, I just thought it might say something more."

Setsu laughed. "You disappointed?"

"It's just not very exciting," Mina admitted.

Setsu was quiet for a moment and then said, "He died early this year, you know, Dr. Nakasone. He was a very nice man, very quiet, good manners."

"You knew him?"

"Oh, yes," Setsu said. "I knew him very well. He helped many Japanese people when they had no money." She paused and looked at Mina. "He was very well respected, you know."

Mina knew Setsu well enough to see that she had liked the doctor and did not want to gossip about him. "What about his son, Akira?"

"Oh, his son was very well educated . . . always such a nice boy, and he took good care of his father when he got old. He has a florist shop down on Beretania Street. They say he is very good at *sumi-e* too, but I don't think he needs to work because his father was very wealthy, and no other children, so he gets all the money."

"He's part of an art exhibit that I'm helping with," said Mina. "I've just met him briefly, but he seems very nice."

"Yes, he was a good boy. He makes nice flowers too, you know. If you want something pretty, you can go to him. He can do *ikebana* too—so nice—everyone wants him to make flowers for Japanese celebrations. Only thing, he's a little bit expensive. But you Mina, you no need worry, neh?"

"I guess he isn't married, is he?"

Setsu giggled. "Oh, no. I don't know, maybe it's only talk, but they say he might be little bit, you know. But who knows?"

Mina parked her car in front of the flower shop on Beretania Street, just past the Ke'eaumoku intersection. She had called Akira about his interview from Setsu's house. He said he had some orders to complete, but she was welcome to talk to him while he worked.

A green-and-gold-striped awning reached over the window of the shop and shaded the sidewalk. The words "Aloha Plants and Florist" were written in tasteful gold script across the window. It was nearly noon, and the awning and luxuriant foliage in the window made the shop look peaceful and inviting. As she and Ollie entered the shop, the bell on the door jangled. Lining the window were two tiers of plants—maiden hair, Boston ferns, blooming anthuriums, and orchids were growing in profusion. In the rest of the shop, galvanized buckets overflowed with different types of flowers—roses, chrysanthemums, irises, lilies, carnations, and other blossoms filled the room with their colorful presence. The plants and flowers, the cool, shaded light, and the quiet that permeated the space made it seem like the cars and concrete outside were a hundred miles away. At the back of the shop, a beaded curtain parted, and Akira Nakasone walked quietly into the room. He was of medium height and slender, and he wore his sleek black hair slightly longer than was currently fashionable. Mina knew he was older than she was, but his flawless complexion made him look young and full of vitality. He was wearing a faded pair of denim overalls and a T-shirt.

"I'm working in here, Mina," he said and beckoned her to follow.

The back room was almost as large as the shop, with a big worktable in the center and a large sink and counter against one of the walls. There were a few smaller worktables scattered around the room, and although boxes and buckets of greenery and flower-arranging equipment filled nearly every space, nothing looked or felt messy and chaotic. Under a window was an old sofa with a quilt thrown over it.

"Please, sit down," Akira said politely. "What a wonderful dog."

She smiled. "I think so."

Akira looked at the dog intently. "He's very happy to belong to you. He didn't like the life he had before. Can I get you something to drink?"

"No, thank you," she answered, wondering what he saw in Ollie.

"If you don't mind," he said, turning back to a newly started arrangement, "I'm going to work while we talk, but don't worry, I'll be listening carefully."

Mina sank into the sofa, which was much more comfortable than it looked. Akira was making the arrangement in a brown metal bowl on legs. He was using only ferns and had several piles of them on the table. Mina recognized the leaves of the bird's-nest ferns, moa, and kupukupu, but there was a curly-tipped fern she'd seen before and couldn't name. She took out her notes and then found herself watching him as he moved around carefully placing a stem in the bowl and then, in slow, graceful movements, looking at it from several angles. He adjusted the fern slightly and then looked again. Mina found herself mesmerized by the secluded and silent room, by the monochromatic greens of the ferns and the subtle and delicate creative process she was watching, and in this womb-like workspace, she found herself feeling more relaxed and open than she had since . . . since she had found Tilda's body.

"I heard you were the one who discovered Tilda," Akira said as if reading her thoughts. "It must have been quite a shock." His voice was soothing and unobtrusive.

"Very," she answered.

"Death has a way of shocking us when we meet it unexpectedly."

"To tell you the truth, I didn't like her very much, and somehow that makes it seem pitiful to me, instead of sad." She didn't know why she was telling him this.

"She was not a very likable human being," he said with no emotion. "She was very misguided. She expected that power and control over others would make her happy, but it was having the opposite effect." He paused for a moment as he placed another fern. "But you're right, we'll all feel pity about her death, but we won't feel the kind of sadness we would if we had any natural affection for her."

"I wonder who killed her?" she said out loud, but it sounded as if she were asking herself.

"She enjoyed making people angry and afraid."

"So I've heard," she said. She was hoping that he would elaborate on the subject, so she said nothing more and looked down at her notes, pretending to be reviewing them. But he was quiet, so she decided to move on. "I see here in the notes you gave to Tamara that you started ink-brush calligraphy when you were a child."

"Yes," he said, "my uncle taught me when I was very young, in Japan. I began with learning to grind the ink."

"And when did you start painting pictures?"

He chuckled. "I can't really say, because calligraphy, to me, is so close to painting pictures. It was through calligraphy I began to cultivate or develop a taste for a certain state of mind, and it's out of that state of mind that the real pursuit of pictures flows. The state of mind becomes the channel."

"And when did this pursuit start?" Mina persisted.

"I think I must have been thirteen or fourteen years old. It was after my father brought me here. We had a quiet life together. We worked together in the garden. He studied his medical books. I worked on my art."

Mina smiled. "So you were never seduced by baseball or the movies or the thousand other things boys get into?"

"You would think I would have been longing for something else, but I wasn't. And my father wouldn't have minded. He just wanted me to be happy."

"Sounds like you always knew what you wanted," she said.

"I consider myself lucky," he said, turning to look at her. "So what do you think so far?" He stood back to look at his creation.

Mina sighed. "So far, it looks beautiful to me. But I know nothing about arrangements, and I'm no expert about art either."

He smiled to himself. "But you have taste and you know what you like, and that's all that matters."

"Your ink-brush paintings are in several important museums and collections. You've had several shows in New York. Those are big achievements for someone out here in the islands. How did that happen?"

Akira shrugged. "One person bought something of mine and showed it to another person. Some gallery wrote to me and asked about a show. I'm not really sure how it all happened. Like I said, I've been lucky. My father gave me a sheltered life, a good education, and left me with just enough money to pursue what I love best. So I don't think too much about art shows and being in important collections. I am drawn to the act of doing things—of picking up the brush, placing the fern, or finding the perfect flower."

"I guess you still have that taste for a certain state of mind," Mina said.

"Constant hunger would be more accurate."

He picked out several of the long leaves of the bird's-nest fern and stood them in the back of the bowl, and suddenly, the arrangement became dramatic, with long, bold lines and the movement of swirling and curling leaves, with both contrast and complement of texture and shape. Mina could not quite believe how everything instantly transformed as if the composition were already there and the viewer just needed the last clue to make the revelation unfold. As she watched him evaluate his work again from different angles, she wondered how much he really knew about Tilda and all of her schemes and escapades—how much had he already put together about her? He obviously watched and noticed things, and Mina didn't think she was wrong in sensing great reserves of raw energy and power just beneath the surface of that calm and cultured exterior.

"People think," he said, "that contemplation leads only to a passive and what some would call a weak approach to life. But all we have to do is look at some of the greatest swordsmen of my former country to see how it isn't so."

After a few more questions and pleasantries, Mina took her leave, and as she and Ollie walked out the door, she was so lost in thought that she nearly collided with a red-headed young man who was going into the shop. She sat in her car for a moment before starting the engine. She had a strange, dislocated feeling as if she were just waking up. She looked at the shady green shop and couldn't decide how she felt about Akira—was he genuinely as he appeared to be, or was he a carefully constructed illusion? Everything was getting more and more tangled, Mina thought as she drove away, and all she could do right now was to watch and notice and try to think of the right questions.

When she pulled into the driveway at Ka'alawai, a great sense of relief washed over her. Today was the day that Mrs. Olivera took a break from Nyla's and came to clean her house while Mr. Olivera did the yard. She couldn't see Mr. Olivera, but she could hear the clattering of the blades as his lawnmower rolled over the grass. He had such a way with plants, and her yard always looked as if it were ready to be part of a garden show. He sometimes had an idea for a new plant or some small change, and Mina had learned to never question his judgment because the result was always perfection. Mrs. Olivera behaved as if she were a part-time mother. She did it with Nyla too, and they had both learned not only to deal with it but, more often than not, to appreciate it. Until the arrival of Ned on the scene, Mrs. Olivera had been full of suggestions about places where Mina might meet a prospective beau, but now that Mina was officially engaged, she had turned her attention to Nyla's pregnancy and the soon-to-arrive baby.

Mrs. Olivera was sitting on the lanai knitting, which meant she had finished in the house and was waiting for Mr. Olivera. Ollie ran up to her and wagged his tail.

"Oh, that dog loves it here," said Mrs. Olivera as she looked up from her knitting. "I saw your name in the paper yesterday. So frightening for you."

"I guess everyone is talking about it."

"You look tired, dear." Mrs. Olivera looked concerned. "Sit down, and I'll get you something cool to drink."

"That would be very nice," Mina said as she plopped down in one of the lanai chairs, feeling like she could use some mothering, "if it's no trouble."

"Of course it's no trouble. I made some iced tea, and I was thinking of having some myself."

She got up, put down her knitting, and headed for the kitchen. Ollie nuzzled up to Mina, put his head on her lap, and looked up at her with his big brown eyes. She scratched him behind his ears, and he made a soft noise of appreciation.

"I noticed that about Ollie when he stayed with us," Mrs. Olivera said as she returned with two glasses of iced tea. "He makes all kinds of noises—like he wants to talk to us."

Mina cocked her head and looked at the dog. "What would you tell us, huh, boy?"

"You know these dogs in Portugal were so clever. When I was a girl, they used to help the fishermen by swimming with the nets. They could herd fish too and carry things between the boats. Some of them were good divers too, and they used to watch out for pirates." Mrs. Olivera nodded her head for emphasis.

Mina laughed. "So if a pirate ship pulls up on the beach, Ollie will let me know."

"Oh, yes," said Mrs. Olivera. "Mina, did you know this girl who died?"

"I only met her once or twice."

"It's terrible to think you might not be safe in your own home. But some of these young women—not you, of course, my dear—some of them are not careful who they talk to. They say things, and men take them the wrong way, and then when they don't do what the men want, they get hurt. Maybe that's what happened to her."

"Maybe," Mina said and took a sip of her tea.

"Your sister asked if I could find someone to clean house for Ned. I'm too busy myself, but I'm going to ask my friend Mrs. Perreira. She might like to have extra money. I don't know. But she was so happy the way you helped her and her nephew."

"That's a wonderful idea," Mina said.

"I was going to suggest to Ned that she comes on Tuesdays, like me, and then we can pick her up."

"It sounds perfect. I'll talk to Ned and call you tomorrow at Nyla's."

"So what did you think of the two sailing artists?" Nigel asked Ned as they drove back to town from the yacht club in the late afternoon.

"I quite liked Bill," Ned replied. A very light rain was blowing down from the mountains, and he turned on the windshield wipers. "I thought Desmond a bit full of himself."

"He is a smooth character, isn't he?" Nigel rolled up his window halfway. "It would be easy for one of them or both of them to be making maps, to keep track of ships and airplanes. If military types frequent that club, they could be finding out about troop movements too."

"Bill is so proficient at capturing the landscape. He could easily make drawings of ships and planes on these sailing excursions. I just don't see what motive either of them would have in doing any of this."

"Enough money can always tempt most people. Especially these Yanks, right?" There was a touch of anger in his voice.

Ned frowned. "What?"

Nigel laughed. "That was a joke, old man, a jest."

"It sounded sardonic."

"Sardonic," Nigel repeated.

"As in mocking, scornful, derisive. Not like you, my friend."

Nigel looked out the window. "It's a sign of the times, Old Trout." He was quiet for several minutes, and when he finally spoke, he was still gazing out at the passing scenery. "I got a letter from Enrico Balban's widow yesterday."

"I see," Ned said quietly.

"Oh, it was very nice, thanking me for the money we sent, thanking us for offering to always help with her son's education, telling me how much my friendship meant to Enrico." Nigel paused, and his voice became hard and sharp. "And while I'm reading this kind and lovely letter, all I can think about is how I want to take a hot poker and stick it down the throats of the people who killed him right before I chop their heads off."

Ned kept his eyes on the road. He didn't speak right away, wanting to give Nigel a bit of breathing space, but he finally said, "Are you all right, Nigel?"

"What?" Nigel looked at him.

"That didn't sound like you. Maybe you needed a longer break."

"No, I need to work," Nigel said in a decisive voice. "It's the only thing that's keeping me sane."

# 14

# WEDNESDAY, DECEMBER 11

**A**RE **YOU SURE** you don't mind me tagging along with you, darling?" Ned asked as he and Mina were about to get into her Packard coupe. "I thought it would be a good time to look at Bill's work. He'd be occupied, and I could look at things without him hovering about."

"I told you, it's fine with me, and I meant it." Mina chuckled. "My sister is right. You Brits are meticulously polite."

"Good manners are essential to civilization. They reflect the state of our spiritual evolution."

Mina smiled and gave him an indulgent look as she started the car. "I love it when you moralize."

The car purred steadily up the driveway and through the luxuriant garden while Ollie panted happily. There was just enough room in the narrow space behind the seats of the coupe for him to sit or lie down. The December day was bright and diamond clear, and the air was as still as the glassy ocean. It was one of those days, Ned thought, that was so heartbreakingly beautiful you had to wonder why anything went wrong in the world. They were driving to the east edge of Black Point, and Mina seemed to know exactly how to get to Bill's house, even though she had never been there before. He knew it was near the art studios, but to get there by car, they had to take a very different route on several twisty lanes. Mina parked the car close to a high, weathered fence made of unpainted, horizontal wooden boards tacked onto posts. It blocked the house and yard beyond from the narrow street. They opened a creaking gate that was just about to fall off its hinges. A ramshackle house stood a good distance away, and all along the fence that surrounded the large yard were trees and bushes, screening out the neighborhood, so that one had the feeling this house stood alone and apart. There was a wide, patchy lawn that sloped down to the lava cliffs, and as they got closer to the house, Ned could see a striking view of the southeast coastline. They stopped for a moment to take in the expansive scene, which brought Ned to an immediate awareness of the powerful forces that created the island. The lava peninsula that they were standing on had flowed from Diamond Head just behind them, and looking east, they could see Koko Head, another crater that reached out into the sea. In Honolulu, one was never far from the visual evidence of volcanism and the constant reminder of the violence that gave birth to the land. Before they walked up to the battered front door, they looked back and noticed Raymond Morgan setting up his camera in a corner of the yard near an old log. Raymond gave them a wave and continued working. Just then, Tevai came in through the gate with Eva. They were both carrying several brown coconuts.

"Just go in the house." Tevai smiled and then laughed with a schoolgirl's delight. "Bill is putting on his funny clothes. We're going to make some Hawaiian lu'au with the he'e that Rahiti caught." She pointed to a clothesline where an octopus was hanging by clothespins. The two girls walked around to the back of the house, and Ollie bounded after them.

The front door opened into a large room, sparsely furnished, with a big salt-stained window that faced the sea. The whole house felt old and thin, and the walls looked as if they might fall down if someone leaned against them or the wind blew too hard. The smell of the ocean permeated everything with a strong eau du salt. Ned guessed that the main room must have begun its life as a fishing shack and over time rooms had been carelessly tacked on. A basic kitchen lined the back wall, with a sink and counters on each side, a rusty stove, an old-fashioned icebox, and a food safe. Bill emerged from a door just next to the food safe.

"Hi, Mina," he said and looked startled to see Ned with her. "And Ned! Good to see you too."

"I thought I would tag along and have a look at your work," said Ned.

"Great! Come on back here to the studio," he said as he eagerly led the way. "I'm just getting into my duds."

They entered a light-filled room. The back wall, from floor to ceiling, was made of discarded windows cleverly pieced together. There were tables and easels and paintings leaning in stacks against the walls. Marguerite Morgan was there to help Bill into his costume. It didn't look very complicated—a pair of khakis, a nineteenth-century-looking shirt, a black vest, boots, and a straw hat. Marguerite said hello but concentrated on her task.

"Tamara said you were doing a Winslow Homer painting," Mina said, "but she didn't say which one."

"It's *The Whittling Boy*," Bill said. "It was my mother's favorite. She had a print of it over her bed. Our log in the backyard gave me the idea."

"So you picked it because of your mother?" Mina asked.

"My mother is the reason I'm an artist," Bill answered. "She loved everything that was beautiful."

"She's no longer alive?" Mina tried not to sound nosey.

Bill shook his head. "No, just my father. Although he might as well be dead for all I care."

"There," said Marguerite. "You are all dressed, and we can go outside."

"If you want to look at any of the paintings," Bill said to Ned, "just go right ahead. You can prop them up on that empty easel. Sorry about the crowding, but space is tight. The watercolors are on that table in a pile." He pointed across the room. "Just make yourself at home while we carry on."

Ned went over to the stack of watercolors and began to look through them, slowly. In the far corner of the yard, he could see the distant figures of Mina, Marguerite, and Raymond clustering around Bill as he posed on the log. He gave a look back into the main room, and through the big window, he saw Eva and Tevai watching Rahiti as he husked their coconuts. He slipped into the bedroom and began to swiftly go through the drawers and closet, not even knowing what he might be looking for. He did this kind of work out of a sense of duty to what he thought was some kind of greater good, but he hated it. Finding nothing in the bedroom but worn-out clothes and piles of magazines, he crept back into the studio and went through all the cupboards and drawers as fast and as thoroughly as he could. He was almost about to give up when he saw a small inlaid chest on a table. He hadn't noticed it before because it was propping up a painting. He carefully lifted away the painting and lifted the lid of the box. He could hear the tinkling laughter of Eva and Tevai floating through the air from the backyard. Inside the chest were passports and other papers and a cardboard gift box with flowers and vines drawn on its cover. Ned opened the gift box and found some pictures of a young boy and a beautiful woman sitting in a flower garden. She had stunning blonde hair and a face that radiated sunshine. There were other pictures of the woman and the boy, whom Ned recognized as Bill. There was a birth certificate for an Elsa Engle that was dated 1885 from Hamburg, Germany, and another drawing of a family tree showing Elsa's German roots and revealing an obvious military tradition in the family. Her three younger brothers all had officer titles. There was a dried flower, a locket, and a lace handkerchief. Ned closed the gift box and the chest, and just as he had placed the painting back in its place and stepped away to look at it, Tevai entered the room.

"Would you like a drink, Ned?" she asked with her French accent.

"Thanks, I'm fine," Ned answered. "I was just admiring this painting."

"You like this one?" Tevai's eyes brightened.

"Well," he answered, "yes, I do."

"Oh," she said excitedly. "There is another one like this but much better that you must see. Bill made it in Tahiti. It is very good. You must look."

While he looked at some watercolors, she began to search through the stacks of paintings, saying something to herself in Tahitian that Ned could only guess was a grumble about Bill's messy habits. She finally found the one she was looking for, deliberately moved an easel into a particular spot, and placed the painting on it.

She called him. "Come, Ned, look here where the light is nice."

He walked over to look at the canvas and was immediately taken with it. It was a scene from the islands. He knew it was painted in Tahiti, but it just as easily could have been Sāmoa, Rarotonga, or even rural Hawai'i. It was done with such an exquisite feeling that Ned could not really think for a few minutes because of the resonances the image invoked in him. Tevai came, stood next to him, and innocently took his hand as she looked at the painting.

"This is why I love Bill," she said softly. "This is on the road that goes all around Tahiti Nui."

There was a road of crushed white coral that vanished in graceful curves. The shadows of the palm trees fell across the road in a complex and delicate mixture of blue, lavender, and pink shades. There was a glimpse of blue water beyond verdant green foliage and a sky with colors that Ned had only seen in the islands. The closest label he could find for the style was a kind of individualized impressionism, but it was the way the harmony of color, light, shade, and shape all fell together in this one painting that made it significant regardless of labels. He appreciated how perceptive Tevai was about her husband's artwork and how remarkably well she had placed the painting for him to look at—with just the right angle of light to show it at its best.

"It's the Broom Road?"

"You have been to Tahiti?"

"When I was a boy," he answered. "I remember someone said they used to call it the Broom Road because people who committed minor crimes had to sweep the road clean with brooms for punishment."

"But now the French have changed all the names," she said with a note of sadness.

"Do you think Bill would sell this painting to me?"

"Yes, I think so, but let me go out to ask him." She gave him one of her radiant smiles and walked out into the garden.

While Ned was in the house, supposedly looking at artwork, Mina had seated herself on the grass to one side of Raymond Morgan's camera and was watching and talking to Bill between shots. She had a reprint of the painting to look at and understood immediately what angle of light Raymond wanted to capture. It surprised Mina that Bill would choose to place himself in such an idyllic and somewhat nostalgic image. She had imagined that, like Desmond, he would choose something dynamic and assertive. Instead, he had chosen this image of a boy, definitely adolescent and innocent—a far cry from the image Bill had created of himself in real life. He had said it was a kind of tribute to his mother, and it amused Mina to think that bohemian Bill Hitchins might have been so attached to his mommy. That could explain why he liked women so much. It was one of the things she had noticed about him from the beginning—he was one of those men who genuinely liked women. He didn't just like them for what he thought he might get out of them, physically, or because he wanted to be admired and gushed over. He liked them because he found them interesting, and he felt comfortable with them.

"So, Mina," Bill said while Raymond adjusted his camera, "what has Tamara decided to do with Tilda's paintings? Is she going to have them in the show?"

"I don't know," Mina answered. "Maybe she hasn't decided yet. I suppose it would be a nice tribute."

"I hope she lets us know," Raymond chimed in. "Because if she doesn't, we'll all have to come up with more pieces to fill the gallery."

"I didn't even think of that," said Bill. "But you're right." He paused, did some fake whittling with the knife and the twig he was using for a prop, and said nonchalantly, "It must have been a horror for you to find her, Mina."

"You could say it was one of the more horrible things that's happened to me," she replied in the same tone.

"You must excuse me," said Marguerite as she turned and rushed toward the house.

Bill pushed back his straw hat and watched her leave. "Did we say something wrong?"

"She's very upset," Raymond sighed, "about Tilda's death and Ari's death too—especially Ari. Marguerite has some Jewish relatives, so she's extremely sensitive."

"I hope we didn't sound flippant," Mina said.

"It's a lot of things." Raymond shook his head. "Finding me with a bullet in my leg gave her a real scare too. She'll get over it. Bill, pull your hat down and get into place. The light is about to be perfect."

Bill quickly got into place, pulled the hat down, lowered his head, got his knees in the right place, and froze as if he were whittling. Mina wondered if the weeds and overgrown grasses around him had been purposefully trimmed to approximate those in the painting, because they matched perfectly. As she looked down at the print and back up at the scene before her, she saw that the light *was* perfect, and the shadows were falling over Bill almost the same way they fell over the boy in the painting. Raymond took several pictures and then declared the session successfully over. He quickly packed up and left, saying he wanted to "see to" Marguerite.

Mina managed to get some information from Bill about his stint in the navy, his early art career on the East Coast, his migration to Tahiti, and his attachment to the Pacific. Bill sat in the grass and leaned back against the log as he spoke, still whittling with the twig and the knife he had used in the photograph and now and then flashing a flirtatious smile at her. He was telling her how ideally he wanted to divide his time between Honolulu and Tahiti, but it might take some doing, because now his wife loved being in Hawai'i.

"And anyway," he said, "there's more moneymaking opportunities here than in Tahiti."

"I guess it must be tough making a living as an artist," she commented.

"You have no idea," he responded. "Desmond is a lucky bum, being able to live on his inheritance."

"When I spoke to Tilda," Mina confided, "she gave me a big lecture about how artists had to promote themselves."

"She would, wouldn't she?" he said with a derisive laugh. "Well, she certainly promoted herself in a variety of ways." He gave Mina a dark look and half whispered, "But I guess it didn't pay off the way she expected it would."

Mina couldn't tell if it was anger, menace, or resentment behind his words, but she instinctively decided to change the subject. "I've noticed," she began, "that some of your recent watercolors are all about Hawaiians fishing."

His countenance suddenly brightened. "There are still some old-time fishing families in the neighborhood around here," he said. "You can't believe how much these guys know about the ocean and the fish. I love to go diving, and sometimes they invite me to go with them or to go out on the reef at night with a torch. I'm learning how to make a net from one of them. I think he's really amused that some haole wants to learn all these things, but to me, it's amazing. I like to paint the things that interest me, not just what I think might sell."

Just then, they both looked up to see Tevai almost running toward them from the house. She looked so fresh and happy, and as she moved toward them, Mina thought that she must bring a tremendous amount of simple goodness into Bill's complicated personality.

Tevai could barely contain her excitement. "Oh, Bill," she said, "Ned has found a painting to buy!"

"Really?" Bill jumped to his feet. "Which one?"

Tevai gave him a satisfied smile. "The one I told you was very good. The one of the Broom Road."

Bill laughed and looked at Mina. "Your fiancé has excellent taste." He started to leave but stopped himself. "Oh, sorry, were we finished?"

"Pretty much," Mina said as she stood up and brushed off her skirt. "I might have to fill a few things in, but we can take care of it later. I'd like to see your work too."

As the three of them walked toward the house, Mina saw that Raymond and Marguerite were walking out through the gate. It was hard to tell from a distance, but Marguerite still looked upset. Mina asked where the bathroom was, and Tevai pointed to a small building that stood apart from the house. She was happy when she finally got there to see that it had a real toilet and wasn't an outhouse. There was a shower there too, and just outside, she saw a *furo*. On her way back to the main house, she heard the familiar sound of a coconut being scraped on a grater, and just around a corner of the house, she found Rahiti sitting on a grating stool, hard at work, while Eva sat on the grass, watching. Ollie was near them, chewing on and dragging around the discarded coconut husks. Eva stood up as soon as she spotted Mina coming toward them.

"Hello," Mina said with a warm smile. "Is Rahiti teaching you how to make coconut milk?"

"I didn't realize it was so much work," Eva replied.

"That's why the men have to do it," Rahiti said as he flashed Mina a dazzling smile.

Mina frowned at her dog. "I hope Ollie isn't making a mess."

"Our dogs in Tahiti like to do that with the husks too," said Rahiti. "Just let him play."

"I saw your parents leaving," Mina said to Eva. "I hope your mother is all right. Bill and I said something about Tilda and Ari that set her off."

"I'm sure it's not your fault. She's been somewhat nervy lately."

"I know," Mina began carefully. "Your father said she was upset about the deaths, especially Ari. I didn't know she had Jewish relatives. It must be hard on her."

"He told you that?" Eva asked with a look of amazement.

Mina felt slightly confounded but said, "Of course, I won't tell anyone if you don't want me to."

"Uh, no," Eva stammered. "I mean, I don't care. I'm just surprised he told you, that's all."

"Will you tell her I didn't mean to upset her or be disrespectful?" Mina asked.

"I will," Eva nodded. "I'm sure she's okay. She still thinks about that day she found my father, you know."

"Of course." Mina smiled at both of them. "Well, have fun."

On her way back to the studio, Mina felt slightly unsettled about the conversation, but once she saw the painting Ned had chosen, she forgot about Eva and Rahiti and decided that she might like to buy something too. She found several watercolors and paintings that she liked and finally settled on a dramatic painting of a moonrise over Maunalua Bay with a shimmering path of light over the water and the dark outlines of Koko Crater and Koko Head.

Bill showed them several styles of frames and offered to arrange for the framing.

That afternoon, after lunch, Mina sat at her desk, with Ollie curled up at her feet, in the spare bedroom she now used for an office. She had just finished a draft about Bill Hitchins for the catalog. Ned had gone off to practice fencing with Nigel for the big demonstration at the yacht club on Saturday morning. She read the piece on Bill once again and decided to set it aside for a day or two. Technically, she only had two more people to write up, Akira and Raymond, and then she would be officially done. But she toyed with the idea of including one on Tamara, just so she could have an excuse to interview Tamara too. There were things about Tamara and her husband in Ari's files that could definitely have been blackmail material for Tilda. Yes, she thought, she would convince Tamara and write a piece on her too. She yawned and stretched and bent over to pet Ollie. These people, this situation, it seemed like there were smoke and mirrors everywhere, and it left her feeling continually unsettled. Todd's words about the files, *don't tell anyone, not even Ned,* kept echoing in her head. Even though Todd hadn't included Ned in solving these murders, she felt uncomfortable about not being able to talk to him about it freely. And Mei's words came back to her too: *maybe Ned and Nigel are up to something.* She wondered what in the world they would be up to and why Ned wouldn't tell her.

Outside the window over her desk, the lovely afternoon light was spreading over the garden. She had heard on the radio that a Kona storm was expected to roll in that night and that clouds and rain from the south could linger for a couple of days. She decided to take advantage of the sunny afternoon by changing into her swimsuit and heading down to the beach. Ollie trembled with excitement and ran circles around her in the sand. The calm ocean mirrored the lazy white clouds and sent thin ribbons of waves rippling up on the shoreline. Mina felt a tingling coolness as she waded into the sea. It was so still that she could hear the cars along the cliff road and muffled voices coming from neighborhood houses. Mina swam away from shore and back and then swam along the shoreline toward Diamond Head while Ollie followed. She could feel the water washing the film of clutter out of her mind, and as she swam harder and began to breathe more rapidly, she sensed the freedom and relief that always came with being in the ocean. She turned over into a rhythmic backstroke so she could see the sky and Ollie as he paddled along behind her.

She had just glided into shallow water, where her toes could touch the sand, when she heard a loud whacking sound and, a few seconds later, a powerful exhalation of water. She walked on to the beach and looked out to see a humpback whale breeching offshore, and when another whale beside it blew a burst of water high into the sky, she realized there were several of them making their way towards Koko Head. She saw a great tail slap the water, and then another immense whale breeched and made a huge splash that echoed against the Diamond Head cliffs. In childhood, she had developed an emotional attachment to these magnificent visitors, looking forward to their arrival every winter, and now, even as an adult, her heart always skipped a beat and she nearly shed tears whenever she saw them—as if they were long-lost relations come home again. Koholā, she remembered, was the Hawaiian word for "whale," and their ivory, when it washed ashore in ancient times, had been used to fashion the prized lei niho palaoa. Because she and Nyla loved the whales so much, their mother had made a special trip to the museum when they were children to see these lei. Carved into a crescent shape that resembled a hook or a tongue and strung on innumerable strands of human hair, these lei of whalebone were worn only by people of high rank and handed down as great treasures from generation to generation. They contained the great, accumulated spiritual power of all the chiefs who had ever possessed them, and it was fitting, she thought, that their origin lay with these extraordinary creatures that roamed the sea. The whales had known the waters surrounding the islands long before the first Polynesians arrived, and she had always thought of them as the older and wiser residents. She stayed on the beach and watched them move through the still and tranquil water until she could no longer see them, and as the late-afternoon sun began casting its long shadows, she reluctantly wrapped up in a towel and walked toward her bungalow, arriving there just as Ned's car pulled into the driveway. She stood with her white towel around her, and in a moment of sharp clarity, she looked at Ned as he walked up to greet her and said, "We have to talk."

Ned stopped in his tracks a few feet away from her and replied, "Yes, we have to talk. Get changed, and I'll make the cocktails."

"How about we flip a coin to see who goes first?" Mina suggested as she sipped her gin fizz. She was sitting on Ned's rattan sofa with her knees tucked up. Her hair was still damp, and she wore an old, thin pullover sweater and a comfortable pair of cotton pedal pushers.

"Here's a nickel." Ned threw a coin up in the air and let it land on the lauhala mat, where Mina couldn't see it. Ollie ran over and sniffed at it. "You say what it is."

"Heads!" she declared.

"It looks like I'll have to go first." He took a big sip of his drink and sighed. "Where to begin? Where to begin?"

"Take your time," she said. "We have all night, a bottle of gin, and I have some soup in the refrigerator that Mrs. Olivera made for me that I might be willing to share."

Ned smiled. "Is this a bribe?"

"It's her very special Portuguese bean soup that she makes with ham hocks."

"I guess I better be on my best, most honest behavior."

"Yes, your best, most politely honest British behavior."

"Well," Ned began, "you know that Nigel and I were childhood friends and that at various times in our adult lives I have done not-to-be-mentioned work for the British government."

"This I know."

"Nigel has made a career out of it."

"I figured that too."

"So then you know that everything I tell you is not to be repeated to anyone without my permission. And I am telling you everything against the wishes of Nigel, so you can't let him know I'm sharing this information with you."

"Goes without saying, darling."

"Very well," he said with a nod. "You already know that when I went to Shanghai, I went to get Nigel out of a very dangerous situation. We got through it. I got him out. He and Mei decided to try their luck here, and they're not here for even a month when suddenly our government and the US Naval Intelligence recruit Nigel to do another job. On his request, our government also recruits me—the very big carrot on the stick for both of us being that if we do this job well, the US government promises to let us stay in the United States forever if we choose. I know I haven't said anything, but my immigration status is something I've been worried about."

Mina tried to act nonchalant when, in fact, she was burning with curiosity. "And the job is?"

"The job is to discover who is regularly providing all kinds of information to the Japanese about ships, aircraft, troop movements in Hawai'i, especially the activity around Pearl Harbor."

"Spying!"

"Wait," Ned put up his hand in a stop signal, "it gets better. The navy gave us photos of their prime suspects, everyone they wanted us to investigate first, and it turns out that to a person, they're all the members of your artists' gang."

"What?" Mina sat up and put her feet on the floor.

"That's right." Ned cocked his head in a way that reminded her of Ollie. "They're all to do with that catalog you're writing."

Mina drained her drink and set the glass down on the table with a bang. "Another gin fizz, please." She followed Ned to the kitchen and watched him make the drinks. "This is incredible and sheds a whole new light on the murders. You know, that's what I'm helping Todd with. I'm his undercover spy into the art group."

Ned smiled at her. "This I know, darling."

"Yes," she said, "but you didn't know about the files."

"The files?"

"The files that Ari kept on everybody showing their connections either to Nazis or to Japan and other criminal things that we think Tilda was using to blackmail people with, but now, of course, there's another dimension to everything."

"Another gin fizz, please," Ned said as he poured their second cocktails and carried them back to the parlor.

"And there are other things too," Mina went on, "personal grudges and sexual intrigues. We'll have to sort them all out together." Mina stopped and looked at Ned. "And what will I tell Todd?"

"We'll have to think hard about that one, but first we can get each other up to speed. Any chance I could have a look at those files?"

"Maybe," Mina answered, "but it depends on how much we tell Todd."

They finished their cocktails and moved over to Mina's house, where they ate hearty bowls of Portuguese bean soup. All the while they talked, trading information, speculating, and trying to contain the nervous excitement they each felt as they put what they knew together. They decided to sleep on the information they had shared and talk again in the morning.

After dinner they walked out on the beach. The cloudless sky betrayed no signs of an impending storm, and the ocean lay motionless and silent. Under the full moon, they sat down in the sand, which still held some warmth, and tried to identify the constellations that were visible. Mina had to call Ollie back to her side several times to stop him from taking a swim. He finally came and curled up next to her.

"Ned, do you think another war is inevitable?" Mina asked while looking up at the night sky.

"Nothing is inevitable, but there are things going on in the world that make it seem like war is a distinct possibility."

After a few moments of pointed silence, Mina spoke in a clear voice. "I've been paying close attention to the news about Japanese politics in the last few years, and I can see why the navy would be concerned about spying. I thought for a while that democracy and the party system would have a chance in Japan, but after the Depression, the trade barriers, the internal violence, it seems the people there think the military will be the answer to all the internal and foreign threats."

"Japan isn't the only nation to embrace that kind of jingoistic nationalism—look at Germany and Italy. What worries me on the European front is that Britain and France are ignoring the fascism in their backyards. This year, Hitler instituted conscription again, a definite violation of the Treaty of Versailles, and now Mussolini has invaded Abyssinia, and no one seems to be willing to stop either of them."

She sighed. "And the League of Nations has proven itself useless."

"If other nations keep ignoring these acts of aggression, another war *will* be inevitable."

"I guess," she said, "what I'm coming around to realizing is that stopping the spying that's going on right here is part of a much larger scenario that could affect the whole world."

"That's right, darling. We have a supporting role in a big and complex plot."

"Is it my imagination," she said, "or do you have a tendency to gravitate to literary metaphors?"

"It's very apropos in this instance."

"And why is that?"

"Because, my love, in literary plots, only conflict is interesting."

# 15

# THURSDAY, DECEMBER 12

**IT WAS STILL** dark when Mina woke from the dream. She turned the light on for a split second to look at the clock. It was nearly six in the morning. She could not actually hear the rain, but the gutter on the roof was dripping the way it did when the raindrops were gentle and fine. Off in the distance, she could hear thunder, and outside the window, she saw faint flickers of light in the sky. She had dreamt that war had come to Honolulu. Bombs were dropping from the sky, objects were flying, and the ground shook as she and Ollie ran outside and stood on the lawn. In the distance, she could see a strange, giant airship flying slowly in the sky, with a huge metal rake attached to it sweeping up the hills and houses. She looked up and saw a bomb about to fall on her house and woke suddenly from the nightmare to a peal of thunder. She called Ollie's name softly, and the dog instantly roused himself from sleep and came to her side with his warm breath and his eager affection. As she reached out and lightly scratched under his chin, she felt an instant comfort in his physical presence. He placed his head on the bed next to hers and gave her face a lick as if to tell her things were fine.

"Good boy, Ollie," she whispered.

Still feeling unsettled, she turned the light back on, sat up in bed, and waited for the images of the dream to fade away. The curtains moved almost imperceptibly as the first hints of a south wind announced the coming of a Kona storm. She could feel the humidity increasing, and she imagined the storm crawling through the sky toward the island, with its mountain chain of heavy gray clouds, holding thunder, lightning, and so much rain. Warfare was something she had only heard about through newspaper stories and newsreels, and it was troubling to think that such violence might come to the islands. After last night's conversation with Ned, she was more than aware that Japan had turned a focused eye toward Hawai'i and Pearl Harbor—watching, waiting, and trying to keep a record of what was going on. She felt a hollow and almost queasy sensation in her stomach. What would happen if she found herself in the midst of destruction as she had in her dream? It would be easy to give way to the kind of fear that she experienced in the dream and felt even now, pressing on the fringes of her waking life, but if there were dark forces taking root and growing in faraway places, forces that could one day find their way to her island home, only a clear head and a sturdy heart would see her through. The investigation had escalated into something more than a challenging puzzle. She and Ned had the opportunity to help maintain a shield of protection for everything she loved. By unmasking the person or persons spying, who in her heart of hearts she thought was also a murderer, they would be doing what they could to help keep things safe.

Ollie jumped up just before Mina heard Ned knocking and calling at her front door. She got up, threw on her robe, and opened the door. He stood there in his own robe, with a sweet, sleepy smile on his face, poised with a black umbrella. "I saw your light on," he began, somewhat sheepishly. "I don't mean to be a bother, but I had a very bad dream and could use a cup of tea and some company."

"A handsome lost soul out in the rain," Mina smiled. "How could a girl resist?"

Several hours later, Mina smeared liliko'i jelly on one of the warm scones Ned had made for breakfast. They had moved to his bungalow after the first cup of tea and were sitting at his kitchen table. It was now raining, and the wind had picked up, making whistling noises that filled the air when it gusted.

"Well," Mina said, "we each have a crime to solve—yours is espionage, and mine is murder."

"And they may or may not be related," Ned added as he stirred some milk in his cup of tea. "Milk?" he asked as he lifted the creamer.

She made a face. "I don't think I would ever want milk in my tea, Ned."

"I promise I'll never force you, darling."

"So," she went on, "you think they may not be related."

"Let's tick off the possibilities," he began. "One, Ari Schoner's death was a robbery. Tilda Clement's death was because she was blackmailing someone, or someone was jealous and/or hated her for other reasons, and the espionage is unrelated."

"Two," she continued, "Ari had figured out who was spying and got murdered by the spy. Tilda knew or guessed who it was and tried to blackmail the spy. The spy murdered her too."

"Three," he added, "Tilda was the spy. Ari found out, and she killed him. And then she was considered a liability and killed by her employers—unlikely, but possible."

"Or," she said as she picked at the crumbs on her plate, "Ari did actually know things about people. He could have confronted one of them about something and gotten murdered for it, and it could have had nothing to do with spying."

"And maybe Tilda knew what he did and threatened or blackmailed the murderer."

"Whichever one of these we pick," she said, "some of the suspects are candidates for espionage and murder. Appy has a motive for killing Tilda out of revenge and anger, and so does Molly, but I think it unlikely that they would kill Ari. I mean, those things in the files were not about them. They were about their fathers, and I can't see Ari threatening to use that information against them."

"Unless," he interjected, "he suspected Molly of spying for the Japanese and having political affiliations with the Nazi Party. So many of the people I know in this kind of undercover work could put the finest stage actors to shame."

"Yeah," she said as she reached for another scone, "I did see Molly in a heated discussion with Ari at the Halloween party, and there's her close relationship with Akira. They could be in it together. But so far, Appy only fits number one."

"Things would be less muddled if we knew who Tilda was blackmailing. Actually, we have no real proof she was blackmailing anybody, but going by what you've found in those files, she had a rich field. She could have been going after all of them or only one of them."

"And now," she added, "there's Bill's connection to the Free Teutonia Society and the German military."

"Desmond is connected to that society as well. They could be partners. And didn't you say both Desmond and Molly were late for your interview the day Schoner was killed? One or both of them could have been committing murder. We could speculate even further and say the three of them could be working as a team."

She looked at him, tightened her lips, and then said, "We might have to do more of what you did to Bill."

"What's that?"

"Don't be coy, Ned. I believe Todd would call it breaking and entering."

He groaned. "Oh, Mina, no."

"What do you mean, 'oh, Mina, no'?"

"It's too dangerous for you."

"If it's not too dangerous for you, it's not too dangerous for me. Look at what you found. His mother's brothers are all German officers. That's useful information."

"And Todd wouldn't like it at all."

"Unlike you," she retorted, "I'm not working for anyone. I'm just doing Todd a favor, and what I do on my own time is my own business."

"If he found out, he might never ask for your help again."

"Maybe and maybe not." She frowned, leaned back in her chair, and crossed her arms. "Look, right now all we have are a whole bunch of threads. I say we need to follow all of them and see where we end up. If you have any other ideas, please tell me."

He looked at her for a moment and burst out laughing. "You're incorrigible, aren't you? Just don't count on me to bail you out if you get caught."

"I think we need to talk seriously about taking Todd into our confidence."

"And I think Nigel would not approve. He'd have a fit if he knew I'd confided in you."

"We can explain that to Todd," she said. "Things are bound to overlap in these two investigations. We can just keep quiet about what we know until you get Nigel to change his mind."

"I'll think about it," he said. "But please, I've already compromised my relationship with Nigel by telling you, so let me make the decision about Todd." Ned was quiet for a moment and then said, "There is something else we should talk about—totally different subject."

"What's that?" she yawned.

"Our wedding plans. Do you have any thoughts about the date and the place?"

"Hmmm, that is a totally different subject," Mina replied. "Well, if it were up to me, I would say we should run away, get married by some justice of the peace, and avoid all the fuss, but I guess our families would kill us."

He laughed. "Right, any other ideas?"

"Since I've been married before," she began, "I think it should be a small, quiet wedding, and because I'm hoping that we'll be living mostly in the islands, it would be only fair of me to offer to go to England—or to Sāmoa, for that matter—to get married, if you want to."

"Actually, I was hoping we would get married in Hawai'i. My mother could bring my grandfather from England. He's mad about tropical plants, and I've wanted him to come to the islands for a long time. This would be perfect. And my grandparents from Sāmoa would be much more inclined to be at our wedding if it were here."

Mina sat up. "Oh, Ned, how about the ranch? We could get married in the wooden chapel there. There's enough room for our families to stay, and we could find a place in Waimea for a few friends."

Ned frowned. "I'd forgotten about that chapel on your father's ranch. I think it's a marvelous idea, as long as you're sure that's what you would like."

"Honestly, it would be a big relief to me," Mina said as she placed her hand on his shoulder. "It would be simple, and we would only have to invite our family and closest friends."

"And," Ned said as he covered her hand with his, "the next thing to decide is when."

"How long do you think your mother and grandfather need? They have to come the farthest."

"Three or four months should give them more than enough comfortable planning and travel time."

"Ned," Mina said excitedly. "Let's get married on May first, May Day. Once when I was a girl in the fourth grade, we had a maypole, and I fell in love with the idea of May first and springtime. And for the last few years, it's become a kind of unofficial holiday in the islands."

"May first it shall be, my darling," Ned said as he leaned over to kiss her. "It's a much better choice than April first."

Mina laughed. "Oh, I don't know, we could dress up like jesters, and after we said 'I do,' we could scream 'April fool!'"

"No," Ned shook his head, "if I have to wear a jester's outfit, it's all off."

"Ned, there's one thing I've been meaning to ask you."

"Sounds serious."

"This fencing thing on Saturday," Mina began, "is it men only, or are women invited to watch too?"

"I've been thinking long and hard about the exhibit and the Tilda question," Tamara said as she tapped her nails on the table.

It was mid-afternoon, and outside a sudden gust of wind whipped the rain against one of the windows in Tamara's upstairs workroom, where she and Mina were meeting. It seemed to Mina that the dark storm, now swirling around them, had elicited a response of warmth and safety from the house—causing the lamp light to take on an affectionate glow, the carpets to appear rich and inviting, and the grain of the wood in the library table to have much more depth and luminosity. Mina found herself once again magnetically attracted to Tamara's home. The playful grumbles and growls of Jocks and Ollie drifted up from the living room as they engaged in a gentle mock battle.

"And have you decided anything?" Mina asked as she pulled her unbuttoned cardigan tighter across her body.

"I've decided to go ahead and include her work. We can feature one of her paintings—I'm asking Desmond to find the self-portrait she painted—in the foyer, and I'll have a plaque made with a simple memorial inscription on it. The self-portrait she did was very fine. She had already given me a list of the things she wanted in the exhibit, so that won't be a problem."

"So then we will be including her in the catalog too," Mina stated.

"I gave her a copy of the piece I wrote, and she corrected it before she . . . before she was killed. I took it from the house that night." Mina paused and looked away. "I know I wasn't supposed to take anything, but it wasn't any kind of evidence or anything. And it did belong to me."

"Poor Tilda," Tamara said, shaking her head. "She was not the most popular person in our group. I think Ari was the only one who genuinely liked her."

"Why is that?" Mina asked. "Why do you think he liked her when no one else did?"

"Well, I think she was very different with him. He was gentle with her, and she trusted him. He had a way of making people feel safe." Tamara gave her a serious look. "Not to speak ill of the dead, but she simply asked for trouble. She always pushed her luck. I'm not sure what led to her death, but to tell you the truth, I'm not that surprised."

"Tilda's piece just needs polishing. I've finished all the others, except for Raymond's. I'm meeting him tomorrow afternoon at the Kamaʻāina Club to interview him."

Tamara laughed. "Raymond must be making a day of it at the club. He's quite the social butterfly. I'm meeting him and Marguerite for dinner there."

"I wondered why he wanted to meet at four," Mina said. "It seemed so late in the afternoon."

"I'm meeting them at six. That will give him time to have your interview and then a few drinks with his cronies before I get there.

Now, would you like a nice cup of coffee or tea before you venture back out into the maelstrom?"

Mina smiled. "A cup of tea would be great."

"I'll just go down and ask Janet to bring it up to us."

As soon as Tamara was out of sight, Mina stood up and looked around the room. She spotted some filing cabinets in the corner and took note of drawers and cupboards that could be explored. She walked to a small hall with two doors. She opened one and saw a half bathroom, but the other one opened to a set of stairs that she guessed led up to an attic. She heard Tamara coming back up the stairs and quickly ducked into the bathroom, flushed the toilet, and then turned on the water in the sink and rinsed her hands, stepping back into the room just as Tamara was sitting down.

"That's a lovely bathroom," Mina commented. "So convenient."

"At my age, it would be absolutely dreadful to have to run up and down the stairs every time I had to go."

Tamara's maid brought them a pot of tea on a tray and two slices of gingerbread cake with a dollop of whipped cream.

"I hope you don't mind me asking," Mina began, "but how long have you been a widow?"

Tamara sighed. "It will be three years in May, but it seems longer. Sometimes I think I should give up this big house, but not just yet."

"What did he do?" Mina asked, seeing that Tamara was open to talking.

"James manufactured lots of different things—parts and pieces of machinery. I could never keep track of what he was doing. To tell you the truth, it didn't interest me. As you know, he did have dealings in the Orient, and sometimes I went on marvelous trips with him."

"You have so many beautiful Japanese prints."

"Asian art is a passion of mine," Tamara smiled, "and an interest James shared."

"You must miss him."

"Yes." A look of determination washed over Tamara's face. "He was more than just a wonderful husband. We both had very strong, shared values, the same sense of purpose, and a vision."

The wind howled outside. The two dogs ran up the stairs and lay down near their mistresses. As Mina sat, sipped her tea, and enjoyed the ginger cake, she wondered exactly what kind of vision and values Tamara and her late husband shared.

"That man in the photograph!" Alika exclaimed as he burst through the door of the Kuakini Street flat in his yellow raincoat. "I saw him! He got out of the car with his bags and everything. I bet he's staying at the embassy!"

Ned and Nigel both lowered their rapiers and lifted off their fencing masks. They had shoved all the furniture out of the way to practice. Alika stood there, holding his bag of schoolbooks and looking at them, and then he noticed the room.

"Boy, you sure made a mess in here," Alika said as he closed the door, took off his wet coat, and hung it up on a wall hook.

Ned shrugged. "It's not so untidy. We could straighten it up in a few minutes."

"Better not let Reggie see it like this," Alika warned. "He likes everything in its place."

"Not to worry about Reggie," Nigel said as he moved his rapier around in small circles while rotating his wrist. "*He* works for *us*. Now tell us who you saw."

Alika walked over to a chair that was up against the wall and sat down. "Remember those pictures you showed of the people to look out for?"

"Yes," Nigel responded. He was now practicing a forward move with a short thrust while Ned watched. "I remember."

"And," Alika continued, "remember the one of the two Japanese men drinking tea with the older haole lady?"

"Of course," Nigel answered, still moving with his rapier.

"Well, it was the younger Japanese man," Alika stated.

Nigel stopped and turned to look at the boy. "Are you sure?"

Alika frowned as if insulted. "Of course I'm sure."

"Where are those photographs?" Nigel moved urgently around the room. "He didn't destroy them, did he?"

"I know where they are," Alika said, disappearing into one of the bedrooms and returning with a folder. "They're in here."

Nigel took the folder and flipped through the pictures. Ned, who had been observing this exchange, pulled the table away from the wall and out into the room. Alika scooted his chair up, and Ned sat next to him while Nigel hovered over them and placed the photo on the table.

"This is the man you saw?" Nigel asked, pointing to the younger man in the photo.

Alika nodded. "Yes, I told you, that's him. He got out of the car under that big cover in the driveway. The driver got out and took out two suitcases and a set of golf clubs and then carried them up to the front door of the big house—the one the ambassador lives in. The servant opened the door to let them in, and then I couldn't see anymore."

"Do you remember what he was wearing?" Ned asked. "Was it a uniform?"

"No," Alika shook his head, "it wasn't a uniform. He had on dark pants, a white shirt with no tie, and he had a coat slung over his shoulder. Oh, and he was wearing dark glasses, you know, like he was a movie star or something."

The door opened, and Reggie walked in. His eyes widened as he saw the furniture spread out in disarray. "What the—" He stopped himself when he saw that Nigel and Ned were there. "I mean, what happened in here?"

"We were just going through a routine for our fencing demonstration," Nigel said calmly. "No need to panic. Everything will return to its proper place. Come on and pitch in."

In no time at all, everything was put back, and they were all sitting around the table. And Reggie, noting that it was four thirty, went to the kitchen and came back with three bottles of beer and a cola for Alika. Ned immediately went back to the kitchen to get glasses for him and Nigel, and then Reggie was apprised of the arrival of the young Japanese man. He then reported some news of his own.

"So," Reggie began, rubbing his right hand over his short, carrot-colored hair, "I've been going to that flower shop in the afternoon for three days in a row now."

"And?" Nigel asked as he tilted his glass and poured his beer into it.

"Well, before I went the first time, I borrowed a book from the library on *ikebana* and read it the night before. There's way more to it than just arranging flowers."

"I should think so," Ned agreed.

"So anyway," Reggie continued, "I go in there the first time on Tuesday afternoon, thinking I would just introduce myself to the guy and tell him I was interested in *ikebana* and get around to maybe setting up a lesson and stuff. But instead, he grabs me by the arm, hauls me in the back, gives me this vase, throws some twigs and leaves and flowers at me, and tells me to make something. Boy, was I ever sweating it out. So I just took a deep breath and tried to remember some of the things I read in the book, like the scalene triangle and all that heaven, earth, and man stuff. And I tried to remember how some of the pictures looked and the line and form of the arrangements. I just took my time and did my best, and when I was finished, Akira came over and looked at it for a long time, not saying anything. Then he gave me another vase and some other stuff and told me to make something else. So I made something else, and then I made something else after that, and after the third time, he looks at me suspiciously and asks me if I'm fibbing him about never doing this before. I guess he was more convinced by the shocked look on my face than by the fact that I said no. Anyway, I went back yesterday, and he gave me more things and a bigger vase, and today he gave me some weird things to work with like green bananas and a breadfruit. I'm guessing he thinks I have some talent."

"Certainly sounds like you might," Ned agreed, "but has he said so?"

Reggie took a long sip from his beer bottle, put it down, and smiled at Ned and Nigel. "No, but he did invite me to go with him to the Japanese embassy tomorrow to do the flowers because his usual helper has something else she has to do."

Nigel chuckled. "It's hard to believe we have an 'in' to the embassy because of your flower-arranging skills, Reggie."

"There's something else too," Reggie said excitedly. "That Tamara Morrison has dropped by twice in the last three days to see Akira. It appears to be friendly and all about fresh flowers, but I can tell they're as thick as thieves."

"Well done, Reggie," Ned said and raised his glass.

It was nearly six and already dark when Ned parked his car in front of the Chang residence on the edge of Chinatown. It had stopped raining for the moment, and the water on the road and sidewalks glistened under the streetlights. He could see a light on in the back of the store, past the beautiful antique *tansu* and the lovely Chinese paneled screen that were displayed in the window. Cecily Chang and her Hawaiian mother ran the antique store and also sold fireworks on the side. Cecily's parents lived above the store, and Cecily and her new husband, Tom Porter, had recently renovated another part of the building for their own home. They both liked the liveliness of this unusual neighborhood, and Cecily liked the convenience of being close to the shop. Mina and Nyla had been friends with Cecily since childhood, and Ned had become very fond of Cecily's father, Wing Chang, or Uncle Wing, as he insisted Ned call him. Uncle Wing had left the running of the business to the women in the family, while he devoted himself to writing poetry, conjuring up French cuisine in the kitchen, and keeping his finger on the pulse of Chinatown. Ned walked down the alley alongside the building and knocked on the door.

Cecily, Mina, and Tom were gathered downstairs in the office looking at some photographs of Cecily and Tom's wedding, which had taken place earlier in the year. The group left the office and walked quickly through the wet streets. Around the corner, just a few blocks away, there was a noticeable change in the neighborhood. There were restaurants, bars with loud music, pool halls, and shops that kept late hours. Neon signs blinked and glared, and Ned noticed they had walked past a few "ladies of the night." It was Thursday and not as loud or reckless as he suspected it might be on a Friday or Saturday night. There were a few American sailors strutting around in their uniforms and clustered under the awnings of some of the bars, standing and talking and smoking cigarettes the way confident and cocky young men did when they were out for a night on the town. It had begun to drizzle again, and flimsy curtains of rain blew in transparent waves over the scene, making car tires whoosh along the streets and throw off small sprays of water as they passed. Each couple raised an umbrella, huddled close together, and hurried along the sidewalk.

The restaurant was on the corner and up a flight of wide but ancient stairs. When they arrived, Ned recognized it as the restaurant where he, Mina, and Cecily had eaten dinner nearly a year ago. There was the familiar painted dragon that curled around the inside of the entry, framing all those who stepped in with its glistening green and golden scales. It was a popular spot and nearly full, but Cecily had the foresight to call ahead and reserve one of the round, shiny black tables. Ned and Tom let the women do the ordering while they happily shared a large bottle of beer.

Ned hardly had time to finish his first glass of beer before the food began to arrive: crisp wontons, noodles, fried rice, roast duck, stuffed tofu, shrimp in ginger and onion sauce, spicy thin-sliced beef, fried oysters, and chicken with some kind of black beans. Ned thought he remembered many of these dishes from his last meal here and surmised that the women must have favorites.

"Don't forget," said Cecily, "that my father has made a special dessert for us that he expects us to eat when we get back. It's French, of course."

"Where does he learn to do all this French cooking?" Ned asked.

Cecily shrugged. "I'm not really sure. He has people he writes to and shares recipes with, and he's sure to make friends with any talented chef in town that cooks French cuisine."

"I've heard him complain several times about the lack of a real French cookbook," Tom said while helping himself to the fried rice, "but it doesn't seem to have slowed him down."

"I wish we could talk him into cooking a real Chinese dinner like he used to," Cecily sighed. "Remember, Mina?"

"I am not going to complain," Mina answered.

"Looking around here," Tom commented, "you would never think we were in the middle of a depression."

"Well, *we're* not, exactly," Mina countered, "not compared to the mainland. Our territorial unemployment is around 7 percent, higher I'm sure in Honolulu. Compare that to 20 percent on the mainland, and we can count ourselves lucky. The sugar and pineapple industries have kept our jobless rate down."

"Don't tell me," Cecily said. "You've done an article on it."

"No," Mina grinned, "I've just kept up."

"Speaking of jobs, Tom, how is the new job going?" Ned asked. "I understand that now you're managing Tamara Morrison's gallery."

"It's wonderful," Tom answered. "She's very open to me expanding the gallery to include more than just visual art. She's given me a very free hand in creating new directions. I'm surprised and delighted."

Ned smiled. "So she doesn't hang about, peer over your shoulder, and ask you about everything you do?"

"Just the opposite," Tom said. "In fact, I wish I saw more of her. Her only regular call is to come in on Mondays with that Akira fellow to change around the fresh flowers. She's big on flowers and greenery in the gallery."

"Akira." Ned feigned a puzzled look. "That name sounds familiar. Have I met him, darling?" Ned asked Mina.

"I don't think so," Mina answered, "but he's one of the artists in the show."

"They seem to have a certain kind of relationship," Tom commented.

"What do you mean," Cecily asked. "You don't mean to tell me they're—"

"Oh, no, no," Tom broke in, "nothing like that. It's just that it's not an employer-employee relationship. It's more like she mother hens him. I guess I can't quite put my finger on it, because I'm not explaining it very well."

"No," Mina said, "you explained it perfectly. It's a certain kind of relationship."

Tom laughed. "Right, that I'm not really certain of."

"My father knew Akira's father, I think," Cecily said. "If I remember, he was a doctor or something."

Ned gave Mina a quick wink across the table.

"Look at that, Tom," Cecily smiled at Ned. "Ned is making eyes at his fiancée."

"And speaking of being a fiancée," Mina said as she reached for a fried oyster with her chopsticks. "We've set a date and a place."

"So tell us," Cecily said, just before she ate a mouthful of noodles.

Mina smiled with self-satisfaction. "The date will be May first, and the place will be my father's ranch. And of course you are invited, but we are keeping it very small."

"Family and close friends," Ned added. "My mother and grand-father will be coming from England."

Cecily frowned and tapped her chopsticks on her plate. "That only gives you four months to plan, Mina."

Mina laughed. "I'm sure I'll get more than enough help and advice from you and Nyla."

After dinner, they made their way back to the Chang residence. It was raining steadily, and the only people out on the street were those rushing from one place to another. The south wind had picked up by the time they arrived at the alleyway lined with red bricks and the door that opened to the back of Cecily's shop. They were all slightly damp and in need of a towel. A set of stairs near the alley door led up to Cecily's parents' apartment. At the other end of the long narrow space behind the shop, another staircase led to a formerly unused area upstairs that had been renovated into a home for Cecily and Tom. Her parents' apartment was above the antique store, while the new apartment stood above two shops that the Changs leased to a seam-stress and an herbalist. They climbed the stairs and gathered around the long wooden table in Wing Chang's kitchen, where he served each of them a piece of a scrumptious *tarte aux poires à la bourdaloue* and a tumbler of cognac.

"Perhaps cognac is not the correct after-dinner drink for a Chi-nese meal," said Uncle Wing, "but I thought it would be welcome on such a rainy and blustery night."

"It's as perfect as this pear tart," Ned said. "The frangipane is marvelous."

A broad smile spread over Uncle Wing's face. "You are welcome to eat in my kitchen for the rest of your life, Ned, just for knowing what frangipane is."

"What is it?" Cecily said in a loud whisper.

"It's the delightful almond-custard-like filling under the pears," Ned whispered back.

Uncle Wing rolled his eyes. "My daughter never remembers anything I tell her."

"She does," Tom said. "She just likes to torture the opposite sex."

Uncle Wing smiled and shook his head. "This is the thanks one gets for buying her a good education."

"Hey, Pops," Cecily said, "where's Mom?"

Her father frowned. "Please do not call me Pops, Cecily. This is not a Charlie Chan movie. Your mother is playing mahjong with her friends."

"Do they play for money?" Mina asked as she took the last bite of her pear tart.

"Not much money," Cecily said, "just nickels and dimes, but they play a long time, and I guess I should plan on opening the shop on my own tomorrow."

"That would be wise," Uncle Wing agreed.

"Ned hasn't seen your new digs yet," Mina said to Tom.

"Would you like the grand tour of the battle site, Ned?" Tom asked.

"I would be delighted," Ned answered, "but only if your lovely wife comes along to tell her side of the story."

Cecily smiled and pursed her lips. "I can see I better go along to defend myself."

"I'll stay here," Mina said, just before she gave her fork a lick, "and maybe I can sweet-talk your father into giving me another piece of pear tart."

"That would be my great pleasure," said Uncle Wing.

When the others had gone, Mina took a small bite of her second piece of tart and said, "Uncle Wing, can I ask you about someone?"

"Oh, dear," he sighed, "and here I thought you loved me for my tart. What is it you want to know? Is it in connection with these recent murders?"

"How did you know?" she asked.

"A simple deduction," he answered, "since Cecily has told us you are helping with the exhibit catalog, and two people closely connected to the artist's group are now dead."

"It's about Tamara Morrison."

"Ah, a most interesting woman."

"And Akira Nakasone."

He nodded thoughtfully. "A most interesting relationship."

Mina said nothing more, waiting for Uncle Wing to decide what to tell her. She could see he was carefully thinking something over, and she did not want to seem rude or demanding. She could see he knew something interesting.

"I must ask you to use this information judiciously, Mina," he began, "because some of it is speculation and based on hearsay."

"I promise," she said softly.

"Tamara married this Morrison fellow. As you know, she is from here, but he was not. He was already wealthy and a successful businessman. She quickly had two children, a boy and then a girl, I think. I've only met her a few times because of her interest in Asian art. I do not know her well, but I've always found her to be polite and respectful." He paused for a moment and then began to clear the table of the dessert dishes as he spoke. "Dr. Nakasone, however, I knew very well. He was an excellent physician and a kind, intelligent, and refined man. I know nothing about his life in Japan, but he was colored by a kind of sadness. It was a twist of fate that brought the two of them together—Mrs. Morrison and the Japanese doctor. There was an accident, you see. It was in the country somewhere near Kahuku—I don't know exactly where—but the Morrisons and their crowd were fooling around at someone's country estate with horses and a particular horse that wasn't quite broken. They had been drinking and daring each other to ride it. Apparently, Tamara took the dare and mounted the horse, which quickly proved to be too much for her, and the horse took off with her hanging on. I don't know how long it ran or how far, but at some point, it ran close to a fence, where a sharp, narrow piece of wood stuck out, and the piece of wood pierced right through Mrs. Morrison's leg, snapping off from the fence, as the horse flew by. Dr. Nakasone and his son happened to be in the neighborhood. After visiting one of his patients, the doctor was treating his son to a walk on the beach when the wild horse and its rider came charging toward them. The horse reared and threw her off onto the sand. The doctor could see she was badly hurt and sent his son for help. He had no idea who she was or where she had come from, but with the help of his friends, he got her to a small plantation hospital nearby. And through his skill, he was able to save her life and her leg. Of course, she was very grateful to him, and that was the beginning of a very close relationship."

"Would you say it was very, very close?" Mina asked in a way that left no room for interpretation.

Uncle Wing nodded. "I would guess they were very, very quietly in love."

"And Mr. Morrison? Did he know?"

Uncle Wing was quiet again for a minute and then said. "Mr. Morrison is where the speculation and hearsay come into play."

Mina frowned at him and looked bewildered.

"By this time, they had two children, and the hearsay is that he went off women. That is, that he 'discovered' he preferred other kinds of relationships. I only know this because he was said to pursue his other interests here in Chinatown. They were primarily Asian— Japanese or Chinese—often somewhat younger than himself. I make no judgment about it, and I trust you will treat this information with the utmost discretion."

"Of course I will," she said.

"In other ways, he was a devoted partner to his wife. When she became interested in Asian art, he did everything he could to see that she acquired the pieces she wanted. Perhaps he felt he had to make up for his abandonment of her as a true wife—whatever their arrangement was, it was clear that he was a loyal friend to her. He let her spend money and helped her in any way he could to further her art collection. As to her relationship with the doctor, she was heartbroken when he died. Because of my friendship with Nakasone, I can say no more, only that she was very good to him and to Akira. She helped the doctor plan his son's education very much to his advantage, and while her real children have married and moved away, she and Akira have common interests, a common loss, and have remained very close."

Mina had been listening, spellbound to Uncle Wing's story. "Isn't it amazing," she said, "how things can be so different from the way they appear?"

# 16

# FRIDAY, DECEMBER 13

I**T WAS JUST** past four in the afternoon when Mina pulled her Packard into the Kama'āina Club grounds and walked from the parking lot toward the main entrance. The remnants of a recent rainsquall dripped unhurriedly from the red tiled roof of the single-story Mediterranean building with its spotless whitewashed walls. She strolled past the Moorish fountain at the entry, through the archway of bougainvillea vines that framed the open door, and into the lobby with its carpets, sofas, tasteful artwork, and fresh flower arrangements that she now recognized as the work of Akira Naka-sone. She made her way toward the back to the terrace and outside bar that overlooked a manicured garden and the tennis courts beyond. Today, because of the rain, there was no laughter and no sound of tennis balls against racquet and court drifting across the garden. She saw Raymond sitting alone at a round table, with a plate of cheese and crackers in front of him and a beer. The jacket of his white linen suit was draped over the back of his chair, and he had rolled his white shirtsleeves up to the elbow. He was staring out at the lawn, lost in thought and smoking a cigarette in a short holder, but he jumped to his feet when he saw her approaching.

"Sorry I'm late," Mina said as she sat down.

"I've gotten quite used to your Hawaiian time," he said as he signaled the waiter. "What would you like to drink?"

"An iced tea would be perfect!" she said.

"One iced tea for the lady," Raymond said to the waiter.

"This shouldn't take much of your time," she said as she took out a notebook and a pencil. "I see you listed several shows that you had on the East Coast, but I was wondering if you had any formal training in photography?"

"While I attended Columbia University in New York, I was fortunate to study photography with Clarence H. White. Have you heard of him?"

"Yes," she replied, "he's quite well known."

"I was very lucky," Raymond said. He took a sip of beer and stared off in the direction of the tennis courts.

"And are there any photographers you admire?"

He looked back at her. "Well, everyone admires Ansel Adams, don't they? And this woman Dorothy Lange, the photo journalist."

"She went to Columbia too. Did you know her there?"

"No, unfortunately we weren't there at the same time. I would have liked to meet her."

"And what are your preferred subjects?"

"Landscapes and portraits," he answered. "You'll see that in the show, of course."

"And the island landscape? What do you think of it?"

"It's most intriguing to me. Especially the way the light hits the mountains. The moods here change so frequently and so vividly."

"I suppose you must be interested in the various ethnic groups in the islands, being fond of portraits."

"Of course," he said as he reached for a cracker with some cheese and moved the plate toward her. "Please, help yourself."

Mina's iced tea had arrived, and she stirred some sugar into it and then took a sip. She could see that any further questions would result in similar useless and boring answers, so she decided to give up and change the subject, hoping he might be willing to gossip.

"How is your leg doing?" she asked.

"Oh, very well, thanks. It's come along nicely."

"And Marguerite? She was very rattled the other day."

He shook his head. "Marguerite is a very sensitive person. These deaths, my being shot—it's made her anxious and afraid."

"Was she a particular friend of Tilda or Ari?"

"Tilda preferred men, there's no question about that. She didn't have many women friends, but Marguerite was very fond of Ari and felt more than a little simpatico on account of her Jewish relatives."

"I hope they're all safe in Switzerland," Mina said as she pushed the pineapple slice in the tea around with her straw.

He smiled. "They are."

"How's Eva doing?"

He sighed. "I wish she would go to the university. She's very intelligent, and I think she's wasting her time working in that beauty shop. I suppose she'll get married one day, but until a girl is married, I think it's better to stay in school. She'll meet young men her age who are more ambitious about life."

"Tamara said she was meeting you for dinner here tonight," Mina said.

"Oh, yes, you're more than welcome to join us," he offered politely.

Mina smiled. "Thanks very much, but I've promised to meet Ned here for a drink. He's meeting a friend for dinner too, but I can't stay. I have some work that needs to get done."

"Perhaps some other time," he said.

"Perhaps," Mina said, and just as she was wishing she had an excuse to leave the table before she had to make any more small talk, she saw Ned walk out onto the veranda. He smiled at her, and it felt as if sunlight had entered a dark room. In no time, he was at her side, and she stood up quickly, thanked Raymond for the interview, and herded Ned inside.

She whispered to him as they walked away. "Let's go inside where we can be alone."

They walked across the lobby to the inside bar that adjoined the formal dining room.

"I guess Mr. Morgan was exceedingly charming," Ned said as they sat down.

Mina laughed. "He's got to be one of the most boring men on the island. And," she added, "I think his photography is boring and uninspired to boot. I don't know what Tamara sees in him other than that he's had shows in some prestigious galleries."

Ned shrugged. "It's a common occurrence in the arts. Just because you have a production at a well-known theatre doesn't mean you can actually write a good play, but it impresses people who depend on other people's opinions—like that story."

"What story?"

" 'The Emperor's New Clothes.' It happens in London and New York as well."

Mina sighed. "All you have to say in Honolulu is 'London' or 'New York,' and everyone would agree that the naked man was the best dresser in town."

"It's a mind-set of people living in the colonies."

She frowned. "Living in the colonies?"

He laughed. "Nobody here realizes it, but they all behave like they're living in one of the British colonies, only it's American. Perhaps you have to be an outsider to see it."

Mina looked taken aback and couldn't say anything.

"I'm sorry, darling," he said when he saw her reaction. "I shouldn't have said it. I didn't mean to make you angry."

She was quiet for a minute and then said, "I'm not angry. It's just that I never thought about it that way—all the phony stuff that can go on here. No one has ever pointed it out so bluntly."

"It's only that I've seen it before," he said gently.

"Well, thanks, Mr. Playwright, now I really do need a drink."

They waved down a waiter and ordered their drinks, and when Mina saw that sashimi was on the pupu menu, she ordered that too and some dry boiled peanuts. Their drinks and pupus arrived in no time, and Mina immediately began mixing the hot mustard and shoyu together for the sashimi.

"So Todd agreed to meet you here for dinner?" she asked.

"He did."

"And how did you get him to do that?" she asked as she took a piece of raw fish with her chopsticks and dipped it in the shoyu mixture. "He can't stand this place."

"I told him that I had something to tell him about a case I happen to be working on that might interest him." Ned used his own chopsticks to take a piece of fish.

She gave him a cautious look. "You mean you're going to tell him everything?"

"I am going to tell him everything. I don't know what Nigel would say if he found out, but I'm doing it anyway because I think it's in everyone's best interest. And if Nigel doesn't like it, he can let me go." Ned chuckled. "Or dock my pay stub."

"I'd like to see the look on Todd's face when you tell him," she said with a smile.

He sipped his gin and tonic. "I will describe it to you in minute detail this evening."

"While you're talking, just remember to keep an eye on Tamara. If she leaves before seven thirty, you have to warn me. You have the directions to the house from here, don't you?"

"Yes, of course," he said impatiently, "but so many things could go wrong with your plan."

"Like what?"

"If she decided to jump up and leave well before your appointed time, how could I explain to Todd, take care of our bill, and manage to get to the car before she gets to hers?"

"Well," Mina began, "before I leave, I will go with you to the dining room, introduce you to the maitre d', Mr. Kent, sign a blank chit for you, and tell him that you are my guest and that you may be called away suddenly. He knows me, so it won't be a problem."

"I just hope she's a very slow eater and nothing goes wrong. You realize, of course, that I might have to tell Todd what you're doing?"

"But don't do it unless you have to," she said as she picked up another piece of fish.

"And if I do," he added with a grin, "I'll also describe the look on his face in minute detail later this evening."

"Just remember," she said, "you drive by the house and honk the horn really loud three times."

Mina parked her Packard up the hill from Tamara Morrison's house where the road ended in a turnaround and there were no houses. It was already dark, but she wore a trench coat and wrapped her head in a scarf to be sure she would be hard to recognize. She dashed down the street and slipped quickly through the gate with the bell and into the courtyard of Tamara's house. Once away from the street, she took out her flashlight and checked her watch. It was six fifteen. She had waited until she saw Tamara pull into the Kama'āina Club before she drove as fast as she could up to Pacific Heights. She calculated that she had over an hour to get the job done. Rain was beginning to fall as she walked around the right side of the house, using the flashlight to make her way along a path of stepping-stones set in gray pebbles. She had just come around to the back door off the dining room and opened it, so thankful that no one in Honolulu locked their doors, when Jocks ran toward her from around the other side of the house, barking loudly. From her coat pocket, she pulled out a meaty bone and dropped it just outside the door. Jocks picked it up and ran off. There were lights on in the kitchen and one light on that looked like it might be in the foyer, but the rest of the house was dark.

She crept through the dining room, the living room, and up the stairs to Tamara's study, going straight to the door that led up to the attic. The attic stairs were surprisingly wide, and she found a light switch at their base. As she closed the door, she decided to take a chance and turn on the light. At the top of the stairs, she made a quick survey for windows but saw that there were only two small windows, both thickly curtained. The light from the stairwell dimly illuminated the room—with just enough light to see but not enough to attract any attention from the street. She took a deep breath and looked around. The large attic was set up like a storage room in an art museum, and it took her a moment to realize that the air in the attic was much cooler than it should have been. She surmised that somewhere there was a unit to cool the air. They were unusual in the islands but not unheard of in the homes of wealthier residents. Tamara must have had one set up to protect her artwork. There were wooden shelves with slots where canvases were stored and many large drawers, which when opened revealed *ukiyo-e* prints. She was not a great aficionado, but she knew enough to recognize some of the names—Utamaro, Hokusai, Hiroshige. It looked like there were hundreds of them. There were metal shelves that stored scrolls on silk and delicate rice paper, porcelain bowls and figurines, and beautiful lacquered boxes. The size of the collection was overwhelming, and she couldn't even begin to guess how much time and money had been poured into acquiring all of these objets d'art. Certainly, the Morrisons could not have done this without considerable help.

At the far end of the room, up against a wall, Mina found several filing drawers. She opened them all and made a quick survey. They contained folders about art purchases and included personal correspondence—between Tamara's husband and different Japanese people. Mina decided to start with the year of Mr. Morrison's death and work her way back. She settled down on the floor and used her flashlight for better reading, and by a glance at the first folder, she could tell that the reading would be very interesting.

Even though the dining room of the Kama'āina Club was at least half full, there was a discreet quiet and a sense of privacy. Ned had waited with Todd in the bar until Tamara and the Morgans were seated, and then he made sure that he asked for a table that kept them in full view. Tamara had given him a friendly wave when he and Todd Forrest walked into the dining room, and they had stopped to say a brief hello. He and Todd ordered their dinner, and as they ate, Ned proceeded to tell Todd about his own investigation and how it might relate to the murders. Almost an hour had gone by, and if Tamara and the Morgans were going to have coffee and dessert, the timing should work out perfectly.

"It seems unbelievable," Todd said as he cut into the last of his steak.

"I know," Ned agreed.

"Taking into consideration everything you've just told me, it seems we have a lot of people with motive and opportunity and almost zero evidence. How's the fish?"

"It's overdone, actually," Ned said, "but it's still not bad."

"I couldn't prove it, but of course the murders and the espionage must be connected."

Ned poked his fork at the cooked vegetables on his plate. "I'm hoping I could see those folders Mina found that belonged to Ari Schoner."

Todd finished his steak, put down his fork and knife, and leaned back in his chair. "There's something I haven't told Mina, because I wasn't sure what it meant, but now it makes sense."

Ned put down his cutlery in the four o'clock position, pushed his plate a few inches away, and said, "What's that?"

"We recovered the bullets from the shooting at that arty place on Black Point. One of them we dug out of the floor. It went right through Morgan's leg." Todd glanced across the dining room at Raymond Morgan, who was listening intently to something Tamara Morrison was saying. "The other one was in Schoner's chest. Anyway, the guy at ballistics said they were an odd caliber—7.65—and he thinks they could be German. It's the kind of ammo they use in the older Lugers. He's checking on it."

"Not the kind of information you would want to be made public."

"No, sir."

"Maybe we should be looking for someone with a Luger."

Todd reached for a toothpick from the glass container in the middle of the table. "Right. Too bad we can't just ask for warrants and search through everyone's house."

Ned watched as Raymond Morgan left the table. "I hate to tell you," he said, keeping an eye on Tamara's table, "but we've proceeded without official warrants."

"Oh, cripes." Todd took the toothpick out of his mouth. "I'm not sure I want to hear this. Hey, why are you watching those people?"

Ned laughed. "Is it obvious?"

"Only to a seasoned flatfoot," Todd replied.

Raymond Morgan had returned to the table. He didn't sit down but said something to his wife and Tamara. Next, Marguerite Morgan stood up, and the couple left Tamara sitting there. Tamara waved for the waiter and was obviously calling for the check, which to Ned's horror, the waiter produced instantly.

"We have to go," Ned said to Todd. "Stand up slowly and start walking out with me."

Todd frowned. "Hell's bells, I guess I better not even ask why."

Ned smiled pleasantly. "I'll tell you in the car. Just get your bum out of the chair now, Detective."

"I hate to alarm you, but we're running out on the check," Todd whispered.

"A word to the maitre d', and it will all be taken care of," Ned said just before he stopped to speak to Mr. Kent.

When they were in the lobby, Ned told Todd to get his car started and to wait out front for him. As soon as Todd was out the door, Ned spotted Tamara walking out of the dining room. He checked his watch. It was only five minutes after seven.

"Tamara, it was lovely to see you this evening," Ned said in his most charming manner. "Did you enjoy your dinner?"

"Barely," she said. "Ray and Marguerite got a call from Eva. Apparently their son has a fever and threw up, and Eva was beside herself. So of course Marguerite felt they should go right home."

"It's a shame your dinner was spoiled."

"Oh, it wasn't spoiled," Tamara assured him. "I just didn't get to eat dessert, which I don't really need anyway."

"Are you sure? We could have an after-dinner drink in the bar, and you could order dessert."

"Oh, thank you, Ned," she said, "that's very sweet of you, but I actually have some work I really want to get done at home. But it's so nice of you to ask. I've already asked Mr. Kent to call for my car, so it should be out in front in just a minute."

"Well, I'll be saying good night then," he said and walked quickly out toward the door.

Outside, Todd was waiting in the car with the motor running. As Ned jumped in and they pulled away, he could see Tamara coming out of the club and the parking attendant holding open her car door for her.

"Get up to Pacific Heights as fast as you can," Ned said.

"What's going on, Ned?"

"Just drive as fast as you can, old bean," Ned replied.

Todd accelerated the car. "Okay," he said, "but what the hell is going on?"

"Mina is in Tamara's house, looking for evidence, and we have to warn her that Tamara is on her way home."

Even in the dark, Ned could see Todd's face turn red. "Of course, breaking and entering! I should have guessed! And just how are we going to warn her without breaking and entering ourselves, may I ask?"

"We're going to drive by the house and sound the horn as loud as we can three times."

"Great," Todd said in a sardonic tone, "then the neighbors can all see us get arrested."

"We won't get arrested," Ned said, "but your sister-in-law might."

"My sister-in-law? Oh, you mean your fiancée? Is that who you mean?"

"You Americans are extremely excitable, aren't you?"

"Is that her behind us?" Todd looked in the rearview mirror and nearly floored the accelerator. "That old lady is driving like a demon."

Thoroughly engrossed in reading another letter in one of the folders, Mina was jolted back to reality by the sound of three sharp horn blasts. She looked at her watch. It was seven twenty. She jumped up, shoved the folder back in the file, and ran to turn off the light, just as she heard Tamara's car pull in the garage. She opened the attic door to run down the stairs, but halfway down toward the living room, she heard Tamara enter the kitchen. And realizing it was too late, she retreated back to the attic stairwell. She put her ear to the door and heard Jocks running up to the study, followed by Tamara's footsteps. She closed her eyes and tried to keep very still as she broke into a cold sweat. She could hear Jocks sniffing around the bottom of the attic door.

"Come here, you silly dog," she heard Tamara say. "Mommy has a treat for you."

Jocks pattered away from the door. Mina heard a sound like a chair being pulled out and then the radio being turned on. Oh, God, she thought, she's sitting down to work, and I could be trapped here for hours. She tried to pretend she was a stone statue or a rock or a brick wall, something hard and silent and immovable, and she couldn't tell how long she sat there, frozen in place in the dark, before she heard the sound of the chair move and Tamara's footsteps pass just outside the door. She held her breath until she heard the door to the bathroom open, and as soon as she heard it close, she counted silently to three as she took off her shoes, opened the attic door, and as quietly as she could, tiptoed down the stairs. In her peripheral consciousness, she registered Jocks giving a halfhearted bark, but he instantly returned to chewing something on the floor. She sprinted through the living room and dining room, managing to miraculously avoid bumping any furniture, and when she made it out the back door, she flicked on her flashlight, flew around the house, over the stepping-stones on the side path, and through the front courtyard, and slipped out the gate that she had left ajar when she entered. It wasn't until she was running up the street toward her car that she realized it was pouring rain.

She recognized Todd's car parked just behind hers. She waved at Ned, got in her own car, put it in neutral, and released the brake, steering the car away from the curb and allowing it to silently coast downhill. When she was well away from the house, she pulled over and waited for Todd and Ned, who were just behind her. Ned got out of the car and came toward her as she rolled down the window.

"Everything all right?" His voice was calm but full of concern.

"Can we go to the Harbor Grill?" she asked. "I need a warm drink and some food."

His hand reached to caress her cheek. "I'll have to get my car first from the club," he said, "but then I'll be right there."

"Yes, well, I need to get away from here, now."

"Righto," he said, giving her a quick kiss, "on your way."

Mina was seated with a steaming cup of tea and eating beef stew and rice when Ned and Todd walked into the Harbor Grill. Ned and Todd sat down and ordered dessert and coffee, and both sat there politely waiting for her to finish her stew. She polished off the food in no time, put down her fork, took a sip of tea, and said, "That was cutting it pretty damn close. What happened?"

"All was well," Ned began, "until the Morgans got a phone call about their son being sick and decided to leave right away. I tried unsuccessfully to delay Tamara, so we had to rush up to warn you. Did she see you at all?"

Mina shook her head. "Nope," she said, "but I'm sure the dog recognized me."

Todd looked supremely irritated. "Why did you pull such a foolish stunt?"

Mina looked at him, unsurprised by his admonition. "You won't call it a stunt when you hear what I found out."

"And what exactly did you find out?" Todd asked.

The waitress appeared with three pieces of apple pie à la mode and the check, and everyone fell silent until she left.

"First of all," Mina said, "with the stash of artwork and objects she has up in her attic, she could open a museum. They look mostly Japanese, but I can't really tell because I'm no expert. But then I found these files—her husband's files—with records of all the purchases, all the correspondence, and everything. It looks like he used his influence and money to further Japanese business interests in the East, and in exchange, they got big help acquiring all kinds of stuff. Some of the things were 'gifts' from various grateful associates. He was chummy and corresponding with all kinds of people—business tycoons, diplomats, and lots of military types. He was giving advice, helping people to cut deals, and sometimes applying pressure to help them get what they wanted."

"Was there any evidence that he was passing information?" Ned asked.

"Not in anything I saw," Mina answered, "but I didn't have time to see everything." She ate a spoonful of vanilla ice cream. "I can tell you this, though: he certainly had friends that might ask for it."

"There's nothing illegal in what he was doing," Todd commented, "unless he was knowingly buying stolen goods, but even then, if no one in Japan complained, there's nothing we could do about it. Did you find customs papers?"

"Yes," she said, "it looked like he declared everything. Although it would be difficult to know if the purchase price on his receipts were real. It would be easy enough to have his friends fix that up."

"It's possible that he was trading information too," Ned said, "and that his wife is continuing to do so for the same kinds of favors."

"Highly possible," Mina agreed.

"More motive and opportunity without real evidence," Todd added.

"There is one more thing," Mina said. "I'm not sure how relevant it is."

"What is it?" Todd asked.

"I found a stash of letters of another sort," Mina said. "They were in a box in the back of one of the file drawers. They were love letters written to Mr. Morrison from another man. There were pictures too. I recognized the name from some of the business letters. He was a pretty high-ranking Japanese military official."

Todd shook his head. "That's just ducky. I wonder if the wife knew about it."

"According to one of Mina's sources," Ned said, "she had an outside interest of her own."

"Look, okay, so you found some valuable information," Todd said. "But what was the risk? I just don't like it at all. What if she is a spy and connected to the murders. You could have ended up dead."

Mina folded her arms, sat back, and looked at Todd. "Ned took a similar risk just the other day, didn't you, Ned? And not only that, but he did it while people were only a few steps away, and he found out a lot."

"That's different," Todd said.

"Because I'm a woman?" Mina retorted.

"Yes," Todd answered back with conviction, "because you're a woman."

A mischievous grin swept over Mina's face. "I'm going to tell my sister you said that. Then you'll be sorry."

# 17

# SATURDAY, DECEMBER 14

**R**EGGIE WAS STILL in his pajamas watching Ned and Nigel pack up their gear. "Oh, that's right," he said. "Today is your sword-fighting show."

"That's right," said Nigel, "but we also want to know what happened yesterday when you went with Akira to the embassy."

"I'm sorry to say it, but he could be the one." Reggie yawned and had a sip from his steaming coffee cup.

"I gather you like the chap, then?" Ned asked as he folded a pair of white pants and placed them under his face mask.

"Yeah, I guess I do," Reggie said, sounding very disappointed. "He's odd but very nice and encouraging. He thinks I have real talent."

Nigel laughed. "You could have a second career arranging flowers."

"Don't laugh," Reggie fired back. "There's way more to this *ikebana* stuff than you could ever imagine. You should try it, and you'd see what I mean."

Nigel grinned. "I think I'll leave it to you, thanks."

"He's right, Nigel," Ned said. "It's a highly developed art form, and the people who are good at it are well respected in Japan, and here too, I imagine."

"We need to know what happened yesterday," Nigel said, changing the subject as he sat down at the table and poured himself a cup of coffee. "Everything that happened. We have some time before we have to leave."

Ned had finished putting his things together and sat down too. He opened a bakery box of glazed doughnuts before he helped himself to coffee.

"Well," Reggie began as he immediately reached for a doughnut, "I guess that Molly woman usually helps him, but she had to do something this Friday. So anyway, I met him at his shop. He had all his stuff organized in boxes. He's very organized. I helped him load it into his delivery truck, and we headed for the embassy. We get there and go in with the first load of boxes, and we unload everything onto a table on the porch of the embassy residence. Then he takes me around and shows me where the old arrangements are—there's three of them: one in the embassy office, in that front building right when you walk in; another in the embassy residence, right when you go in the door in the big living room or whatever you call it; and the last one, upstairs in the private sitting room. The last one is much smaller than the other two. Akira asks me to take them apart, starting with the one in the office. He tells me what things to save so that he can use them again, and then he says he has to meet with the ambassador and his wife to discuss the following week's plan. He's always a week ahead, see. Then he says something to the housekeeper—they're talking Japanese, so I can't understand—and he disappears upstairs. Oh, yeah, and he takes this briefcase with him. I go to the office place first, take down the arrangement, put the vase in a box, do everything there, and then go back and start in on the big one in the downstairs of the residence. While I'm doing that, that guy in the picture, the one Alika spotted, is sitting out on the veranda with his coffee, polishing up his golf clubs. He speaks English pretty well and starts up a conversation with me while I'm taking down the arrangement. His name is Takeo Tadashi, but he tells me to call him Jimmy. He laughs and says all his American friends call him Jimmy. He says he's in the diplomatic service, and that's all he tells me about what he does. He seems happy when I tell him I'm just a student at the university, and he asks me if I play golf. I say yes, and I'm not lying to him because I like to play—and I'm not bad, if I do say so myself. So then he invites me to play golf with him this afternoon."

"And you said?" Nigel asked.

"Of course I said yes," Reggie answered. "I acted like an excited college student who was eager to make new friends."

"This Jimmy fellow is staying there, I presume?" Nigel asked. "Did he say how long?"

"I'm sure he's staying there," Reggie nodded. "I'd bet anything he's stayed there before too. He showed me the lawn in the back where he sets up his putting green. They keep the grass trimmed for him, just so. The only problem was where to tell him to pick me and my golf clubs up."

"What did you do?" Ned asked.

"I picked a place at the university. I'll just park my car in another place and walk over there. I should act poor and hungry, and maybe he'll buy me dinner or something."

"Well done, Reggie," Nigel said as he stood up. "See what else you can find out about him this afternoon. We've got to be off now."

Ned gave Reggie a smile as he picked up his gear. "For our sword-fighting show."

Mina and Nyla sat in the garden at the Pearl Harbor Yacht Club on a curved marble bench that was behind a tall, semicircular hedge of mock orange. In front of the bench was a small lily pond surrounded by a stone inlay that extended well beyond the pond in a neat rectangle. It was an area, Mina remembered, that was used for outdoor picnics and other events. She and Nyla had driven out to see the fencing demonstration and had arrived a bit early. While Nigel and Ned were setting up and doing their warm-up, she and her sister had taken a lazy stroll and come to rest at this pleasant spot. The day was sunny and still.

"It's a shame Todd couldn't come," Mina said as she watched the goldfish swimming around in the clear water of the pond.

"A policeman's work is never done." Nyla sighed. "I just hope he finds some time to see his child grow up."

"I was thinking, if you're not too tired, we could stop downtown on the way home. I want to pick something up from Liberty House."

"Only if we can eat lunch at the Harbor Grill," her sister said.

"I was counting on it."

"I'm sorry we're not going to the ranch for Christmas. I hope its not spoiling things for you."

"Don't be silly," Mina assured her. "There's going to be so many more Christmases at the ranch—missing one won't matter. What matters is that you and the baby are safe and healthy."

Nyla frowned. "But really, Mina, how dangerous could an overnight ride on a cattle boat be?"

"It's probably not dangerous at all, but can you imagine the fuss Grandma Hannah and Dad would make? Not to mention your husband." Mina shook her head. "It wouldn't be worth all the grief you'd have to put up with. Besides, I'm looking forward to spending Christmas in Honolulu for a change. We may not get to do it for another umpteen years."

"I was surprised that you wanted to get married at the ranch," Nyla said, fingering the heart-shaped locket on her necklace and watching for her sister's reaction.

"Why? Because Len and I lived there after we were married?"

"Something along those lines."

"You're the only one who knows that I wasn't happy with Len. Trying to be the kind of wife he expected me to be nearly drove me crazy."

"Maybe Dad and Grandma Hannah might have guessed, even though they don't say."

"Then, when he died in the accident, I felt even worse, and ever since then, the ranch hasn't been the same for me. Even though that whole episode was a short part of my life, the ranch hasn't been the place I loved when we were kids. I thought this might change things."

"I hope it will."

"And the chapel is only a couple of years old. It wasn't there when . . . when Len and I were there."

"I guess we'll just have to make this wedding break the bad spell."

"Ned's already cabled his mother and heard back that she and his grandfather *will* be coming."

Nyla had found some pebbles to throw in the pond. "How about his grandparents in Sāmoa? I would love to see Tavaʻesina and George again."

"He hasn't heard from them yet," Mina said, "but I'm sure they'll come." Mina was quiet for a moment. "I called Len's mother when Ned and I first got engaged. I wanted to tell her myself before she heard it from anyone else."

"How did Mrs. Bradley take it?"

"Did I ever tell you how miffed she was when I took my maiden name back after Len died?" Mina laughed. "But then, when I started writing for the paper, she was relieved that their family name wasn't associated with some of the things I wrote."

"To tell you the truth," Nyla said, "I always thought she was stuck up . . . for nothing."

"Anyway," Mina continued, "when I told her I was going to get married again, there was this big pause, and she said something like, 'Don't you think it's a little soon for that?' And I said, no, it had been three, almost four years, and I wasn't getting any younger."

Nyla laughed. "You said that to her? What did she say?"

"What could she say? She mumbled something about how she was sure Len would want me to be happy, she congratulated me—very insincerely—and then said good-bye. She didn't even ask who I was marrying."

"Well," Nyla said, "you did your duty, and you can't help it if she's a cow."

The two sisters were laughing, but when they heard angry voices approaching from the other side of the hedge, they immediately became quiet. At first they couldn't hear exactly what was being said, but as the couple approached the other side of the hedge, their voices became clear.

"Don't you just walk away from me when I'm talking to you." It was a woman's voice, and Mina was pretty sure it was Molly Rivers.

"You're such a nag, Molly. I'm sick of it." Mina definitely recognized Desmond Rivers.

"Oh, you're sick of it, are you? Well, I'm sick of you. First you're screwing that cheap waitress at the Kamaʻāina Club, and then it's Tilda, right in our own backyard."

"And do you know why? It's because I have to live with a cold fish."

"You're such a pig, Desmond. I could kill you."

There was the sound of a hard slap. Mina waited a few seconds before she stood up and peered around the hedge to see Molly running toward the parking lot and Desmond sauntering into the clubhouse. Neither of them looked back.

"Is the happy couple gone?" asked Nyla.

"Both gone their separate ways."

"There seems to be something extremely poisonous about that artists group," Nyla commented. "I've met Molly and Desmond at a cocktail party or two, and you would never guess they could go at it like that."

"You would if you got to know them better. It's just about time for the fencing. Let's walk over there."

Mina sat next to Nyla on the very end of the semicircle of chairs that curved around the length of the pavilion. The glass doors were wide open and let in the fresh air. She hoped no one, even Nyla, had seen her surreptitiously drop her name on a folded piece of paper into the bowl labeled "experienced fencers" near one of the doors. Every chair was quickly filled, and late arrivals were standing behind the row of chairs. A drone of conversation filled the room as Ned and Nigel finished putting on their gear and sorting out the foils, épées, and sabres, but Mina sat silently taking in the faces in the audience and watching her sister review her Christmas list. Christian Hollister had walked in and was standing on the opposite end of the room. With his straight blond hair and wire-rimmed glasses, he always looked like a tall, East Coast Yankee, even though he had been born and raised in the islands. Tamara had brought Akira with her, and Molly was sitting with them—far away from Desmond, who was talking to Christian Hollister like they were old chums. She could tell Chris didn't like him. Bill Hitchins had given up his chair to April Fraser, who appeared to be there by herself. Mina was surprised to see her and gave her a friendly wave, but a few minutes later, when scruffy Andrew Halpern appeared in the doorway, she understood Appy's presence. Mina surveyed the crowd, thinking that someone sitting here was very likely a murderer or a willing accomplice.

Ned and Nigel were about to begin, as a few more spectators straggled in—Louis Goldburn and Johnny Knight were among them. Nigel began by explaining something about classical fencing. He talked about the history of fencing and dueling and how the modern fencing movement now used an electronic scoring device for the épée. He had a lot to say about fencing as an elegant practice that developed the mind, body, and character of those who practiced it. He also announced that those who had experience fencing could drop their names in a bowl by the door, and hopefully he and Ned could do a teaching and coaching demonstration with people from the audience.

Nyla leaned toward Mina. "Don't think I didn't see you drop your name in that bowl," she whispered. "And don't think I don't remember how you were the female champion at all those fencing tournaments at that club you used to belong to."

Mina smiled. "College was a million years ago. I hope I haven't lost my touch."

"You mean your touché."

Nigel went on to show and talk about the three kinds of swords they were using—the foil, the épée, and the sabre—and then spoke about the rules of fencing. Afterwards, he and Ned moved right into doing demonstrations with each sword type. They would first do a mock match very slowly while Nigel explained the moves, and then they would do it at a normal pace. They ended with an unrehearsed match of two out of three touches. Just as they had lowered their masks and begun, Raymond Morgan and his daughter, Eva, entered. Raymond looked around the room, as if checking to see who was there. Raymond watched for a short time, and then, after giving what looked like a minor scolding to his daughter, turned around and left. Poor Eva, Mina thought. She was going to have to work very hard to ever get away from home.

The sound of the épée blades ringing out as they struck together resonated in Mina, and she found herself yearning to pick up a sword.

She wondered how many other names were in the bowl, and if her name were picked, she wondered if Nigel would give her a chance. There were men who thought women fencers were a joke, and she hoped that Nigel wasn't one of them. She wondered now if putting her name in the bowl was a mistake, but as she watched Ned and Nigel carefully, she decided that with practice, she could be up to their standard. She certainly was at least that good, if not better, in her college days. The demonstrations seemed to fly by in no time, and before she knew it, Nigel had retrieved the bowl with the names in it.

"Well," Nigel began, "it looks like there are only two names in here. One of them," he said as unfolded the first paper, "is Christian Hollister." Nigel looked at the second paper and grinned at Ned. "And the other one is Mina Beckwith."

A ripple of laughter spread through the audience, but Mina did not flinch or betray the least bit of embarrassment. Eva Morgan gave Mina a thumbs-up. Nigel carried on unaffected by the turn of events. "Would our volunteers step forward and tell us about their fencing experience?"

Both Christian and Mina said that they were on teams in college but had not fenced since then. Nigel took the opportunity to remind the gathering that women's foil competition had been part of the Olympic Games since 1924. He said he would more than welcome female students and that although the art of fencing did require some strength and stamina, it had nothing to do with brute strength. Fencing required good timing, balance, grace, quick wits, and concentration—things every woman was capable of. He went on to say his own fencing master ranked his students, both male and female, by skill alone, and though his master's conduct was considered outlandish by many people, Nigel thought him to be ahead of his time. No doubt, Nigel added, his teacher's wife, an excellent fencer in her own right, was no small influence in opening their school so equally to women. While he was talking, Ned gave Christian and Mina each a white jacket and breeches, a mask, and a fencing glove. Fortunately, Nigel had quite a collection of gloves, so Mina was able to find one that fit her. Nigel designated himself as Christian's "coach" and said that Ned should coach his fiancée, as it would be good practice to try and get his future wife to listen to him. The remark brought the expected twitters of laughter.

"You're full of surprises, aren't you?" Ned said to Mina as he helped her to secure her jacket. They were standing to the side and speaking quietly.

"It's far better than being a bore," she answered.

Ned gave her a small, suspicious smile. "Just so I'm not too surprised, how good were you?"

Her face fell. "I've never told anyone this, but my coach wanted me to stay and train after college and try for the 1932 Olympics."

"Why didn't you?" Ned asked in amazement.

"My mother was sick, and I needed to be with her."

"It's a shame you had to give up the chance."

"You can't tell anyone, Ned," she said seriously. "Especially anyone in my family. I don't want them to add any more sadness to the memory of that time. And I don't want anyone to think I made some big sacrifice either, because I would have walked away from anything to be with my mother."

"I suppose you must have some ribbons and trophies hiding somewhere."

"I took first place in almost every tournament I entered. Of course, in the tournaments my opponents were strictly women, but we practiced a lot with the men's team, and I did pretty well if I do say so myself."

"Good," Ned said. "I'd love to see you take Christian Hollister's ego down a few pegs in public."

She winked. "I'll do my best for you, darling."

Nigel then announced that he would be coaching Christian outside for about fifteen or twenty minutes, and Ned would be working with Mina in the pavilion, and in about half an hour, they would have a match. People were free to wander back and forth to watch or to take a break and return for the match. But before they broke up, he said he would flip a coin, and either Christian or Mina would then decide which kind of swords they would use.

"There's no need for a coin," Christian Hollister said, smiling. "I'm perfectly happy to leave the choice up to my most worthy opponent."

Mina looked at him and tilted her head ever so slightly. "In that case, I'll choose the épée."

For the next twenty minutes, Mina worked with Ned, while Nigel worked out on the lawn with Christian. Ned ran her quickly through some standard moves. At first, her responses were stiff, but after ten minutes or so, she felt things coming back of their own accord, as if her body had not forgotten the moves that had slipped out of her mind. She and Ned ended with a few practice matches, one of which she won.

"Mina has wonderful balance and superb footwork," Ned said out loud so that those who were watching could hear. "She also wastes no space and energy in the way she moves her blade. You don't need big, hacking movements in fencing. You need speed with grace. Her concentration may be a bit rusty because she hasn't fenced in years, but if her opponent hasn't either, he had better be very careful. We'll gather back here in ten minutes."

Mina and Ned then stepped aside to speak privately.

"So how was I really?" Mina asked.

"You're bloody good, Mina. We could do this together, and it would be great fun, don't you think?"

Her laughter revealed her exhilaration. "Right, we can settle all our marital arguments this way."

"Listen," he said in a very confidential tone, "I think Nigel is planning on going to a five-point win. I would let Mr. Hollister win the first one. It will make him feel overconfident, and then you can do your best to surprise him."

She gave him a sly smile. "How about if I let him take the first two?"

"You don't want to play it safe?"

"I'll decide after round one."

Soon everyone had returned. Mina was surprised that no one had left, and just before they got started, Johnny Knight came up to inform her that people were placing bets on who would win.

"And who are you betting on, Johnny?" she asked.

He grinned at her. "I'm backing a winner."

Nigel then gathered everyone together. "Mina," he announced, "has chosen the épée, the sword that was formerly used for settling matters of honor through a duel. If this were a real duel, any part of the body that was hit would be cut, and so with the épée, a strong defense is crucial. Unlike the foil, which has a limited strike area, with an épée, any touch on the body counts as a hit. The protective tips covering the points of the swords now have red dye on them so we can see when a hit is made. The first person to get five points will win. So, are our two swordsmen ready?"

Mina and Christian stepped up to salute Nigel and then saluted each other, and Nigel called, "*En garde.*" Mina and Christian put on their masks and assumed the fencing stance. Nigel then called out, "*Prêt,*" and then "*Allez,*" and the bout began. Christian launched an aggressive attack. Mina parried and made a halfhearted riposte, and Christian, encouraged by her apparent hesitancy, scored a hit. He took the second point too, and to the audience, it appeared that Mina was not up to the challenge of her male opponent.

Before the third bout started, Mina glanced at Ned through her mask and wondered if he could see her smiling at him. She confidently assumed her fencing stance, and when Nigel called "*Allez,*" she advanced on Christian with an *appel* that startled him and upset his already sloppy balance. She was easily able to score a hit. She effortlessly took the next two hits with quick and confident footwork that confused and disoriented his attention. The room had become as quiet as a night sky. She scored her fourth point with an impressive *fleche,* delivering the red mark to his rib area just as her front foot touched the ground, and she made her fifth point with a graceful lunge that left a red dot on his heart. The room stayed quiet for a few seconds as if everyone was stunned, and then there was a long and loud applause. Mina and Christian saluted the audience, and then Mina retreated to Ned and removed her mask.

"You're a formidable opponent, Miss Beckwith," Ned said before he gave her a kiss on the cheek.

Men and women were crowding around Nigel, and Mina could hear them asking when and where he was going to have his classes. As soon as she could, she made an escape to the locker room, where she took off the fencing clothes, washed her face, and tried to do something with her hair. She purposefully took a long time, hoping that most of the people would leave so she wouldn't have to talk to anyone. What she really wanted to do was to put the fencing gear back on and spend the rest of the morning practicing. When she did get back to the pavilion, Nigel and Ned were busy packing up.

"Mina," Nigel said as she walked into the room, "several women are asking if you're going to be one of the instructors in the fencing classes. That was very impressive."

"It was rusty," she said. "I was just lucky that he was rustier."

"If that's rusty," said Nigel, "I'd love to see polished."

"You will see polished," Ned chimed in. "I'm going to recruit Mina to keep us on our toes."

"I see you had a fan and supporter, before we even began," Nigel said.

"Who was that?" Mina asked.

"That lovely blonde girl who gave you the thumbs-up," he answered.

"Oh, Eva," Mina said, "Eva Morgan."

"I saw that she met a much older man on the lawn, and they went off together. Was he her husband or her father?" he asked.

Mina laughed. "That's her father, Raymond."

Nigel laughed too. "That's good. For a moment, I was feeling sorry for her."

"Didn't you meet the Morgans at the luncheon, when we were here before?"

Nigel shook his head. "No, I must have missed them."

"He's a photographer, one of the artists in the exhibition."

"She came up to me afterwards," Nigel explained. "She was asking all kinds of questions about taking a class, and she seemed like a lovely girl."

"She is, and I think her father is having trouble with her growing up," Mina said as she scanned the room. "Hey, where did my sister run off to?" Mina asked.

"She went over to the clubhouse with Johnny," Ned said. "She wants you to meet her there."

Mina walked over to Ned and kissed his cheek. "Thanks for coaching me, Ned. I'll see you this evening. Nyla and I are going to have a sisterly day."

Nigel smiled. "It sounds like they plan to get into trouble, Ned."

Ned gave a nod of agreement. "They've been getting into trouble since they were tadpoles."

As Mina strolled across the lawn, heading toward the clubhouse, enjoying the shadows that the palm trees cast over the grass, Christian Hollister walked up behind her.

"Mina," he said, "could I talk to you for a moment? Great fencing, by the way."

"Thanks," she said, surprised that the irritation she had felt towards him for several months was now completely absent.

"I wanted to talk to you," he began slowly, "about coming back to the paper. I know we don't see eye to eye on a lot of things, but we need you. Our readers need you. You can write about things that go on in the islands with a special perspective, and besides that, you're just a damn good writer." He looked away, embarrassed. "You wouldn't have to come in every day if you didn't want. We could make some kind of freelancing arrangement—whatever it takes to make you happy."

"And what if I told you in order to be happy, I would like to be able to sometimes write a second point of view to an editorial I didn't agree with?" she asked.

He looked as if he had been expecting her pointed negotiation, but he paused before he carefully answered. "I guess that's the sticking point, isn't it? The best I can do is to promise to work things out on an issue-by-issue basis. I still am the editor and the place where the buck stops. So I couldn't give you—or anyone else, for that matter—carte blanche. But I can be open-minded about it."

"I'll have to think it over," Mina said.

"Will you really?" he asked as if he had expected a total refusal. "I mean, will you please think it over and call me as soon as you make a decision?"

"I will," she said.

"Great." He smiled his charming smile. "That's great. I'll look forward to hearing from you."

Mina watched him as he walked away toward the parking lot. She felt overwhelmed by these events—the euphoric exhilaration of the fencing match and now this invitation to go back to the newspaper. Christian Hollister wasn't exactly begging, but he was a bit like an ex-lover asking her to come back. Her own metaphor startled her. He may have flirted with her, but he was never her lover. And now he was a married man. And what she loved and what was important to her about being at the paper had nothing to do with him. She continued to the clubhouse, where Nyla and Johnny were waiting for her at a table on the veranda.

"Here she is," Johnny said, as he stood up to hug her, "our own musketeer! Hey, I made fifteen bucks on you. Let me buy you lunch."

"I promised Nyla I would go to the Harbor Grill, so it's up to her," Mina said as she sat down. "But I could use one of those lemonades."

"Let's eat here instead," Nyla said, "because now I'm starving."

"Great," Johnny said, "I hope you don't mind that Louis is with me."

"No," Mina said. "We love Louis, right, Ny?"

"Love him," said Nyla as she laughed and took a sip of her lemonade.

"So who's the bookie who started the betting?" Mina asked.

"Oh, let me guess," Nyla said, tapping her chin with her finger. "Could it have been our second, or is it third, cousin?"

Johnny laughed and jumped to his feet. "Listen, sisters, I'll bet that is the most fun some of those people have had in years. Money changing hands just doubled the excitement. I'll go and get your lemonade and see if I can scare up a waiter."

"That was pretty terrific, Mina," Nyla said. "Everyone was so impressed. I knew you fenced all those years at school, but I never saw you."

"You were at Mills. I was at Antioch College. We were miles apart."

"Still," Nyla said, "I'm sorry I never got to see you compete."

"After you have the baby, I'll show you how it's done. It'll be a great way for you to get your shape back."

"Don't look now," Nyla whispered as she smoothed the cloth napkin on her lap, "but there's an incoming artist right behind you."

Mina turned around to see Desmond Rivers approaching.

"Mina!" Desmond said in his affable manner. "This must be your twin sister I've heard so much about."

"Yes," Mina answered. "This is my sister, Nyla. Nyla, this is Desmond Rivers."

Desmond stared at Nyla. "I'm sure Nyla and I have met somewhere before. Remarkable, two identical beauties."

Nyla smiled at him. "Don't flatter us, Desmond. It might go to our heads."

Desmond placed his hand on Mina's shoulder. "Fabulous fencing, Mina. You're going to make all the other women on the island feel inadequate."

"I seriously doubt that," Mina said.

"I wanted to tell you that Raymond has almost finished developing the photos he took for the catalog. He's going to give them all to Tamara, but he's making extra prints that he's dropping at our house. There's a copy for you to borrow if you like."

"Thanks, Desmond. Maybe I could get them late this afternoon."

"I'll be at the studio at Halemana, and I'll expect you to come and have a drink." Desmond flashed them both a smile. "And you would be most welcome too, Nyla."

Nyla smiled politely. "Thank you."

Desmond stepped away from them and made a mock bow. "Then, I hope I see you both again soon."

"I can see why he must infuriate his wife," Nyla commented as soon as he was out of hearing range. "He has 'rake' written all over his face."

Johnny came back with lemonade for Mina, four menus, and Louis Goldburn in tow. It was just before noon, and the shady veranda with its expansive view of the gardens created, for Mina, a veneer of luxurious safety and tranquility. Out on the peninsula, removed from the daily hustle and bustle of town, surrounded by calm water, the yacht club existed in a peaceful world of its own. As a kind of reward—for doing well in the fencing and for being wanted back at the paper so badly—Mina decided to give herself over to this soothing illusion and do nothing but enjoy her lunch and the pleasant company.

"Good boy, Ollie," Ned said as he unfastened the long, makeshift leash he had tied on the dog's collar.

He had started teaching Ollie to track a human scent trail, something he had done with the family dogs on his grandfather's estate when he was a boy. Ollie could now track a couple of hundred yards, and Ned suspected he could go much further but held him back to make sure the dog was successful at every session. Ned was hot and a bit tired and decided he needed to take a long shower. He left Ollie happily lapping up a bowl of cold water on the lanai and went inside the bungalow to have a nice long wash.

The hot water from the showerhead hit him between the shoulder blades and ran down his back. He was relieved that the fencing session was over and that it had been such a success. Nigel had certainly stirred up an interest and possibly the beginning of a great occupation if he decided to make Honolulu a permanent home. Mina's surprise triumph added a touch of excitement and drama to their enterprise, and thanks to her, fencing as a competitive sport was given quite a showcase. He thought about Mina giving up the possibility of the Olympics and returning home to a dying mother. He turned off the water and stepped out of the shower, reaching for one of the fresh towels that hung on the rack. As he dried the droplets of water off his clean skin, he wondered what Christian Hollister had thought of the morning's events. Hollister looked surprised but not upset by losing to Mina. And after she scored her first two points, it seemed like he realized she was the better fencer, and he lost graciously and with good humor. Ned wrapped himself in his bathrobe and went to the kitchen to make a cup of tea. His mind held the image of Christian Hollister speaking to Mina on the lawn of the Pearl Harbor Yacht Club. He had seen Hollister stop her as she was headed toward the clubhouse. He could tell from Hollister's posture that although the conversation wasn't long, it had been intense, and judging by Hollister's confident gait as he walked away, Ned presumed that he had been happy with the outcome. Ned couldn't help but feel sorry for Christian Hollister. It was obvious to everyone but Mina that the man harbored feelings for her. Mina had worked for Hollister for nearly two years before Ned had met her. In two years, Ned figured that Hollister could have done his best to try to win her, but it looked as if Hollister had been unaware of his own feelings and that his interest in Mina had only surfaced when Ned had engaged her affection. Yes, Ned thought, he felt sorry for Christian Hollister because Mina was a gem and a prize, and Hollister had only recognized that when it was too late. Compared to Mina, Lamby Langston, no matter how physically attractive she might be, no matter how expensive her clothes, was like cheap costume jewelry. Ned couldn't understand why Hollister had married her—some people just seemed to stumble from one foolish error to another.

Ned watched the steam rising as he poured hot water into a cup and over a tea bag. Americans had certainly taken to using tea bags with enthusiasm. He heard some whining at his door and turned to see Ollie begging to come in. He opened the door, and the dog's countenance immediately switched from forlorn to joyously happy. Ollie did not like being left alone. Ned whistled in the hall as he carried his cup of tea back to his room to dress with Ollie trailing at his heels. He couldn't help but be pleased with himself as the husband-to-be of Mina Beckwith, and she even came with a great dog. He picked up his watch. It was nearly five, and he realized he had to hurry, as he had promised Mina to stop and pick up some photographs for her from Desmond Rivers before he met her at her sister's house. Mina and Nyla had decided to end their sisterly day together with dinner and Christmas-tree decorating, and he had been summoned by phone to join them.

A few minutes later, he was dressed and in the driveway, loading Ollie, whom he had been instructed to bring, in the backseat of the car. The sky was already fading into its evening colors as he drove over to Black Point and pulled into the parking lot, which thanks to Mina's precise directions, he easily found.

Ned let Ollie out, and the two of them made their way through the ironwood grove toward the old wooden buildings. The sky colors were quickly changing to brilliant oranges and pinks as the sun fell toward the horizon. An offshore breeze made a lonely, singing sound as it moved through the long needles of the ironwood trees. The light fell at a muted angle, illuminating everything in a soft glow, and for a moment, he could believe he might have stumbled into an enchanted forest. Ollie ran ahead to the lawn in front of the buildings, straight up to the edge of the grass, and then froze, taut and tense, staring toward the lava coastline. He admired the dog's silhouette against the green grass, now bright and glowing in the setting sunlight. Rough white surf rolled against black lava rock as the dark-turquoise sea heaved and swayed. Transfixed by the evening colors, he had nearly reached the lawn when he heard the first shot. Ollie took off toward the lava coastline, and Ned ran after him. Against the dazzling sunset, he saw the figure of a neatly dressed man in a white shirt and dark jacket just beginning to turn toward him when a second and third shot rang out in quick succession. Ned stopped and stared in shock, watching time slow to a crawl, watching the figure flail, watching him spin and turn, watching him sink down against the jagged rocks into a crooked, seated pose.

Ollie's bark startled Ned back into action, and he broke into a run toward the fallen man. As he ran, he saw a dark, hooded figure moving into the brush along the shoreline to his right. The dark form turned, pointed, and fired at Ned. Ned dropped against the sharp lava stones as the bullet struck rock about a foot away. He rolled and pressed himself into a depression in the rough stone that was filled with seawater. The cold tide pool saturated his clothing and shocked his senses just before another bullet cracked and whizzed close by. Ollie was barking and dashing wildly back and forth. Surf sprayed and surged into the pool where Ned lay. He counted to ten, then raised himself into a crouching position. He scanned the vegetation line, and seeing no one, he got to his feet and ran over the lava to the lifeless figure.

He knelt down and saw Desmond Rivers with his head back, eyes empty and staring straight up into the heavens. Ned looked up to a firmament smeared with high, mackerel-skinned clouds changing from vermillion to a more delicate pink and, beyond them, another cloud layer of white wisps that coiled in thin ribbons. The colors of the sky were seeping into the tide pools surrounding the empty shell of Desmond Rivers, and Ned found himself trapped in a tableau of violence and beauty. Ollie approached silently from behind, licking the back of his neck, helping him to regain the composure he needed. As he stood to walk back to the art studios to find a telephone, an old sailors' adage his father used to recite popped into his head: mackerel skins and mares' tails, lofty seas, lower your sails.

Twenty minutes later, Ned was in the midst of confusion and chaos in the parking lot. Todd had arrived, followed closely by his retinue from the police department. Molly had run out at the first arrival of the police cars, and Todd had insisted she wait in her house until he could speak to her. The police had begun to go about their routine—made difficult by the location of the body and the fading light—when one after another, all of the artists began to arrive for a meeting they had scheduled to work out some of the details of their show. Todd had a couple of his assistants herd them into their meeting hall while he went with Ned to speak to Molly. She had left the back door open and was pacing nervously behind her purple couch.

"What's happened?" she said as soon as she saw them. "What's going on out there?"

"We have some very bad news," Todd said calmly, "and you might want to sit down."

"I don't want to sit down," she retorted. "I just want to know what the hell is going on!"

"I'm afraid it's your husband," Todd replied. "He was shot and killed out on the lava."

Molly stopped pacing and stared at Todd. "He was what?"

"He was killed by an unknown assailant. Ned found him and saw what happened."

She turned to look at Ned. "Is he dead? Are you saying he's dead?"

"Yes," Ned said very quietly. "I'm sorry, Molly. I know it's a great shock." He moved to her, took her by the hand, and sat her down on the sofa. "Todd, why don't you find us a bottle and two glasses."

Todd obediently found a bottle of brandy and two glasses. He set them down on the coffee table in front of them and sat across from them in an easy chair. When Ned and Molly had both emptied their first shot, Ned asked if she would like to know what happened. She said nothing but nodded, and Ned went through his story. When he had finished, he poured them each another round.

"I know this is difficult for you," Todd began, "but as a matter of routine, I need to know what you were doing and where you've been in the last few hours."

Molly, with a vacant look, turned her gaze to him. "I went to the store. I came home and put the groceries away. I took a shower and then went to read in the bedroom."

"You didn't hear any shots or notice anything else out of the ordinary?" Todd asked.

"No," she answered in a monotone. "I had the radio on as I was reading. I didn't hear anything but the music. I didn't hear a thing until the sirens of the police cars."

Todd continued. "And where did you think your husband was?"

She took a big sip of brandy. "An hour or so before I went to the store, he said he was going to the studio to work."

Todd stood up. "Thank you, Mrs. Rivers. I'll need to speak to you again, perhaps tomorrow. Ned, can you wait here for a few minutes until I send someone in?"

Ned nodded yes.

Molly sank back into the sofa as Todd walked out the door. She was quiet for a minute and then said, "Did you see who did it?"

"No," Ned answered.

"Who do they think did it?" she asked.

"They don't know yet," he answered.

"But who do they suspect might have done it?"

"They just don't know yet."

"They don't know yet," she repeated. "Not yet. Did it happen quickly?"

"Yes," he said, "it happened very quickly."

She furrowed her brow. "How did he look? How did he look when he was dead?"

Ned thought for a moment and then said, "He looked like he wasn't there."

Tamara Morrison entered the room and told Ned that he was wanted in the meeting room and that she would stay with Molly. Ned said again to Molly that he was very sorry, but her only response was to look up at him as if she didn't quite understand. When he stepped outside the door, he found Ollie waiting for him with a worried and melancholy look, and Ned felt bad that in all the confusion, he had forgotten the dog.

"Come on, lad," he said as he scratched the dog under his chin. "We've both had a hard evening, haven't we?"

Ollie looked up at him with his soft brown eyes and wagged his tail. And as they made their way through the ironwoods toward the meeting hall, Ollie stuck close, and Ned felt the warm comfort of his physical presence with every step.

Todd was standing outside the meeting hall waiting for Ned. "I already broke the news to the group," Todd said, "and one of the guys is taking statements from all of them about their whereabouts this evening. I told them that they all have to come down to the station in the next few days and that they're welcome to bring their lawyer if they like."

"How did they react?" Ned asked.

"They balked and protested."

"You mean they don't like being treated like suspects in a murder case?" Ned said in a mildly sarcastic tone.

Todd shook his head. "I'm not fooling around with this lot anymore. This is the third one of their arty gang to buy the farm. They can kick and scream all they want, but no one gets off the hook on my watch."

"I think," Ned said, "that it's time to bring Nigel into the fold. You're going to be questioning all of our suspects, and I'll put it to him that not joining forces now would be foolish."

"Very foolish," Todd agreed. "Just so you know, I'm posting some men here tonight so no one goes out on the lava. I want to try to recover the bullets that missed you. It's too bad you didn't get a better look. By the way," he added, "I called the sisters on the hill."

"And?"

"Mina said she'd meet you at home, and she'd bring some food."

Ned managed a smile. "That's one thing about us being with the sisters."

"What's that?"

"We'll always be well fed."

# 18

# SUNDAY, DECEMBER 15

**T**HE NEXT AFTERNOON, Ned and Nigel sat in the parlor of Ned's bungalow at Ka'alāwai. Nigel had agreed that they would partner their investigation with Todd's, and Ned had admitted to collaborating with Mina. Even though Nigel had consented to the partnership, he was not happy about it.

"It can't be avoided," Ned reasoned.

Nigel frowned. "I suppose not."

"Todd has to conduct this murder investigation. He's going to be questioning all of our suspects—something we can't do. He's in a perfect position to help us by passing along and maybe even ferreting information out for us. We would be remiss to pass up this opportunity."

"Yes," Nigel said, "but it could muddy up our side of things."

Ned could not understand Nigel's persistent, irrational resistance, and he had to try hard to hide his exasperation as he stood and went to look out the window. The morning had started out bright and sunny, but clouds had come in from the north and colors of the garden were now muted and soft under the overcast sky. He marveled at how if one stopped to listen, bird sounds were always present in the islands, ready to soothe and help one to maintain equanimity. After being shot at yesterday, Ned needed all the equanimity he could latch onto, and now Nigel was being difficult. He just couldn't understand this reluctance on Nigel's part to collaborate. It was clearly the most logical and advantageous thing to do, but Nigel was doing it grudgingly.

"And," Nigel went on, "I'm very uneasy about Mina being involved."

Ned kept looking out at the garden. "And why is that?"

"Because it makes things awkward."

Ned couldn't believe what he was hearing. He turned to Nigel and managed not to raise his voice. "Nigel, we've known several women who do our kind of work as well or better than we do, and we've known several couples who work very well as a team. I don't see why all of a sudden this is bothering you."

Nigel pouted and said, "I just don't like it, and that's all there is to it."

Ned sat down, faced Nigel, and spoke calmly. "Well, you can't very well tell Todd how to conduct his investigation or who he can and cannot work with. Mina is engaged with that group of artists and doesn't need any kind of pretext to watch them. It's the perfect cover, and as far as I can see, she's provided some crucial information. And I don't like having to mention this, because she is my fiancée, but as a working partner, she is as competent as anyone I've ever worked with, including you."

Nigel looked away. "I just hope this doesn't end up in our losing control of our own investigation."

Ned said nothing more and surmised by his comment that what was really bothering Nigel was the fact that he would not be in absolute command. Ned had not worked with Nigel for several years now, and he supposed this could be a new development in his character. It didn't sit well with Ned. This behavior wasn't like the old Nigel he knew and trusted. In fact, Ned had learned to mistrust people who were obsessed with control. They had trouble listening and were often prone to serious errors of judgment.

Ned heard a car rolling into the driveway and stepped again to the window. It was Todd. He was followed just a minute or two later by Reggie. And just as they both stepped into the house, Ned heard Mina's screen door slam, and he saw her walking across the arbor to join the group. Reggie was introduced, and a fair amount of time was taken sharing background information. It pleased Ned to see that Nigel betrayed none of the pessimism he had expressed to Ned before everyone's arrival and, in fact, behaved in a courteous and cooperative manner, and Nigel seemed impressed by Mina's discoveries in Tamara's attic.

"Here's something else," said Todd. "Early this morning we found the two bullets on the lava that missed you, Ned. It's definitely the same gun that was used to kill Schoner and to shoot Morgan in the leg, and it looks for sure like it must be a German Luger."

"What?" Mina looked surprised.

"I didn't want to say until we were reasonably sure, and we are definitely keeping that fact out of the press," said Todd.

"I think we have to agree," said Ned, "at this point, it's still difficult to tell whether we're looking for one person or a pair of conspirators.

"Well," Nigel began, "we can say with a great degree of certainty that the Japanese embassy is receiving information, but for diplomatic reasons, we can't confront them, much less ask them who gives it to them. Our job is to work from the other end and to identify and provide evidence on the person or persons who are doing the collecting."

"But what happens then?" Mina asked. "The person or persons are most likely going to be arrested by Todd for murder."

"I haven't the foggiest," Nigel answered. "We were just hired to identify them."

"It's something the territorial government will have to work out with the ONI," said Todd. "Believe me, the aftermath will be out of our hands. We need to focus on apprehension. I was hoping one of the things we could do this afternoon is to go through our list of suspects and then maybe come up with a plan."

"The list of our suspects has dwindled a bit," Mina said. "Now, there's Tamara, Akira, Molly, and Bill Hitchins."

"What about that photographer?" Ned asked. "What's his name? And the girl, April. They weren't among *our* given suspects, but perhaps they were overlooked."

"They're low on our list," Todd explained. "Morgan, because he was on the receiving end of an attack. April does have some personal motives and could have well-hidden political motives, so maybe we should include her on the list."

Mina tapped a pencil on her pad of paper. "Tamara certainly qualifies as a candidate for spying."

"So does this Japanese fellow, Akira," Nigel added. "I mean, he is Japanese, and he does frequent the embassy. Reggie here is keeping a close watch on him."

"And Bill Hitchins," Ned said. "From what I saw of his family tree, he could be closely allied with the Nazi movement—and what an excellent cover. He's a beachcombing artist who just happens to be sailing around Pearl Harbor all the time with his sketchbook."

"Then there's Molly," Mina said. "She's infuriated with her husband. She's complex and hard to read, and her father just happens to be a major proponent of eugenics—something that could endear and tie him to the Nazi Party."

"And," Nigel added, "from my experiences in the East, I can assure you that the Japanese-Nazi alliance is not an idle fantasy, and it is very likely that one of these people is a Nazi sympathizer working here for the Japanese military."

"To me, Morgan is an unlikely person," Todd said. "Not only was he attacked, but there was nothing on him in Schoner's files, and his wife is Jewish."

"I'd have to agree with you there," Nigel said to Todd. "He was not one of our suspects either. I think we should turn our attention elsewhere."

"That brings us back to the girl, April," Ned said, "although I don't know why we call her a girl when she's actually a grown-up."

"Because Appy acts like a child," Mina chimed in.

"Didn't you go to school with her?" Ned asked Mina.

"She was in school at the same time I was, but she is a lot younger than I am, so I hardly knew her. I know she had some very hard feelings about Tilda and that she does know an awful lot of what goes on between the artists, but if she's up to something this complicated, I would be genuinely surprised."

"It's just as Mina and I were discussing the other night," Ned said. "We have information and no real evidence, so perhaps we should just keep digging as deep as we can until we find some evidence or force someone's hand."

"Look," Todd interjected, "I am questioning all of these people down at the station next week, and I'm calling the wives in too. Three people from their group have died in the last few weeks, and nobody can protest too much about being a suspect. And I could ask questions that might help in uncovering espionage, if I knew what those questions might be."

"Well, I think we can safely say when we've found one, we've found the other," Mina said. "When we find the murderer, we've found the spy."

"Is there a place at the station where we could listen and not be seen?" asked Ned.

Todd nodded. "Yeah, we have a room, but maybe it should just be one of you. I don't want to arouse the curiosity of too many of my colleagues on this one. I'm trying to keep a lid on things."

"Ned, why don't you look after that? I still need to keep an eye on the embassy," Nigel said. "And Reggie needs to keep up his friendship with both Akira and this Jimmy person. He seems like the perfect information carrier, and we really need to monitor where he goes and who he meets."

"I did play golf with Jimmy yesterday," Reggie reported. "He mentioned we should play a foursome with a couple of artists he knew, Desmond Rivers and Bill Hitchins. I acted like I'd never heard of them."

"I'd like to be able to have a look at Ari Schoner's files before the suspects are questioned," Ned said. "I want to make sure we don't miss anything."

Todd smiled. "Be our guest. So I'm going to question the suspects, and I'm thinking our best strategy is not to hold back," Todd said with a grim look on his face. "I intend to start rattling some cages. I'm just warning you—it may upset some of the beasts."

"Let's agree to meet up again after the questioning, then," Nigel suggested. "Perhaps in the middle of the week."

"While you're doing the interrogations," Mina said as she looked at Todd and Ned, "I have a few lines of inquiry I'd like to pursue."

Todd shook his head and gave Mina a half smile. "I think the less I know, the better."

Mina sat waiting in her Packard with Ollie in the narrow space in back. She watched Ned as he closed the door to his bungalow and walked toward the car. He had a physical grace that she liked to watch, and she thought how he could just as easily have become a dancer instead of a playwright. He fenced beautifully as well, and she anticipated many happy hours of friendly competition.

"Sorry I'm late," Ned smiled as he climbed in the car. "I had almost forgotten about our dinner. For some reason, I thought your grandmother had gone back to the ranch."

"Grandma has been off visiting her friends all over the island, but now she's back at Nyla's. And she's staying through Christmas. My father is coming later, probably at the eleventh hour, if I know him. Everything is different this year. We usually have Thanksgiving here, then go to the ranch for Christmas and come back here for New Year's."

Ned rolled down his window. "I think you mentioned a change of plan because of the baby."

Mina was about to start up the car but stopped herself and turned to him. "Ned," she said quietly as she took his hand, "are you okay? Yesterday must have been brutal. I don't know what I would have done if you had gotten hurt—or worse."

For a moment, he sat without saying anything, then he smiled a weary smile. "I'm bloody tired of being shot at. That's twice in the last few months."

"Not to mention three dead bodies in the last few weeks," she added.

"It's a difficult business," he said as he rubbed his fingertips over his forehead. "And something queer is going on with Nigel."

She gave him a perplexed look. "What is it?"

"That's just it," he answered. "I have no idea. I can feel something grating on him. I thought it was this partnership with you and Todd, but I don't think so. It's something else."

"Maybe he's having trouble at home—something to do with Mei," she suggested. "I mean, you never know."

"It could be, I suppose."

"She and Nyla are spending quite a bit of time together," Mina said as she started up the car. "Why don't I ask her if Mei has mentioned anything in their girl talk?"

"On a brighter note, I've heard from Sāmoa," said Ned as they got under way, "and my grandparents will be here for our wedding. Maybe an aunt or two, if that's all right."

"It's not only all right; it will be lovely. And we've gotten word that my brother will be home soon."

"You know, I've known you for almost a year, and I've never met your brother."

"Let's see," Mina said as they pulled out of the driveway. "He spent most of last year traveling and was only back here when you went to Sāmoa, but he's supposed to appear shortly after the New Year. I think he wants to be here when the baby arrives."

"What's he like?"

Mina frowned. "That's hard to say. He's brilliant, in his own way, and he's different. I would say he's one part island boy, one part bohemian, and one part humanitarian. You'll love him."

They said no more but shared a comfortable silence as they drove around the old crater of Diamond Head, through Fort Ruger and Kaimukī, and then wound their way up Sierra Drive to Maunalani Heights. Night was stealing across the sky as they made their way past the carnation farms to the very top of the hill, and by the time they had reached Nyla and Todd's house, it was nearly dark. The lights in the city below blinked on as the last glimpses of the sea faded with the light. As they stepped from the car, Mina felt a rush of cool, invigorating air.

"Let's forget about guns and murder for the rest of the night," Mina said.

"I can more than endorse that course of action," Ned said as he wrapped his arm around her waist. "It will all be there for us to think about tomorrow."

They entered through the back door off the kitchen, where they found Nyla taking a cake out of pan. She looked particularly domestic with her flowered apron and her voluptuously pregnant belly.

Nyla smiled. "At last, the lovebirds have arrived. Come right in. Grandma Hannah is anxiously awaiting you in the living room."

"Where's the governor?" Ned asked.

"He's out picking up our dinner," Nyla reported. "I hope you don't mind I'm not cooking. I have a big craving for Chinese food."

"Yum," Mina said. "Now I've got one too."

"But I am making dessert," said Nyla. "And it's not quite finished, so go and have a drink and talk to Grandma. I know you could do with a drink after your wild weekend, Ned."

"Righto," he replied, "just point me in the direction of the malt whiskey."

Mina sat on the sofa next to Grandma Hannah, and Ned mixed cocktails for the ladies and poured himself a double shot of whiskey before joining them. A huge Christmas tree with lights stood to the left of the fireplace. Boxes full of decorations surrounded it. Grandma Hannah was working on a baby quilt but put her work aside when Ned brought their drinks.

"I shouldn't sew at night," said Hannah. "It's not good for my eyes, and it's easier to make a mistake."

"It's so cute," Mina said, admiring the fine stitching. "And such a lot of work."

"I'm happy to be here to do it," Hannah said, raising her glass. "Here's to the new baby coming into our family and to your wedding in May."

They all touched their glasses together and took a sip from their drinks.

"Oh, Nyla told me all about the fencing, Mina," Grandma Hannah said with a mischievous smile. "And how you beat that Christian Hollister."

"I used to fence in college," Mina reminded her.

"I know, and I'd forgotten about it," Grandma said. "You know, Ned, she was very good—always winning this and that."

"She's still very good." Ned said.

"And what is the club like now?" Grandma asked. "Your father used to spend so much time there. He was always sailing or racing. The club was in a lovely spot, as I recall."

"Nothing much has changed really," Mina said, "at the club, that is. There's more military activity in the area. They're building another air force base on the Diamond Head side of the harbor entrance. Grandma, didn't you tell me something once about Ford Island, Moku'ume'ume?"

Grandma Hannah laughed. "I must have told you it was named for that naughty game, ume. People would go there and play a partner-swapping game. The old folks in my time said it was a game for couples that couldn't have children. They would just go there to try with someone else for a child. I don't know if it's true or if people just wanted to be naughty."

"Would you like to go out to the club while you're here?" Mina asked. "Ned and I would be happy to take you. I'm sure Dad would like to go when he gets here."

Grandma sighed. "Yes, my dear, I'm sure Charles would like to go, but to tell you the truth, I would rather remember it the way it was long ago." Grandma paused for a moment, lost in thought. "Ka'ahupahau and her brother Kahi'uka are guardians of those waters. They're the sharks that live in a cave near the mouth of the harbor and protect it from intruders. They were helpers to the people of that district, and the people fed them and kept them clean by scraping the barnacles off their backs. "Ke awa lau o Pu'uloa," she whispered, and then looked at Ned and Mina. "That's how we used to refer to Pu'uloa, Pearl Harbor. It was once an 'āina momona. Its lands were said to be fat or rich because there were so many fish ponds, so many taro lo'i, and fields of sweet potatoes."

"It certainly is a different place now," Ned commented, "with a definite military presence."

"Oh, yes, and when I was a young girl, there were so many arguments and debates about Pu'uloa and whether the United States should be allowed to use that place for their military. I was a teenager when the first Reciprocity Treaty was signed in 1871 by the king, Lunalilo.

That treaty was to allow the exchange of certain goods back and forth from the United States with no duties charged. There was some talk about giving America the exclusive right to use Pu'uloa as part of the treaty agreement, but there was so much protest among the people that the king refused."

"What were the objections?" Ned asked.

"It was a long time ago, and I was very young, but the main objections, I think, were that it was too much land to alienate from the kingdom and that if America was given Pu'uloa, it would be the first step towards losing our independence. It *was* finally given to America in the 1880s under Kalākaua. He was under so much pressure from the sugar planters, who wanted to ensure that their sugar would be imported to America duty free." Grandma Hannah took a sip of her drink. "It was such a different place in my day. Queen Emma had a house near the entrance to the harbor, on the Diamond Head side. The Bishops had some property out there. And the beach on the 'Ewa side was so lovely. As you came into the harbor and looked back toward the land, it was so beautiful and peaceful, looking up at the green hills. The water was still and clean. That's why I don't want to go there today. I have a lovely memory, and I want to keep it."

"It must be difficult for you," Ned said, "to see so many changes, not all for the good."

Grandma Hannah shrugged. "I suppose you could say that to any person my age anywhere in the world."

"I suppose," he said, "but like Western Sāmoa, your country lost its independence. People in Sāmoa are still upset being under New Zealand and are still talking about getting their independence back."

"No one talks about it nowadays, because now we're all supposed to be good Americans, but at one time, there were big, organized groups among us to keep Hawai'i independent. We had rallies and speeches, and people spoke and wrote about the importance of independence in our newspapers. Did you know, Ned, that nearly every living Hawaiian signed a petition against annexation to the United States? There was never any vote here about whether we wanted it or not, and if it weren't for the Spanish-American War, things might be different." Grandma Hannah's voice was full of emotion, and everyone fell silent.

Then Grandma Hannah let out a laugh. "How did we start on this gloomy subject? Let's talk about something happy, like your wedding. Mina, everyone at the ranch is so excited about the wedding. And Ned, the paniolo are all talking about having a bachelor party for you. They still remember your last visit. You made a big impression on them when you went on that pīpī 'ahiu hunt."

Mina rolled her eyes. "Heaven help us."

"What time of day will you have the wedding ceremony?" Grandma Hannah asked.

Nyla marched into the room. "Are you making wedding plans?"

Mina chuckled. "No, Grandma's just asking what time of day the ceremony will be. No need to get excited."

Nyla put her hands on her hips and looked at Ned and then Mina. "Well?"

"Well what?" said Mina.

"Well, what time will the ceremony be?" Nyla asked.

Ned shrugged and looked sheepish. "I'm leaving it up to the bride."

Mina laughed. "Or the bride's sister."

"If the ceremony is around four," Nyla went on, "it's a perfect time for cocktails and dinner to follow. And that gives lots of time in the day for preparing things. You need to think of things like that."

Mina turned to her grandmother. "What do you think, Grandma? What's the best for everyone at the ranch?"

Hannah nodded in agreement. "Oh, I think four o'clock would be lovely, but it's up to you and Ned."

"It's up to you, Mina," Ned said. "Just tell me when to show up."

"Actually, four sounds fine to me," Mina said.

"Good," Nyla said, "we're making progress. Now, have you thought about what kind of food you want? Or do you just want us to take care of it?"

"I haven't thought about any of that stuff," Mina confessed. "Do you want to just take care of it?"

"How about Grandma and I plan a menu and run it by you and Ned?" Nyla suggested. "You can be thinking about the guest list and the invitations, which I suggest you get out right after the New Year."

"We don't want a lot of people. Just our family and very close friends." Mina looked to Ned for confirmation.

"Oh, right," Ned agreed.

Nyla went on. "Well, Daddy and Grandma might want to include some of their neighbors. That's how everyone gets extra help for these special parties."

"It's also good because then we'll get offers to help put people up," Grandma said. "Everyone is so good about helping each other out."

"We'll make our list soon, and then you and Daddy can add to it," Mina said to her grandmother.

"Of course," Ned added, "we want to do whatever we can to make sure things go as smoothly as possible."

"That's why planning is so important," Nyla said. "Things go smoothly if you try to think of everything in advance."

Ned looked at Mina. "Maybe we should go and look for some rings."

"And Mina," Nyla went on, "have you thought about what you're going to wear?"

"No, Ny," Mina answered. "We just picked a date last week!"

"I'm warning you," Nyla said as she turned and headed back to the kitchen, "if you're going to have a dress made, better start thinking about it now so you don't end up with something junk at the last minute."

Grandma Hannah broke out in a big grin as she watched Nyla retreat to the kitchen. "She loves to be in charge of the parties, Ned."

"See, Ned," Mina explained, "we just have to act helpless and incompetent, and she'll take over for us."

"But is that a good idea, asking her to help us so much with the new baby coming?" Ned asked.

Mina took the last sip of her gin and tonic. "I'm telling you, if we don't let her do it, she'll be furious and hurt."

"Don't worry," Grandma Hannah added, "there will be lots of other people to help. And Nyla is very good at making other people happy, so she'll do her best to please you."

Ned got up to freshen everyone's drink, and Todd arrived with the Chinese food. They all served themselves in the kitchen right out of the boxes and then sat at the dining room table to eat. Nyla could not stop talking about the wedding, and both Ned and Mina and even Todd enjoyed channeling their thoughts into something bright and cheerful. Nyla was making proposals about how to decorate the chapel and talking about how they could use one of the outbuildings that was like a large hall for the dinner.

After dinner, they decorated the tree, while Grandma Hannah played some Christmas carols on the baby grand piano. Nyla gave each person a box of decorations and supervised from the sofa, and Todd nearly knocked over the tree when he placed the star on the top branch. When they had finished, they turned out the lights and stood back to admire their handiwork. Nyla went into the kitchen and brought out a luscious Boston cream pie, dripping in chocolate.

"It looks too beautiful to cut," Mina said to her sister.

"I'll bet you could do it," Nyla said as she handed her a cake knife.

Everything about the cake was perfect, from the fluffy yellow cake to the cream filling and the chocolate coating. Todd brought out a bottle of brandy that he and Ned indulged in while the ladies shared a pot of jasmine tea.

On the way back to the bungalows, Ned drove while Mina looked out the window at the night sky. "I'm wishing something, Ned," she said.

"What's that, darling?"

Mina yawned and said, "I'm wishing we can be finished with this ugly business before Christmas and that there will be no more intrigue in our lives until way after our wedding."

# 19

# MONDAY, DECEMBER 16

NED SAT IN a wooden chair at the downtown police station, in a hidden narrow space looking down into the interview room. He had a clear view of the table, and he was surprised that he could hear everything quite clearly. From the other side of the room, his observation portal appeared to be a kind of slatted wooden vent, but backing the vent was a darkened screen, nearly impossible to detect. Todd had just seated Molly Rivers and was pretending to look through a file before talking to her, a tactic he used to try to give his subjects the impression that he was the authority figure in the room and in control of the conversation. Ned could see Molly's fingers fidgeting with her skirt. The tall and usually stately woman looked worn, with dark rings under her eyes and a pallid complexion—even the startling blonde streak in her dark hair appeared dull and washed out as she sat with her shoulders slouched and her head slightly bent. The room was not exactly dark, but the light level was low and the blinds were drawn so that the time of day was not apparent. Todd closed the file, paused for a moment, and spoke.

"I'm very sorry to have to ask you these questions so soon after your husband's death," he began.

"You mean murder?" Her voice betrayed her anxiety.

"I was trying to be discreet. This is the third death in your gang of artists, so we are looking very carefully at the inner circle of the Halemana group."

She said nothing and stared at her hands folded on her lap as Todd opened the folder again and uncapped his fountain pen, ready to take notes.

"When was the last time you saw your husband alive, Mrs. Rivers?"

"We drove back from the yacht club together. We had gone to that fencing demonstration and eaten lunch. I guess we got back at about two or two thirty. Desmond said he was going over to the studios, so I guess that was the last time I saw him."

"And you say that was around two or two thirty?" Todd asked.

"Around," she said. "I didn't really look at a clock."

"And where were you from that time until you were informed of the incident?"

"I went to the store. I came home, and I took a shower," she began. "I turned on the radio in the bedroom and read. I think I drifted off for about half an hour or so, but when I woke up, I went back to my book until I heard the police sirens. Then you came to the house to tell me about . . . to tell me about what had happened."

"Did anyone drop by or call you?"

"No," she said quickly.

"Now, if I remember, weren't you out taking a walk when Ari Schoner was shot?"

The question took her by surprise. "Well, yes, I mean, I don't know. I did go out walking, but I don't know exactly when he was shot."

"Well, it appears he was shot right before you got home." Todd paused and looked at her. "Did you see or speak to anyone on that walk?"

"No. I mean, I don't know. I don't remember."

"And," Todd continued, "on the evening of the Halloween party, did you have words with Ari Schoner?"

"What?"

"An argument," Todd said. "Did you argue with him out on the lawn?"

"It wasn't really an argument."

"What was it, then?"

"Why are you asking me about Ari?"

"Just answer the question, please."

There was a hint of defiance in her voice. "It was something personal."

"Do you recall the late afternoon or early evening of December eighth? I believe you had a photo shoot earlier up around the Pali. What time did you get home?"

"I don't remember exactly. We took the photos. We ate lunch by a waterfall. I came home and did some sketches for a piece I'm working on. Then I ate dinner and listened to the radio. I read and went to sleep."

"Your husband was with you?"

"No, he was out."

"Where was he?"

"I don't know. He doesn't always tell me."

"No one came over? No one called you on the phone?"

"No."

"You were aware that your husband was having sexual relations with Tilda Clement?"

"Yes."

"Were you angry about it?"

"Yes, all right, I was angry. That's what I was trying to tell Ari— that his favorite pet wasn't so wonderful—and all he wanted to do was make excuses for her."

"And on Saturday, earlier in the day at the club, a witness said they heard you and your husband arguing."

"Well, lately we've argued a lot."

"You were heard to say you could kill him."

She raised her voice. "I was just saying it. I didn't mean it literally."

"Is there a gun in your household?"

"I don't think so. I mean, not that I know of, but Desmond has a lot of junk. He has things over at the studio too."

Todd paused and shuffled through some of the papers in his folder. "How long have you been in Hawai'i, Mrs. Rivers?"

"About five or six years now."

"And," Todd went on, "you moved here from San Francisco?"

"Yes."

"But you are originally from Sonoma, California, aren't you? Where your father is a doctor."

"Yes, he runs a clinic in Sonoma."

"The Sonoma Institute for Research. Is that it?"

She frowned and spoke sharply. "Yes. Why are you asking me about my father?"

"What kind of research does this institute do?"

"I don't see what that has to do with anything," she answered angrily.

Todd shrugged. "It's not any secret. The Sonoma Institute for Research is one of the leaders in the research and promotion of eugenics."

She glared at him. "Then why are you asking me if you already know?"

"What I would like to know, Mrs. Rivers, is do you subscribe to this theory of eugenics?"

"That's none of your business." She jumped to her feet, all her tiredness replaced by fury. "You leave my father out of this. Do you hear me? And if you want me to answer any more questions, then I want my lawyer. I'm not stupid. I came here voluntarily, and now you're badgering me. I know I don't have to take this, and I'm leaving."

Todd stood up and said calmly, "Fine, Mrs. Rivers, and I'm telling you officially that you are a suspect in a murder investigation, and any attempt on your part to leave town will be taken as an indication of your guilt."

As she walked out of the room, Todd cast a glance toward the false vent, and as soon as Molly had left the room, he signaled Ned to come down.

"Well, well, Detective," said Ned as he entered the room, "you certainly know how to rattle cages."

"Well, well," Todd replied. "If we make the beast—or beasts, as the case may be—nervous enough, they just might do something foolish."

"And let's just hope," Ned added, "that it's only foolish enough to get caught."

"Stop and drop me off here," Mina said to her sister. "And pick me up in exactly one hour."

Mina opened the car door, got out in the parking area for the Halemana art studios, and quickly slipped through the gate into the Rivers' home. She knew exactly what time Molly was going to be interviewed at the police station, and looking at her watch, she figured that she had a safe hour for her search. She headed straight for the bedrooms, thinking that a bedroom closet would be the first chosen hiding place of anything secret. She quickly ascertained by the décor and the clothes in the drawers and closet that only Molly slept in the master bedroom. Mina gave everything a once-over and found nothing very interesting tucked away among the clothes or shoes, but on a bookshelf, there were several books on the subject of eugenics. Three of them were by a Dr. Adam Madison. Mina opened one up and read the inscription: "To my darling daughter with admiration and love, your devoted Dad." There was a picture of a handsome, intense-looking man standing before the archway of some important-looking building. Mina wondered how she would feel if she found out her father was doing something she deemed morally reprehensible—ties of love, particularly those formed in childhood, ran strong and deep. But maybe Molly had no problem with her father's beliefs and research. She remembered when she worked on the series of articles on eugenics, how firmly and passionately some of its followers believed they could make a better world for all human beings and how they saw themselves as people of vision on the cutting-edge of social change. Many of them were highly intelligent and charismatic. But she had come to realize that these people believed themselves to be an aristocratic intelligentsia with upper-class rights over "lower classes." They were completely cut off and disconnected from their "subjects" and had conveniently made them objects instead of recognizing them as real, complex people. Mina felt a wave of revulsion, replaced the book on the shelf, and moved on.

She found the bedroom that Desmond had used. While Molly's room had been spare and neat, his room was a messy spread of magazines and clothes, ashtrays, and empty glasses. As she went through his things, she was glad she had worn gloves. She did find a twenty-two-gauge rifle in his closet, but the most incriminating thing she uncovered, stashed way back in a closet, was a cigar box with some condoms and old snapshots of scantily clad women. One of them was Tilda. Mina left the messy room, went to the living room, and sat down to think for a moment on the purple sofa. She stared out at the sea, so blue and crisp this morning. She looked around the room, her eyes lingering on Desmond's prints of Hawaiians engaged in different traditional activities. He might have been a rogue, but he had an artist's eye, creative style, and the technical skills to capture beauty in his printmaking. All these things he had rendered—a man mending a fishnet, women weaving mats, and a family harvesting taro from their lo'i—touched her.

She got up and left the house, the same way she had come, still thinking about Desmond and how she hadn't really liked him but admired his artwork. She stopped herself and realized she was standing at the edge of the ironwood grove looking toward the art studios. It was a quiet morning with no wind and no cars in the parking area. The old wooden buildings looked silent and forgotten. She looked down at her feet, nudged the sandy loam with one of her shoes, and looked back up at the studios. Of course it was more than worth a try, she thought, and headed through the trees.

She called out at the painting studio and next the printing studio to see if anyone was around, checked the meeting room, and then went back to the printing studio, where Desmond did his printmaking. While going through the drawers, she found sheets of sketches— some detailed and finished and some less so—faint images emerging from the white realm of the drawing paper. Other drawers held finished prints numbered and signed by Desmond, and Mina saw several that she would like to have for herself. Mina searched all of the cabinets and shelves and found nothing of interest, but suddenly she remembered the room in the other studio—the room where Tilda and Desmond had their illicit tryst.

Mina walked down the shaded concrete breezeway that connected the two buildings to the screen door of the studio, which was slightly ajar. The drawing benches and the easels stood around the room looking lost and abandoned, and she imagined that some of the figures in the drawings tacked to the wall were staring and accusing her of trespassing. She was aware of the slight scent of mildew as she stood for a moment in the doorway that led to the room. Along the opposite wall was a small bed covered with a rose-patterned bedspread. Even though it was old and faded, the red, pink, and yellow roses still emanated a wild vibrancy of color. Several silk cushions piled at the head of the bed made it look soft and inviting. The makeshift vanity consisted of what looked like an old door supported by two nightstands placed in front of a framed oval mirror that hung on the wall. On the vanity were hairbrushes and combs, bottles of lotion, cold cream, scent water, and a bunched-up piece of red silk. A wooden stool arrayed in a variety of paint drippings served as a seat.

Mina's attention was drawn to something she hadn't noticed before—a wooden wardrobe in the corner to the right of the door. She checked her watch and saw that she had to hurry. She looked through the drawers of the vanity first and then turned her attention to the wardrobe. She found hanging in the closet a silk robe, several sexy negligees, an Elizabethan costume, and a quilted bathrobe. She reached out and fingered the soft fabric of the silk robe. On a high shelf were assorted hats and a feather boa, and on the wardrobe floor were several pairs of shoes. She was examining a pair of boots when she accidently dropped one. The heel of the shoe struck the wardrobe floor with a hollow thud. On a hunch, Mina took a second look around the edge of the wardrobe floor, and sure enough, in the dark left-hand corner, there was a hole big enough to stick a finger in. She cleared out the shoes and lifted up the piece of floor wood. In the narrow empty space lay a little black book. She snatched it up, replaced the floorboard and the shoes, and quickly ran to meet Nyla. Once at the agreed meeting place, Nyla's car came quickly into view.

"Where have you been?" Nyla scolded. "I've been driving around in circles hoping the neighbors don't see me and call the police."

"Sorry," Mina said. "I just had to check out one last thing."

Nyla smiled and gave her a sideways glance. "And?"

Mina laughed. "And bingo, jackpot!"

"So what now?" Nyla asked.

"I'm starving," Mina answered.

"Let's go to the Green Lantern in Waikīkī," said Nyla. "I think today is the day they make that really good oyster stew."

Only fifteen minutes later, the two sisters were in the restaurant being seated in a booth with plush leather seats. They asked the waiter for two glasses of iced tea, and then they both ordered large bowls of oyster stew and decided to split a grilled cheese sandwich.

"So what did you find?" Nyla asked her sister.

"A certain black book," she answered. "I hope it's full of dreadful secrets."

"How can you stand to sit there and not read it?"

"I don't really want to look at it now," Mina said. "I'm nervous and keyed up from illegally searching a house, and I need to eat and calm down."

Nyla furrowed her brow. "Oh," she said and then burst out laughing. "I swear, sometimes I think I have the weirdest sister in town."

Mina stirred some sugar into her iced tea. "You probably do."

"Yeah," Nyla said, "I bet you think it would be really romantic to save it and look at it with that boyfriend of yours."

Mina grinned. "Ah yes, a loaf of bread, a jug of wine, Ned, and a black book of criminal activity. You have no idea what you're missing."

"Hmmm," Nyla said thoughtfully, "maybe I could get Todd to bring home some case files to spice up our marriage."

"Speaking of marriages, how are Mei and Nigel getting along in their new digs? I know you've been seeing a lot of her."

"Well, their house is starting to look lovely, and Mei bought a baby grand and already has a couple of piano students—neighborhood kids." Nyla eyed her sister. "What? What do you want to know?"

"Has she said anything to you about Nigel? Ned's worried about him."

Nyla nodded. "As a matter of fact, she has made these remarks."

"Like?"

"Like, 'Nigel hasn't been himself lately,' or 'Nigel is physically recovered, but I think he has some emotional scars,' or 'I hope this or that thing will cheer Nigel up.'"

"Ned did say that Nigel lost a working partner in Shanghai. Sounds like he hasn't gotten over it."

"I don't pry," said Nyla. "I figure if she wants to tell me something, she will."

"I'm sure she appreciates your friendship."

"She did tell me one very juicy, very confidential thing that I might let you in on, seeing as I know I can depend on your silence."

Mina perked up in her seat. "What?"

"She suspects she might be pregnant, but she's not telling anyone, not even Nigel, until she talks to a doctor. I think she just told me because I'm in the same state."

"That is pretty juicy," Mina agreed. "Could you tell me if she says anything else?" she asked as she scanned the menu. "Are you going to eat dessert?"

Nyla sighed. "Why not? I've driven the getaway car for your illegal activities, and now I'm agreeing to spy on our friends for you. I deserve a treat."

"It's not really spying. I'm only asking because Ned's worried, and he cares about his friend."

"Okay," said Nyla with a smile. "As long as it's for a noble cause." Nyla's eyes were suddenly alert, and she raised her menu to cover her face. "Don't look behind you, but Lamby Langston, excuse me, Lamby Hollister just walked in."

Mina abruptly raised her menu to mirror her sister. "Does she see us?"

"I don't think so," Nyla answered in a half whisper. "Uh-oh, I was wrong. Take cover, enemy fire." Nyla smiled in Lamby's direction.

Mina managed to still the urge to burst out laughing and fixed a pleasant smile on her face. Without turning around, she could hear the clack of Lamby's high heels and the jingling of her charm bracelet announcing her presence.

"Nyla!" Lamby's voice rang out. "I haven't seen you in ages. Oh, and Mina too," Lamby cooed as she posed with her left hand on their table, displaying her sparkling diamond rings.

"We hear congratulations are in order," said Nyla.

"Yes," Mina chimed in, "we're so happy for you and Chris. Congratulations."

"Thank you," Lamby replied. "We had a very small wedding, but we'll be having a big party in a few months before we leave for Europe."

"Europe, how lovely," said Nyla.

"Yes," Lamby said as she ran her hand over her blonde hair. "I'm so looking forward to shopping in Paris and Italy. It's just impossible to find anything decent here."

"Well, I'm sure you'll have a great trip," said Nyla.

Lamby turned to Mina with a phony smile. "So, Mina, are you still engaged?"

"Yes," Mina answered, "we're getting married in May."

Nyla gave her sister a quizzical look. "Say, Mina, when you marry Ned, will you have one of those English titles too? Will we have to call you Lady Something-or-Other?"

"I have no idea," said Mina.

For a passing instant, Lamby looked shocked, before the next insincere smile returned to her face. "Well, so nice to see you both. I better get back to my friend. Bye now."

"Bye," Mina and Nyla said at the same time.

When Lamby was well out of earshot, Mina groaned and said with a drawl, "I'm so looking forward to shopping in Paris and Italy. It's just impossible to find anything decent here."

Nyla shook her head. "What could Christian possibly see in her?"

"A prize knickknack," Mina responded. "And speaking of Christian, he's begging me to come back to the paper."

"Oh, brother! He already sees he's made a mistake, and he wants you around again."

Mina frowned. "What? Doesn't it occur to you that he might want me back because I'm a very good journalist?"

"Sorry," Nyla apologized. "It goes without saying that you're a great journalist. I just said the first thing that popped into my pea brain. But I wonder if Lamby knows. Maybe on the way out, we should stop and tell her."

Mina laughed. "You're such a cat."

"Meeow, meeow, meeow," squeaked Nyla, putting her hands up like paws. "What's for dessert?"

At the police station, Ned looked down from his hidden perch as Todd ushered April Fraser into the interview room. To Ned's surprise, she was accompanied by Andrew Halpern. Mina had mentioned that April had a crush on Andrew, but it looked as if it had blossomed into something more. Ned had met Andrew nearly a year ago when his father, Abel Halpern, had been murdered and a valuable historic portrait had disappeared. Almost a cliché, Andrew was a talented but troubled artist from a rich and troubled family. He was well known around town for his unkempt appearance and his sulky, angry attitude. Ned thought the interview might be very entertaining, as everything about Andrew irritated Todd to no end.

"I hope you don't mind," April began, "I'm bringing my friend Andrew for moral support. All this murder business is frightening."

"I suppose it's all right," Todd answered in a bland voice while giving Andrew a cold look.

April and Andrew both sat down, and Andrew immediately crossed his arms and looked defiantly at Todd. Todd ignored him and looked into the file folder on the table and then spoke to April as if Andrew weren't there.

"Thank you for coming, April," began Todd. "This is a very serious business. Three people associated with the artists' group are dead. I hope you'll answer my questions fully and honestly. Can you do that?"

"Appy's not a child," said Andrew. "You don't have to talk to her like she's five years old."

"I'm not speaking to you," said Todd without looking at Andrew. "And if you're here to interrupt this interview, you'll have to leave."

Andrew made an exasperated noise and looked away, and Ned observed a smile of admiration pass over April's face. She thinks he wants to protect her, Ned thought, but does he? Or is he simply enjoying an opportunity to be belligerent to an authority figure?

"I want to start with your relationship with Ari Schoner," said Todd. "What was it?"

April shrugged. "He was just a nice old man who hung around the group. He was always helping out and stuff. He was just nice to me, that's all."

"Did he ever mention or question you about your past or the past of anyone in your family?"

The question took April by surprise. "What?" she blurted out. "No, he never asked anything like that."

Todd spoke sharply. "What about Tilda? Did she ask or bring up things like that? Did she ask about your family?"

April's face turned red. "Who's been talking behind my back?"

"No one," Todd said calmly. "Ari kept some information that he passed on to Tilda. Can you answer my question?"

"You don't have to answer his questions," Andrew said as he took April's hand. "You can just leave and get a lawyer."

April looked at Andrew and back at Todd. "She threatened to say certain things about my mother that weren't true. And she knew things about my father because she'd had an affair with him on the mainland. He's an artist too. I don't know if my father lied to her about my mother or if Tilda just made it up."

"I guess you were angry with her," Todd said.

"Hah! I wanted to kill her, but I didn't."

"Did you know she was having an affair with Desmond Rivers?" asked Todd.

"Yes. And Molly knew too. She and Molly had a big fight about it."

"And," Todd continued, "do you think she might have told these true or untrue things to Desmond?"

"I have no idea," said April. "She was poison."

"And where were you on the evening of December eighth, the evening Tilda was killed?"

She answered flatly, "I was at home, painting."

"Can anyone corroborate that?"

"I can," said Andrew. "I called her at half past five, and we talked for an hour."

Todd looked at April. "Is that true?"

"Yes," she answered.

"And Desmond Rivers," Todd went on, "what was your relationship with him?"

April paused before she answered. "I don't know, I just knew him—like I knew everybody else. We weren't big friends or anything."

Ned could see Todd calculating what direction to push her in. "Did he ever make improper advances? Did he ever pressure you that way?"

The question agitated her. "He did it to everyone. I wasn't the only one. Just ask Eva Morgan."

"Did he threaten you?"

"No, he just tried to—you know—get what he could."

"And where were you," Todd asked, "on the evening that Desmond was shot?"

April gave him an incredulous look and said nothing.

"She was with me," said Andrew, "at my place."

Todd looked at him. "At your place," he repeated.

Andrew gave him a tight smile. "Yes, sir, at my place."

"Why are you asking where I was?" April demanded. "Do you really think I could kill somebody? I just wanted him to leave me alone, and I wanted Tilda to shut up about my mother and my father. She was a liar, and I hated her, but I didn't kill her or anybody else."

"Your artists' group is small," said Todd. "Three of you have been murdered. I think any one of you could be the killer, and I'm going to find out who and why."

April stared at Todd. Her nervous demeanor faded into something cold and detached. When she spoke, she no longer seemed like a helpless young thing. "Well, I'm sure you have no real evidence against me," she said, sticking her nose in the air as if she smelt something bad. "You're just digging around, aren't you?" She stood up. "Let's go, Andrew. And I think I'll take your advice: if he wants to talk to me again, I'll just go get a lawyer." She turned and left the room with Andrew close behind.

Ned waited a few minutes before he went to the interview room. "The lawyers in this town are going to love you with all the business you're sending them," Ned said with a laugh.

Todd sat at the table looking puzzled. "Did you see that?" he asked.

"You mean the instant change from scared naive girl to cool and in control?"

"Yeah," said Todd. "It gave me the creeps. Maybe she's schizophrenic."

"Or maybe," Ned mused, "she's a very good actress."

That evening, Ned and Mina sat on the pune'e in her living room, propped up against a pile of pillows with their legs comfortably stretched out. They had eaten roast beef sandwiches and coleslaw for dinner and were now sipping Ned's excellent port and reading the black book that Mina had found. She had immediately recognized Tilda's handwriting from all of the handwritten notes that Tilda had made on her artist's statement, but some passages in the book were underlined with a blue-colored pencil and some had check marks next to them.

"Do you know what I think?" Ned asked.

"No," Mina replied before sipping her port. "Who knows what goes on in your superior brain?"

"I think," he said as he moved closer to her, "that someone else made all these blue marks."

"Hmmm, you mean someone like Desmond Rivers?"

"Excellent deduction, my love. I think Desmond Rivers found this after she died. Or perhaps he knew where it was before she died, and once she was gone, he took up where she left off."

"And where would that be, I wonder?"

"That would be," he said, "close enough to scare the guilty party into another murder."

"This stuff makes me feel like I want to wash my hands," she said. "Even though she's clever and calculating, there's something so desperate and pathetic about it."

Ned got up and poured himself more port. "Let's go back and just concentrate on the things that are underlined."

Mina relaxed back into the cushions and closed her eyes. "Okay, read them," she said. "But not all of them—start a few weeks before Ari was killed."

"Very well," he said as he sat back down and found a starting place in the book. "This is about three weeks before Halloween. I'm going to skip the dates and just read through. 'Who would have thought Ray was such a tiger in sheep's clothing? Too bad he's so off again/on again. Tamara is a pretentious prig. She should be making this a solo show for me. I would love to cut her down to her no-talent size. Bill Hitchins is an arrogant pig, but that Tahitian boy looks pretty tasty. I saw him looking at a certain part of me yesterday when I was bending over. Too bad Ari is an old geezer. He's the only one of this crappy bunch that really likes me. Desmond has proven to be delicious. I wish he would dump that frigid wife of his. He doesn't even like her. And she thinks she's so much better than me.'"

"It sounds even worse when you just read those parts," Mina mumbled.

"There appears to be a big gap in the underlining, but then it picks up again right after the first murder."

"Go on," she said.

"These look like they're all to do with blackmail: 'Finally found the files in an unlikely place. Told Y about the articles and expect some money soon. Lots on X but haven't figured out exactly how to use it. Leaning on W will be for pleasure, not for profit. Z has agreed to pay for the photo clippings—think I could make lots more there. U is pretty much worthless moneywise, but V could amount to something.' That's it," Ned said as he closed the book."

Mina sat up and opened her eyes. "She certainly had an appetite for men and money."

"I'm sure Desmond did all this underlining," he said.

"Yes," she said, "but if that's so, Tilda must have told him things, because he never saw the files. How else would he know who those letters stood for? I mean, I don't even know that, and I've seen the files."

"She would only have to have told him about one person."

Mina nodded. "It looks like that's exactly what she did."

Ned opened the book and looked at it again. "Z and Y are the ones she's sure she can get money out of. I'd place them first on a suspect list."

"Yes," she agreed, "but just mentioning photos and articles is nothing to go on. They all had photos and articles in their files."

"Still," Ned said, "we do have a few other bits to go on. We know for sure now that Tilda was blackmailing people. We can be reasonably sure that Desmond found out, either through this book or because Tilda told him or both, and that he must have said something to the murderer or murderers because now he's dead. But it looks like neither of them knew about the spying."

"As far as we know," Mina reminded him.

"Yes, darling," he said as he picked up her hand and kissed it, "as far as we know."

# 20

# TUESDAY, DECEMBER 17

**N**ED STOOD IN his kitchen making himself a cup of coffee. He had gotten up early and laid a fairly long and complex track for Ollie, aged it for about twenty minutes, and then took the dog to run it. Ollie had been performing so well that Ned couldn't help but wonder if someone had trained him to track before he came to Mina. As he poured his coffee and stirred in the cream and sugar, he heard a car rumbling down the driveway and then Ollie barking with excitement. It dawned on him that it was Tuesday, the day the Oliveras came to work—Mrs. Olivera cleaned Mina's bungalow while Mr. Olivera took care of the yard. Then he remembered that today was the day they were bringing Mrs. Perreira along to clean his bungalow for the first time. In a panic, he set down his coffee cup and ran to his room to get dressed. He threw on a clean pair of khakis and a white undershirt and then made for the bathroom to brush his teeth. He could hear Mrs. Olivera and Mrs. Perreira talking to Mina outside and fussing over Ollie. He had just finished his teeth and was smoothing down his hair when Mina and the ladies came knocking on his door.

Mrs. Perreira was overjoyed to see Ned and told him all about her nephew and how wonderfully things were going for him. Mina and Ned had solved a murder over the summer that had affected Mrs. Perreira's family and at the same time opened new doors for her nephew.

"Oh, yes," Mrs. Perreira said with pride. "David is getting along so well with his new sisters, and he's such a favorite with his grandmother. He's a good boy, you know. He deserves to be spoiled just a bit."

Ned offered to take Mina out to breakfast so they could get out of the way, and Mina thought it was a splendid idea. They left Mrs. Perreira in the capable hands of Mrs. Olivera, who assured them that she would tell her everything she needed to know.

Ned and Mina met in the café at the Alexander Young Hotel on Bishop Street. She had first suggested her old standby, the Harbor Grill, but then remembered the wonderful pastries and the eggs Benedict at the hotel. He was only too happy to consent. After his father died, he and his mother had stayed at the hotel on their way to Britain. He was a timid child, but he fondly remembered the kindness of the elevator operators who allowed him to ride up and down with them as long as he liked. He also remembered it was the first place he had ever had an apple turnover and how his mother allowed him to eat one every day after breakfast. After the waitress in the starched pink uniform had seated them in the plush leather chairs, he was delighted to see that the apple turnovers were still listed on the pastry menu. The café was softly lit, and even though one could look out through the large glass windows at the bustling scene of the business district, the room was enveloped in a sedate hush. People spoke in quiet voices, and the thick carpet allowed the waitresses to move silently from table to table—a stark contrast to the noise and clamor of the Harbor Grill.

Ned asked for an apple turnover and coffee to be followed by scrambled eggs, pan-fried mahimahi, and rice. It was one of the things he loved about Honolulu—you could almost always find fresh fish on any menu for any meal. Mina decided she wanted an almond croissant, tea, and the eggs Benedict. He proceeded to eat his turnover with a knife and fork, while she cut her croissant in two and ate it with her fingers.

"I got up and did a track with your dog this morning," said Ned.

"I guess we should start to think of him as our dog," she said.

He smiled. "Our dog is very good at it."

"Thanks for doing it with him."

"He loves it," he said.

"So," she said, "just to be sure, Akira's interview is at nine thirty?"

"Right," he said.

She checked her watch. "I don't have to meet Reggie until nine, so we have lots of time. He's helping me today."

"Tamara follows Akira," he said before he ate another piece of his turnover. "These pastries are as good as I remember them."

"I don't need to go back to Tamara's house," she said, "so maybe I can go Christmas shopping afterwards."

He laughed. "So you'll go from illegal entry and search to Christmas shopping."

She gave him a rueful smile. "All in a day's work. And while we're on the Christmas subject, I hope you haven't forgotten the Christmas party tonight at the theatre."

"Johnny Knight has kindly reminded me several times," he said as he put down his fork and watched her in silence.

"What serious thing do you want to say to me?" she asked as she started on the second half of her croissant.

"How did you know it was serious?"

"Because," she answered, "you always get that quiet, poetic look just before you want to tell me something important."

"It's about my work," he began, "the unmentionable work I do for the supposedly nonexisting section of His Majesty's government."

"Are they asking you to do something else for them?"

"No," he said. "You know, I don't *have* to do things for them. I'm not employed or obligated in any way except by a sense of duty and doing my bit—wanting to be useful in the world."

She dropped two sugar cubes in her tea. "I think you've told me that."

"Well, the thing is," he said, "as we've talked about, the way things are going in the world, it's likely that sooner or later I *will* be called on. Actually, it's more than likely. If I agreed, I might have to be away for months and have little or no opportunity to communicate with you, and since we're about to be married, I thought we should talk about it."

"I gather that sometimes you're placed in very dangerous situations?"

"Sometimes, yes, we are."

She tilted her head slightly as her brow wrinkled. "And are you thinking I might not want to be married to you if you continued to do that kind of work?"

"Something along those lines. I guess I'm wondering how you feel about it. As I said, I don't *have* to do it."

Mina put her right elbow on the table, cupped her chin in her hand, and leaned forward. "Yes, you do. If it was important to the world, you would feel you had to do it, and if I disapproved and tried to stop you from doing things you felt you ought to be doing, eventually you would feel resentful and stifled, as well you should. Of course I know it won't be easy. Of course I'll worry, and of course I would miss you. But I would rather live with all of those things than keep you from doing work that was important and meant something to you."

Ned stirred his coffee. "I do only agree to things that I think are important."

"Do they ever ask you to do violent things?" she asked as she finished her croissant.

He winked. "Don't worry, darling, I'm not a hired assassin."

She sighed. "That's disappointing. There are so many people I was counting on you to bump off."

The waitress glided up to their table, removed their pastry dishes, and replaced them with their breakfast orders. The food looked comforting and delicious. Mina asked for a glass of lilikoʻi juice, and Ned decided to have one too.

"I guess this is a good time to tell you," said Mina, "that Christian Hollister wants me to come back to the paper."

"Is that what he was asking you at the yacht club?"

She smiled. "Ned Manusia, were you spying on me?"

He grinned. "No, I wasn't spying on you. I was just watching what you were doing through the window."

"I haven't said anything yet. It looks like I could dictate my own terms. I could freelance for the paper instead of showing up every day at a desk."

"I thought you didn't like the politics of the newspaper," he said.

"I don't particularly, but Christian said he might give me the opportunity to present other views."

He gave her a skeptical look. "And you think he'll actually do that?"

"I think I might be willing to give him a chance because," she paused for moment, "because I really miss the work."

"Are you sure you feel comfortable with Christian Hollister? You have to see that he fancies you."

"No," she retorted, "I do not see that, and even if I did, that would be his problem." She gave him a mischievous smile. "Don't tell me you're worried."

"I'm not worried," he answered quickly, "especially now that he's married to Lambykins or whatever her name is."

An hour later, Mina and Reggie were parking Mina's car on a quiet street in Pauoa Valley.

"If we walk one block over and up the street, we'll be at his driveway," said Reggie. "I came here with him last week to pick up some stuff."

They walked past front yards full of growing things—past mango trees, vegetable gardens, banana patches, papaya trees, and more than one henhouse. The working-class neighborhood had a rural atmosphere even though it was only a few minutes from downtown. They turned up the next street, which ended in a gravel driveway with a "no trespassing" sign. They looked around to make sure no one was watching them and then ran up the private road. Fortunately the road curved right away through overgrown brush, and they were quickly out of sight. The driveway ended at an open garage with lava-rock pillars and a gravel roof. Next to the garage was a tall bamboo hedge, and in the middle of the hedge was a wooden gate with a tall door.

Both Reggie and Mina slipped on gloves, and Mina laughed and said the world should be glad they weren't professional burglars.

Mina opened the door and stepped through into what seemed like another world. A pebble path wound through a green lawn shaded by the canopy of an old monkeypod tree that stood off to the right. The path led to a bridge that arched over a curving pond and continued up to the old wooden house, set back in the distance like something from a Japanese storybook. The dark tiled roof hung over a narrow porch that fronted the first floor. A second story with its own roof was set in the center of the house, and a pillared portico, also centered, covered the wide stairs that led up to the massive double wooden doors. The house resembled a sad and lonely temple, set in the middle of a lovely garden. Mina thought it would be a happier place if there were children running and tumbling on the lawn or skipping over the bridge. They walked along the path, and as they crossed the bridge, a colorful school of koi swirled beneath them. A bell was mounted next to the front doors, and Mina promptly rang it, just in case someone might be in the house. When no one answered, they tried the door, which was not locked, removed their shoes, and stepped inside.

To the right was a tatami area with pristine mats and a long, low table in the center. Sitting on the table was one of Akira's exquisite arrangements, made with slender sticks of driftwood, dark-purple irises, and green ti leaves. A koto and a floor cushion sat near one of the walls. Mina stayed on the dark wooden floor and signaled Reggie to follow her to the back of the house. After peering in all of the wide, sparely furnished rooms, Mina decided she should focus her search in the room that looked like it had once been the doctor's study, because it was the one room with a desk and drawers and places where papers and books were stored. Reggie went to investigate the rest of the house.

As Mina surveyed the room, she saw an old doctor's bag and, on the bookshelf, a few medical books in English and many books in Japanese. On the desk was a picture of the family while they were still in Japan. In the picture, there was a man standing next to a woman who looked like his wife, a young girl of about fifteen, and a small boy of seven or eight whom Mina instantly recognized as Akira. The women were dressed in beautiful kimonos, and they all stood in front of some kind of shrine. There were a few birds on the ground in front of their family group, and as Mina looked closer, she was drawn to the vibrant smile of the young girl, who looked so much like the older woman. She guessed that Akira must have had an older sister. There was only one other photo on the table. It was a picture of Akira in a cap and gown holding up a diploma. Mina looked up from the desk and out toward a wide covered patio and the garden beyond and thought how sheltered and serene the whole room felt.

She then began to open the desk drawers. In the bottom right-hand drawer, Mina came upon an old scrapbook with neatly mounted family photos, and beneath that, on the very bottom of the drawer, was a kind of folded cardboard envelope with articles in kanji and a photo from a newspaper of Dr. Nakasone in a military uniform standing next to a young soldier. Mina thought she had seen the same picture in Ari's file. There was another worn picture of the same young girl in the photo on the desk. It was faded and foxed, but Mina recognized the same dazzling smile. There was a very small envelope of folded rice paper, holding a pressed chrysanthemum. Mina was looking at all these things when Reggie entered the room.

"There's nothing I can see," he reported. "In fact, this room is the only one with anything in it, except for the kitchen, and I couldn't find anything there. I'm telling you, it looks like nobody lives here."

He walked over to the desk, looked over Mina's shoulder, and pointed to the newspaper photo. "Hey, that looks like Jimmy," he said, indicating the young soldier who stood next to the doctor.

"Jimmy who?"

"Jimmy, Takeo—the guy I'm supposed to be cozying up to at the embassy."

"Are you sure?" she asked.

"Of course I'm sure," he replied. "He must be in cahoots with Akira. They must be the ones!"

"Don't get too excited," Mina warned him. "I'm taking this packet to someone who can tell us what all this says. It looks like it's been in the bottom drawer forever, and it doesn't look like it's going to be missed anytime soon. I might have to ask you to sneak it back, so do you think you can remember that it goes right here?" She showed him where to place it.

He smiled agreeably. "I can remember that."

"Right now," she said looking at her watch, "we need to tidy up and leave."

They took a quick look around the back of the house and discovered a greenhouse full of orchids and ferns and a shed full of garden tools. Birds sang and swooped over the yard as they made their way back to the front of the house. While walking away, over the koi-pond bridge, across the lawn, and out the gate in the bamboo hedge, Mina wondered how she could get Setsu to tell her everything she knew about the Nakasone family.

Ned looked out from his hiding place at Akira sitting in the interview room waiting for Todd. Akira's long black hair was combed neatly back, and he sat very still but relaxed and composed, as if he were an experienced performer taking a break backstage. He seemed younger than his thirty-two years, with his clear, innocent face that looked as if he had just rinsed it with spring water, and Ned wondered if that vulnerable, aesthetic demeanor could be masking something ruthless and terrible. When Todd entered the room, Ned smiled at the way the two men stood in contrast to each other—the cynical, blustery redheaded detective, and the peaceful and detached artiste.

"Thank you, Mr. Nakasone," Todd said as he sat, "for coming here voluntarily."

"These murders are disturbing," Akira said. "I hope you find whoever is responsible for them."

"As you're aware, the victims all belong to your art group, so we're questioning all of the principal members."

"I understand," he replied.

"I want to start with Ari Schoner," Todd began. "Was he a close friend of yours?"

"I would say he was a close acquaintance, but like anyone who has a deep fear of being persecuted, he kept everyone at an amiable, observable distance."

"An amiable, observable distance?" Todd looked like he didn't understand.

"He watched everyone, while he smiled and smoked his pipe. He watched everyone very carefully, and he didn't miss much."

"And you think he did that because he was afraid of being persecuted?"

"I think he saw it as a way to protect himself, yes."

"What about his relationship with Tilda Clement?"

"I don't know much about it," he answered. "I had as little to do with her as possible."

"And why is that?" Todd asked.

Akira gave him a wry look. "Did you ever meet her? She was a very disturbed woman. I'm sure I'm not the first person to tell you."

"Why do you think Schoner was so fond of her?"

"I think he saw a confused, somewhat self-destructive soul, and he felt sorry for her. She was his project."

"Where were you on the morning Schoner was killed?"

Akira answered without flinching. "I was at the shop, working, all alone. And," he continued, "on the evening Tilda was killed, I was at home in Pauoa tending my plants, alone. And when Desmond Rivers was shot, I was also at home and alone. But you won't find any evidence to link me to any of those crimes because there isn't any."

"And what kind of relationship did you have with Desmond Rivers?"

"I don't think he liked me," Akira answered, "and I really didn't want to be his friend either."

"How about his wife? Did you want to be her friend?" Todd asked with an edge in his voice.

Ned saw the tightness in Akira's face. "I'll always be Molly's friend, Detective."

Todd leaned back and asked, "What exactly do you do at the Japanese embassy?"

Akira tilted his head, trying to figure out this turn in the questioning. "They're one of my regular customers. I make new arrangements for them every week."

"Are they friends of yours? The ambassador and his staff?" Todd's voice had an aggressive edge.

"Only in a business sense," Akira answered.

"And flowers, is that the only business you do with them?"

Akira frowned. "What other kind of business would I be doing with them?"

"You tell me," said Todd.

Akira looked at Todd and considered what he had just said. He smiled only with his lips, slowly rose to his feet, and spoke as if he were slightly amused. "I think you're conducting what's known in crime fiction as a fishing expedition, and as of now, my voluntary cooperation is all used up. So unless you have something you want to charge me with, I'll be leaving."

Todd just folded his arms and looked up at him. "You're free to go. Just don't even think about leaving the islands."

As soon as Akira left the room, Todd looked up at Ned and said, "Let's go get some coffee."

A few minutes later, the two of them were in Todd's third-floor corner office. Ned held a warm cup of coffee between his two hands as he gazed out the window at the activity on the corner of Merchant and Bethel Streets. Patrons were going in and out of the Yokohama Species Bank, and people with letters and parcels were walking up on the portico of the old post office.

Todd was sitting with his feet up on his desk. "He was a smarty-pants, wasn't he?"

"He's very smart," Ned said, still looking down at the street scene. "I hear his father saw to it that he got an excellent education."

"I wonder if the old man thought he wasted his money. I mean, you don't have to go to school to arrange flowers or sticks and leaves, or whatever he does."

Ned laughed. "No, but it comes in handy when you're being questioned by a slick detective."

"I'll say," Todd agreed. "And guess who's up next? The demon driver of Pacific Heights."

"I just don't see why all these terrible things are happening," said Tamara.

Ned could see her clearly from his hiding place. Her gray hair fluffed out in untidy waves. She sat across from Todd, looking concerned and waving her hands around as she spoke. Ned saw Todd shift in his chair as if he were uncomfortable.

"Ari!" she went on. "How could someone harm that kind old man? You know, he was very generous to our Halemana group—donating his time and money. Oh, and he was so encouraging to the younger artists like April. I just don't understand what the world is coming to."

"So you can't think of any reason why someone would want to kill him?" Todd asked.

"Heavens no!" she exclaimed. "It must have been some deranged person."

"And Tilda Clement, do you know why anyone might want to harm her?"

"Well now," she replied, "Tilda was a different animal altogether—very pushy and ambitious, always craving attention, especially from men. Perhaps that's what got her into trouble."

"And just how far would she push people?"

Tamara tapped the table with her fingernail. "I would say she could be reckless. She got a thrill from treading on dangerous ground. And I suppose you want to know about poor Desmond too—such a shock to think he's gone and so hard for poor Molly—not that they didn't have their troubles. Every couple has troubles, of course. I think she's too fond of Akira myself, but then Desmond had a roving eye too. But if you want to know about why Desmond was killed, I simply have no idea—no idea at all. Our art show is practically ruined, but I intend to go through with it anyway. We can't let these violent things defeat us. We just have to carry on and—"

"Mrs. Morrison," Todd interrupted, "I'm sorry to have to ask you this—I am asking everyone—where were you when these people were killed?"

Ned saw Tamara's head twitch ever so slightly, and he noticed her immediate use of a polite smile to disguise her surprise. He immediately thought of Mrs. Worlan-Burke in Shanghai and wondered if Tamara also had a cleverly crafted persona.

"I understand perfectly," said Tamara in a cheerful voice. "Of course you have to do your job. On the morning Ari was killed, I was at home, and I remember that clearly because my dog Jocks had just dug up a recently planted hydrangea just before I heard the news. Now, I was at home on the Sunday evening Tilda died and the same for when Desmond was killed, because I'm always at home on Sunday evening. My daughter sometimes calls at that time, you see."

"Did she call you on either of those Sundays?"

"No, she didn't, but I always like to be at home, just in case."

Todd pushed his chair back and crossed his legs. "Now, you and your late husband traveled quite extensively in the Orient, I understand."

"Yes, we did," she answered with the first sign of wariness.

"Including Japan?" Todd asked. "Did you spend a lot of time in Japan?"

"Yes, we did."

"What sort of business was he in?"

"He had things manufactured, machine parts and other things, I think." She paused for a moment. "You see, I really don't know much about what he did. He never discussed his business with me. I can't help you much there, I'm afraid. He kept me in the dark, so to speak. As a couple, we met socially with his business associates, but no one ever discussed their work. I mean, I may have been told the names of companies that people worked for, but I never paid much attention because it didn't interest me at all."

"So do you still maintain any social contact with his former business associates?"

"Yes," she said as she gave him a cautious look.

"For instance," Todd went on, "I imagine he knew the Japanese ambassador? Are you still socially acquainted with him and his wife?"

She looked at Todd as if he were a small boy in need of a scolding. "Whatever has any of that got to do with these terrible murders?"

"Please, ma'am," Todd said in a most polite manner, "we've been told to follow several lines of inquiry. I hope you're not offended."

Tamara softened. "Well, yes," she said, "the ambassador and his wife are social acquaintances of mine, but certainly that's not a crime? I mean, relations between our countries may be strained, but we still try to maintain pleasant diplomatic relations for the good of all, don't we? The ambassador and his wife are lovely people, and as you may know, I have a particular interest in Japanese art and culture. The Japanese have such a refined and tasteful aesthetic, don't you think? Really, it makes so many of our Western habits look boorish and clumsy."

"That may be," Todd said, leaning forward as if he were telling her a secret, "but did you know that the Japanese are very interested in the military activity at Pearl Harbor? Our military officials are keeping a watch on things very closely."

"Oh, my goodness! I don't know anything about things like that! I'm interested in building cultural bridges through mutual understanding." She recited the last phrase like a slogan.

Todd smiled pleasantly. "Well, thank you, Mrs. Morrison. Those are all the questions I have for you today, so unless you can think of anything else that might help our investigation, I won't take up any more of your time."

"I can't think of anything," she said as she stood up. "But if I do, I will be sure and tell you. I just hope you clear all this up soon."

Todd stood up and opened the door for her. "Thank you, Mrs. Morrison, and drive carefully."

She smiled at him with confidence. "Oh, don't worry about that. I'm an excellent driver."

As soon as Ned saw her walk out of sight, he slipped out of his roost and into the interview room. Todd gave him a sly smile.

"Well done, Detective," said Ned. "You put her on the defensive with the utmost courtesy. And now she more than suspects that you think she might be up to something—whatever that might be."

"I have to say," said Todd, "that she plays the benevolent Honolulu socialite role so well that she could be onstage."

"Speaking of being onstage, are you and Nyla going to the Christmas party at the theatre tonight?"

Todd shook his head. "Not me. I'm staying home with a cigar, my whiskey, my feet on the couch, and jazz night on the radio, but Nyla and her grandmother are going."

"Johnny Knight practically got me to sign an oath in blood that I would be there," said Ned. "I can't imagine why."

"What? You can't imagine why? You're the big star of the Honolulu theatre set, that's why. He's probably running all over town saying, 'Ned Manusia, the playwright, will be at the Christmas party. You simply *have* to be there.'"

Ned laughed. "I doubt that he's saying it exactly like that."

Todd wrinkled his brow. "Hey, today's Tuesday."

Ned gave him a quizzical look. "And?"

"It's fish chowder day at the Mermaid Café. Do you remember how good Duncan McKenzie's fish chowder is?"

Ned nodded. "I do remember."

Todd raised his eyebrows. "Then I say, if we waddle our culturally boorish and clumsy butts over to the Mermaid now, we'll just beat the lunch crowd."

Mina opened her car door and stepped out into the parking lot of the Aliʻi Theatre. The theatre sat on a small hilltop in Kaimukī just behind the fire station and had one of the loveliest views in the city. To the west was an expanse that swept over the city and beyond to the Waiʻanae mountain range. As the last of the daylight drained out of the sky, Mina could see city lights coming on here and there, and when she turned to look in the other direction, she saw the coastline of the south shore and the dark silhouette of Koko Head fading into night. She was wearing the same simple gown she had worn at Thanksgiving but had given it a Christmas look with the addition of a forest-green velvet jacket embroidered with red flowers meant to resemble poinsettia. Just as she reached the entrance to the theatre, she saw her sister's car pull into the lot and decided to wait.

"Where's Ned?" Nyla asked as she and Grandma Hannah walked up.

"Johnny insisted on picking him up himself," said Mina. "I think he wanted to be absolutely sure that Ned would be here."

Grandma Hannah shook her head and smiled. "That Johnny-boy. He must be up to something."

They found the Christmas party in full swing on the theatre stage. The festivities spilled out into the wings and the adjacent greenroom and patio. Johnny Knight was playing Christmas music on the piano in the middle of the stage while the party swirled around him. He had a cigar stuck in one side of his mouth and a glass of champagne balanced precariously above the keyboard. He brought his song to an end when he saw them approach and extracted a promise from Nyla to take over as musician in a few minutes, after she had a chance to socialize.

Grandma Hannah and Nyla were then swiftly caught up in a conversation with old friends, and Mina set off in search of Ned. She found him in the greenroom talking to Louis Goldburn and his wife, Doris. As soon as Ned saw Mina, he took her hand and pulled her into their circle. They greeted Mina and kept on talking.

"So I told Lou," Doris said, "'I don't care if you're Jewish. This year I'm getting a Christmas tree.'"

Louis laughed. "Well, it's not like I'm religious, but I do like to give her a hard time."

"Is the Jewish community here very large?" Ned asked.

"Tiny," Doris answered.

"Almost nonexistent is more like it," said Louis. "What I wouldn't give for a deli."

"I'd bet there's more Jewish people here than we think," Doris said. "They just prefer to keep quiet about it."

Louis nodded. "There is a definite undercurrent of anti-Semitism in Hawai'i, especially with the island elite."

"Do you know Raymond Morgan?" Mina asked Louis.

"I've met him a couple of times, but I've never really talked to him," he answered.

"He told me the other day," Mina said, "that his wife had some Jewish relatives, and I was wondering if what he was really telling me was that she was Jewish."

Louis rolled his eyes. "He was probably telling you that she's Jewish. She doesn't want to publicly identify herself as such, but she's sympathetic to Jewish issues."

"Oh, cripes!" said Doris. "Why do people have so much trouble accepting who they are?"

"I guess sometimes it's complicated," said Ned.

"It would behoove us all," Louis said, "to work to make the world a place where no one feels they have to be ashamed of who they are or where they came from."

Ned looked at Louis with admiration. "We could all raise our glasses to ideas like that."

"Except," said Mina, "some of us don't have a glass."

"Well, that's a problem I can easily fix," said Ned. "Anyone else need anything?" he asked before he left.

"I've met Raymond Morgan's daughter," Doris said. "She works at the beauty parlor where I get my hair cut."

Louis grinned. "Doris goes all the way to Pearl City to get her hair cut."

"Because my New Zealand friend Raewyn owns the shop, and she cuts my hair. Us kiwis have to stick together. The number of people from New Zealand in Honolulu is even smaller than the number of Jews. Right, dear?" Doris jabbed her husband with her elbow.

"Oh, absolutely," Louis answered.

"Raewyn is seriously thinking about moving her shop to town, though. There are so many military wives out there, and they're always moving. Raewyn feels that just as she's getting to know them and their hair, they leave. She thinks she wants a steadier clientele. That Eva is a lovely girl, so friendly and personable. Of course, she's not a trained beautician. She does the hair washing and the comb-outs."

Ned returned with Johnny Knight in tow and a drink for Mina.

"Mina, my dear," said Johnny, "I'm stealing your boyfriend now and making him circulate with me."

Mina turned to Louis and Doris. "This is what we get for not being playwrights—left out of the social limelight."

Johnny winked at them. "For not being *great* playwrights."

Mina decided to stroll over to the buffet table and found herself with a plate in her hand standing next to Tamara Morrison. Tamara was dressed in a long red silk Chinese top and matching wide-legged pants with a Christmas-tree broach made from very expensive-looking emeralds.

"Mina," Tamara smiled, "how lovely to see you here."

"Merry Christmas," said Mina. "I'd forgotten that you're a big supporter of the theatre."

"I love plays," said Tamara, "and your Ned is such a talent. I heard he was recently lecturing in Shanghai."

"Why yes," Mina replied, unable to disguise her surprise. "How did you know that?"

Tamara laughed. "I have my sources, you know. This chicken looks delicious," she said as she placed a piece on her plate. "I'm going to stop and see Molly on my way home. She's usually always at these theatre parties."

"Does she volunteer here?" Mina asked.

"Didn't you know?" Tamara asked as she scooped some chow fun onto her plate. "She's a marvelous actress. She's been in several productions here."

"I didn't know that," said Mina, "but I don't go to every production."

"Bill's been in several productions too, but only in minor roles," said Tamara. "He's very good too, but he's not to be counted on for a major role because sometimes he shows up tipsy. Still, he's never missed a performance, although I have seen him miss a line or two. Of course, Desmond never wanted Molly to be in anything Bill was in."

"Why is that?" Mina asked.

"Didn't you know?" Tamara spoke in a half whisper. "Molly was Bill's girlfriend, and Desmond stole her away."

"I didn't know that," Mina said.

"Molly told me once when she'd had too much to drink," Tamara said with a laugh. "It all happened long ago on the mainland. They all belonged to some kind of club or something when they were art students. Oh, look," said Tamara as she gazed across the room, "there's Christian and the new Mrs. Hollister. He's a fine actor too. I don't know what he sees in that empty-headed glamour-puss."

Mina tried to think of something kind to say. "I'm sure she'll make a very good society wife for him."

Tamara made a noise that was something between a laugh and a snort. "I'm sitting with your friends Tom and Cecily," she said. "Why don't you come along and join us?"

Tamara was not the only one who saw the arrival of Christian Hollister and his wife. Ned, who was allowing Johnny to shuffle him around like a raffle prize, spotted the Hollisters as soon as they entered the room. He couldn't help but notice the smooth and charming way Hollister moved through the crowd, as if being admired and deferred to were as natural as breathing, and he wondered how much real sincerity mattered to a person like Christian Hollister. Perhaps Hollister didn't care as long as people did what he wanted. Always polished and polite, Hollister gave the impression that he was slightly above it all and looking down from a height. Ned was nodding and smiling at an eager young man Johnny had introduced him to who was going on and on about some play, and although Ned was trying his best to listen, his attention was drawn to Christian Hollister. The young man who was talking to him didn't seem to notice. Ned saw that Hollister was politely making small talk, but all the while he was scanning the room like a searchlight. And Ned also saw the unmistakable twinge of longing that flashed over Hollister's face when he finally spotted Mina sitting at a table with her friends. Ned shook hands with the young man, who seemed very pleased, and Johnny began steering Ned to the next group of people. As Johnny was ushering him along, Nyla appeared and slipped her arm through his.

"Don't worry, Ned," Nyla whispered in his ear. "As you can probably see, it's all one-sided. She might like him, but she's never cared for him that way."

For a moment, Ned was worried. "Was I being so obvious?"

Nyla gave him a peck on the cheek. "Only to the doppelgänger twin sister."

# 21

# WEDNESDAY, DECEMBER 18

**T**HE NEXT MORNING, Ned found himself back at the police station in his observation room, watching Todd question Bill Hitchins. He felt sorry for Bill, who looked vulnerable and worried. He hadn't shaved in a few days, his clothes were wrinkled, and it looked like he had forgotten to comb his hair.

"Yes, I belonged to the Free Society of Teutonia, but Desmond and I only joined it because of the girls," said Bill.

"The girls?" Todd looked confused.

"Yeah," Bill said, "there were these really cute girls who belonged to the club. We never believed in their wacky ideas, but we got some great dates with the women in the club, if you take my meaning."

"So you didn't join in their marches and pass out leaflets or things like that?"

"Yeah, we did things like that with the girls," Bill admitted. "I mean, you had to if you wanted to be in the club."

"And how is it that you met Molly?"

Bill flinched. "What?"

"Molly," said Todd. "She was your girlfriend first. Where did you meet her?"

"Right," Bill said bitterly, "she was part of the Free Society of Teutonia."

"She was the reason you say you joined?"

Bill shook his head. "No, I met her afterwards. She was one of the serious ones."

"She took it seriously?" Todd asked.

"Her father made her join up. She was young and worshipped her father. She was trying to be the kind of daughter he wanted her to be."

"You met her father?"

"Yeah, he was this really strict doctor type. He had to screen anyone she wanted to go out with. He's at the top of the research heap in the eugenics field, and he attracted some major funders for his work—big-name American foundations. She started questioning some of his ideas, and one day he just cut her out."

"How did he do that?"

"He disowned her. He didn't want to have anything to do with her. She took it pretty hard and was looking for someone to save her. I think she knew I wasn't ready to be that serious."

"And is that when Desmond moved in on you?"

"Yeah," Bill said, "and I was pissed off, but it was a long time ago. Desmond helped her through a bad time. He encouraged her interest in art. It's all water under the bridge now."

"Is it?" Todd persisted.

"Yes. I said so, didn't I?"

"Is that why you took off to Tahiti? Because your best friend took away your girl?"

"What does it matter why I went to Tahiti?"

"And how did you and Desmond get along lately?"

"Desmond was a good friend. We did a lot of things together. We didn't have any bad feelings anymore, except—I guess I thought he didn't appreciate Molly the way he should."

"Do you know if Molly gets along with her father now?"

"I've seen letters from him around their house, so I guess she must."

"Where were you when Desmond was shot?"

"I was at home taking a nap."

"Was anyone else there?"

"How should I know?" Bill said. "I was asleep."

"So you belonged to this Teutonia society because of the girls and not because of your relatives in the German army?"

Stunned, Bill stared at Todd in a stony silence.

"Did you understand the question?" Todd asked.

There was no mistaking his anger. "My mother and her relatives have nothing to do with this."

"Do you keep in touch with them?"

"Sometimes," Bill said. "They loved my mother. She wanted me to stay in touch."

"And how often do you sail around Pearl Harbor?"

Bill gave him a confused look. "I don't get why you're asking me all these weird questions."

"You can cooperate or not," Todd responded impatiently. "We have our reasons."

"I go sailing out there at least a couple of times a week."

"I guess you have a pretty good idea of what goes on in the harbor there. With the navy ships and so forth."

Bill looked perplexed. "I see them, if that's what you mean. I can't help but see them. They're right there."

"You were in the navy, I understand, so you must be pretty good at identifying all the different vessels."

"Right," said Bill with a touch of sarcasm. "I can make out a battleship from a submarine."

"And do you keep track of all the vessels? Do you draw them or something?"

"I only draw them," he answered, "if they happen to be in the landscape I'm looking at. I don't draw them for their own sake, and I certainly wouldn't paint one."

Todd paused and made a pretense of looking through a file folder. "I'd like to ask you a few questions about Tilda Clement."

"What about her?"

"And how did you get along with Tilda?"

"I did not get along with her," Bill answered.

"Why?"

Bill looked disgusted. "I made her furious because her sleazy sex routine didn't work with me, and it offended her that I didn't want to sleep with her. And she purposefully picked on Tevai whenever she could."

"Because?"

"Because that was her way of getting back at me."

"Did she ever threaten you or try to blackmail you?"

Bill answered slowly. "No, not really."

"Not really?"

"She did kind of hint around once that she knew things about me. She said I better be nice or she might decide to broadcast it. When I asked her what it was she thought she knew, she just laughed and walked away."

"When was this?" Todd asked. "Do you remember when she said this to you?"

Bill thought for a moment. "I can't be sure, but I think it was a few days after Ari died."

"And when she died, you were where?"

Bill sighed. "I was at home working in my studio, and no one was there. I'm sure that's what you want to know. And the morning Ari was killed, I was walking on the beach in Kahala, by myself."

Todd was quiet and opened a folder, ignoring Bill and pretending to read something. After a few minutes, he casually looked up at Bill and told him that he could go but that he might be wanted for further questioning. Ned watched as Bill left the room, and he couldn't help but feel that something was weighing on Bill. Perhaps, Ned thought, he felt bad about the death of his friend, compounded by the fact that he had killed him.

"What did you think of the beachcomber?" Todd asked as Ned entered the room.

Ned pulled out a chair and sat down. "He's hard to read, like all of the others. It's hard to tell who is telling the truth and who isn't."

There was a knock on the door.

"Come," Todd called out.

A young man in uniform stuck his head in. "There's someone downstairs to see you, sir. He says it's urgent, and he won't talk to anyone else. His name is Reggie."

"Send him up," said Todd.

Reggie came bursting into the room and paced around excitedly. "You'll never guess what happened! Someone was taking potshots at Jimmy—I mean, Takeo—on the embassy lawn!"

"Hey, cut your motor," said Todd. "Just sit down."

Reggie sat down at the interview table.

"Good," said Todd. "Now take a few deep breaths. First of all, was he hit? Was anyone hit?"

Reggie shook his head. "No, sir."

"Okay, then start from the beginning. What were you doing on the embassy lawn?"

"Well, remember, Ned and Nigel wanted me to get chummy with him? He invited me to play an early round of golf, and we did. And then we went back to the embassy, and we were fooling around on the lawn out in the back. The gardeners kind of keep this one spot trimmed and manicured so the ambassador and his guests can use it as a practice putting green. It's between the embassy residence and the bushes along the stream. We got back around ten thirty and were out there playing around, and someone started shooting. A bullet went flying, right through Jimmy's shirt sleeve just before he was about to hit the ball, and he jumped. And then another one almost got him in the leg but hit a nearby tree. So I grabbed him and brought him down and covered him with my body, and then I thought, 'What the hell am I doing? I could get shot!' But the shooting stopped. I waited a few minutes and then got up and checked the stream as best I could without taking a really big risk, but I couldn't see anyone. People in the residence heard the shots and came out. I wanted to call the police, but they wouldn't let me. They were all jabbering away in Japanese, and I couldn't tell what the heck they were saying, but every time I mentioned the word 'police,' they said, 'No, no police.' I thought it was very odd that they wouldn't want some kind of legal protection."

"They'll probably find their own protection," said Todd.

"So then we went into the residence, and everyone was fussing over Jimmy, who kept insisting that he was all right. But I could see he was shaken. They gave us each a couple of shots of sake, and then Jimmy started thanking me so much for trying to save his life. I didn't tell him that if I'd thought about it, I probably would never have covered him like that."

"That is a very curious incident," Ned said almost to himself. "It's obvious he was the intended victim. No one could mistake him for you."

"There were no other witnesses?" Todd asked.

"Not that I know of," Reggie replied.

"Who knew you two were going to play golf this morning?" Ned asked.

"People at the embassy knew because I met Jimmy there with my clubs, and they saw us go off together. We used an embassy car, so the driver obviously knew, and he had time to tell someone else while we played golf. It must be someone at the embassy wants him out of the way."

"Or," said Todd, "he could be involved in our murders somehow from the other end."

"But if he were," Ned speculated, "let's say he's involved in eliminating a chain of evidence that traces the spying activities to himself and the embassy, why would the people spying for him want to kill him? Certainly he wouldn't try to incriminate anyone who could turn around and incriminate him."

"There's not much I can do if no one reports the incident to us," said Todd. "Hell, I can't even go up there and look for the bullets."

Ned shook his head. "Obviously they don't want any officials poking around the embassy. It can only make one think they have something to hide."

Reggie looked back at Todd and then at Ned. "But what should we do?"

"I think you should try to keep close tabs on this Jimmy character," said Todd. "Give him a ring, check in, say you're worried about him, and see if you can find out anything more."

Ned looked at Reggie and stood up. "May I please use your telephone, Todd? I need to make a call."

"You know where my office is," Todd said to Ned and then turned to Reggie. "Can you believe how polite he is?"

Ned laughed as he walked out of the room. "Can you believe how rude he is?"

Mina sat at the table in her sister's kitchen. Her grandmother was making her pancakes. The familiar smell of pancakes cooking in butter sent her straight back to her childhood and the comfort of eating something sweet and warm in a very safe place. Ollie lay nearby, looking as if he were hoping someone would give him a treat. Grandma Hannah was humming an old tune as she stood in front of the stove with a dish towel thrown over one shoulder and a spatula in her right hand. Mina could see embroidered carrots on the corner of the dish towel and recognized it as one of the patterns her grandmother used when she tried to teach her how to do needlework. Nyla had always been much better at it. Grandma Hannah still loved to sew and made all kinds of things for them—monogrammed pillowcases and handkerchiefs, quilts, and dish towels with cross-stitching or embroidery. When she and Nyla were children, Grandma Hannah made them beautiful dresses, pajamas, play clothes, and the best Halloween costumes on the block. Grandma Hannah placed a stack of three pancakes in front of Mina.

"Put the butter and syrup on now, dear, while they're still warm," said Grandma as she went to pour herself a cup of coffee.

"Aren't you going to have any?" Mina asked as she watched the melting butter spread into her pancakes.

Grandma sat down with her coffee. "We ate before you got here. When Nyla is hungry, she wants to eat right away."

"What is Nyla doing anyway?" Mina asked. Her sister had said hello to her when she first arrived and then disappeared.

"She's upstairs looking for something and being very secretive," said Grandma Hannah as she reached for the creamer. "I saw you talking with Tamara Morrison at the Christmas party. I didn't get a chance to say hello to her. How is she?"

Mina swished a fork full of pancakes in the syrup on her plate. "She's fine."

"I haven't seen her in years. She's younger than I am, of course, but when we were girls, she used to go to the Daughters of the Islands meetings with her mother. And they went to church at St. Andrews, so I saw her there sometimes too."

"Did you know her husband?"

"We knew her first husband, but I never met the second one, Mr. Morrison."

Mina gave her grandmother a surprised look. "She was married before?"

"Yes, she was married to Derek Potter. He was in the construction business, and he used to hang around Waikīkī Beach too, because he loved to surf and paddle canoes. He was not a very nice man, and your grandfather didn't like him at all."

"Why not?" asked Mina, waiting until her grandmother looked away so she could slip Ollie a piece of pancake.

"He was one of those big talkers—always telling everyone what his opinion was on this and that and always bragging about things. And you know how people are here. They feel if you're good at something, you shouldn't have to say so. He had a mean streak too, and more than once, Tamara was seen with black and blue marks on her face."

"I can see why Grandpa wouldn't like him," said Mina. "But what happened? Did they get a divorce?"

"Oh, no, he had an accident and died. He used to drink quite a bit, and he got drunk and fell down the stairs in their house. They were living in Mānoa at the time, not far from where we used to live. The police looked into it too because his father accused Tamara of pushing him. There was no proof, so nothing ever came of it, but you know how people can talk. Old man Potter was not a nice person either. Did you get enough, dear?"

"More than enough," said Mina. "Nobody's pancakes taste as good to me as yours."

"That's because nobody's pancakes are as good as Grandma's," said Nyla as she entered the kitchen. "I have something I want to show you, Mina. It's in the living room. You come too, Grandma, so you can tell us what you think."

Mina and Grandma Hannah dutifully followed Nyla into the living room.

"Okay now," Nyla said as she took the cover off a long cardboard box. "This is just a suggestion—a possibility of what you could wear for the wedding. It was Mommy's. I'm not sure what she wore it for, but it's gorgeous."

Nyla parted the mounds of carefully folded tissue paper and lifted out a lace dress. It was a dark, unusual green like emeralds or ferns growing in the shade and had obviously been hand dyed. The style was late Edwardian, elegant in its simplicity and timeless with a ballet neckline and short, gossamer sleeves. The bodice, a modified empire cut, ended just above the waist, with the skirt flowing out to a scalloped hemline with a modest train. The most dazzling feature of the dress was the lace itself and its pattern of ferns and roses curving in sensual lines. Nyla put the lace dress and its matching silk underdress on a padded hanger and handed it to Mina, who could only stare in astonishment at the garment. "Just try it on," Nyla said.

Mina went into the spare room just behind the staircase with Ollie trailing after her. She slipped out of her sweater and trousers and slipped into the silk underdress. The green fabric felt cool and soothing on her skin. The dress had several lace-covered buttons on the back that she carefully unbuttoned, and then she put the dress on. Like magic, her sister appeared in the room, buttoned her up, and then turned her to the full-length mirror on the closet door. For a few seconds, the image in the mirror confounded Mina. It was so unlike the image she had of herself in her own mind. She wasn't sure if she imagined it, but she thought the faint scent of her mother's perfume lingered in the lace.

Nyla cocked her head to the side. "Well?"

"It will be perfect," said Mina. "I can't believe you've had this hidden away all these years."

"It's been waiting for you and Ned and your wedding day," Nyla said as she took her sister's hand. "Come on, let's go and show Grandma."

"Oh, darling," Grandma said, as she wiped away a tear. "You look so beautiful. The last time I saw that dress, your mother was wearing it at her engagement party."

Nyla looked surprised. "Mommy wore this at her engagement party?"

"Yes," Grandma nodded. "It came from Paris. Someone had brought it back for their daughter, but it didn't fit, and so your mother bought it because it fit her like a glove. You look just as lovely in it, Mina dear."

Mina looked at them. "If it was Mommy's engagement dress, how could I not wear it? It will be like she's with us."

"What do you think?" Grandma asked. "We could have a delicate lei poʻo made for you with ferns and pink baby roses, and you could wear some of your mother's Niʻihau-shell lei."

Ollie gave Mina several barks as he jumped back and forth.

"Sounds like the 'what do I wear to my wedding' questions are pretty much answered and approved." Mina smiled at her sister. "Thank you, Ny, for saving this dress and for giving it to me to wear."

Just then the telephone started to ring. "What's a sister for?" Nyla said on her way to answer. She picked up the receiver, said something, laughed, and then called out, "Hey Mina, the boyfriend wants to talk to you."

Mina parked her car on the street in front of Setsu's cottage. She and Ollie walked up the path past the vegetables and the flowers, growing with a vigor and enthusiasm that rivaled all the gardens in the neighborhood. Beans climbed up panax hedge poles; carrot tops erupted in raised beds next to radishes and lettuces. Blooming marigolds grew along the edges of the garden and between the vegetables, and she remembered that Setsu had once told her that the flowers kept the bugs away. Ollie's eyes traced the flight path of a honeybee.

"Come inside," said Setsu from the front porch, as she waved Mina toward the door. "Let's go out to the back. It's so nice outside today."

Mina followed her through the house and out to the back porch to the familiar lanai table. Ollie wandered over to the fishpond, lay down in a shady spot, and watched the goldfish. This afternoon Setsu had set out a pitcher of iced tea with mint leaves and a plate of sugar cookies.

"Funny kine, that dog," Setsu said. "He's watching fish."

Mina chuckled. "He always does that. Those dogs used to work for fishermen. Maybe that's why he likes fish."

"It's terrible, what you told me on the phone," Setsu said as she sat down and adjusted the lacquered sticks that were holding her graying hair up in a bun. "And these horrible murders—everyone in town is talking, you know."

"Yes, it is terrible," Mina agreed as she wondered how to begin.

"I guess you want me to tell more about Dr. Nakasone?"

"If you would, it might help us," said Mina, knowing that Setsu was very sensitive about the doctor. Mina took out the things she had found in Akira's house. "I was wondering if you could tell me about these things and if you think they mean anything."

Setsu moved the tray with the tea pitcher and the cookies and spread the pictures and the articles out on the table, and taking her glasses out of her apron pocket, she began to look things over, shaking her head every once in a while and saying something under her breath in Japanese. When she finished looking over everything, she put it in a neat stack on the table, took off her glasses, and looked at Mina. "It's a very sad story, and before I say something, what does it have to do with what you told me on the phone?"

Mina took one of the newspaper clippings out of the stack. "The man at the embassy who was being shot at is this young officer in that newspaper picture with Dr. Nakasone."

Setsu frowned and shook her head. She sighed and leaned back in her chair. "I see. Better I tell you everything then, just in case, but first, you pour some tea for us."

Mina poured two glasses of tea and put two sugar cubes in each glass, stirring them around with the long teaspoons. She handed Setsu her glass, and then took a long sip from her own glass. The familiar taste of Setsu's tea with its hint of pineapple juice soothed her, and she sat back in her chair to listen to what her former nanny had to tell her.

Setsu picked up the faded photograph of the Nakasone family. "I'm not the only one who knows these things," she said as she ran her finger over the photo, "but people don't mention them because the doctor was so good to people. And many Japanese people who came here, they had things they wanted to forget about. I hope Akira Nakasone has not done something foolish." Setsu paused. "Mina-chan, you be sure you eat some cookies, now. I know you like them."

Mina picked up a cookie and took a bite. "These are delicious."

Setsu turned her attention back to the old photograph. "This photo was in Japan. Look, here is Dr. Nakasone. He looks so young. This was his wife, and here is Akira when he was a small boy, and this must be the sister. She's the wife's sister, you see, not Akira's sister—pretty, no? Such a shame what happened."

"What did happen?" Mina asked as she took another cookie.

"Dr. Nakasone was in the military before, and the young man in the newspaper, he was the son of a military man who was very high up. The father was promoting Dr. Nakasone's career, and so the doctor had to treat his son very well. You know how those things go. So one day he invited the son to visit with his family and the son— what did you say his name is now?"

"He likes people to call him Jimmy," Mina said, "but I think they call him Takeo too."

"I don't know the family names, but anyway, he meets the young sister. You can see she was beautiful," Setsu said as she ran her fingers over the photograph. "They say she was a simple country girl, and he starts to flirt with her and, you know, make advances. Then one day she goes to her sister and says she's pregnant. She tells the sister how many times he forced her, and she didn't know what to do because he threatens her. He says if she tells, his father will ruin Dr. Nakasone's chances to succeed. The doctor finds out, and he goes to the boy's father, who blames the poor girl. The Jimmy person—or Takeo or whatever his name—says she seduced him, and he calls her very bad names. Then, a few days later, the poor girl kills herself. She hangs herself in the shed, and her sister finds her. The doctor is very angry, and to avoid scandal they let him go from the military service. He just goes away to be a country doctor. After the young sister dies, the wife is very sad and becomes ill, and then she dies some months later. That's when the doctor decides to take his son and come to Hawai'i to try for a new life."

"That's terrible," Mina said. "I can see why Akira would hate him."

"Yes," Setsu agreed, "he has good reasons."

As Mina left Setsu's cottage, she decided to drive by her childhood home on Kamehameha Avenue. She drove down East Mānoa Road, past the triangular-shaped park, and took a sharp left onto the wide avenue. Then she parked across the street from the house and rolled down her window. Ollie sat up as if he expected something interesting to happen next.

"Let's go for a walk, Ollie," she said as she picked up his leash from the passenger seat.

Ollie happily jumped out of the car, and she snapped on his leash. He didn't really need to be on a leash, as he came as soon as she called him, but she thought it better to keep him close to her, because some people didn't like strange dogs wandering into their yards. Also, Ollie often found a cat or a mongoose a very tempting chase. The large monkeypod trees hung over the street and the grass lawns along the roads, making it shady and pleasant. As she strolled past the houses, she tried to recall the names of the families who lived in each one. She knew that some of them still lived there, and she supposed she could knock on a few doors to say hello. But she just didn't feel like talking to anyone. She thought about the things that Setsu had said, and it occurred to her that although Akira might have a motive for shooting at the Jimmy character, it was unlikely, in view of his father's rejection of his military career, that he would ever want to spy for the Japanese government. That left Tamara, Molly, and Bill as prime suspects. Tamara could easily gather information in exchange, not for money but for valuable pieces of art. Mina knew the avarice that easily overwhelmed collectors, causing them to lose any moral restraint they might have in order to get the piece they wanted. And Tamara, for all her very nice social mannerisms, had large amounts of determination and drive. She wondered if that drive included the capacity to kill. Tamara's former father-in-law apparently thought so. Mina had also seen Molly's temper flare up in an instant, a characteristic that pointed to a chaotic inner life. Molly could be furtive and sneaky too, and she remembered the flush and nervous look on Molly's face the day that she had been late for Desmond's interview—the day Ari had died and Molly said she had been out walking. And Bill—so enthralled with the memory of his mother—was he equally devoted to her family and the ideals of the Nazi Party? His hard-drinking, beach-combing, and artistic lifestyle would be the perfect cover for a political assassin and spy. His involvement in the yacht club gave him plenty of opportunity, and she wondered if anyone had ever bothered to check and see if he was really ever even in the navy or if everyone was just taking his word for it.

Lost in thought and looking down at Ollie and the grass at her feet, she suddenly looked up and found herself standing in front of her old home. The house stood back from the street. Her eyes followed the plain concrete walkway up to the five stairs and the wooden lanai that led up to the front door. The lanai continued and widened along the right side of the house, where Mina could see a set of rattan furniture. To the left of the front door, the wide bay window protruded, and she remembered the Christmas Eve she had spent lying there on the window seat at the edge of the living room because she was sick. The smell of the Christmas tree came back to her, as did the taste of eggnog laced with bourbon that her father let her sip. The radio had been on and tuned in to a reading of "A Christmas Carol." She remembered how her mother had come to check on her, and as she stood there, she could almost feel her mother's cool, smooth hand on her forehead. Ollie looked up and barked at her, and she turned away, not wanting to alarm the neighbors by lingering too long. She walked across the street to her car and took a last look at the house before she opened the car door. Her grandmother and Nyla went frequently to her mother's grave with flowers, but instead of the sad graveyard, she preferred to come here, to walk down this street, to look at their old house, and to remember her mother in this place, because it was where they all had been happy together.

As she started to drive away, she worried that Akira might make a second attempt and get himself in real trouble. She wanted to find a pay phone and call Ned right away to tell him what Setsu had told her. She told herself to calm down. Surely this Jimmy person would be well protected by the embassy. Ned would be at the station with Todd at least until midafternoon, and she would just have to wait to talk to him when he got home. But maybe then they could do something before it was too late.

As Ned looked in on the interview room at Raymond and Marguerite Morgan, he thought they were a very odd couple. Raymond, in his white linen suit and crisp white shirt, exuded an air of sophistication, while poor, chubby Marguerite, in her white, blue-flowered dress with puffed sleeves, looked as if she would feel more comfortable milking cows. There was no accounting, Ned thought, for how people chose each other, and perhaps Marguerite had some very fine qualities that her husband admired. Todd had chosen to interview them together, as he felt their only use might be that they had noticed or seen something that could be useful. Ned could see that Todd's attitude was relaxed and casual.

"Thanks for coming in to speak to me," Todd said. "I'll try not to take up too much of your time."

"We're happy to help in any way that we can," Raymond said as he placed a cigarette in a jade holder. "I have a personal interest in seeing you apprehend whoever is responsible for these murders."

Marguerite nodded. "Yes, my husband could have been killed too."

"Well, I certainly know where you were when Ari Schoner was killed," Todd began, "but could you tell me where you were when Tilda Clement and Desmond Rivers were killed? You understand, I'm asking everyone this question. It's just a formality."

"I believe," Raymond said as he lit his cigarette with an engraved silver lighter, "that the deaths occurred on two successive Sunday evenings?"

"That's right," said Todd as he pushed an ashtray toward Raymond.

"Oh, on Sunday evening, we are always at home with the children," Marguerite offered. "We always have a nice meal on Sunday evening, and then sometimes we sing together. Eva is very accomplished on the piano."

Ned smiled to himself. He had trouble imagining Raymond Morgan singing with his family after dinner.

"I see," said Todd. "Did you know Ari Schoner well?"

"Of course, we saw him at art events and meetings, but we didn't socialize with him outside of the artist's group," Raymond responded.

"He was very helpful with the arts group," Marguerite added.

"Did he have any enemies that you know of?" Todd asked.

"No," said Marguerite. "He was very well liked."

Raymond shook his head. "I don't know why anyone would want to harm him."

"And Tilda Clement?" Todd looked at both of them.

From where Ned was sitting, he could see Marguerite blush at the mention of Tilda, and he realized that she must have known about her husband's indiscretion. Raymond remained perfectly calm and seemingly unaware of his wife's discomfort. Or perhaps, Ned thought, he didn't care and was one of those husbands who expected their wives to tolerate their extramarital affairs.

Marguerite lifted her chin and said, "She was a woman with no morals."

"I've gathered that," Todd said with a half smile.

"Who knows who she had relations with?" Marguerite went on. "It is terrible how she died, but that kind of loose behavior can lead to very bad things."

Raymond said nothing as he sat and blew his cigarette smoke nonchalantly up in the air. He curled his right hand over and examined his fingernails.

"And Desmond Rivers," Todd continued, "do you think he was one of Tilda's conquests?"

"Well," said Raymond, "yes, they were having an affair."

"It was shameful," said Marguerite.

"Desmond had quite an eye for the ladies," Raymond added. "He and Bill had a big blowup too. I think Desmond had been making advances on Bill's wife."

"When was this?" Todd's interest perked up.

"It was on Saturday at the yacht club, just after the fencing exhibition," Raymond answered. "They were upstairs in one of the meeting rooms, and I happened to hear them because I was walking by in the hall. I thought they might start fighting."

"What about Desmond's wife, Molly?" Todd asked. "How did she feel about his philandering?"

"She never spoke about it," Marguerite said. "Perhaps she did not know."

"Don't be silly, Marguerite," said Raymond. "Of course she knew about Tilda. She's not stupid."

"And doesn't Molly spend quite a bit of time with Akira Nakasone?" Todd persisted. "Do you think there's anything going on between them?"

"No," said Marguerite, "she's just very interested in the *ikebana.*"

"I don't think he's Molly's type at all," Raymond added, "being an Oriental."

Todd frowned as if thinking. "Do you know if Desmond owned a gun?"

"I don't think so," Raymond said. "At least I never saw one, but he could have."

"Do you know if anyone in the artists' group owns a gun?"

"Well," Raymond said thoughtfully, "Tamara said once her husband used to hunt on the outer islands, so perhaps she still has some of his guns. I have never been to Akira's house, but I believe at one time his father was in the Japanese army."

"I don't think April would have a gun," Marguerite added.

Raymond shook his head. "No, she wouldn't know the first thing about guns."

"And, of course, we never allowed a gun in our house—because of the children," Marguerite said with resolve.

"And Ari or Tilda?" Todd asked.

"Tilda had a gun," Raymond said, "a small thing, a ladies' gun. She showed it off to me once. She said it was for protection."

"Yes," said Todd, "we found that among her things."

"As for Ari," Raymond said, "I really don't know. That's all I can think of on the gun issue."

"But Raymond," Marguerite said, looking at her husband.

"But what?" he responded with irritation.

"Don't you remember that time we went to Bill's house?" she said sheepishly.

"What are you talking about?" Todd cut in and addressed Marguerite. "What happened at Bill's house?"

Marguerite looked startled and didn't answer. Todd spoke calmly and quietly. "Mrs. Morgan, this is a serious murder investigation. If you remember something that you think is relevant, you need to tell me."

"Many months ago we were there for a barbecue one evening, and Bill showed us a gun," she said. "Maybe Raymond wasn't in the room—that's why he doesn't remember—but Bill showed off a gun. He was very proud of it. I remember because it was a German gun that belonged to his grandfather."

Raymond frowned. "Are you sure, Marguerite? I never saw it."

"Yes," Marguerite insisted, "I am very sure of what I saw."

"Well, thank you for telling me, Mrs. Morgan," Todd said in an even voice. "I don't have any more questions for you. Unless there's anything else you can think of that might be useful for me to know, I won't take up any more of your time."

Raymond laughed as he stood. "We could use your advice, Detective Forest, since you are used to enforcing the law, on how to handle our young daughter."

Todd looked at him and smiled. "I'm afraid you're on your own there. Young ladies, in my experience, are a law unto themselves."

Ned went right down as soon as Todd gave him the signal that the room was clear. Todd was already yelling down the hall for his assistant.

"I guess you're about to call for a search warrant," said Ned.

"Damn right I am," Todd said.

"It's very odd that I didn't come across it while I was going through his things," Ned said. "He must have it very well concealed, or maybe it was in one of the more public rooms. I didn't look in the kitchen or the parlor."

"Don't blame yourself, buddy," said Todd. "You're right. You couldn't look everywhere. With a search warrant, we can take the house apart if we like. I'd invite you to the party, but I don't think it would look good."

"No, no," Ned agreed. "At this point, I think it's better for me to appear to be a disinterested party, but you will ask your men to watch for anything that may be relevant to our other interests, won't you?"

"Don't worry, pal," Todd assured him. "We'll go through the house with a flea comb."

# 22

# THURSDAY, DECEMBER 19

**T**HE MORNING SUN had just reached the beach at Kaʻalāwai when Mina emerged from the sea after a morning swim. Ollie was still frolicking along the shoreline and digging holes in the wet sand. Her sleep had been restless and her mind crowded with thoughts about Bill Hutchinson's arrest the evening before. Last night, Ned told her about the report of the gun. Later in the evening, Todd called and said they had recovered a German Luger at Bill's house, and they had him in custody. It was only a matter of ballistics confirming the gun was the murder weapon before he would be formally charged. For reasons Mina couldn't quite articulate to herself, this turn of events grated on her and made her feel unsettled. She was still worried about Akira and hoped that somehow they could intervene and talk to him today. The December sea had chilled her, and she wrapped up in her beach robe, lay back on her towel, closed her eyes, and welcomed the warmth of the morning sun. She concentrated on the murmuring sound of the very small waves that washed up on the sand until her body began to feel warm and heavy and her mind less troubled. She wasn't sure how long she lay in what felt like restful oblivion, but found herself enticed into reality by the smell of freshly brewed coffee. She opened her eyes to see a tray next to her with a cup of coffee and a note that read, "Will wait for your arrival to put scones in the oven." She smiled, sat up, and sipped the warm brew. Ollie appeared, ran around her a couple of times, and then took off toward the house.

On her way to Ned's bungalow, she passed Ollie, who was lying in the shade under the hau arbor that separated the two bungalows, near a table set for two. There was a tiny vase of weedy flowers in the middle, a sugar bowl painted with a hula girl, a matching creamer, a dish with a gleaming slab of yellow butter, a small bowl of Setsu's liliko'i jelly and egg-shaped salt and pepper shakers. The smell of bacon drifted out of Ned's house, and when she peered in the screen door, she could see Ned taking a tray out of the oven. She went in to see if she could help, and he handed her two plates of perfectly scrambled eggs and strips of bacon. He popped the fresh scones into a small basket lined with a clean dish towel and followed her outside to the arbor. The morning sun was just high enough to cast the shadows of the heart-shaped leaves over the table.

"Ned, you're a dream," she said as they sat down.

"I think it's going to be a rough day," he said, "so we should be kind to ourselves and have a nice breakfast."

She sighed. "It was already a rough night."

"I didn't sleep very well either," he said as he sliced a scone in two and placed it on her plate.

"Thanks, darling," she said. "You know what I think my problem is with this case?" she said as she carefully buttered her scone. "I like all of our suspects, and I don't want any of them to be murderers. Tamara is guilty of collector's avarice, but she seems like a nice person. Molly is dark and troubled, but I find something deep and genuine about her. Akira is strange but vulnerable, and Bill—well, I just can't see him being so vicious."

"Why do you think that is?" he asked. "I'm not necessarily disagreeing. I'm just curious."

She paused for a moment in thoughtful silence. "I know this might sound strange and not objective at all, but I can't help it. It's his art. I just don't see any trace of malice in it, and I imagine if he were a hardened killer, it would show up somehow in his creative work."

"I have trouble seeing him as a killer too—for a reason that's even more subjective than yours."

"Let's have it," she said just before she took a bite of her scone.

"It's Tevai. Even though she appears to be, and maybe she is, naive about many things, she's highly intuitive about people, and I don't think she would marry or love anyone who had a nature that was excessively violent." He waited to see her reaction.

She smiled at him. "I think you have a soft spot for her, Ned."

He laughed. "Maybe I do, but I still think I'm right. And I have another, more evidence-based reason to think he's innocent."

She gave him a suspicious look. "Have you been holding out on me?"

He looked at his watch. "For about an hour and a half."

"I'll forgive you then," she said, "but only because of this delicious breakfast."

"I spoke to Todd this morning, and he said that the gun is a match for two of the murders. So they'll be charging Bill and are going to try to get him to confess to strangling Tilda. But then I asked him where he found the gun, and he said he found it in the studio, in the chest with all of those papers about Bill's mother and his family. Bill claims the gun went missing and that he hadn't seen it for at least a month. The thing is, it certainly wasn't there when I looked in the chest. Of course, I know he could have had it hidden somewhere else in the house, but I think we have to ask ourselves, if he did use that gun to commit two murders, don't you think he would hide it in a better place?"

Mina frowned. "You're right. Whoever killed those people isn't stupid and certainly isn't careless. If I were the murderer, I wouldn't put it in an unlocked chest in my painting studio. I wouldn't even keep it on my own property. If I were Bill and I were a murderer, I would stash it somewhere like the yacht club."

"You sound like an actress who was trained by Stanislavski."

"Who's that?"

"A theatre director who got his actors to use what he called the 'magic if.' You're supposed to use your imagination to gain insight into the character you are going to portray by asking yourself things like, 'If I were a peasant in the dark ages, what would I be wearing on my feet, and how would it make me walk?' and 'What would I be looking forward to eating for dinner?' and so on."

"Sounds like it could be useful for other things too," she said as she ate her last piece of bacon.

"That was a very simplistic explanation," he added.

"I've got the gist of it."

"Then," he said, "I guess we both agree that we don't think Bill is a killer."

"Yes," she said, "but do you think he could be a spy?"

"I think it's more likely that he would be a spy than a murderer, but Todd found no evidence of spying. I must call Todd and remind him to be sure to look at any kind of locker Bill might have at that yacht club. Surely Desmond had one too, and we may have overlooked them."

"Have you spoken to Nigel about the arrest?"

"Yes, I called him this morning," he said. "We still have the big problem of tying Bill to spying."

Mina had finished her breakfast. "What shall we do? I know what I want to do. I want to go with Reggie to Akira's house and have a talk with him. I don't care if he gets mad or causes a fuss. I just don't want him to take any more potshots at anyone. I don't think he's dangerous, and I really don't think he's your spy or the murderer. What do you think?"

Ned groaned. "I think it sounds dangerous, but I don't suppose it will stop you."

"No, it will not stop me."

"If Nigel finds out about this, its bound to send him into a rage."

"I'm willing to deal with his rage. Even though he's put on the good-manners act, I can tell he doesn't like dealing with Todd, much less me."

"It's true. He has been unusually resistant."

"Really, Ned, can you see Akira as a murderer? Or a spy?"

"I agree it seems very unlikely, but we just don't know. He could be under Molly's sway and very unlike the person he presents himself to be. You should know that by now. In these situations, the lake looks calm—"

Mina laughed. "But underneath, there could be dragons!"

Ned shook his head. "Why do I even bother? Well, I do insist that Reggie should go along. Maybe he could show up in advance on some other pretext. Reggie will be there, and Akira doesn't know you're working with him. Will you at least do that for me?"

"I'll call him and arrange it," she said. "What are you going to do?"

"I'm thinking I might go over to Bill Hitchins' house to pick up our paintings. I'm sure that Tevai will tell me what happened, and maybe I can ferret out something helpful."

"Let's meet afterwards and compare notes," she said.

"Yes," he said, "I know just the place. Just tell Reggie to take you to our hideaway."

Ned parked his car in the lane just outside the gate that opened to the Hitchins' house. He had called earlier and asked Tevai if he could come and pick up the two paintings that he and Mina had bought from Bill. He felt certain she would agree, as it looked like they could certainly use the money, and he could take the opportunity to see if there was any way he could help Tevai. He opened the creaky gate and walked across the lawn. The waves broke lightly against the black lava today. Without steep faces, the swells moved in and out almost rhythmically. Rahiti waved to Ned from a far corner of the yard, where he was working with a pair of shears to trim one of the hedges.

Rahiti flashed him a dazzling smile and called out, "Ia Orana, Ned."

Ned raised his hand and called back, "Ia Orana, Rahiti."

Ned saw that the door of the house was open, but he stood on the threshold and called out before entering. Tevai appeared dressed in a blue and white pareo around her waist and a white cotton blouse. He could tell she had been crying. As they walked through the living room and kitchen area, Ned saw Eva Morgan sitting in one of the faded easy chairs looking at a magazine. Tevai took Ned straight into the studio and showed him the framed pictures that she had nicely displayed on two easels next to a worktable.

"I hope you like the frames," she said in a small voice.

"They're perfect," Ned said as he took out an envelope from his jacket and placed it on the table. "Here's the money we agreed on. We're so happy to have these."

"I think they make the pictures look very nice," she said as she ran her fingers over the frame of the painting of the Broom Road. "I will miss this painting very much."

"Maybe you can get Bill to paint one just for you," he said.

"Let me wrap them in brown paper, and Rahiti will help you carry them out to the car," she said as she moved to find the paper.

"Wait, Tevai," he said, "before you do that, sit down. I want to talk to you about Bill." He found two chairs and placed them as if they were viewing the paintings. "I know that the police came yesterday and arrested him."

Tears came immediately to Tevai's brown eyes. "I don't know how they think he could do such a thing."

"I want to help Bill," he said, handing her his handkerchief, "so do you think you could answer some questions?"

"If you think it will help," she said.

"This gun they found," he began, "it did belong to Bill, didn't it?"

"Yes," she said, "but what Bill told the police was true. We couldn't find it for a long time, and Bill was very upset. He walked all over the house looking and yelling, but we still couldn't find it."

"Who knew he had the gun?"

"Oh, everybody knew. He was always taking it out and showing everyone."

"And when did the gun go missing?" he asked.

"I'm not sure, but maybe it was around the Halloween party. That's when we saw it wasn't there, but Bill didn't look at it every day."

"And the gun, the house, were never locked up?"

Tevai shook her head. "No, we never lock anything."

"So anyone could have come in here at any time and taken it," he said as if thinking out loud.

"Is it bad for Bill?"

Ned looked at her. "It's too bad he had that fight."

She looked confused. "What fight?"

"The fight," he said carefully, "that he and Desmond had at the yacht club after the fencing demonstration."

"I don't know about any fight," she said. "Desmond came back here on Saturday afternoon. He drank a beer, and they were laughing and talking just like always. Bill was asleep when I left for work at four, and Desmond had gone."

"Someone said that they had an argument because Desmond made improper advances to you."

She frowned. "Desmond? He never did things like that to me."

Ned suspected she could be covering up for Bill. "I guess the person who said those things must have misunderstood," Ned said as he stood up. "Do you know if Bill has got a lawyer?"

"I don't know anything about those things. Will they let me see him?" She looked at him like he was the one who was making the decision.

Ned nodded. "Yes, I'm sure they'll let you speak to him for a few minutes. If you want, I can drive you there right now and make sure you get to see him."

A smile brightened her face. "Thank you, Ned." She jumped up and took his hand. "Can Rahiti come with us?"

"Of course," he said. "And while you're visiting with Bill, I'll go and speak to someone I know who's a lawyer. Bill needs to have a lawyer."

The sound of the gate creaking turned their attention to the yard. Through the window, they saw Raymond Morgan steaming toward the house. Rahiti saw him and put down his shears. Raymond walked in the front door without knocking or announcing himself, and Ned and Tevai could hear him yelling at Eva in the living room. Ned put his finger to his lips, signaling Tevai to be quiet so they could listen.

"What the hell do you think you're doing here, young lady?" Raymond bellowed. Get up right now. You're coming home, and you're never coming back here."

"But Tevai—"

Her father interrupted. "She's not suitable company for you anymore. Her husband has been arrested for murder!"

"And I know he didn't do it!" she yelled back.

Through the half-opened door, Ned saw Raymond grab Eva by the shoulders and force her toward the front door. Rahiti was standing just outside and made a move to help Eva. Raymond let go of her for a second and gave Rahiti a violent push to the ground. He then caught hold of his daughter by the wrist and dragged her across the yard and out of the gate. As soon as they were out of sight, Tevai ran outside to her brother with Ned following. Rahiti had hit his head on a rock as he fell and appeared to be dazed. They took him inside, and Tevai gave him a cloth with some ice for the bump on his head.

"Are you all right?" Ned asked.

"Yes," Rahiti answered. "He is cruel to his daughter. Right, Ned?"

"Yes, Rahiti, that was very cruel," Ned answered, and he couldn't help but feel touched by the trust these two young people had placed in him because they instinctively saw him as one of their own.

The bamboo hedge clattered in the breeze as Mina checked her watch and took a deep breath before she pushed open the wooden gate at the entrance of Akira Nakasone's Pauoa Valley home. Reggie's car was parked in the drive, so everything was going according to their plan. When she had phoned Akira and asked if she could come and speak to him about something important, she was more than surprised that he seemed very willing to talk to her. The sky was now overcast, and clouds had gathered above the mountains, looking as if it might rain. She walked slowly along the path and over the wooden bridge, as she looked at the waiting house. From the bridge, the haunting music of the koto drifted on the air, and she supposed that in addition to his brush painting and *ikebana*, Akira was also a talented musician. She walked up to the door and knocked, and the music stopped. Akira opened the door and smiled. After taking off her shoes, she entered and followed him to the room in the back of the house. She cast a guilty glance at the desk where she had pilfered the family papers. They sat in two chairs looking out into the wide lanai. Light rain began to fall on the lawn and garden and the trees beyond, and she could feel a slight change of temperature and moisture in the air. She noticed Reggie working on an arrangement down at the other end of the lanai, out of earshot but not out of sight.

"One of my students had a sudden inspiration and wanted me to critique his idea," Akira said to explain Reggie's presence. "Don't worry about him. He can't hear anything we say."

"It was good of you to agree to see me," she began.

"I'm intrigued," he said. "What is it that is so important?"

"First," she said, "I want you to know I'm doing this because I'm concerned about you, and I don't want to see you make a mistake and do something that might ruin your life."

He shifted in his seat and gave her an interested look. "And just what big mistake do you think I'm about to make?"

"I've found out from certain sources about the attempted shooting at the Japanese embassy yesterday morning," she said.

"An attempted shooting?" he asked. "Who was the target?"

"Someone who calls himself Jimmy but whose Japanese name is Takeo Tadashi."

Akira's expression changed for a split second to one of alarm, but his mask of calm instantly returned. "And you think I am the person who was trying to shoot Takeo Tadashi?"

"Yes, I do," she said.

"And why would I want to do that?" he asked.

She did her best to sound calm and kind. "Because of the despicable things he did to your aunt and because of your mother's early death. And I agree that what he did deserves punishment, but not at the cost of you spending the rest of your life in a prison cell."

"The memory of someone in the Japanese community has a long reach," he said quietly.

"They only told me because they knew I would try to help you," she said. "I understand that you may be angry, and if you want me to leave, I will. But please don't ruin the life your father worked so hard to give you for the sake of revenge."

He smiled at her. "How could I be angry with someone who is so concerned about my welfare?"

She just looked at him and didn't know what to say.

"I appreciate it very much," he said, "but I'm afraid I have to disappoint you. It wasn't me who was shooting at him. I don't even know how to shoot a gun. If I were going to go after him, I'd be more likely to chop off his head with a sword."

"He's right," said a female voice from the doorway.

Mina looked up to see Molly enter the room. She was wearing a Japanese cotton robe, and she looked as if she'd just gotten up.

"He spent the whole morning—the whole day, in fact—with me. And I would swear to it in any court of law," she said as she sat down next to Akira.

Mina looked away and then looked back at them and smiled. "Well, that makes me a fool, doesn't it? But I'm a happy fool at any rate."

"Actually," Akira said, "even though I didn't try to kill the bastard, I'm very interested that someone else did. Besides what he did to my family, do you know anything else about him?"

Mina took a deep breath and realized she had to make a very quick decision. "I know that Navy Intelligence has their eye on him as someone who could be receiving information for the Japanese military about Pearl Harbor—troop movements, ships, and things like that."

"And are you in touch with Navy Intelligence?" he asked.

"In a way."

Akira was silent for a moment. "I hear and see things at the embassy, when I go to do their flowers. I'm very quiet and polite, and no one notices me. Takeo has come there before, and I know just before he goes back to Japan, the ambassador always arranges a lunch or dinner party at the Sakura Teahouse in Alewa Heights. Once before, after one of those parties, I looked in Takeo's room and found things that make me sure he must be carrying information. I had plans to follow him this time to see who was giving it to him."

"And then what were you going to do?"

"I was going to tell someone, but I didn't know who," he said. "So it's quite a fortuitous coincidence that you have come here today, because the next teahouse party is tomorrow afternoon."

"Have you ever heard of synchronicity?" Mina asked.

He shook his head. "No, what is it?"

"It's a new idea by a Swiss psychiatrist, a former disciple of Freud's. It describes exactly what's just happened—this fortuitous coincidence."

Molly, who had been listening quietly, finally spoke. "This whole thing sounds dangerous."

"It's very dangerous. I think whoever is doing the spying may have committed the three murders. I don't know if you've heard, but they've arrested Bill."

"Bill?" Molly jumped to her feet. "Bill couldn't kill anyone. I know him. He couldn't."

"You've just given me some very valuable information," Mina said to Akira. "I think I need to tell the people in charge of this investigation as soon as possible."

"I'll walk you to the gate," said Akira. "Just let me go and talk to my student for a minute."

"Mina," Molly said when Akira had left the room, "I hope you don't think too badly of me. Desmond and I had been on the outs for a long time, and then when I found out about his affair with Tilda, I just couldn't take it anymore."

"I don't think badly of you, Molly," Mina said. "I hope you find some happiness in life."

Akira returned and walked Mina out the front door, over the bridge, and across the lawn, and when they got to the gate, they turned around to look back at the house.

"Do you see the way the house looks from here?" he asked her.

"It almost looks like a storybook house, with a Japanese flair," she said.

"When my father bought this property, there was no house. He brought me here to this spot and asked me what kind of house I thought we should make here. When we got home to our rented house—we lived down in the lower part of the valley then—I went to my room and started to draw a picture of a house. I worked on it for days, and when it was finished, I showed it to my father, who had forgotten he even asked me the question. But he was so impressed by my effort that he showed it to the builders and had them build a house like the one in my drawing."

"I hope you still have the drawing," she said.

Akira smoothed back his straight, dark hair. "My father changed when my aunt and my mother died. He was always a good man, but before that, he was ambitious and wanted to get ahead in the world. Their deaths pushed him into a daily awareness of the impermanence of life, and he would constantly tell me to try to appreciate each day and to not waste my time pursuing activities and things that had no meaning for me. I loved my father and would never dishonor him by murdering another human being, even though the person might deserve it, but if there is some way I can help to do what needs to be done, please let me know. That would be an honor to my family and my father."

Mina looked out over the lawn and turned to him. "I'll be sure to let you know, and thank you for everything."

Mina drove down the driveway and parked down the street where Reggie would be sure to see her. In about fifteen minutes, she saw him coming down the street in her rearview mirror. He pulled up next to her and asked her to follow him, and she put her car in gear and pulled away from the curb—intrigued and curious about what Ned had meant by a hideaway.

Mina and Reggie were eating plate lunches with wooden chopsticks and drinking colas when Alika walked in. Mina, with her chopsticks in midair, stopped and smiled at him.

She let out a laugh. "Why am I not surprised to see you here, Alika?"

"Because like a germ, I'm everywhere?" he laughed.

"Schoolboy humor," she said. "The world could use more of it. So I guess you've been helping these jokers out?"

"Yep," he replied.

"And would you like a plate lunch? We have an extra one." She pointed with her chopstick to a plate wrapped in brown paper.

"Sure, thanks," Alika said as he sat down.

Mina had purchased the lunches downstairs in the store and had been unable to resist buying several of the oversized almond cookies from the big glass jar on the counter. When Ned arrived a few minutes later, he was only too happy to have something to eat, and they were just finishing up when Todd showed up, followed a few minutes later by Nigel. Mina reported what Akira had told her about Takeo Tadashi and also told them about his alibi. Just as Ned predicted, she could see Nigel's anger. Ned related what Tevai had told him about the gun going missing and how she didn't think Bill and Desmond had any kind of argument after the fencing demonstration.

When Ned had finished, Nigel turned on Mina. "Just what did you think you were doing, going over to Nakasone's house? Did you know about this, Ned?"

"It doesn't matter whether he knew about it or not," Mina said. "He's my fiancé, not my keeper."

"You've overstepped your bounds. He could be the spy we're looking for, and now you've gone and alerted him to the fact that the navy is investigating. He could easily be lying, and this Molly could be his willing accomplice or even the ringleader. It certainly seems like now she has a reason to want her husband out of the way."

"Come on," interjected Todd. "At this point, it's more likely that the murders and the spying are two different parties."

"But we won't know that," Ned said, "until we see who shows up at the teahouse. And it will be very interesting, because if we eliminate Akira and Molly, Tamara is the only one left."

"Besides Bill," Todd reminded him. "If no one shows up, it has to be Bill."

"And there *is* a pile of evidence to suggest that Tamara could very well be a spy," Ned said.

Todd looked at Ned. "What are our plans, then? Since this seems to have more to do with your job, I'll follow your lead."

Ned looked at Nigel. "I say we go to the teahouse, be prepared, and see what happens. It's certainly worth looking into. Todd could provide some unobtrusive backup."

"I'll agree to that," said Nigel with an edge of hostility, "but remember, the ONI has not authorized us to make any kind of arrest. They only want us to positively identify the person responsible for passing information. And Todd already has a person in custody for the murders."

Todd looked at Nigel for a few seconds before he spoke. "A person is arrested on the *suspicion* of murder, but we could always have made a mistake."

Undaunted, Mina moved right on. "Akira will arrange a private party room for us at the teahouse for lunch tomorrow before the time he thinks the embassy party is going to be there. He and Reggie can show up early to make a special flower arrangement for the table in our room. You know, there's one huge advantage to having him help us."

"And what's that?" asked Todd.

Mina smiled. "He's Japanese, and everyone at the teahouse trusts him."

"Of course," Todd said as he looked at Ned. "Does she ever make you feel like you're stupid, Ned?"

Ned chuckled. "Not more than three or four times a day."

"So what do you want me to do?" Todd asked.

Nigel shrugged. "Ask Ned."

"I'd like you to be in the teahouse with us," said Ned, "and have a couple of men in plain clothes placed just outside the grounds. I'll drive over there after this so I can get a feel for how things are laid out."

Todd popped the cap off of a bottle of cola. "Do you think we need to be armed?"

Ned thought for a moment. "I think it would be wise if you had a concealed weapon. If this person has spied and committed the other murders, it could be dangerous."

Todd sipped his cola and put it down. "You really think Hitchins isn't guilty, don't you?"

"I could be wrong," Ned said, "but I don't think he's guilty."

Todd looked at his watch and stood up to leave. "I need to get back to the station to fix things up, but why don't we all meet tomorrow morning?"

"Why don't we come round to your office tomorrow?" Ned suggested. "Around nine."

"Fine," said Todd as he eagerly made for the door.

"I guess tomorrow Akira will know that I've been lying to him," Reggie said in a dejected voice.

"When I call him," Mina said, "I'll explain things to him. Do you want me to tell him that you've really become interested in *ikebana?* Have you?"

Reggie looked embarrassed. "To tell you the truth, I have. Do you think that's weird?"

"It's art, Reggie," Ned said, "and you don't have to be embarrassed just because it involves flowers."

Reggie got up and wandered over to some of the fencing equipment that had been left in the living room area. He picked up one of the foils. "Say, Ned, do you think you could give me a fencing lesson one of these days? I'd like to try it out."

"I'd be happy to," said Ned. "I'm sure Nigel and Mina would too."

"I'm rusty," Mina said, "but I'm ready."

"Jimmy said he likes to fence," Reggie said.

"Really?" Ned asked.

"Yeah," said Reggie as he waved the foil around in the air, "he learned it at some club in—"

"Be careful!" shouted Nigel. But it was too late. Reggie had accidentally knocked a dusty vase off a shelf, and they all watched it crash and shatter on the floor.

"On that note," said Mina, "I think I'll be leaving. Don't forget, Ned, we have a dinner date at the arbor."

Nigel waited until Mina had left before he spoke. "Ned, I need to have a word with you about Mina."

"What's that?" Ned asked, determined to remain calm to Nigel's anger. He went over to help Reggie pick up the pieces of the shattered vase and place them in a trash bin.

"How could you just let her go and talk to Akira Nakasone like that? If you can't control her, I want her off this case."

"Then speak to Todd. She's not working for me."

"This is exactly what I mean about outside interference."

"Nigel, Mina may just have uncovered some valuable information for us by going there to talk to him. Surely you have to see that."

Nigel shook his head. "And I'm telling you that he may be totally misleading us. And she could have seriously compromised our objectives."

"Well," said Ned as he threw a piece of the broken vase into the bin. "I guess tomorrow we'll find out."

The sun was setting, and Mina turned the lights on to illuminate the arbor. She had just started a fire in the hibachi. She was happy that there was not much wind. But the December evening was chilly, so she had put on a sweater. The birds were chirping away in the trees, having their last hurrah before nightfall, and Ollie was dashing around the bungalows carrying a stick of driftwood in his mouth as if he were on a mission. She could tell by the way the waves sounded breaking in the distance that the ocean was calm. Ned wandered out to the arbor with a cocktail shaker and two glasses on a tray. He poured something pale and frosty into the two glasses, and they toasted each other and drank.

"This is delicious," she said. "Thank you."

"It's the least I can do for the cook. Nigel phoned. He was in a state and nearly yelling at me. He was adamant that Naval Intelligence doesn't want us to arrest the suspect, just to witness and identify the illegal activity. He said he couldn't be at the police station in the morning, but he would meet us at the teahouse."

"That's odd," she said. "I mean, even if he's angry, he should be there."

"Something is not right with him. I'm worried and puzzled. I keep feeling like there's something I should be seeing, and I'm not."

She frowned. "Here's another thing I don't get. Why isn't the ONI more interested at this point? Why aren't they participating?"

"I don't know," he said. "Nigel is the one who has contact with them."

"You don't?"

"I've met them, of course, but everything passes through Nigel."

"That's convenient," she said as she stirred the charcoal.

He gave her a curious look. "What does that mean, darling?"

"I don't know exactly," she said, staring at the glowing coals. "It just slipped out. It's going to take a while for this to burn down. So in the meantime, could you do me a favor?"

"Anything your heart desires," he said.

"I think there's a mouse underneath my stove. Do you think you could catch it for me? I don't want you to kill it or anything. I just don't want it in my house."

He laughed. "Ah, my specialty, rodent removal. Do you have a torch?"

"A torch?"

"Sorry, what you Yanks call a flashlight."

"I do, but the batteries are dead."

"Not to worry," he said. "You'll find one in the glove box of my car."

Mina walked up the driveway to Ned's sedan, opened the glove compartment, and reached for the flashlight. Stuck in the glove compartment was a file folder, and it took her a moment to remember that it was the folder she had taken from Tilda's house on the evening of the murder. Mina remembered the reason they had gone to the house was to pick up this version of the piece on Tilda for the catalog. Tilda had been so insistent about having editorial control over it. Mina opened the folder and looked at the first page. There weren't many notes—mostly added adjectives that flattered the artist. She took the folder and the flashlight and went into her bungalow, where she found Ned on the floor, peeking under the stove. She threw the folder on the pune'e and handed him the flashlight. Ned turned it on and looked again.

"He or she looks like a very friendly creature," Ned said as he switched off the flashlight. "Do you have any cheese?"

"I think there's some in the Frigidaire," she said. "Do you want it?"

"Why don't you give me the cheese and a paper bag and wait outside?" he suggested.

"Why?" she laughed. "Do you think I'll start screaming and jumping up on chairs?"

"No," he replied, "I don't want you to spoil the communion between myself and this noble creature."

"Okay," she said as she opened the refrigerator door. "I can take a hint. Here's your cheese. I'm going to take the teriyaki steak and go outside to cry in my cocktail. The paper bags are in the drawer."

She went outside and distracted Ollie, who knew something exciting was going on in the house. The charcoals had reached the perfect state, and she had just put the teriyaki on the grill when Ned marched out of her house with the paper bag, headed for the brush at the edges of the yard.

"The deed is done, my lady," he announced proudly when he returned.

"And so is the steak, my lord," she said as she placed the sizzling meat on to a plate. "Your timing is impeccable."

They went into the house, where she had a bowl of potato salad. They happily sat at her dining room table and devoured everything before them. She remembered there were almond cookies left from lunch, and Ned said he would just run over to his bungalow for his bottle of port. She put the dishes in the sink and went to stretch out on the pune'e. As she lay back waiting for Ned, she opened the file folder she had thrown there earlier and began to thumb through the papers. Behind the piece she had written, she found an envelope. She opened the envelope and found a folded newspaper article. It was from a German newspaper dated about three years ago. There was a short article and a big picture of four people. Mina could not stop staring at the photo, as she clearly recognized three out of the four faces. She didn't even notice that Ned had come back and was rummaging around the kitchen. From what sounded like a distance, she heard his voice.

"Mina? Is everything all right?" he asked.

"What?" she said.

He frowned. "I've asked you twice what glasses we should use, and you haven't answered."

"Use any glasses," she said. "Pour us doubles. You won't believe what I just found."

He poured the port and went to the pune'e. She handed him the newspaper clipping. "I took this folder from Tilda's on the evening we found her body. It had my piece on her in it, and I just stuffed it in the glove compartment and forgot about it. Can you believe it? Can you read German?"

Ned saw a German officer smiling out from the photograph, with his arm around Eva Morgan. Marguerite and Raymond stood next to them. Raymond's hair was blond instead of the dark color it was now. Ned's German was good enough to read the caption.

"This is from some kind of social occasion," he began. "It identifies Raymond as a Dr. Gerhardt Hirsch, with his wife, Marguerite, and their daughter, Eva. This other man is Joseph Goebbels. He's high up in the Nazi Party and very close to Hitler."

Mina stared at the photo. "Oh, Ned," she said, "the mind *is* like a camera, taking random pictures. I know why Ari was killed. That night of the Halloween party, Ari, Tilda, Eva, and I were sitting at the table and eating. Ari was talking to Tilda about this man, Goebbels, and saying how he loved the young girls. Eva was looking at Bill, and all of a sudden she blushed and jumped up and left. I thought it was because she saw Bill flirting with Molly, but it must have been because of what Ari had said. She must have run straight to her father and told him."

"Something else might be very wrong too," he said anxiously. "It came to me while we were eating. Didn't Reggie say today that Takeo, Jimmy—whatever we want to call him—had learned to fence at some club?"

"Yes, but what has that got to do with this?"

"I need to make a couple of phone calls, right now," he said. "I'm going to use the phone in your bedroom, and I'll be right back."

He stepped out of the room, and she continued to look at the photograph. Eva smiled a nervous, girlish smile, while the man with his arm around her looked smug and possessive. Raymond's smile reeked of superiority, and poor Marguerite wore the plastic obligatory smile of a politician's wife. Mina suddenly felt very sorry for Eva and slightly sick when she thought about what Raymond might have forced his young daughter to do. When Ned returned, he looked more troubled than she had ever seen him.

"What is it?" she asked as she reached for his hand. "Who have you been talking to?"

He reached for the glass of port that he had left near the puneʻe, drank the whole thing, went back to the kitchen, and poured himself another before joining her. He sat down next to her and let out a long, deep sigh. "Where to begin?" he said as he caressed her cheek.

"I don't care where you begin," she said. "Just talk."

"Well, then, he said, "let's start our narrative in Shanghai. Nigel was undercover in Shanghai working at a Japanese men's club teaching fencing. He had a partner, Enrico Balban, from the Philippines. Their employers didn't know that both men spoke Japanese. But then a German doctor appears on the scene. This doctor is very friendly with a young Japanese officer, and on the doctor's suspicion, Nigel and his partner are found out. Nigel barely escapes with his life, but his partner and dear friend is brutally murdered. I got Nigel out by the skin of our teeth. Nigel, on my advice, comes to Honolulu, where he's given this job that he drags me into. He then discovers that the doctor and the Japanese officer who are responsible for his friend's death are the very people whom he's been hired to identify. Raymond must have made a trip—or several trips—to Shanghai from Honolulu, making sure to change the color of his hair when he got back here."

"But wait," Mina stopped him. "Wouldn't Raymond have recognized Nigel if he saw him before in Shanghai?"

"I don't think Raymond has ever actually seen Nigel. He may have glimpsed him at that first luncheon at the yacht club, but I think Nigel and Mei were in the corner when Raymond walked in. And if you remember, Raymond only stood around for a minute and then went right out and didn't come back. I don't think Nigel saw him that day either. I think the first time Nigel saw Raymond was at the fencing demonstration, when Nigel had his mask on. Nigel saw Raymond, but Raymond couldn't see Nigel's face. In fact, I remember Nigel asking about Eva and Raymond."

"So," she said, "what starts the chain of murders is a remark Ari made to Tilda at the Halloween party. Raymond must have thought Ari was onto them and dropped the remark on purpose, and who knows, maybe he did. Up until that time, Raymond is just doing his spying and passing information to that Jimmy guy." She paused for a moment. "Ned, he must have murdered Ari and then shot himself or had Marguerite do it."

"Either way, he was a doctor and could have figured out how to do it without causing serious injury."

"And," she added, "they must have stolen Bill's gun to use."

"Right," he said. "Ari dies, but he's mentioned his files to Tilda, who inherits all of his property. She finds this picture and decides to blackmail Raymond. He kills her next and then finds out she's been having an affair with Desmond. Desmond then threatens or drops some kind of hint to Raymond."

"So Raymond eliminates him too."

"Nigel couldn't have prevented Tilda's murder, but Raymond killed Desmond on the evening of the fencing demonstration."

"You can't blame him for not saying anything to you right away," she said.

"No," he said angrily, "but he could have said something the next day, or the next day, and he hasn't because what he wants isn't justice. It's revenge."

"It's very easy for people to get the two mixed up," she said. "You have to see that he's under a tremendous strain and not thinking straight, and he definitely should never have been working on this case. The important thing now is that *we* think straight. We have to figure out what to do and who to inform, which means going over Nigel's head and not telling him. You can decide whether you want to protect him or not from being reprimanded."

"He must be the one who was shooting at Tadashi."

"No wonder he was so angry with me for talking to Akira."

"I'm afraid that Nigel is about to try to bring down Raymond by himself. I have to stop him before he ruins his life."

Mina rubbed her forehead. "Do you think we can stop him?"

"Can I count on your help?"

"Do you have to ask?" Mina stood up, opened a drawer in the kitchen, took out a paper tablet and a pencil, and moved to the table. "I think we should talk seriously about what to do and who to ask for help. Come on. Finish your port, and I'll make some coffee. It's going to be a very long night."

# 23

# FRIDAY, DECEMBER 20

**M**INA PUSHED DOWN the alarm clock button at seven thirty and immediately heard the arrival of a car in the driveway and someone knocking on Ned's door. She peeked out of her bedroom window and saw a Western Union deliveryman return to his car and leave as quickly as he had come. She went straight to shower and dress and in twenty minutes was dashing over to Ned's to see what the morning held in store. She knew he had placed several long-distance calls last night and sent some urgent telegrams to his contacts. She could hardly contain her curiosity as she knocked on his door. Looking through the screen, she could see him on the telephone. He motioned for her to come in as he spoke.

"Yes, thank you, Commander," Ned was saying to someone on the phone. "I'll call you as soon as I speak to Detective Forest. Goodbye now."

"I thought," said Ned as he hung up the phone, "that we should keep Navy Intelligence informed from this point on. It was pretty tricky to find out who to contact without involving Nigel."

"Did they ask about Nigel?"

"I lied and told them he was very ill and had asked me to take over," said Ned as he poured two cups of steaming coffee.

"And how did you find out who to contact?" she asked.

"By sending several telegrams and disturbing the sleep of several others," he answered. "And I hope this telegram reveals something else." He tore open the missive that had just arrived.

"Do you have any eggs?" Mina opened the Frigidaire. "I see you do, and you have some bread too. I have just enough time to make us a couple of fried-egg sandwiches before we have to leave."

Mina fixed the egg sandwiches in record time and even managed to include some cheese slices, while Ned read every word of the telegram carefully. Just as he had finished reading and poured their second cups of coffee, she placed their sandwiches on the table.

"What did it say?" she asked as she sat down and cut her sandwich in two.

"It answers some questions about Gerhardt Hirsch, or Raymond Morgan, as we know him." Ned paused to take a bite. "He was born in America of an American father and German mother. The father died when he was about ten or eleven, and the mother took him back to Germany to live."

"That explains his total lack of any accent," she said. "He must have taught the children American English as they were growing up."

Ned continued. "He became a doctor, prominent member of the Nazi Party, and huge proponent of the eugenics movement in Germany. It's thought that his daughter was a mistress of Goebbels, the Reich minister of propaganda for the Nazi Party, and through that connection, Morgan was able to advance his career. My sources knew that he dropped out of the scene in Germany a couple of years ago but didn't know where he went. And I happen to know something else about this Joseph Goebbels person," he said as he stirred his coffee. "He's a frustrated author whose literary work never really got accepted."

"In other words," she said, "he's an angry beast."

"Exactly," Ned responded.

She shook her head. "Isn't it amazing how easily people like Morgan can pass themselves off in Hawai'i as someone they aren't?"

"But," Ned said excitedly, "there actually was a Raymond Morgan who was a photographer of minor success from the East Coast. He disappeared around the time the doctor showed up here, and he's still considered a missing person."

Mina had finished her sandwich and was wiping breadcrumbs off her skirt. "I suppose Marguerite is German and not Swiss and definitely doesn't have any Jewish relatives."

Ned nodded. "Right, and according to this, she was a nurse in one of the clinics the doctor worked in."

"You called Nigel this morning?"

"He and Mei are having some kind of meeting with their real estate agent about the house."

"Let's pray he's not really off somewhere assassinating someone."

Ned looked at her over the rim of his coffee cup. "Great minds think alike, darling."

Mina sighed. "I feel like my head is spinning, but I guess we just have to take a deep breath and get on with it."

"You'd make a great general, my love," he said as he stood. "That's what we'll be doing right now, getting on with it."

She smiled and also stood. "But only after we brush our teeth."

Mina had just dropped Ned off at the police station on the corner of Merchant and Bethel so that he and Todd could meet with an officer from Naval Intelligence. She parked on Merchant Street with an hour to kill before she would come back, joined by Reggie and Akira, for their final briefing before they left for the teahouse. She was just getting out of her car when she happened to see Louis Goldburn and his wife, Doris, pulling up to park in front of his law office, which was only half a block from the police station. They greeted Mina with warm smiles and insisted that she join them in their Friday-morning ritual of coffee and pastries at the Mermaid Café.

"It's an indulgence of ours," Doris explained, "to celebrate getting through another week at the office."

"And sometimes," Louis added, "we have more than one pastry."

The three friends walked down Merchant Street, over the granite stones in the sidewalk, and past the post office and the Yokohama Species Bank and turned down toward the Boulevard. Just a few blocks on, they stepped through the gate, with the Mermaid Café sign swinging and creaking in the wind overhead. There was something comforting about coming through the gate in the rock wall and seeing the familiar lawn with its bamboo grove in the corner and the two carved mermaids hovering over the doorway. Mina knew it had once been someone's residence and over the years must have gone through several transitions until its present incarnation as a restaurant on the ground floor and a comfortable apartment on the second floor. The covered patio stood lonely and deserted today, probably on account of the wind, but inside, the café sparkled with conversation and activity. They took a table in the corner, and in an instant, Maggie McKenzie, with her flaming red hair, appeared. Mina and Doris decided they wanted to have tea, but Louis stuck to his usual coffee. Maggie then returned with three plates and a tray full of pastries to choose from. Mina decided on a bear claw. Doris picked a Danish, and Louis took the last glazed doughnut. As usual, Mina's eyes couldn't help but drift over to the centerpiece of the room—the life-sized carving of the lovely mermaid, posed like a figure on a ship's prow.

"You can't imagine," said Doris, recognizing what held Mina's attention, "how many people have tried to buy that carving from Duncan."

"Of course, he'd never sell it," added Louis. "I wouldn't either, if it were mine."

"Me either," Mina agreed.

"I guess you know that Ned came to me yesterday about Bill Hitchins," said Louis. "I went to see Bill that afternoon. He's insisting that he's innocent."

Mina wished she could tell them everything but just said, "We're pretty sure he is innocent."

"Still, it looks pretty bad for him," Louis said before he picked up his doughnut.

"Well," Mina said, leaning forward and speaking softly, "I can't say any more, but by the end of the day, it might not look so bad."

Doris laughed and winked at her husband. "I think she means the game's afoot, dear."

"Can't you give us one teeny hint?" Louis pleaded.

Mina let out a laugh. "Sorry, no peeking at presents before Christmas. New subject."

"Speaking of new subjects," said Doris, "my friend who owns the beauty shop said our lovely Eva Morgan is in a royal dilemma."

"Why is that?" Mina asked with obvious interest.

"I don't know all the details," Doris confided, "but apparently Eva has fallen in love with someone and is desperately afraid her father will find out and do something awful. Apparently the father has a horrible temper, and everyone in the family is terrified of him."

"You'd never know it from meeting him," Louis commented. "He's always had the best manners and never calls attention to himself. But then, I've known more than one socially gracious man who beats his wife and children in private."

"Poor Eva," Mina said with genuine concern. "I hope there's a way someone can help her."

Maggie appeared again with the tray of pastries, and Mina and Doris decided to have another cup of tea and share a second bear claw, while Louis helped himself to a long john. Doris and Louis asked about Ned, and Mina shared their wedding plans and asked them to think about coming to her father's ranch for the ceremony. They agreed to try to get together over the holidays, and feeling warm and full of sugary treats, they all walked back together. Mina said good-bye at the police station, and as she watched them walk away, huddled close together against the wind, she thought about how happy she was to have found Ned.

She climbed the stairs to Todd's office. Everyone had just arrived, and she was relieved to see Akira and Reggie having a friendly conversation without any ill feeling on Akira's part. Ned took Mina aside and told her that Naval Intelligence had weighed in on their proceedings, agreed with everything they planned to do, and would make themselves available to help as soon as there was indisputable evidence. Two of Todd's best detectives, Pat Murphy and Hiram Kealoha, joined them, and Todd and Ned explained the setup to everyone. There were several questions and speculations about possible scenarios, but Ned reinforced the idea that the main objective today was to identify the person passing information and to try to collect some hard evidence. Akira and Reggie would be the first to leave. They were to arrive about an hour early and, under the guise of arranging flowers, try to find out as much as they could about the embassy party. Nobody from the embassy would be surprised to find the *ikebana* master and his assistant doing an arrangement for a friend and private party.

When the meeting finished, Ned asked Mina if she would take a stroll with him before they had to leave. Outside the police station, he took her arm, and they walked across Ala Moana Boulevard toward Aloha Tower. The cool wind energized her, and she was grateful for the chance to walk with Ned in the midst of the unfolding events. She felt sharp and intensely alive as they strolled past the tall white building along the pier. She looked up at the big clock on the tower, which now read ten thirty, and she laid her head on Ned's shoulder as they walked.

"Mina," he said, "I haven't told anyone, even Todd, that Morgan is a Nazi—just in case Nigel happens to get to him first. I'm sure we'll be able to arrest him today and connect him to the spying business. Then we can make the discovery."

"And if today results in nothing?"

"Then I'll have to have a serious talk with Nigel. He's one of my oldest friends, and I just can't bring myself to—what do you say in America?—rat on him."

"I understand," she said.

They had just reached the tower elevator, and he pressed the call button. The elevator arrived, and they stepped inside the cramped space. He pushed the button for the top.

"I wanted to ask you to keep an eye on him today and to try to keep him from doing anything foolish if you can. You might not be able to stop him, but I know he would never hurt you. He's as close as I've ever come to having a brother, and there's no one else I can trust but you."

She kissed him on the cheek. "Of course I'll watch out for him, and I'll do my best to keep him from doing anything stupid—because he means something to you and because Mei is a wonderful person who doesn't deserve the grief."

The elevator doors opened, and they stepped out. Aloha Tower was the tallest structure in the city, and the observation decks offered unobstructed views of the harbor, the city, and beyond. They first walked to the mauka side, and looking back above the town, they could see steel-gray clouds sweeping up, getting thicker and darker as they gathered in the Ko'olau Mountains. She liked the way things appeared to be so different in this gloomy light and windy, chilly air. It was as reasonable a facsimile of winter as there could be in Honolulu, and she hoped it would last through Christmas. They watched people and cars below on the sidewalks and boulevard pass below as they walked to the west deck. The view of the city gave way to the canneries and then the distant sea of cane fields that surged up to the base of the Waianae mountain range. On the south deck, with its view of the harbor, they watched the boats chugging by, and they ended on the east deck, looking toward Diamond Head, now cloaked in green because of the winter rains. She took his hand, turned to him, and smiled. He raised a finger and brushed it softly over her lips.

"Yesterday," she said, "I got an invitation to Ginger Raymond's New Year's Eve party. I think we should go since that's where we met last New Year's Eve."

He put his arm around her and pulled her close. "Only if you promise I'll get to see the girl dressed up like a harlequin again. I can't quite get her out of my mind."

Mina laughed. "I'll see what I can do, but this year I think we'll have to get you a better costume than that sack you were wearing."

"That was Todd's fault," he said and then added in a quieter voice, "You will be careful today, won't you? Promise me you won't take any unnecessary risks."

"I'll promise," she said, "but only if you promise to be careful too."

Everyone was seated in the private room at the teahouse. Akira had learned, by talking to the staff, that their party and the embassy party were the only patrons for lunch, along with someone called Mr. Smith, who was already installed in a private room upstairs. Akira had not seen the man, and apparently he frequented the teahouse. He always arrived very early, always asked for the same room, always ate by himself, and usually stayed until late afternoon. Ned was afraid this "Mr. Smith" might have seen them, but Akira assured him that the private rooms faced away from the entrance.

The silhouettes of the two kimono-clad women appeared on the shoji doors just before they entered the room. Floating like swans, their white *tabi* gliding silently over the tatami mats, the ladies served each person a bowl of steaming miso soup and a small side dish of grated radish and carrots over bits of green lettuce and watercress and then disappeared as swiftly as they had come.

Mina, Ned, Todd, Reggie, Akira, and Nigel were seated on *zabuton* cushions on the floor around the shiny, black lacquered table. In the center of the table, Akira had created a centerpiece using red Christmas berries as a sculptured base with tall sinuous sticks and a few lacy pine leaves rising up to form wonderful flowing lines. They could hear the embassy party in the next room, and Akira, who sat nearest the adjoining wall, pulled a stethoscope out of a satchel and placed it on the wood panels to listen to what was going on next door.

"This was my father's," said Akira, as he placed the chest piece against the wall.

"Can you hear?" Todd asked

"Perfectly," Akira answered. "They're just talking about the food. The ambassador is apologizing, saying it's not as good as the food in Japan."

Nigel kept his eyes on the shoji doors. "I'll let you know if the women are about to come in," he said.

"We should try to act normal and eat our food too," said Mina, "so we don't arouse suspicion."

"I can hear the ambassador in there," said Akira. "His wife is there, Takeo, three other ladies—one of them is the ambassador's personal secretary—and the other two men appear to be visiting from Tokyo, because they're thanking the ambassador for making their stay so pleasant. Maybe the other two women are their wives." Akira managed to drink his miso soup from his bowl while listening. "I'll tell you if they say anything important."

They all sipped on their miso soup and then ate the side dish. Reggie had trouble using the lacquered chopsticks and finally resorted to one of the forks that had been thoughtfully placed on the table. "Hmm," he said, "this tastes pretty good once you can get at it."

"Ladies!" Nigel hissed as the two outlines of the waitresses appeared on the other side of the screens.

Akira whipped the stethoscope under the table just as the shoji door slid back. The women came in and smiled as they whisked away the empty dishes and placed a tray with the second course in front of each guest. The trays held plates of perfectly sliced sashimi on a thin bed of julienned cabbage. This was accompanied by a dab of wasabi in a flat, round dish and a small bottle of shoyu. Once everyone had been served, the ladies vanished, and Akira went back to listening. Mina showed Reggie how to mix his wasabi and shoyu and was trying to make a quiet conversation with him by asking him about his family and where he was from. When she asked him if he had plans for Christmas, Todd chimed in and invited him to Christmas dinner.

Reggie cracked a smile. "That would be great," he said. "I hope we won't be using chopsticks."

Todd shook his head. "Nope," he said, "there's no eating roast beef with chopsticks at our house."

The kimono ladies came and went once more, leaving behind big lacquered trays at each place with separate compartments for shrimp and vegetable tempura, miso butterfish, beef sticks, sushi, rice, and tossed greens. Ned tried not to forget about the job at hand, but it was hard when confronted with the delicious food. He decided he should eat the tempura first in case he was interrupted, and just as he had finished the sweet potato tempura, Akira waved at him and Todd.

"Takeo Tadashi is excusing himself for a few minutes," Akira said in a loud whisper.

Todd, Ned, and Nigel jumped up, and Ned cracked open the shoji door and peered outside.

"As soon as we leave," Todd said to Nigel, "run outside and tell Murphy and Kealoha to be on alert."

"Why can't you do that?" hissed Nigel.

"Because I'm calling the shots here," growled Todd. "The rest of you stay put."

"Yes, sir," Reggie said as he opened his coat to show Todd that his firearm was tucked into a shoulder holster. "I'm ready."

"He just walked out of the room," whispered Ned. "He's turning into the hall. Let's go."

Ned led the way. He glimpsed down the hall and signaled Todd to follow when he saw Takeo going up to the second story, while Nigel stole off in the opposite direction. Walking slowly and softly, Ned and Todd made their way to the bottom of the stairs just in time to hear Takeo knocking at a second-floor door. They heard the door open for Takeo to enter and then close again. As they crept up the stairs, trying to keep them from creaking, they could hear muffled voices coming from one of the rooms. They tiptoed down the upstairs hall, and Ned put his ear to the door and very gingerly twisted the doorknob to make sure it wasn't locked. He looked at Todd, mouthed the word "now," and charged through the door.

Raymond Morgan, who had been sitting at a table on the floor with Takeo, jumped up, and just as Todd called out, "Police!," Raymond pulled a gun from a briefcase next to him. Turning on Ned and Todd, he took up the briefcase and swiftly backed toward an open window. Todd and Ned froze. He easily swung his right leg outside, planting it on the slanting shingled roof that shaded the lower story. But as he moved to hoist his left leg over, his right leg slipped, and he started to tumble. The gun flew into the air. His left hand, which held the briefcase, slammed on the window edge, causing him to drop the case inside the room. Then there were thudding sounds as Morgan expertly tucked up his body and rolled off the roof. Landing onto the grass below, he uncurled and took off into the jumble of tall grass and koa haole thickets.

Takeo held his hands up as if to surrender. "I don't know anything," he said lamely. "He only asked me to come up here to help him read the Japanese menu."

"Grab the case!" Ned shouted to Todd as he raced down the stairs.

As Todd moved to recover the case, Takeo Tadashi made a hasty retreat from the room.

In the downstairs hall, Ned had trouble finding his way in the confusion of rooms and corridors, and once outside, he could find no trace of Morgan. He ran to Todd's men, who reported that no one had come past them, and then he ran back to the place where Morgan had rolled off the roof, and looked carefully around. He spotted the gun in the croton hedge under the overhang, and then he walked back and forth along the waist-high rock wall that bordered the tea-house. On the other side of the wall were overgrown and empty lots that stretched up a hillside. Todd came out, and Ned pointed out the gun. After a couple of minutes, they heard some rustling and Mina's voice calling out. She emerged from the brush, out of breath, with grass stains on her clothes and a few twigs in her hair.

"I thought I told you to stay put," Todd scolded. "Oh, I forgot, you're Nyla's evil twin."

"Nigel went after him," she said. "I followed, but I lost them both."

Todd shook his head. "Ten to one he'll hide in the brush and then make his way through the neighborhood by weaving through peo-ple's backyards. Hell, he could be anywhere. I'll get my men to start searching around and call for some backup, but the guy is clever. I think he's probably long gone."

As Todd walked back, Mina detained Ned under the guise of hav-ing him brush off her clothes. "Nigel had a gun with a silencer," she told Ned. "He fired it several times at Morgan, but I don't think he hit him. I don't think he saw or heard me either. He was so focused on his prey."

As they went back to their room in the teahouse, they encoun-tered the members of the embassy party making a hasty retreat and the inn owners in a tizzy. Todd was showing them his credentials and demanding to use the telephone. Inside the private room, they found Reggie and Akira pouring over the contents of the briefcase.

Mina looked up at Ned and smiled. "There are lovely things in here that should make your employers very happy."

Reggie whistled. "Lists of ship arrivals and departures, destina-tions, routes, number of troops, commanding officers, maneuvers— I wonder where he got all this information?"

"Find anything?" Todd asked as he entered the room.

"There's more than enough evidence in here to have him arrested and charged with espionage," said Ned, "but not murder."

"The men are scouring the neighborhood," said Todd. "The am-bassador stuffed Takeo in the car, claimed diplomatic immunity, and sped off. I have someone watching Morgan's house, but so far, it's busi-ness as usual. The wife's swept the house and hung out the laundry."

Ned sat back down at the table. "I think if you wait a bit, she'll be on the move."

"Yeah," Todd agreed as he also sat down, "and while we're waiting a bit, I'm going to finish this lunch, just in case I don't get to eat dinner."

They all went back to Todd's office to wait for further developments. Nigel did not return to the teahouse, and no one knew where he had gone. At four, it was reported that Marguerite had left the house, picked up her son from a Boy Scout meeting, picked up Eva at the beauty shop in Pearl City, and now looked as if she were heading toward the Pearl Harbor Yacht Club. Ned, Todd, Reggie, and Todd's two detectives were organizing calls to the ONI and getting ready to leave. In the flurry of activity, Mina slipped away. It was drizzling outside, and she had changed into some old dungarees and a long-sleeved shirt that she kept in the car. She took along Ollie, who was grateful to be getting out of Todd's office, where he had waited patiently most of the day.

There was little traffic as they drove out of the downtown area and past the pineapple canneries in Iwilei with their pungent smells. The rain had let up, although a dark sky remained, and as Mina looked up toward the Koʻolau Mountains, she could see that the clouds were clinging to the ridges and creeping down low into the valleys. Moisture hung in the air, tangible and cold.

She was nearly overcome by anxiety. The idea that war might come to the islands was not something new to her, but after seeing the documents in Morgan's briefcase, what was once an abstract thought now had become something concrete and possible. War was not part of her experience, and the reality of it was hard for her to imagine. But the thought that things could spiral so far out of control that survival and escape from death might be all that mattered sent a wave of fear through her. She gripped the steering wheel and forced herself to think about the business at hand—watching out for Nigel and devising a way to stop him from shooting Raymond Morgan if she had to.

By the time she turned off the main road and headed down the Pearl Harbor Peninsula, a light rain had begun to fall. She drove slowly when she got near the yacht club, and once in the parking lot, she looked for Nigel's car. It wasn't in the main parking lot, but then she remembered the smaller lot behind the pavilion and turned down the gravel drive. She found his car parked close to the building and not readily visible from the main lot and grounds. He didn't appear to be anywhere in sight. She put on her rubber boots and rain jacket, and then from under the driver's seat, she slipped her pistol into one of the oversized jacket pockets and its silencer in the other. She had found the Baretta M418 in a pawnshop. After inquiring about a "lady's pistol," the proprietor brought the gun and its custom-machined silencer out of a back room. She didn't want to think about its history.

When she got out of her car and peered in the window of Nigel's car, she saw a box of rifle cartridges sitting on the front seat. It was open, and more than half of them were gone. She couldn't decide where to look, but when she looked back in his car and saw an undershirt that looked dirty and unwashed, it gave her an idea. She let Ollie out, snapped a leash on his collar, took the dirty shirt, and then presented it to Ollie to sniff. "Come on, boy," she said. "Let's see if you've learned anything from Ned."

Ollie sniffed at the shirt, wagged his tail, and looked at her. For a moment, she thought it was too much to expect from him, but then he put his nose to the ground and began to sniff around the car. And after a minute or so, he set out across the grounds, casting around every so often and then setting off again purposefully. She held onto the leash and let him guide, amazed that he actually seemed to be following some kind of scent. The soft rain made the ground smell musty and earthy, and as they walked, she kept looking around to see if she could spot Nigel, not wanting him to see her first. Ollie led her to the front door of the clubhouse and began to whine and look at her. The building sat in a perfect and eerie silence. She opened the front door very quietly, took the shirt out of her pocket, and let Ollie sniff it again. He put his nose down, and she found herself following him up the staircase. She placed slight tension on the leash to get him to slow down. He took her upstairs, turned to the left, went to the end of the hall, and sat down in front of a closed door. Mina opened the door, slowly and carefully, just enough to be able to see. One side of the room was lined with sets of French doors that opened up to a balcony. On the balcony, Nigel sat on a chair, with the barrel of his rifle resting on the railing as if he were waiting to take aim.

"Good boy, Ollie," Mina whispered, as she scratched under his chin.

Mina opened the door, thankful that it did not squeak, and walked softly into the room. As she came up quietly behind Nigel, she could see beyond him to the pier on the loch. Marguerite, Eva, and the boy, Paul, were sitting nearby on the lawn under umbrellas. They had a couple of small baskets and a box, and it looked as if they were ready for an evening picnic in the rain. Calmly, Mina called out Nigel's name.

Startled, he turned, and when he saw it was only her, he gave her an irritated look.

"What are you doing here?" he said, standing and leaning the rifle up against the railing.

"Ned sent me," she answered.

"Well, there's no point, is there?" he said, moving toward her abruptly.

Mina eyed his rifle, deciding the best course of action would be to maneuver herself between him and the weapon. She kept her focus on him and edged slowly to one side. "I don't know," she answered. "I don't understand why you're doing this."

He answered defensively in a raised voice. "He's responsible for my partner's death—he and that fop Tadashi! Enrico was one of the kindest men that ever walked the earth, and he didn't deserve to die that way."

"I'm sorry," she said as she moved around and slightly closer to him at the same time.

"You don't know what it's like to think that I might have been able to save him, if only I'd been sharper, if I'd paid more attention to what was going on."

His agitation bordered on manic, and she realized that because he was not thinking clearly, she had to be extra careful. "I'm sure it wasn't your fault," she said, moving slowly in front of him so that she now stood between him and the rifle.

"I was the senior partner," he yelled. "It was my job to see what was going on!"

She sighed, and not really knowing what to say, she just said the first thing that came into her mind. "If your partner was as good as you say, I don't think he would want you to do this. What are you going to do? Kill Morgan's family?"

"No," he said emphatically. "I'm just waiting for him to show up." Nigel paused before he spoke again, and his voice caught in his throat. "Enrico was *my* friend, not yours."

"And I'm sure he was a good friend," she responded. "That's why if he were here, he would be saying what I'm saying."

"It's none of your business," he retorted.

"Can't you see how valuable Morgan could be if he's taken alive? Think about the information they could get out of him. I know the navy has its ways of extracting information. They might be able to use what he knows to save some lives, and even if you did kill him, your friend is still gone."

He shook his head. "You can't stop me!"

"Oh, yes, I can," she said as she expertly pulled out her gun and twisted on the silencer.

He looked at her gun and laughed. "You wouldn't kill me, and I know it."

"No, I wouldn't kill you," she said as she fired at his foot, purposefully missing by an inch, "but I might shoot you in the foot."

"What! Are you crazy?" he yelled, jumping back.

"I might be," she said, shooting at his other foot. "So I think you'd better just go into the room and sit down before I do something insane."

He backed into the room and sat down. Mina stood, keeping her gun pointed at him. Ollie ran to her side, looking up anxiously at her.

"How did you know where to look for Marguerite?" Mina asked him.

"I followed her, just like the police did," he answered. "She got here first. I haven't seen him yet, but I expect the bastard is about to show up."

Tires spun, spitting bits of rock and sand as Ned, Todd, and Reggie sped off the highway and onto the frayed asphalt and gravel road that led to the yacht club.

"Did the navy say they would be standing by?" Todd asked.

"They're going to watch from Ford Island," said Reggie, "and have men and a vessel ready. They're waiting for our signal."

"I just hope we're not too late," Todd mumbled, swerving left and right to evade potholes.

They came to a stop next to Murphy and Kealoha, who had arrived first and stood ready and waiting by their car.

"The lady and the kids are on the other side of the club, near the pier," said Kealoha.

"No sign of Morgan," Murphy added.

"And Mina or Nigel?" Ned asked.

The two officers shook their heads.

Todd nodded, pursed his lips, and said, "Murphy, move the car to the edge of the lot, then you and Kealoha wait behind cover with the car. Don't let anyone leave the lot. If Morgan shows and bolts, honk to signal us, then chase him. If he shows and parks, lie low and keep an eye on him, but don't let him see you. Reggie, you scout around the yacht club grounds. Check any access paths through the dry brush and the dirt roads, and keep your eyes peeled for Mina and Nigel. If you see them, make sure they hang back and keep out of sight. Ned and I will approach the club and pier. If you hear gunfire, everybody come running on the double."

Murphy went to move the car, while Todd parked at the far end of the lot among the few vehicles scattered near the club. Todd and Ned checked their weapons, chambered a round, and made sure the safeties were locked. Reggie headed toward the rear of the club. Todd waved Ned forward, making their way toward the koa haole brush that skirted the parking lot.

Ned was worried about Mina and Nigel, but Todd's gesture reminded him to focus his attention on the here and now. Ned's senses became acute and intense, as if things were happening in slow motion. He became more aware of the light rain falling on his head and shoulders, the damp ground underfoot, the smell of the wet grass, and the shimmering flecks of raindrops that fell from the leaves as he and Todd crept slowly through the brush, toward the water's edge.

He could see the boy, Eva, and Marguerite sitting on a grassy slope, under a tree in front of the pier. They held umbrellas over a huge picnic basket, a few grocery bags, and several small boxes that were spread around them. They hardly spoke, and their mood appeared somber. Raymond Morgan was nowhere to be seen. Todd gestured downward, and he and Ned crouched behind a thick bordering hedge of naupaka.

They had hardly settled when Ned spotted the prow of a sampan rounding the peninsula from the east loch, heading toward the pier. The chug of the diesel engine became more and more audible, until he could clearly see a lone figure at the wheel. Marguerite stood, signaling to Eva and Paul to collect their belongings.

"This is it," said Todd. "Wait for him to tie up to be sure we can grab him."

They watched and waited as the small family made their way to the water's edge, then out onto the pier, hauling their assortment of bags and boxes. As soon as the sampan bumped against the timbers, Marguerite began tossing packages onto the deck of the small boat, swung the boy over the gunwale, and grabbed her daughter's hand, ready to leap together onto the craft and make their escape.

"Bad choice," Todd muttered. "Let's go!"

Todd and Ned bolted. Todd fired a shot in the air to summon the others as they charged toward the pier. Ned kept his focus on Raymond, the man behind the wheel of the sampan.

Todd shouted, "Halt! You're under arrest!" and fired a second shot into the air.

In the confusion, Eva pulled violently away from her mother. She broke free, turned away from the boat, and charged back in the direction of Todd and Ned. Marguerite leapt onto the sampan and pulled a short, fat, twin-barreled gun from the picnic basket. Raymond grabbed Paul from behind, holding the boy between himself and the thundering approach. There was no clear line of fire with Eva and Paul in the mix. Todd and Ned ran harder. Ned's ears rang with the hollow clatter of their footfalls as they raced down the long pier. Morgan pulled harder on the throttle. Marguerite drew down and pulled hard on the first trigger. The shotgun boomed. Ned heard a thud and turned to see Todd falling on the pier. Ned dodged Eva, raced for the boat, and managed to leap the rail and grab the muzzle from Marguerite before the second shot roared. The sampan gained speed as it pulled away from the pier, and Morgan released both the boy and the wheel, turning on Ned, who was wresting the shotgun from the hands of his wife. As they fought, the weapon flew overboard, but Raymond seized a two-by-four that was lying on the deck and swung it with force from behind. Ned's awareness burst into a flash, dissolved into a narrow light, and faded to black.

The sampan made rapid progress away from view of the club, along the channel between Ford Island and the Waipiʻo Peninsula and toward the mouth of the harbor. Marguerite took the wheel, while Raymond struggled with hoisting Ned's considerable weight up and over the rail of the boat and into the gray-green water with a splash, leaving his body to float away in their wake.

Mina and Nigel heard the shots. Without hesitation, Mina dashed into the hall and down the stairs with Ollie charging behind. Nigel grabbed his rifle from the balcony before running after her. As they sprinted toward the pier, they passed Reggie running in the other direction and shouting something about calling the cutter. At the dock, they found Kealoha at Todd's side and Murphy rushing off to call for an ambulance. A moment later, Mina was kneeling beside Todd. Kealoha had torn away Todd's pant leg to expose the wound on his thigh, wadding up the cloth and using it to apply pressure to stop the bleeding. Todd looked drawn and pale but conscious.

"You one lucky buggah, sir," said Kealoha. "The bullet only graze you, bumbye you gonna be just fine."

Todd, aware of Mina's presence, tried and failed to sit up. "Ned," he said in a hoarse voice. "Ned's on the boat."

Mina turned her gaze from Todd to the boat making its way into the bay. "They've got Ned!" she yelled to Nigel. "Get an outboard! Look over by the slips! Now!"

Nigel took off.

Eva, seeing that she had escaped, came back down to the pier, in tears. "He's crazy," she sobbed. "They're both crazy, and I can't stand it anymore."

Mina went to her. "It's all right," she said, holding the girl by the shoulders. "We'll all make sure that you're safe, but right now, I need you to stop crying, run up to the clubhouse, and get a bowl of water and some clean towels for Todd. I want you to help the police officer here in any way you can until the ambulance gets here."

"Yes, Mina," Eva said as she dried her eyes and ran toward the clubhouse.

Just as Mina heard the roar of the outboard motor, Nigel pulled around in a sleek blue racing boat and up to the side of the pier. She made sure her gun was securely in her jacket and jumped into the boat. Ollie began to bark wildly and ran back and forth on the pier.

"Ollie, stay," Mina commanded. "Take care of my dog," she called out to Kealoha.

Nigel opened the throttle to full speed, and the power of the engine lifted the bow of the boat from the water as they sped off after the sampan, leaving a rolling wake of white water behind them. They closed in on the vessel as they neared the west side of Ford Island. In the distance, they could see the high gray prow and deep wake of a US Navy cutter swinging around the south side of the island and heading toward the sampan, cutting it off from the mouth of the harbor.

"Take the wheel," Nigel yelled to Mina when they were just a few yards from their target.

Mina stepped up and took the wheel. Heading straight for the sampan, she cut the engine at the last minute and spun the boat around with precise timing so that the outboard bumped up against the other vessel, allowing Nigel to jump on board. Nigel cut the sampan engine with one hand while shoving the barrel of his shotgun at Morgan's head.

Mina pulled out her gun and trained it on Marguerite, who had made a move to help her husband. "Get back to where you were," Mina growled. As Marguerite moved back and stood near her terrified son, Mina saw that Nigel's hands were trembling as he clutched at the rifle. "Ned?" she yelled. "Nigel, where is Ned?"

"Where is he?" Nigel roared at Morgan. "Tell me where he is, or I'll blow your brains out right now."

"Please don't kill my daddy," the boy said, in a small voice. "The man got hit on the head, and so he fell over."

"Yes," Marguerite hissed, "we fed your friend to the sharks."

"You bastard!" Nigel screamed at Morgan, pushing on his head with the barrel of the rifle. You God-damned—"

"No, Nigel," said Mina. "Leave him, just leave him. We have to find Ned! He could still be alive. He could. Let the navy cutter take them. Please," she pleaded, "Ned needs your help, and we need to go, now!"

Nigel hesitated for one second. Then he pushed Morgan down and whacked him hard on the side of the head with the butt of his rifle before turning to jump back in the outboard. As Nigel and Mina sped away, the navy cutter was closing in on the sampan, and a geyser of spray and foam off the starboard bow followed the loud report of the cutter's deck gun. The ship hailed the sampan with the noise of Klaxons and a booming loudspeaker commanding the boat to prepare to be boarded. Sailors quickly jumped on board and took the defeated Raymond and Marguerite Morgan and their boy into custody.

Nigel and Mina had turned the motorboat around, cut the engine to a slow cruise, and made their way back toward the yacht club, criss-crossing the waters and keeping a steady lookout for Ned.

"I'm sorry, Mina," Nigel said feebly. "I'm sorry for everything."

Mina, sick with worry, couldn't speak and vigilantly scanned the dark-green surface for any sign or clue. She was more than conscious that the light was fading and that after nightfall, their search would be futile. When they had nearly reached the pier, they turned around to retrace their path. It was nearly dark, and Mina could see by the crestfallen look on Nigel's face that he was losing hope. Their craft was just passing the place on the peninsula called Puʻu Peahi when something on the shore caught Mina's eye, and she told Nigel to pull in closer. There, on the silty sand, lay the figure of a man, wet and curled up in a fetal position. Nigel cut the engine, and Mina threw herself into the shallow, murky water and rushed toward Ned. When she reached him, he was drifting in and out of consciousness, but after a few minutes, he opened his eyes and whispered her name. He was weak, and there was blood matted into the hair on the back of his head. He slowly regained consciousness, and she and Nigel were able to get him to stand and hobble very slowly through the waist-high water toward the boat. Even though it was nearly dark, Mina was aware of the tears falling from Nigel's eyes.

"Something," Ned mumbled, "something pushed me. I think something was pushing me in the water, toward the shore."

"Just stay quiet, darling," she said. "We've got you now."

After some effort, they managed to get Ned over the side of the boat. Nigel started toward the yacht club, and Mina, while holding Ned close, glanced out across the harbor. In the very last of the daylight, she clearly saw the fin of a shark heading toward them. It glided gracefully alongside their boat, and just before they reached the pier, it turned to make a wide circle before disappearing into the darkening waters.

## 24

# SATURDAY, DECEMBER 21

**M**INA WOKE UP with a start. She had fallen asleep in the easy chair in her living room. It was very early in the morning, and the first light of day was just creeping into the sky. Ned lay asleep on her pune'e, and she went over to him and listened contentedly to his even breathing. The doctor at the hospital had released him yesterday evening on the condition that she keep a close eye on him during the night. She had gotten little sleep, staying awake with coffee in order to check every hour and make sure he hadn't slipped into a coma. She was looking out the window at the ghostly shapes of the plants in the garden when Ollie, who she had allowed to sleep on the pune'e at Ned's feet, got up, went to the screen door, and whined softly to go outside. She let him out and looked at the rumpled clothes she was wearing, and when she realized that she hadn't changed or cleaned up from yesterday's adventurers, she headed straight for the bathroom and turned the hot water on in the bathtub. When it was filled, she let her body sink into the steamy water and felt her tight muscles melt into a state of relaxation. She thought she would close her eyes, just for a few minutes. She opened them again to realize that the water had gone cold and to see that daylight was now streaming through the window. She could hear noises in the kitchen and decided she had better get dressed and see what was going on.

In the kitchen, she found Ned, awake and dressed, making a fresh pot of coffee.

"I see you're up and about," she said before she kissed him. "How are you feeling?"

"I feel like I had one of the best sleeps of my life," he said. "What time was it when I nodded off?"

"It was right when we got home," she said, "which I think was about eight."

"Nothing like a ten-hour sleep to make you feel like you're in fighting form," he said as he poured two cups of coffee.

She yawned. "I'm awake but barely. Remember the doctor said I had to keep an eye on you through the night?"

He frowned. "No, I hadn't remembered, but now it's coming back to me. And so is the gash on my head."

"Careful, darling," she said, "you have a few stitches."

Ollie began to bark as a car pulled down the driveway. Grandma Hannah got out of the car, took a cardboard box from the backseat, and headed toward the door. Ned rushed gallantly out to relieve her of the box, while Mina held the door open for both of them.

"I thought you would be up by now," Grandma Hannah said as she plopped herself in a chair to catch her breath. "I wanted to make sure everyone had something substantial for breakfast after the terrible things that happened yesterday and the injuries and whatnot. I brought you some chicken hekka and rice."

"Grandma, you must have gotten up at four a.m. to make this!" Mina exclaimed.

"Oh," Grandma replied, "you know us old folks don't need that much sleep. Besides, I had to do something after what everyone has been through. Todd told us all about it."

"How is he?" Ned asked.

"He's already gone off to the police station," said Grandma, shaking her head in disapproval. "I told him he should stay at home and rest, but he just laughed and hobbled off with his cane. Now, I won't leave until I see you two eat some of that hekka."

Mina put rice in two bowls and then topped it with big spoonfuls of her grandmother's hekka. This had always been one of Mina's favorite dishes, and she had decided never to make it because she knew she could never match this taste. She especially loved the aburage and the thin slices of gobo. Ned finished his bowl and then asked for seconds, and after they both had eaten their fill, they sat with Grandma Hannah, who insisted on hearing their account of yesterday's events.

"I remember Morgan hitting me with something," Ned said in his conclusion, "but I just don't know how I ended up onshore. I can't see him taking the time to drop me off."

"He dumped you overboard," said Mina.

"I do have this very vague recollection of something bumping at me and a bit of an ache on my left side," he said. "There's a big bruise too." He lifted his shirt to show them.

Mina looked at her grandmother and told her what she saw in the water when she found Ned. Grandma Hannah looked at both Ned and Mina, gave them a smile that was both sad and joyful, and said, "You see, not everything is lost."

As Mina was clearing up the breakfast things, the phone rang. It was Todd asking if they both could come to the police station for a few hours.

"It's Marguerite," Todd said to Mina. "Raymond has gone silent, but Marguerite is ready to talk in exchange for the kids to be left alone. The thing is, Mina, she's asked for you to be there."

Though Mina felt like she could sleep for a hundred years, she dragged herself into the bedroom to change her clothes while Ned saw Grandma Hannah off. Mina argued that Ned should stay at home and rest, but he refused. And when she was ready, he even insisted that she let him drive.

Todd had Kealoha meet them in the downstairs lobby of the station and usher them up the tiled stairs with the wrought-iron balustrade to Todd's office on the third floor. Kealoha knocked on the thick wooden door, surrounded by its rich warm frame, and Todd called them in. Already present was a representative from the US Navy and a court reporter who would be taking everything down in shorthand for the written statement. When they were all comfortably seated, Todd sent Kealoha to get Marguerite Morgan.

Marguerite entered in a shapeless dull-gray dress, her hair pulled straight back off her face and held in place by a black barrette. Her face looked pale and sallow, and underneath her swollen eyes were dark patches. She sat down on one of the sofas in the office, with no

defiance, as if her body weighed a thousand pounds and she had resigned herself to her fate. Todd sat directly across from her, and all
the others sat farther away.

Todd looked at her and spoke in a calm, even voice. "We've thought
about your proposition, and we've agreed that if you cooperate, your
daughter will not be charged with any crime—even though we know
she is old enough to be charged with aiding you and your husband in
your criminal activities, at least in your espionage activities."

"How can I be sure?" she asked.

"You will have to take our word for it," Todd said, "but I assure
you, our word is good."

"Is this true, Mina? If I tell, Eva will be protected?"

"Yes," Mina answered, "I'm sure of it."

"Very well then," said Marguerite, "I will tell you everything."

"My name is Emma Hirsch, and my husband's name is Gerhardt
Hirsch. I am from Germany, and my husband was born in the United
States but moved to Germany with his mother when he was twelve.
In Germany, he is a doctor of some renown and is a leader in the country
of the eugenics movement. Perhaps you've heard of this movement?
Its purpose is to make a better world. We were asked to take this job
of watching Pearl Harbor and reporting to the Japanese government
for a period of two years, and after this time, my husband was to
have the leading position at a new research clinic for the study of
eugenics in Berlin. They said he was chosen for this because of his
perfect American English, and that may be, but I also think it was
because of our daughter, Eva. My husband made her enter into a relationship with someone high up in the Nazi Party who had a fancy
for young women, Joseph Goebbels. But after a time, he was displeased
with Eva's behavior, and I think he wanted us out of his sight. Maybe
they never really planned to give my husband this research position,
but he believed they would, and so we came here.

"So we collected our information by watching the harbor. We
made friends with military officers and their families at the yacht club.
I made friends with the military wives through the Boy Scouts club
with Paul. Eva chatted and asked questions at the beauty shop, and
sometimes she would date young officers that Gerhardt had picked

out. My husband even sent Paul in a sailor suit to the navy docks to look at the ships. The sailors thought he was so cute, they would take him on the ship, and he would ask the questions his father taught him. He did not know what he was doing, of course. He only thought it was a big game, but Eva did not like anything. Gerhardt was so strict with her, forcing her to do things she doesn't want to. She is almost twenty-one years old now, not eighteen like we tell everyone, and she and her father have been fighting. Sometimes he even hits her because she doesn't want to do as he says, and I can see she is just waiting until she is twenty-one to finally run away from him."

Marguerite began to cry, and Todd handed her his handkerchief. "I have done everything for Gerhardt, but I was so afraid of what he might do to Eva if she defied him."

Todd gave her a few minutes to gain control of herself and then asked her to tell them about Ari Schoner. She was quiet for a minute and then continued in a shaky voice.

"It was because of what Eva heard at the Halloween party," she began. "Eva heard Ari say something about Goebbels and young girls, and she thought somehow he knew all about her, so she ran to her father. Gerhardt said we couldn't take the chance that he might know about us, so that day we were cleaning up from the party, he shot Ari and placed him in that position, and then I went there to meet him and shot Gerhardt in the leg. He showed me exactly where to shoot and how to hold the gun. I hid the gun in our car and then came and pretended I had just found him like that."

"He had stolen the gun from Bill?" asked Todd.

"Yes," she answered, "but our children knew nothing about this. Now they will know everything." She started to cry again.

Todd waited until her sobs subsided before he went on. "And Tilda Clement?"

"She was a terrible person," she said with disgust. "Ari kept some records, and Tilda found something out about Gerhardt—that he was really a German doctor—and she wanted money, so he said she had to die. And then he found out she had told Desmond. You know they were having relations. She had no morals. But after she died, Desmond hinted something to Gerhardt, and so Gerhardt killed him with Bill's pistol and then put the pistol back. That's why I had to mention it when you questioned us." She stopped talking and looked beyond Todd and out the window.

"Is there anything else you want to tell us?"

She spoke absently, as if speaking to someone who wasn't there. "He hates this place, you know, Hawai'i. Gerhardt hates the people here. He can't stand the way you people marry races different that are not your own. He thinks it is degenerate, and he hates that he has to be pleasant and nice to people he finds repulsive. It has been very hard for him, you see."

Todd looked at her. "And you? Did you think it's disgusting?"

"I do not think one way or another," she answered. "I only do what Gerhardt tells me to do. I have devoted my life to him and his cause. The only thing I regret is how I may have hurt Eva and Paul, especially Eva. Perhaps now they will have a chance to be happy. You said you would allow me to see her, didn't you?"

"Yes," said Todd, "you'll be allowed a short visit."

Marguerite turned to Mina. "You will see that she comes to me. Please, Mina," she said sobbing, "it is very important I talk to her once more."

"I'll try," Mina responded.

Todd turned to the navy officer and asked if he had any questions. The officer responded by shaking his head, and so Marguerite was taken out of the room. Todd had some things to discuss with the naval officer, and Ned and Mina ambled back to their car. When Mina checked her watch and saw that it was only nine thirty, she thought about how much could happen in just a few hours. Mina insisted on stepping into Louis Goldburn's office to tell him about Marguerite's confession, and Louis decided to go right to the police station to see about Bill Hitchins' release.

On the way home, Mina fell asleep, and Ned had to shake her awake so that he could walk her into the house. She lay down on the pune'e, and he covered her up with the quilt he had used the night before. As she closed her eyes, she mumbled something about Eva visiting her mother and then fell immediately into a deep and dreamless sleep.

It was early evening, and just getting dark, when Ned woke Mina from her slumber on the pune'e.

"How long have I been napping?" she asked with a yawn.

"Almost eight hours, my love," he said. "What would you like? A cola? A cocktail? A nice cup of tea?"

"A nice cup of tea sounds wonderful," she said.

"Your sister called," he said as he put the kettle on the stove. "She invited us to come and eat with them, and I took the liberty of accepting."

"And when do we have to be there?" she said, sitting up and looking around for her dog.

"I'd say we should get ready to leave right after tea. Nigel came over, just after you fell asleep. We had a long talk. He's formally resigning from his 'unofficial' position with the British government. He apologized profusely, and said his only excuse is that he was under a heavy strain and 'not himself.'"

"How very British," she said.

"He also said to thank you for not shooting him in the foot. What did you do to him anyway?"

She gave him a sleepy smile. "Just some trick I learned from the cowboy movies. If you're nice to me, I might teach it to you. I can't believe how tired I was," she said, yawning once more. "How are you? Does your head hurt?"

"It's nothing a couple of aspirins can't take away," he said. "I took a liberty while you were in the Land of Nod."

"What was that?"

"I found Eva at the Hitchins' house, and I drove her to see her mother."

Mina frowned. "She consented to go?"

"It took persuading," he said, "but she agreed to go, and then on the way home, she seemed quite glad that she had gone."

"Are she and Paul staying with Tevai and Bill? I guess she feels like she needs a friend right now."

"I have a feeling," he said, "that friendship is not the reason she likes to be around the Hitchins' household."

Mina gave him a quizzical look. "What are you talking about?"

"I think she's in love with Tevai's brother, Rahiti. I think she's been hiding it, and her father suspected something."

"The thought must have sent him completely over the edge," she said.

"I'll say," he said as he went to pour the hot water from the kettle into the teapot. "When I went there, her little brother was getting on famously with Rahiti, so I don't think their father's lunacy has ruined his better judgment either."

"Oh, the Lord moves in mysterious ways," Mina said as she flopped back on the pune'e cushions. "Is that what you call irony? The eugenicist's daughter falls in love with the handsome Tahitian male?"

"Yes," he said as he presented her with a cup of tea, "I suppose it is a contradictory outcome of events that is a mockery of everything her father believed in."

"Well," she said, "I hope that Eva and Rahiti get married and move to Tahiti, that Paul grows up there and marries a gorgeous island woman, and that they all have tons of hapa-haole kids."

"And that," said Ned, raising his teacup, "would be poetic justice."

## 25

# CHRISTMAS DAY

**M**INA WOKE UP on Christmas morning and thought she smelled gingerbread. She sat up in bed and took a couple of deep breaths. She definitely smelled gingerbread, and it was coming from Ned's kitchen next door. She got out of bed, got dressed, made some coffee, and went to investigate.

"Oh, so you finally woke up," Ned said as she opened the screen door to his bungalow. He was standing in the kitchen licking batter off a wooden spoon.

"Have you been making gingerbread?" She didn't really have to ask, as the air in the room had a gingery overtone. "Did you know it's one of my favorite Christmas things?"

He smiled at her. "Perhaps you've mentioned it once, or maybe ten times."

"So do we get to have some for breakfast?"

He glanced at the clock. "No, I'm afraid it will have to be after breakfast. It has a few more minutes to bake, and then it needs to cool off."

"Merry Christmas, Ned." She came in the kitchen and kissed him. "Oh, sweet torture, you even taste like gingerbread."

"Happy Christmas, darling."

"Okay," she said, "I'll go over and get the curried eggs and potato salad, and you make the sausages, so we can eat breakfast and move on to the gingerbread."

"Your wish is my command, oh best beloved," he said and kissed her on the forehead. "The table is set under the arbor, and I'll meet you there."

A few minutes later, they were both sitting under the hau-tree arbor eating their breakfast of curried eggs, potato salad, and sausages while Ollie tucked into his Christmas treat of cubed meat in a bowl. The gray and overcast sky made their tablecloth with the red-and-green poinsettia border seem more cheerful than usual, and the chilly northeast breeze had Mina bundled into a sweater.

"I hope you don't mind eating this for Christmas breakfast," she said. "It's one of my favorites."

"It might become one of mine too," he said as he reached for another curried egg. "It's nice and simple after yesterday's chaos. You weren't exaggerating when you said Thanksgiving was your sister's warm-up exercise."

Mina stopped her fork full of potato salad in midair. "I hope she didn't drive you crazy."

He laughed. "Not completely."

She sighed and shook her head. "We're all so used to her Christmas regime. But don't worry. When we go there this evening, she'll have transformed back into the calm and fun-loving hostess, and everything will be perfectly lovely."

"These eggs are wonderful, darling," he said, "and so is the salad."

"I made them both the way my mother did." She tilted her head and gave him a faint smile. "I wish you could have met her. I always miss her at Christmas."

"I always think about my father during the holidays too."

"Do you think the gingerbread is ready?" she said as she stood up and began to clear the table.

"Let's just have a look," he said.

After they had taken care of the breakfast dishes and poured two small glasses of eggnog spiked with bourbon, Ned cut them each a square of the warm gingerbread. They were just sitting down again when an old truck pulled into the driveway and set Ollie barking and running back and forth. They both stood up and saw Bill Hitchins get out of the truck and take a parcel wrapped in brown paper out of the back. He waved to Ned and Mina.

"Mele Kalikimaka," he said as he sauntered toward them.

"Manuia le Kirisimasi," said Ned. "Come and sit down, and have some gingerbread and eggnog with us."

"I don't want to interrupt anything," he said as he leaned his parcel against one of the arbor posts.

"You are not interrupting at all," said Mina. "We're very glad to see you looking so well. Come and join us." She placed her untouched gingerbread and eggnog in front of Bill. "I'll just run in the house and get myself another serving," she said as she dashed off.

"I didn't mean to take her cake," said Bill.

"Well," Ned said in a low voice and with a smile, "she's probably in there cutting herself a bigger piece."

"In that case," said Bill as he picked up his fork, "I'll eat without guilt. It looks delicious."

"How have you been?" Ned asked.

"Relieved to be out of jail," Bill answered, "but stunned and unsettled by everything that's happened. Thank God for painting, because right now, it's saving my sanity."

"Yes," Ned agreed, "sometimes I feel the same about writing. It's a corner of peace in a world of chaos."

"Oh, Ned," said Mina as she came back with her own cake and eggnog, "this gingerbread is beyond perfect." She turned to Bill. "I got quite a catch, don't you think?"

Bill nodded. "My advice is to marry him for his gingerbread as soon as possible before somebody else does."

"How are Eva and Paul doing?" Mina asked. "Are they still staying with you and Tevai?"

Bill was quiet for a moment. He took a sip of his eggnog and then ran his finger around the rim of the glass. "That's one of the reasons I came over here. I need to ask your advice. See, Eva and Paul have skipped town, and Rahiti went with them."

Ned frowned. "Where did they go?"

"I have no idea," Bill said. "The day before yesterday, early in the morning, they said they were going on some kind of all-day-and-into-the-evening party and not to wait up for them. When we got up on Christmas Eve and they weren't there, we got worried. Then I found a letter addressed to me and Tevai in the studio. It was from Eva. It said they were leaving the islands, and they would be in touch when they felt safe."

"What is she doing for money?" Mina asked.

"Apparently," said Bill, "there was a cache of money in the Morgan house and a Swiss bank account that Eva now has access to—at least that's what she told Tevai. When Ned took Eva to visit her mother in jail, Marguerite told her where the money was and gave her instructions about the account."

"She did seem unusually happy for someone who'd just visited her mother in jail," Ned commented.

"She must have sneaked into her old house," said Mina. "I thought it had been closed off for a search."

"I can't blame her for wanting to get away," said Ned. "And who could blame her for wanting to forget about her parents?"

"I'm just not sure if I should tell anyone about them leaving," said Bill. "Will I get in trouble if I don't?"

"I don't think so," said Mina. "I mean, they promised Marguerite they would leave the children alone if she confessed. Isn't that right, Ned?"

Ned leaned back in his chair. "I don't think Naval Intelligence is interested in Eva or Paul. They know Eva was forced into doing things she didn't want to and that the boy was too young to understand what he was doing. I'm quite positive the ONI is happy with the bigger fish and that their word about leaving Eva and Paul alone is good."

"And," Mina added, "I'm sure that Todd isn't going to go after Eva. She had no idea her father was a murderer on top of everything else."

"My advice," said Ned, "would be to say nothing until someone asks, and then you can just tell the truth. After all, you're not legally responsible for her."

"Still," said Mina as she picked at the crumbs on her plate, "you and Tevai must be worried about them."

"Tevai doesn't seem to be worried," Bill said. "She's convinced herself they're somehow on their way to some far-off Pacific island."

"It would be very easy," said Mina, "to check up on passenger liner and freighter departures. Of course, they always could have left on a yacht or something, but people in the yacht harbor or at the club would know if anyone left in the last two days and where they were going."

Bill sighed. "Right now, I think maybe it's better if we just don't know any more."

"I think you might be right," said Ned.

"What are you doing for Christmas?" Mina asked.

"We're going up to Tamara's for dinner," Bill answered. "I think Molly and Akira will be there too. It's very low-key, but that's all any of us want right now, right?"

"Yes," said Mina, "low-key seems like quite a blessing."

Bill stood up, got the parcel that was leaning on the post, and brought it over to the table. "I want you two to have this for helping me when I was in jail—for getting me a lawyer and for reassuring Tevai. I can't tell you how much it meant to me. I hope you like it. I think it's one of my better pieces."

"Thank you so much, Bill," said Mina. "You didn't have to give us anything."

"But," said Ned, "because we both admire your work, we would never refuse one of your paintings."

"Yes," added Mina, "it will be a treasure."

They watched Bill amble back to his old truck and waved to him as he drove up the driveway. Ned turned to Mina. "Do you think what's happened will help to sober him up?"

"I assume you mean that literally," she said.

"His disposition seems affected already."

"I think," she said, "it could either help to sober him up or make his drinking worse. I'd say it's a toss-up."

"Whatever the outcome, we're now the owners of another painting by Bill Hitchins."

"Do you want to open it now?" she asked. "Or haul it up to Nyla's and unveil it when we open the rest of our presents?"

"Delayed gratification is always exciting, darling."

She smiled and kissed his cheek. "I couldn't agree more."

Mina decided she would like to take a walk on the beach, and Ned told her he was going to clean up his kitchen and would catch up with her. When she tried to offer to help, he insisted on doing it himself, saying that sometimes housework actually helped him to relax. So Mina went to change into her swimsuit, and as it was turning out to be a not-so-warm day, she threw on her beach robe and set out with Ollie.

Sometimes she would see one or two other people on her beach walks, but today, perhaps because of the weather and it being Christmas morning, there was no one to be seen. And she thought nothing could be finer than having the whole beach to herself. The wind wasn't harsh, but it was cold. And she turned up the collar to her beach robe as she walked along. The windblown ocean was full of whitecaps and clouds of spray streaming off the tops of the waves as they broke over the reef. She walked slowly, looking carefully in the sand for any shells or bits of sea glass she could pick up and put in her robe pocket. It was a habit she had acquired in childhood from her mother and grand-mother, and she smiled as she recalled the countless afternoons they spent at island beaches combing through the sand for shells and beach glass. She rounded a corner and looked up to see the lighthouse and the Diamond Head cliffs rising up before her. The usual bright, trop-ical colors of the landscape were all subdued under the windy gray sky, and she felt relieved and quieted by the absence of brilliant light. She sat down close to a hedge of naupaka that sheltered her from the wind and stared out across the ocean while Ollie scampered around the shoreline, running in and out of the water. After all of the bad and frightening things that had recently happened, she was puzzled that she felt so happy—delighted about Nyla's baby and exul-tant about her own wedding in May. She was so eager to meet Ned's mother and grandfather in a few months, and more immediately, she looked forward to dinner tonight and the company of her family. Maybe, she thought, seeing terrible things made the good things in life more valuable, and compared to many other people, she was ex-tremely lucky. She got up, called out to Ollie, and was just starting to walk back when she spotted Ned in the distance walking toward her. She broke into a run, and with Ollie chasing and barking beside her, she dashed down the beach and threw herself into Ned's out-stretched arms.

That evening, Mina sat outside on her sister's patio, looking through the French doors at the Christmas festivities going on in the house. Dinner was over, and dessert had been laid out on the buffet amidst a garland fashioned from mock orange leaves and Christmas berries. Mina had come out to check up on Ollie and to let him have the knuckle bone Nyla had gotten him. Ollie had begun to happily gnaw away at his treasure, but instead of returning to the party, she lingered outside in the bracing night air and watched from the outside, a tem-porary voyeur. The scene inside appeared so warm and full, like a movie, only better because at any moment she could give up watch-ing and step into the story. Mei sat at the piano with Nyla next to her, while Ned and Nigel stood behind them. Mei had just begun to play "It Came upon a Midnight Clear," and they all were singing. Their blending voices drifted out into the night, and Mina could see Grandma Hannah looking on and smiling, while Reggie and her father were huddled in an intense conversation. The tall Christmas tree surrounded by a mess of ribbons, wrapping, and opened pres-ents, the crackling fireplace, the glass punch bowl, and the happiness of those whom she was watching made her smile and think of a Dick-ens novel. She looked out at the southern sky, so clear and full of stars, with the beautiful tail of Scorpio curving gracefully across the heavens. The wind had died down, and the air hung cool and crisp. She wished she could identify more of the constellations in the night sky and decided it would be a good activity for her and Ned to pur-sue. Hearing the French doors open, she turned to see Nigel walking toward her. She had been so engrossed in the starry sky that she hadn't noticed the singing had stopped.

"Hope I'm not intruding," Nigel said.

"Not at all," she said. "I was just stargazing."

"It is a lovely night, isn't it?" he said as he lit a cigarette.

"It is."

"Say, Mina," he began, "I haven't properly thanked you for preventing me from doing something foolish."

"You don't have to thank me," she said. "Maybe someday you can return the favor."

"I was in a pretty dark place," he paused and took a drag on his cigarette. "I hope you'll forgive anything I said in anger."

"The important thing is that we got those two horrid people arrested, and now they can't hurt anyone else."

"I do want us to be friends. Mei thinks the world of you and your sister."

"Of course we're friends, Nigel," she said reassuringly.

"I've known Trout for so long. He's like a brother to me."

Mina frowned. "Trout?" She looked at Nigel in amazement and laughed. "Did you say Trout?"

"Oh, no," groaned Nigel.

She smiled and folded her arms. "Explain yourself, Nigel."

"When we were lads—we must have been around eleven or twelve—there was this very big, very crafty, old brown trout in a nearby stream that Ned was obsessed with. He was always going off saying he was going to catch the old trout. I could never understand why it took him so many years to catch it. He was the best fly fisherman of all of us."

"So you called him Trout because of that?"

"Because he was always going on about the trout."

"But he did finally catch it?"

"Well, yes, he did," Nigel said. "He caught it, took it home, and would not allow it to be eaten. He insisted on burying it in the garden. He even planted a rose bush over it. We all thought it was quite strange, and he got very angry if we pressed him about it. I don't suppose you could forget I said anything?"

Mina laughed. "No, Nigel, I don't suppose I could."

"He's going to kill me."

"Who's going to kill you?" Ned said as he strolled up and gave Mina a kiss on the cheek.

"Nothing," Nigel said quickly. "I mean, no one."

Mei stood in the doorway. "Come in now, all of you. Nyla wants us to get busy on the dessert."

"I'll be right in," Nigel said, "as soon as I finish my smoke."

Mina got up from her chair. "Well, I think I'm ready for dessert." She started toward the house. "Are you going to come along, Trout?"

Ned rolled his eyes and looked at Nigel. "I should have left you to die in Shanghai."

Nigel shrugged and grinned. "Sorry, Trout. It just slipped out."

Back in the house, everyone was helping themselves from the buffet of desserts. There was a spice cake, several kinds of cookies in different Christmas shapes, an apple pie, and fresh strawberries that Charles had brought from the ranch. They had all settled down in the living room with their plates of sweets and cups of steaming coffee or tea when there was a knock at the front door.

"Who in the world could that possibly be?" asked Nyla. "Todd, go and see."

Todd got up and went across the room, into the foyer, and opened the door. He spoke to someone for a few minutes, and the next thing everyone knew, a figure dressed as Father Christmas burst into the room. He was tall and wearing a green velvet tunic covered by a rich burgundy cloak edged with fur. The hood of the cloak was thrown back, and voluminous white hair and a white beard streamed away from his face. A velvet eye mask that was decorated with whirls and swirls of gold-colored threads hid his eyes. A wreath of pine and berries topped his head, and in one hand he held a staff and in the other a basket full of mistletoe. From under his cloak, he handed a stick and drum to Nyla and an alto recorder to Mina. The sisters looked at each other and smiled. With verve and spirit, the three of them launched into a rendition of "Good King Wenceslas." Father Christmas and Nyla sang in perfect harmony while Mina accompanied them on the recorder. They performed in perfect unison as if they had rehearsed it, and the whole effect amazed and pleased the others. At the end of the song, Mina and Nyla both screamed "Charlie" at once. They tore off his mask, kissed his cheeks, and took off his wreath, false beard, and wig to reveal a young man who looked very much like them. After the young man had kissed and embraced Grandma

Hannah and Charles, the sisters introduced their brother, Charlie, to everyone else.

It was such a surprise, and there was so much chatter, that it took some time to learn that he had wanted to appear earlier, but his ship had been delayed and he had some trouble finding a ride from the dock, as there were few cabs to be found. Grandma Hannah went to the kitchen and made him a heaping plate of food, and everyone plied him with questions and fussed over him, all of which he took with humor and grace. When Charlie had finished eating and everyone else had finished their dessert, Todd brought out a bottle of brandy and turned down the lights so that only the fireplace and the Christmas tree illuminated the room. There was more affectionate and happy conversation, and as the time for parting company drew near, Grandma Hannah ended the Christmas celebration with the family tradition of reading the Christmas story in Hawaiian from their family Bible.

Ned and Mina left with promises of seeing Charlie the next afternoon, and they started off down the hill with their Christmas presents piled in the trunk and Ollie sleeping peacefully in the backseat. They rolled down all of the car windows to let the cool night air stream through.

"Your brother has quite a theatrical flair," Ned commented.

"He's always been quite the artiste," said Mina, "but he also has a very smart and practical side too. That's why we enlisted him to run the family trust and our foundation."

"I'm surprised one of the Lamby Langstons of the world hasn't snatched him up."

Mina chuckled. "Don't think they haven't tried. Anyway, he doesn't go in for the glamour-puss types."

"What type does he like?"

"He likes the artistic, intellectual girls who enjoy the outdoors," she said. "You know, smart girls that are semi-tomboys."

"Like his sisters?"

Mina gave him a puzzled look. "I'll have to think about that," she said. "Ned, are you sleepy?"

He shook his head. "No, I'm wide awake for some reason."

"Great," she said. "Let's go and sit out on the beach when we get home."

"I'll bring the port," he said.

She smiled. "And I'll bring the cookies. Nyla gave me some in a tin to bring home."

When they arrived home at Ka'alāwai, they unloaded their presents onto the pune'e in Mina's living room. They both changed out of their party clothes. Ned carried a couple of blankets and some pillows. Mina put the port, two glasses, and the cookie tin in a basket, and they headed down to the beach. Ollie, who had been acting sleepy, suddenly perked up and followed them with an eagerly wagging tail. Ned spread out the first blanket and threw down the pillows. Soon the port was poured and the cookie tin opened, and the two of them lay back on the pillows, staring at a calm sea and a still night full of stars while Ollie roamed lazily around in the sand.

"These are very good cookies," said Ned as he bit into one shaped like a star.

Mina smiled. "Yes, Trout, they're delicious."

He sighed. "I can't believe he told you. He promised he wouldn't."

"I think he felt like he owed me."

"What about me? I saved his ungrateful skin in Shanghai."

"He told me all about the fish you finally caught too and buried under a rose bush."

"Well," he said, "he doesn't know everything."

"There's more?"

"Yes, much more, but you, being in league with Nigel, might never get to hear it."

"But darling, we're about to be married, and there should never be any deep, dark secrets between husband and wife."

"All right," he said, "but you have to promise never to call me the forbidden name in public."

"I promise," she said, raising her right hand. "But I might use it in private. I find it quite endearing. Now tell me everything."

"I caught the old trout long before I brought him home and buried him—maybe as many as three years before. He was old even then. Those brown trout can live to be very old, you see, and he had developed quite a reputation for being wily and elusive. But I caught him, and I was over the moon with excitement, as you can imagine. When I scooped him up in the net, he was floundering and flapping about a great deal. And when I looked down at him in the net, it seemed like he was staring at me with his big, wet, fishy eye, and I had the distinct feeling that he was begging and pleading with me for his life. I suddenly felt terribly guilty and very sorry for him, and so I pulled the hook out of his mouth and released him. He gave a jump when I let him go and swam around in a few circles in front of me before he took off, and in my boyish imagination, I took it for a thank-you."

"But what about all those times you told people you were going off to catch him?"

"I would go off by myself," he said slowly, "with all my fishing gear and a book stashed away that no one could see. I would sit around in the place where I caught the old trout and read. And after a while, he would come swimming up, and I would feed him the bait. I shared a hundred secrets and just as many plans with that fish. One day I came and found him dead—floating around in the spot where I used to feed him. So I stuck a hook in his mouth, pretended I caught him, took him home, and buried him. Of course, I couldn't allow anyone to eat him."

"No, of course not," she said. "That would have been so wrong."

"So I buried him and planted a rose bush over him. Everyone thought it was a queer thing to do, but I didn't care. He was a great friend to me."

"Well, darling," she said as she kissed his cheek, "I will call you Trout in private with great pride and affection."

"Now," he said, "pass the cookie tin this way, and I'll see if you've left any for me."

"I was thinking, Ned," she said.

"Not too hard, darling. It's Christmas."

"I was thinking we should learn to find the constellations and learn the names of the stars. It would be something fun and interesting we could do together."

He looked up at the night sky. "It's an amazing show, isn't it? And it's up there every night."

"You can't beat the admission price either," she added.

"Our ancestors knew the skies so well that it kept them from losing their way at sea. It's hard to imagine how well they must have been able to read the sky."

"Do you think we could? Wouldn't it be great to be able to look up at the sky and know what you were seeing and how the stars were shifting?"

"And," he said, "if we ever had children, we could teach them what we knew, so they would never feel lost."

"You are a romantic, aren't you, Ned?" she said as she took his hand.

"The world needs a little romance," he said, "especially now."

"This was our first Christmas together."

"The first," he said, "of many happy Christmases yet to come."

And as the two of them lay there, in silence, transfixed by the brilliance above them, a shooting star suddenly streaked across the dome of the sky and fell toward the southern horizon, and they both took it as a sign that heavenly powers were in agreement.

# ABOUT THE AUTHOR

Victoria Nalani Kneubuhl is a well-known Honolulu playwright and writer. Her work has been performed in Hawai'i and elsewhere in the Pacific, the continental United States, Britain, and Asia. She is currently the writer and coproducer for the television series *Biography Hawai'i*.